CU00408948

DEEP
WATER

DEEP WATER

TIM JEAL

LITTLE, BROWN AND COMPANY

A *Little, Brown* Book

First published in Great Britain in 2000
by Little, Brown and Company

A CIP catalogue record for this book
is available from the British Library.

ISBN 0 316 64684 9

Typeset in Sabon by
Palimpsest Book Production Limited,
Polmont, Stirlingshire
Printed and bound in Great Britain by
Clays Ltd, St Ives plc

Little, Brown and Company (UK)
Brettenham House
Lancaster Place
London WC2E 7EN

Acknowledgements

I am indebted to the late John Garnett CBE for describing to me the missions he took part in while serving in the SIS/SOE naval flotilla operating out of the Scilly Isles and the Helford River during the Second World War. The specific operations described in this novel are invented, so I am entirely responsible for any shortcomings.

CHAPTER 1

O n her daily bicycle ride to the north Oxford girls' school where she taught music and English, Andrea Pauling's eye was caught by a newsstand headline: DOG FIGHTS OVER DOVER. She imagined an enormous dog, floating in the warm July air, high above the fields of Kent. Then she read: LUFTWAFFE BOMBS PORTS, and the surreal image vanished. She felt sick and breathless; any day now, these solid, rust-red Victorian houses in the Woodstock Road could be reduced to heaps of blackened brick.

Andrea thought of her only child, Leo, sitting in an identical building less than a mile away, stumbling his way through Julius Caesar's *Gallic War*. The soft downiness of his cheeks, and the way his hair curled at the nape of his neck, made her weak with love. Andrea sighed. Her son had been her best piano pupil until giving up last term. Now he didn't draw and sing any more either. Instead, at twelve years old, machines and warships absorbed him, as they did his father. The day before, she had been shocked by a newspaper photograph of young evacuees waiting in a train station, looking lost. This must never happen to Leo. If he were banished to a remote village, how would she ever regain the easy familiarity they had known in the past?

Shortly before Mr Chamberlain's celebrated flight to Munich, Andrea's father had called from Baltimore and begged her to

1

come home to America with her English husband, Peter, and with Leo. Andrea had been tempted. Her father, now retired, had been chief of staff at Johns Hopkins Hospital, and could easily have afforded to support his daughter's family for however long it took Peter to find a job. But knowing her husband would never leave his native country with war threatening, Andrea had refused.

When she and Peter had first met, she had been a twenty-one-year-old co-ed at Cornell. Dr Pauling had then been the youngest engineering instructor on campus; and Andrea – whose joint majors were English and Music Performance – had met him after attending one of his lectures in an interdisciplinary series on 'Science and Culture'. Usually mistrustful of assertive male lecturers, she had found Peter's iconoclastic polemics challenging. Even now, individual sentences would come back to her: 'Scientists test hypotheses by experiment. Poets and novelists deal in untested ambiguities that mean one thing to one reader and something else to another.' He had spent much of this lecture mocking the literary world for its naïvety in revolting against the machine age. *That* was the only kind of 'age' Americans were ever going to know.

During questions, Andrea had stood up and asked him to name some 'naïve' writers. He had reeled off the Romantics and some unknown English moderns, throwing in Rimbaud and Baudelaire for good measure. But why should Romantics do anything *except* revolt, she had asked sweetly, confusing him. In days to come they had talked at length, and, after many arguments, had fallen in love.

Their affair had been more than daring, since, as an instructor, Peter would have lost his job if news of it had ever reached the ears of faculty bosses. In retrospect his willingness to risk so much for love in that insecure era amazed Andrea, as did their liking for bootleg whisky and bathtub gin. Her favourite memories were of long walks together in the woods above Lake Cayuga, and returning, tired but contented, to Peter's frame house overlooking one of Cornell's deepest ravines.

They had married in 1927, and, the following year, Leo had been born. In 1930 Peter had accepted a lectureship at Oxford. Today, a decade after their departure from upstate New York, it grieved Andrea that her husband no longer treated her lovingly. In 1938 Peter had contracted polio, and now, two years later, walked with a limp severe enough to rule him out for active service.

Later that morning at school, Andrea was trying to elicit from her class of gently nurtured sixteen-year-old girls why they thought Hamlet had been cruel to Ophelia. Opinion divided equally between some blaming Hamlet's immaturity and others blaming his mother. Long before the bell ended the lesson, Andrea was thinking of Peter, who was in London being interviewed for a job with the Royal Navy's Department of Secret Weapon Development.

From a selfish point of view, Andrea would have preferred him to remain a lecturer in the engineering department at Oxford, thus allowing them all to continue their untroubled existence. But, knowing how desperate Peter was to play a direct role in the war effort, she could not bear to think of him being rejected. To make use of his mind, the Admiralty would surely make allowances for his damaged body, perhaps letting him work a shorter week.

Peter had promised to call her during morning break, so Andrea hurried from the classroom when the lesson ended. In the staff room, she found a note already pinned up.

Mrs Pauling – Your husband is returning to Oxford on the 11.20. Please meet him at the Mitre Hotel at one.

The absence of positive news left Andrea feeling increasingly nervous as she pedalled into the High.

At the Mitre she looked in vain for her husband in the absurdly Dickensian dining room, where she always expected red-faced hunting squires to burst in demanding devilled kidneys and claret. The head waiter directed her to a table next to a party of pink-faced young men. 'Aesthetes', they probably considered themselves, with their long hair and languid voices. Apart from two fur-clad foreign-looking women, the rest of the diners appeared to be local tradesmen and yeomanry officers.

One of these khaki-clad men gazed at Andrea intently enough to make her blush. She was wearing a simple gingham blouse with a plain navy waistcoat. With her red-gold hair pinned back, she reckoned she looked prim and schoolmarmish. Yet surprisingly many Englishmen seemed to like her that way. Recently, one of Peter's engineering colleagues, after an embarrassingly inept pass, had called her MIT – Massachusetts Ice Temptress – and had had the nerve to tell her that she was known by this nickname throughout the university. She might have laughed louder if, days earlier, Leo had not asked her to stop wearing her blue silk dress with 'the splotchy flowers' when she came to his school. He'd overheard his geography teacher saying she'd looked 'a corker' in it on Sports Day.

Peter's uneven step alerted Andrea before he came bustling in, crumpled Burberry over his arm, heavy briefcase bumping the backs of chairs and people. Eyes turned as this broad-shouldered muscular man lurched across the room, using his walking stick to such effect that he seemed to reach Andrea's table in a rush of air.

Peter ordered a bottle of wine, and said nothing until he had drained a glass. Invariably late for appointments, his flushed, perspiring face showed how hard he had tried to arrive on time today. He looked so troubled that Andrea said gently, 'Don't worry, Peter. Just tell me.'

'They want me to start in two weeks.' An uneasy frown lingered on his forceful, yet kindly face.

4

'Isn't it good they want you right away?'

'They want me to work long hours. Even at weekends . . . sometimes.'

'But you'll be home most week nights?'

A nervous hand dragged at his thick brown hair. 'I wish it was the kind of work that starts at nine and ends by six.' A gust of laughter came from the young men's table.

'You mean you'll stay over in London Monday to Friday *and* weekends?' In shock, she hardly noticed the waiter put down a plate of watery soup.

Peter hung his head. 'I'm sorry, darling, but it's top priority stuff.'

'What stuff is that?'

'I'm not permitted to say.' He glanced meaningfully in the direction of the foreign women.

'You can't be serious, Peter,' she cried, attracting the admiring officer's attention.

'Please Andrea,' he whispered, leaning closer, 'you must know why I can't say anything.'

Mechanically, Andrea took several spoonfuls of soup. Three weeks ago before he'd even approached the Admiralty, Peter *had* told her something. He'd been thinking about a floating bridge. It hadn't occurred to her that this casually mentioned idea might be taken up by one of the armed services as a matter of priority. One of the 'aesthetes' announced in an affected high-pitched voice, 'I hate rugby and all games played by men with odd-shaped balls.' Their laughter obliged Peter to wait before continuing, 'This job really matters to me, but I haven't accepted yet, and I won't, unless I know I'm going to be able to go on seeing you.'

Touched, she asked, 'Can't you come home *any* nights, Peter?'

'Not really. I'm scared stupid my leg will let me down. I can't risk putting it to any extra strain. The train delays are awful already.'

'If you can't manage weekdays or weekends, how does Leo get to see you?'

Peter said humbly, 'I hope you'll both visit *me*.'

'What if Hitler bombs London?'

'Then I won't expect you to bring Leo.' He reached out a hand, and clasped one of hers. 'But would *you* risk coming at weekends, darling?'

'How could I leave him alone in Oxford?'

Peter looked at her fearfully. 'Maybe Leo should go to a country school.'

'Go where?' she gasped.

'A school in the country, far from danger.'

She fixed tragic blue-grey eyes on his. 'Unless he goes away, we two won't meet at all? Is that what you mean?'

As Peter nodded, she seemed to see Leo's grief-stricken face, freckles standing out darkly, so pale was he. Will he ever forgive me if I agree to this?

Peter said in his most reassuring voice, 'Thousands of kids have been evacuated. Leo knows that.'

Andrea pushed away her soup plate. 'I hate every goddamn thing about British boarding schools.'

'They're not like they used to be.'

'They're still obsessed with "toughness" and "putting up with things". You know they are. Kindness and sensitivity don't come into it.'

When the waiter removed Andrea's unfinished soup and replaced it with a small portion of nameless fish with some boiled vegetables, she knew she would be sick if she ate any. Already at Leo's day school, which was segregated by sex and social class, he was learning the English way of hiding his feelings, and how to do 'the done thing'. Recently he had warned her not to ask questions when friends came to the house. 'You're too jolly nosy, mother.' (He really did sometimes call her 'mother', and not entirely as a joke.) She had warned him that English aloofness was a thousand times

6

worse than American familiarity. And later he had come and said he was sorry, once more the thoughtful boy she loved, and had even shed a few tears. But away from home, in a place where callousness was praised, what would happen to him? And right now he could be in Baltimore at an ordinary high school, mixing with girls as well as boys.

For Peter, his wife's unhappy face spoke of one thing only: the fact that she cared far more for Leo than for him. Since polio had robbed her of the man she had married, he didn't really blame her. No active man could remain the same person after losing his ability to make love with ease and walk without stumbling. It shocked Peter that she seemed to think him guilty of sacrificing Leo for his own needs. But she'd got Leo all wrong. He wasn't a delicate, artistic boy who would crack up away from home. On the contrary, he was the type who would grow in confidence and self-belief in a tough environment. But Andrea would never accept this in her present mood. He said emotionally, 'I'd refuse the best job in the world, if taking it was likely to stop me seeing you.'

'Shall I rephrase that?' she offered, in a paper-thin voice. 'If I won't let Leo go to Dotheboys Hall, you'll say "no" to the navy. That's blackmail, Peter. I *know* what the job means to you.'

'Dearest Andrea, boarding school isn't the hell on earth you're making out.' He was smiling sincerely. 'He'll fit in fine, I promise.'

Andrea wanted to scream her frustration. Like most of his self-satisfied male colleagues, Peter had been sent away at a tender age, and like them was unaware of any lasting ill-effects. Should these dons hear that she had stopped Peter working for the Admiralty by refusing to let Leo go away, they would think her literally crazy. Children were being sent to live with strangers in Wales and Scotland, and even Canada. Families all over Europe were being torn apart. So what could be so bad about a few terms in a well-run preparatory school? The war had weakened her position; and guilt about Peter's disability completed her defeat. Andrea could not save Leo if, by doing so, she made Peter refuse the only kind of job likely to ease his misery at being unable to fight for his country.

She looked ahead stiffly and sighed, 'Okay, he can go.' Her voice seemed to come from a cold and immensely distant place, and Peter shivered as he heard it.

'Will you ever forgive me?' he asked, scared by her expression. Cripples are not wise – ran one of his new unwritten maxims – to push attractive spouses too far. But despite his unease, tears of gratitude filled his eyes.

'I need to go,' she murmured, pushing back her chair, terrified she might sob if she stayed. She squeezed past the refugees to a muted cheer from the aesthetes.

Only when Andrea was collecting her bicycle from the alley beside St Mary's did the reality of what had happened hit her. In a few months Peter and Leo would have gone, and she would be living alone. A tinny gramophone was bleating jazz from an upper room in Brasenose. An ache of bereavement filled her chest. She had to sit on the steps of the Radcliffe Camera until she felt strong enough to return to school.

CHAPTER 2

Andrea thought it mildly comical that she should not be allowed to enter Peter's office in Archway Block South by the Mall; for how could she, or any other non-scientist, learn anything from the nameless fragments of metal littering his table? But regulations had to be obeyed, and as always she was obliged to meet him at the sandbagged main entrance where soldiers stood guard in their tin hats.

As they walked the short distance to St James's Park in the October sunshine, Peter told Andrea her wide-brimmed hat and dark glasses made her look elegantly Gallic. He himself was wearing a baggy flannel suit, its pockets bulging with detonators and copper wire. On all her visits to town, Andrea was touched by his obvious pleasure in seeing her, though it couldn't make up for the infrequency of their meetings. Soldiers of shattered continental armies – French, Norwegian, Dutch – walked in the park, chatting with office girls, who broke into fits of giggles on finding themselves lusted after.

Tiring, Peter pointed to a couple of unoccupied deck chairs by the lake. He and Andrea reached them just ahead of an elderly civil servant.

'I'm told the Luftwaffe hit St Giles's, Cripplegate, last night,' Peter said, sinking down into one of the chairs. 'Milton's statue was blown off its plinth.'

9

'The fall of Milton, not the fall of Man,' she replied smiling, surprised he had preserved this literary plum for her.

Andrea had been upset by Leo's latest letter and handed the envelope to Peter before unwrapping their sandwiches. Ever since her son's departure she had longed for his half-term. Now, only days before he was due home, he had written to say he wouldn't be returning alone. Peter was soon beaming as he read.

'What did I tell you? He's settled in marvellously.'

Andrea hated these formulaic letters that gave no sense at all of her living, breathing son. 'Why can't he ever write anything remotely personal?'

'He doesn't want to worry us by letting on he's homesick. Of course he *is*, like everyone else, but that's just a fact of life one needn't spell out.'

'But one does spell out that one's making a towel rail in carpentry, and that the stupid soccer team beat Half-wit Hall 3–2, and a boy called Cunningham Minor gave one a slice of stupid birthday cake. For Christ's sake!'

'Food's very important in boarding schools. Cunningham's parents probably saved coupons for months to have enough butter and sugar for that cake. It was a gesture of real friendship to offer Leo some. One has to read between the lines, my sweet.' Peter suddenly looked up from the letter. 'This is splendid! He wants to invite a friend to stay with us during half-term. I'm amazed you're not pleased.' He read on for a few seconds. 'Excellent! This boy's a budding Robinson Crusoe. He's built a hut in the woods and invites his pals round for grub. No wonder Leo likes him.'

Andrea shook her head as if to clear it. 'Leo has a good friend and didn't tell us till now, and we should be pleased?'

Peter reached over and squeezed her hand. 'It's a big compliment to us that he wants to bring a friend home.'

'Sweetheart, I don't want to share Leo. Not on his first visit home.'

'Come on, Andrea. You've read the letter. His friend's dad flies fighters – imagine the life *he's* leading – and his mother's in Kenya. This lad may have to stay at school for half-term if we say no.'

Andrea raised her hands. 'You're right. It was really nice of Leo. Of course I want this boy to come.'

As golden leaves drifted down around them, they ate their sandwiches. Peter, in his generous way, was simply glad that Leo had found a friend. Impulsively, Andrea kissed her husband. As so often these days, she found herself slipping into her 'if only' routine. If only the doctors had never plunged him into despair by saying he wouldn't walk again; if only she hadn't felt obliged to visit the Radcliffe Infirmary day after day for months until drained of every atom of emotion. If only Peter hadn't needed her so much, while simultaneously detesting his dependence.

After throwing a few crusts to the ducks on the lake, they headed for the hotel where Peter chose to live. Being near Victoria Station, a prime target for the Luftwaffe, one wing of the hotel had already been compacted to a massive mound of rubble. The place appealed to Peter because few people wanted to stay there. Along an empty upper corridor, unknown to the Admiralty, the hotel's manager had let him construct an experimental water tank, in which he carried out tests on a model of his floating road away from the eyes of opinionated experts at the navy's research laboratory.

Not for the first time, the siren was wailing as Peter and Andrea arrived. As usual, they waited in Peter's room to see how close the planes came before deciding whether to go down to the basement. Below them in the street people hurried to take shelter.

'Wouldn't it be rather fun to make love with a raid going on?' suggested Peter.

Andrea wanted to agree; this was exactly the kind of remark the old Peter would have made before his illness, if a war had

11

been in progress. But with all her senses attuned to noises off, Andrea knew she would have none to spare for her own body, let alone his. Fear of pain and extinction apart, she would be constantly aware that if they died together Leo would be an orphan.

That afternoon no bombs fell closer than the City, so they talked while the raid lasted, and then, in the early evening, after the 'All Clear' had sounded, they left the curtains open, and Andrea peeled off her stockings by the glow of burning offices and churches. Thirteen years after their marriage, Peter watched as if witnessing one of the loveliest sights in the world. Because lovemaking still meant so much to him, Andrea often forgot his physical awkwardness, though never the distance between them. For almost a year he had kept from her his terror that she would leave him, and for much of that time had subjected her to anger she had found inexplicable and hurtful.

After Peter had eased himself off her body, she stared up at the ceiling. Even now, if they could be together more often, perhaps they could be happy again. But how could she expect to get more time? Women friends thought her lucky to see Peter as often as she did. Their husbands were in the army, or at sea, or even in one case in a German prison camp. 'One has to *expect* one's man to be elsewhere,' the bursar's wife had told her firmly. 'You Americans were hardly in the First War, so you don't understand what's involved.' This woman's husband was in a destroyer escorting Atlantic convoys. Yet Andrea had been unabashed. Because her good-natured, optimistic husband had been changed forever by a cruel illness, he and she deserved a second chance, some special opportunity. Wanting to love him again, she refused to accept that they wouldn't get one.

Andrea planned to collect Leo and his friend from King's Cross Station and then take them to the hotel to meet Peter. The boys would spend the day in London with her and Peter, and then leave for Oxford with her alone in order to spend the rest of the four-day holiday there.

Andrea felt great sympathy for this boy whose mother was abroad, and whose father was a pilot; but she still feared he might monopolise Leo, and felt guilty over this.

Before joining the other mothers near the barrier, Andrea went into the ladies to check her lipstick and powder – not that she expected Leo to notice her appearance. Outside, she exchanged small talk with a woman whose hair was permed into absurd rows of tight little curls. The only question bothering Andrea was whether she would hug and kiss her son in the station, or feel obliged to ape the reticent British, and wait till they were safely inside a taxi.

When Leo came towards her with his friend beside him, one hand thrust deeply in a pocket and the other carrying his case, the kiss she had meant to give him ended as a brush of her cheek against his.

'Mum, this is Justin Matherson.'

'Hello there, Justin.'

'How do you do, Mrs Pauling.' He held out a formal hand for her to shake, reinforcing her impression of him as a small adult. His eyes were dark, almost violet blue with long black lashes, and they held Andrea's for several seconds before flicking away. His face was narrow, with a proud, firm mouth.

Andrea smiled tightly. 'Okay, boys, we're going to get ourselves a cab to Pimlico.'

In the taxi both boys were enthralled by the bomb damage, and pointed to each rubble-filled gap where a house had been, and each boarded-up shopfront concealing a blackened interior. The smell of damp plaster dust and burned bricks filled Andrea's nostrils. On every visit to London from unscathed Oxford, she shuddered to see how fragile all buildings were.

'A pity we can't stop for a better look,' remarked Justin, staring straight at Andrea, as if willing her to tell the driver to pull over. He and Leo were craning their necks to look

13

back at an exposed inner wall, from which a flight of stairs projected crazily over an empty space. A washbasin also hung above a void, suspended only by its pipes.

'Imagine you'd been washing, then BAAM!' cried Leo, pulling a grotesque face.

Dismayed by their excitement, Andrea said quietly, 'Let's hope everyone was sheltering.'

Ahead, there was a notice in the centre of the road which read: WARNING UNEXPLODED BOMB, with an arrow diverting the traffic through several side-streets. Before their taxi driver could return to the main road again, he pulled up at traffic lights right beside a hole in the road.

Justin wound down the window and looked up and down the street. 'No warning here,' he announced.

Deep down in the earth, men were labouring to repair fractured gas pipes. Before Andrea could stop him, Justin had jumped out of the cab. She darted after him and caught him by the arm as he peered at the men, working almost up to their waists in muddy water. One shouted up, 'Are you daft, mate? Just shove off!'

Back in the taxi, Justin was unrepentant. 'I hope there'll be a raid before we leave,' he declared, fixing Andrea with another searing look.

'Gosh, yes,' echoed Leo.

'You can't want that. People may die,' objected Andrea.

Justin said sharply, 'Who cares what *I* want? People conk out anyway, all over the place, worse luck.' And again he fixed her with his fierce eyes.

Guessing the cause of his anger, Andrea remained silent. Leo seemed cowed, too, plainly in awe of his unpredictable friend. Andrea smiled encouragingly at her son. 'Dad's built a kind of tank at the hotel.'

Leo perked up. 'A Crusader tank?'

'A water tank.'

'Oh Gawd.'

'It's for a model of his floating road,' Andrea said brightly, immediately suspecting that she'd spoken out of turn. 'Leo's dad makes wonderful models,' she added, hoping to reduce Justin's interest in Peter's work by making it sound like a boyish hobby.

'You should see the fantastic plane Justin's making in the craft room,' gushed Leo.

'It's good, not fantastic,' corrected Justin.

Reminding herself that Justin was twelve, Andrea smiled at him and said she was sure he was being too modest. But Justin soon put her right. One boy at school made aircraft that really *were* fantastic.

'I guess if you enjoy making things, that's what matters,' suggested Andrea.

'If you're spastic at it, you shouldn't bother,' said Justin, as the taxi drew up at the hotel.

After Peter had given the boys lunch in the cavernous cream-painted dining room, Leo asked his father to show them his water tank.

Peter said edgily, 'I suppose your mother told you?'

'*You* told me about your bridge ages ago, so don't get cross with mum.'

Peter leaned closer to Leo. 'I'm only cross with her because she knew I broke every rule in the book when I built my tank here. She was incredibly indiscreet.' He smiled reassuringly at Leo. 'I had to set up my own model to get away from interfering technicians in the lab. Don't worry. No one will find out.'

'So we can't see it.' Leo sounded terribly disappointed.

'I didn't say that, Leo. In fact I think you'll be less likely to blab if I trust you both.'

To Andrea's immense relief, Peter suddenly relaxed. After making Leo and Justin promise to say nothing to their friends at school, he led them all up the disused backstairs.

On an upper landing, beneath a cracked skylight, Peter paused to unlock a metal fire door. Beyond it, stretching down the passage, was a narrow trough of water supported on columns of bricks. Made from linoleum, the 'tank' was almost fifty feet long. How Peter had set it up, Andrea didn't dare imagine. On the water floated a thin roadway constructed from miniature palings wired together and laid crosswise under a canvas covering. The whole construction was anchored at opposite ends by cables secured to hanging weights.

'Amazing,' whispered Leo.

Peter placed a model truck on the roadway, and even Justin came closer. The vehicle was powered by a battery motor, and, as it moved forwards, the hinged curbs of the road rose up like the sides of a boat on each side of it, dropping down into their former position the moment the weight of the truck had passed.

Justin was frowning. 'It'd be good on a river, but what if it's on the sea and there are waves?'

Peter smiled at him. 'You mean ship-to-shore. Good question.'

'*Would* it be swamped?' asked Leo anxiously.

As Peter flicked down a switch, paddles under the water started to make waves. Andrea expected the roadway to sink at the point where it was weighed down by the truck, but the raised sides moved along with it and protected the vehicle like a mobile boat. Leo clapped and Andrea joined in.

'That's jolly clever,' conceded Justin. 'What happens if a truck breaks down?'

'Another good question,' chuckled Peter. 'Well, if the sea's flat, the truck stays afloat just like when it's moving. If it's rough, that part of the road gets waterlogged, but we get time to tow away the broken-down vehicle.'

Justin said, 'A bomb would make the whole thing sink.'

'You're quite a pessimist,' laughed Peter.

Looking at her son's admiring face and Justin's frown of concentration, Andrea felt immensely proud of Peter. He switched off the waves with God-like authority. 'Another advantage is it can be rolled up, and taken anywhere.'

'Like a gigantic swiss roll,' said Leo. 'You should call it Swiss Roll, Dad.'

Peter clapped him on the back. 'Perhaps I will.'

After wave experiments with three model lorries nose-to-tail on the bridge, they went downstairs to sample the best tea the hotel could provide. Shortly before they left for Paddington, Justin went to the gents. Peter hugged his son.

'A bit of advice, Leo. Don't be too impressed with Justin because his dad's a pilot. It may sound big-headed, but scientists win wars, not heroes.'

'I don't care about his dad. Justin's more daring than any-one.'

'What does he do?' asked Andrea, uneasily.

'I can't say. I'm really sorry, mum. But he stuck up for me in a fight, and we both got our heads shoved in the whitewash bucket.'

'By other boys?' gulped Andrea.

'Of course.'

'I bet you looked a fright,' chortled Peter, suddenly aware of Andrea's confusion. 'They mark the football pitch with whitewash. Just horseplay, darling.'

Peter came down with the boys in the hotel's only working lift. Standing by her husband, Andrea noticed Leo slip his hand into his father's without Justin seeing. Instead of embracing his son again and causing him embarrassment, Peter ruffled his hair as they parted.

In the cab on the way to Paddington, Leo murmured, 'I love the leathery smell of taxis.' After that, neither boy spoke for a long time. Andrea suspected that, if Peter were in her place now, he would know exactly what to say to them. After a few moments of panic, she asked whether they could remember exactly how they met. A howl of laughter greeted her question.

'We were on "big stairs", waiting for Spud to give us the whacks,' explained Leo.

'What had you done, sweetheart?' She had a fluttery feeling in her chest.

'Talking after lights out. Anyway Justin told me to wait for him afterwards because he knew a way to stop your bum hurting.'

'I got him jumping up and down on the beds in Drake dorm – the way the Masai do, really high.'

'They're a tribe in Kenya, mum.'

'Didn't you hate being hit?'

'We loved it, Mrs Pauling,' said Justin. 'Spud goes puce and grunts as if it's killing him. It's a laugh!'

Leo said sympathetically to his mother, 'He's joking. We don't really love it. We have to shake his hand when he's finished. No one likes that.'

'Dead right,' agreed Justin. 'But unlike some squits, *we* don't snivel.'

The thought of Leo being hit by a red-faced, grunting man made Andrea feel sick. Suddenly, the boys became gloomy, as if her reaction had opened their eyes to the truth of their situation. To lighten their mood, Andrea asked them about their teachers' nicknames. This had them laughing again, and Justin asked her whether the girls she taught called her Mrs Appauling.

'Of course they do,' she admitted. 'Do boys call Leo "Appauling"?'

'They don't use long words.'

'At all?' she asked, with deliberate seriousness.

'I meant they don't use long words for *nicknames*,' Justin replied patiently, as if she could not help being stupid.

As their train gathered speed, the howl of a distant siren reached them in their blacked-out compartment, soon followed by the drone of bombers. Both boys groaned their disappointment at having missed a raid. But the next time Andrea looked at Justin, his face was fretful. Was he imagining his father swooping down from the clouds to intercept?

Outside the sky would be dark, with searchlights flickering.

Leo also seemed sad; but just then he turned to Justin and asked him what he thought Spud (their headmaster?) had been doing during half-term. At once they were giggling again.

Three months later, during the Christmas holidays, Peter read in the papers that Justin's father had been killed. When he told Leo his son was obviously shocked, but he did not say much. Expecting him to return to the subject later, Peter would be surprised to find he never did.

At the end of the holidays, Leo and his mother once more ate lunch with Peter in the cream-painted dining room of his hotel. The place looked more tawdry than before – the remaining windows had been boarded up and the chandeliers wrapped in protective sacking. Leo ate lamb which came in minute portions with the kind of mint sauce that left bright green stains on his plate. Towards the end of the meal, his father said with a puzzled sigh, 'You never mention that friend of yours any more. He was a sharp lad.'

'We had a fight. A real one.' Leo raised a fist in illustration.

His father nodded as if he understood, then asked, 'What happened?'

'He wanted me to keep doing more and more scary things.'

'Like?'

'Climbing on the roof; being out all night. He wants to force Spud to expel him. I couldn't stand it any more . . . being in trouble all the time.'

'I can see that,' murmured Peter. 'I suppose he did risky things to take his mind off his dad flying.' Leo sat staring at his plate. 'Cheer up, old man. I'm going to be sent to do tests by the sea in the New Year. If it happens to be somewhere really nice, I'll rent a cottage and keep it on for the holidays.'

'We'll be together?' Leo sounded dazed.

'You bet.'

'Can't you tell us which county?' asked Leo.

'Somewhere near an estuary.'

19

'Sounds wizard.'

In the cab on the way to King's Cross, Andrea was overjoyed when Leo kissed her, without prompting. She realised she didn't feel the wrenching pain that had made his first departure such a misery.

Passing Euston Arch, she touched her son's hand. 'Isn't it wonderful about the cottage?'

'Fantastic. Will you send me a picture of the river?'

'When I get to hear its name.'

'I'll stick it inside my desk lid. It'll bring the hols closer.'

She moved up to him on the leather seat. 'You'd tell me if you were truly unhappy, sweetheart. You do promise?'

He didn't reply at first. Then she detected the faintest of smiles. 'I promise, mum.'

Only when she was watching the rapidly dwindling train, as it curved out of the station, did she think she understood that look. How can anyone say whether they are happy or unhappy? Can you, mother? Life's the way it is, and we must make the best of it.

The following day, as a treat Peter took Andrea to a lunch-time concert at the National Gallery to hear Myra Hess play Brahms and Schubert. While anticipatory chatter rose and fell in the high-ceilinged gallery, Andrea asked her husband to get her a postcard of the estuary near the cottage he would be renting.

'Leo wants one,' she explained.

'I'll try,' he promised. 'Did I tell you I won't be working when we're down there?'

'You can't be serious.'

'I'm absolutely serious. Strictly *entre nous* the navy expects to test Swiss Roll in March, so my job'll be over before Leo's spring holiday starts.'

'That's really wonderful, Peter.'

So *this* was to be their special chance – hers and his. They would be together again for the first time since his illness, on a proper vacation. Leo hardly saw his father, so it would be marvellous for him, too; and Andrea would see enough of her son to feel close again.

When Dame Myra began to play Schubert's *Wanderer Fantasy*, Andrea's feet tripped along the shores of an estuary she had never seen.

There was a snow storm on the third day of term, and, since it coincided with the British capture of Tobruk, Captain Berty, Leo's headmaster, felt sufficiently well-disposed to declare a half-day holiday. During the Twenties he had devised a Great War game which required a huge 'work party' to build a long snow 'trench' – in reality a snow rampart – which would be defended by one 'army' while a second tried to storm it. Snowballs stood in for Mills bombs and grenades. Boys who were hit anywhere above the waist were declared casualties, and forbidden to throw snowballs. Once all the boys on one side or the other had become casualties, that army had to raise the white flag.

On the morning of the day on which Tobruk fell, Leo had not yet spoken to Justin since returning to school. They had eyed one another from a distance, but, when close to, had passed by without speaking. In the war game, Leo found himself on the same side as Justin, defending the trench.

As the attackers advanced, their corduroy jerkins filled with snowballs, the defenders had to rise clear of the sheltering rampart to throw their bombs. Leo was hit on the head early in the action, and then organised a snowball factory to supply the boys still fighting.

Justin was incredibly quick at throwing and ducking down again behind the snow wall; so while boys were hit on every side, he remained unscathed. As Leo supplied his friend with snowballs, he could not help fondly remembering him jumping from bed to bed after their beating. A double bomb finally knocked Justin in a heap at Leo's feet. Out of breath and laughing, they lay in the snow as the attackers stormed the rampart.

A few days later, Justin told Leo that his father had been burned alive, strapped in his seat, before he crash-landed. The day after that, Leo invited Justin to stay with him 'on a river somewhere' for the Easter holidays.

CHAPTER 3

Behind Andrea, in the back of Peter's battered little Standard car, Leo and Justin were chattering away. It was only half an hour since she had collected them from Truro Station, and already she was starting to feel a little like a chauffeur on the wrong side of a glass panel. But to give in would have been feeble, so Andrea pointed out things that appealed to her: primroses scattered in the hedge banks, stunted oaks stretching gnarled limbs across the road, the finials of a Norman church thrusting skywards through a haze of new greenery.

Not that any of this impressed her pink-blazered passengers as much as her ability, after a week in Cornwall, to negotiate a labyrinth of lanes without the help of signposts, all of which had been removed during the invasion scare. By studying the Ordnance map, she had memorised many of these magical missing names: Poltesco, Ruan Minor, Goonhilly, Trezebal, Treworgie, Manaccan in Meneage, and Landewednack, where the last sermon in the Cornish tongue had been preached in 1678. A few miles away, a regiment of dragoons, homeward bound from the Napoleonic Wars had been shipwrecked, and, even now, the bleached bones of men and horses were some-times washed up. With an urgency that surprised her, Andrea wanted the boys to share her latest enthusiasm.

For several days, Andrea had imagined stopping the car at

a particular bend overlooking a secluded creek on the river's upper reaches, so the boys could gaze through the branches of ancient oaks at the jade-green water flowing seawards. If the tide were out, there would be nothing but a narrow channel meandering between tall mudbanks, so Andrea was relieved to find the water up. She cut the engine and wound down her window. They couldn't fail to love what they saw.

'The Polwherne River,' she announced like a showman.

'I'd imagined it wider,' muttered Justin.

'Won't be good for swimming,' sighed Leo.

'How come?' asked Andrea, determined to stay cheerful.

'That pea-soup colour means a muddy bottom, mum.'

'Like the school pond,' agreed Justin.

Andrea said very firmly, 'The river's blue downstream, and a lot wider.'

As they descended to the creek, the road squeezed between the flanks of an old granite bridge before twisting upwards again through more oak woods.

'A civil war battle took place near here. Some kids found a cavalier's shoe and a musket last summer.'

Justin pointed to the main arm of the river beyond the creek. 'How deep is it out there, Mrs Pauling?'

'Please call me Andrea, Justin. I'd guess fifteen feet right now, but who knows for sure.'

'Not enough water for a German sub to creep in.' Justin sounded disappointed.

'Why would a sub *want* to?' asked Leo, with a trace of anxiety.

'To land spies or commandos, twit-face.'

Leo looked doubtful. 'What would they want to blow up in a quiet place like this?'

'They'd land here *because* it's *quiet*. And they'd bring bicycles to get to their targets.' Justin said this with such impressive conviction that Leo was silenced.

Andrea managed to laugh. 'Good thing it's too shallow.'

'It'll be deeper near the sea,' said Justin.

As they skirted heather-clad Goonhilly Downs, Andrea did not mention the Bronze Age barrows in case Leo lectured her on the embarrassment of having a schoolteacher for a mother. Instead she said she had brought his bicycle to Cornwall and purchased another for Justin's use.

'I'm afraid yours is a woman's, Justin,' she added, still distressed that he had called Leo 'twit-face'. She had been moved to tears, on first hearing that Leo had been big-hearted enough to invite Justin to Cornwall, despite their former disagreements. 'I'll need to ride it, too,' she warned. The thought of Justin's loss brought a lump to her throat. If he turned out awkward at times, who could be surprised?

A rope was flapping against the suitcase on the roof, so Andrea stopped. After making minor adjustments to the knots, she was ready to drive on; but, by then, the boys had wandered to the end of a stone barn. Across a field of newly sown spring corn, the land dropped away to a sheet of shimmering water. Leo and Justin were staring at the estuary, mesmerised.

'Can we get a boat, mum?'

'I'll look into it.'

Leo turned to Justin, 'My dad taught me to sail before his leg went bad.'

'He took you out a few times in a sail boat, Leo. That's all. Maybe there's a club some place near, where you can take lessons.' Leo looked crushed. To cheer him Andrea enthused about the nearest sandy beach, without mentioning the barbed wire defences.

The brick villa Peter had rented was neither pretty nor quaintly rustic. Just outside the hamlet of Trevean Barton, it stood at the end of a rutted lane, slightly apart from the older granite cottages. In the neglected garden, daffodils and a laburnum tree in flower banished any sense of desolation.

'Why isn't dad here?' demanded Leo, clumping up the stairs behind his mother, his knee-length socks down by his ankles.

'There's been some minor problem with his roadway. But he'll be back from Falmouth soon.' Leo must not know how upset she was that the tests on the roadway were running almost a fortnight late.

Leo's room was no bigger than a horse's loose box, just large enough to hold a washstand, chair, chest of drawers and bed. Justin was to have the larger attic room with a view of the estuary.

'Sorry about the wallpaper,' said Andrea, frowning at the faded pattern of pink bows and posies.

She showed them the bathroom with its claw-foot bath and copper geyser that had left a rusty stain on the chipped enamel. 'It roars like a locomotive letting off steam.' She hoped for a laugh but got only a faint smile from Leo. Their flashes of enthusiasm and contrasting moodiness reminded her of their ups and downs during half-term.

The house was not as primitive as she had anticipated. Expecting paraffin lamps, she had been surprised by the flickering electric light powered by a generator at the nearest farm. But there was no refrigerator and an ancient oil-burner served for a stove. The telephone, installed by the navy for Peter, was a rarity in the village. For three weeks, Peter had been looked after by a local girl, who had managed to obtain eggs, milk and butter from the farm in scandalously large quantities without recourse to coupons. But since she had just joined the ATS, Andrea hoped to find another village girl.

After tea, Leo and Justin went for a bicycle ride. An hour after their arrival at the house, Andrea found herself alone again. She was expecting Peter to be delivered home by a Wren driver at any time. He had sworn to her that for the rest of the week he would be free to be with his family, and she did not believe he would break this promise.

Waiting for the boys, she walked to the brow of the hill outside the hamlet. Against a sky of penetrating blue the trees on the ridge stood out in silhouette. A large elm reminded her of those on New England village greens – though the English tree was more thickset than the spreading American variety. Hitching up her skirt, she clambered onto the bank. A grey-blue stripe marked the spot where sea met sky. Many times, returning from visiting her parents, she must have steamed by without noticing this coastline, as she wandered among showcases holding jewellery and expensive clothes, while an orchestra played. And now all sailings were suspended.

Two tiny figures appeared, zigzagging wildly as they pedalled up the long hill towards her. Andrea waved to them.

They were still wearing their awful pink blazers and she could hear them laughing. The wind was caressing her hair and singing in the phone wires above her head. A bubble of happiness swelled inside her.

When Andrea made love to Peter, she often closed her eyes and imagined him as he had been before his illness – not just slimmer and more mobile, but more cheerful, too, and less driven. She still found him attractive, although his body had become thicker and stronger above the waist and in the arms. Inevitably perhaps, given the pain he still suffered, he had become more serious and less able to relax. It was Andrea's dearest hope that, in this remote village, he would manage to become more like the man she had first met.

Peter's favourite recreation remained walking. But though most of his friends applauded his 'guts for not giving in', Andrea wished he could sometimes be happy to sit quietly with her in the garden, or to admire a country view from an automobile. Secretly, she wished that he would come to terms with his losses, and try to develop new interests to fill the gap: reading novels perhaps, or listening to music.

But whatever the future might hold, their first full day together in Cornwall was to be devoted to walking. Peter's mind was made up. He assured Andrea that the day before he had managed to walk a mile without harming his leg. So she bit her tongue when he suggested a more ambitious hike along the cliffs. Everyone at the hospital had told her that he should be encouraged to be enterprising. He had studied the map carefully, Peter told her, so she needn't worry. If his leg hurt, he would walk through the fields to the nearest road and wait for her to return with the car.

Peter liked to have definite objectives and today he aimed to reach a Celtic earthwork on a headland near the mouth of the river. He would achieve this, he said, by walking across fields, rather than attempting to follow the lower coastal path. In this way, all steep slopes and streambeds would be avoided.

Andrea had never forgotten him saying, shortly before leaving hospital, that a man on two crutches was a cripple but a man with a single stick was only lame. His success in ridding himself of his crutches had been achieved at the cost of so many falls that his every unaided descent of the stairs had made Andrea fear he would break his neck. And all the time he had been deaf to her pleas for greater caution. Today, as he swung his stiff left leg over a stile, with help from both hands, she experienced the same old mix of admiration and misgiving.

By the time they came to a gate where adhesive mud lay between the granite posts, he was already breathless and sweating. After negotiating this quagmire, he was obliged to rest, perching on the shooting stick Andrea always carried for him. It had been overcast earlier but now the sun shone with real warmth. Only days before the young blades of corn had seemed unable to push themselves above the earth, and larks had been flung like scraps across hail-filled skies. Today, in fields ahead, kingcups glowed and the hedges were white with drifts of hawthorn.

Peter took out his binoculars and trained them on the distant headland. A frown puckered his brow. 'That's odd. Looks like they've laid some kind of railway track.'

'In such an out of the way place?'

'Maybe they're trying to fool the Germans into dropping

bombs here instead of on Falmouth docks. Smart idea. If they light up the track at night and build a few sheds, it could even work.'

'Unless the Germans hit our house instead.'

Andrea felt depressed by the war's spreading tentacles. Peter lurched ahead of her again, his broad shoulders dipping from side to side as he limped across the tussocky grass. At last he stopped again and dabbed at his dripping face. His hair was shining as if with brilliantine.

Outside the estuary the sea was ruffled with white-capped waves. Andrea asked, 'Will Leo be safe out there if I rent a boat for him?'

'Why on earth not? There's a naval patrol to fish him out if he capsizes.'

'Could a German sub come in?'

'Most unlikely. There's a net across the estuary.'

'Might submarines *want* to come in?'

'Of course. The river's a perfect spot to lie up before hitting a coastal convoy.'

Andrea understood why Justin had resented her automatic dismissal of his theories. Between the Channel and the Atlantic, Cornwall's ports and airfields would be strategically important, especially since German airplanes in France were only an hour's flying time away. The headland still looked beautiful, though the surrounding sea seemed destined to be a graveyard for scores of young sailors and airmen.

As Peter's limp became more pronounced, he knew from Andrea's compressed lips that she longed to ask him to turn back. But if *he* could put up with a little pain in order to achieve something special, why couldn't *she* turn a blind eye to his occasional grimaces? Her anxiety made everything more difficult for him, taking away the joy he felt in having crossed rugged country through his own efforts. For months he had lain in hospital fearing that he would never again enter a wild landscape on his own two feet, and now that he was actually standing in such terrain with the wind and sun on his face he was not going to give up because Andrea was worried. Bathed in warm sunlight the headland beckoned, tantalisingly closer than it had been even minutes earlier.

As they reached the farm track that provided the only realistic access to the headland, someone shouted at them to halt. The local Home Guard had rolled coils of barbed wire across the track, and an elderly corporal and two other khakiclad figures approached from the side of a low farm building. Peter's naval identity card caused these uniformed shopkeepers and farm labourers only momentary doubts. Returning them, the corporal said, 'Us can't let 'ee go down there, sir, whatever papers 'ee do have.'

Peter could have wept with frustration. It was out of the question to try to reach the shore and scramble over the rocks. Knowing that Andrea thought him obsessive about carrying through his plans, he hid his disappointment and even smiled at her. 'That's that then,' he remarked.

Andrea smiled back thankfully. Believing Peter had been in agony, she imagined he must be delighted to have this unexpected excuse to turn back. She wanted to cheer. Because Peter could quit now without any sense of personal failure, his temper would not be foul for the rest of the day.

As she hurried away to collect the car, Andrea's relief gave way to depression. She had hoped for so much from their holiday. Ever since his heroic fight back against polio had begun, Peter's leisure time had been swallowed up by challenge and struggle, just as his working hours had been for years. That was almost the worst thing his illness had done. I'm thirty-five, she thought, and this is how my life is passing. How can I respond to a man who has no idea of the impact his behaviour is having on me? From woods near the river, the twin notes of a cuckoo pulsed on and off as if urging her to make haste while she still had time.

*   *   *

Justin jumped onto the shingle from a barnacle-encrusted rock. Because all his holiday clothes were in Kenya, he was wearing an aertex school shirt with grey shorts. Leo's well-meant offer to wear school clothes too had only made him laugh.

'Perhaps we'll find a German mine,' cried Justin, glancing along the beach, as if such an object might suddenly float into view.

'What would you do?' asked Leo, continuing to pop the bubbles in a strand of seaweed.

'Fetch the navy and watch them disarm it.'

'How would they?'

'A man looking like a plumber comes, though he's a naval officer really. He gets out lots of tools, and opens it up.'

'How do you know?'

'One got washed up near my aunt's place in Sussex.'

Leo wished that occasionally *he* could tell Justin something he did not already know. They had left their bicycles in the woods behind the beach and were walking along the shore towards a fishing village on the estuary. Earlier that morning Andrea had promised to find a sailing boat for them.

A fishing boat with red-brown sails was coming in from the sea with clouds of circling gulls in pursuit. Further out, a grey fast-moving vessel was entering the estuary. The throb of its engines soon became continuous. Slanting through broken clouds, a shaft of sunlight caught the little grey ship as if in a spotlight. It looked brave and festive with its fluttering white ensign, and bright sheaves of spray curling from its bows.

'That's a motor gunboat,' said Leo, delighted to be able to recall in detail the model of an MGB in the school craft room. As the ship came closer, he could make out a stubby gun turret in the bows and people on the bridge.

'Could be an MTB,' countered Justin.

'We'd see the torpedoes if it was.' Leo was the proud owner of *Warships of the British Empire*, a well-thumbed volume packed with photographs and silhouettes of ships of all sizes.

As the gunboat passed a few hundred yards out in the river, machine guns were clearly visible on the wings of the bridge, as were Oerlikons amidships. Further astern, a row of black barrels looked like depth charges. Before the warship could disappear upstream, the boys had clambered onto a rocky promontory and from there saw it sweep in a broad arc upwind, towards a large cylindrical buoy. A deeper roar filled their ears as the engines were put astern, making the water froth and boil. Four other naval craft were shackled onto adjacent buoys: an MTB, two fishing boats painted in naval grey, and a minesweeper. A launch now sped away towards the MGB from a pontoon attached to a stone quay.

'What's going on?' muttered Justin. 'They're in one hell of a rush to get out to that ship.' Behind the quay was a rough lawn dotted with sheds and Nissen huts, and, behind these, a white house dwarfed by a tall flagstaff. 'Some kind of headquarters.'

'So what?' Leo suddenly felt irritated by his friend's breathless fascination. 'It's not the Grand Fleet, is it?'

Justin scowled at him, so Leo did not go with him to investigate the pontoon. Nor was he with Justin when the launch returned from the MGB, filled with officers and men. Instead Leo sat alone on the rocks poking at anemones for a while, before wandering along the beach towards Porthbeer village.

The fishing fleet was in and some of the boats had not yet lowered their russet sails. A man on the quay was tipping fish guts into the harbour while gulls screeched and dived. On a weed-stained slipway, a fisherman was scraping barnacles from his boat's hull, while another was painting the keel with red lead. A reek of drains merged with the stink of lobster pots.

'What a pong,' said Justin, joining Leo on the quay.

Below them in the harbour, two boys were swimming between the boats. Leo was amazed they should want to swim in such a smelly place. A woman in a black shawl shouted at them to get out. The incoming tide slapped against the boats, making the boys' heads bob up and down. When they stumbled up the steps, Leo saw that they were naked.

The boys towelled themselves and dressed in guernseys and corduroy trousers that just covered their stockings. Justin strode towards them along the harbour wall, past swathes of drying nets.

'Those navy boats,' said Justin, pointing, 'what do they do?'

'Who be 'ee?' demanded the taller of the two boys.

Justin gazed blankly at his questioner. Leo said quietly, 'He's asking who you are.'

'Oh, I'm a Jerry spy,' snapped Justin. 'Donner und Blitzen!'

'We're on holiday at Trevean Barton,' said Leo.

The Cornish boys laughed. 'Do 'ee think they be all right?' one asked the other, grinning.

'Don' see why not.'

The taller of the two said, 'Them sailors be rescuin' pilots and fishin' for mines, ol' boy.'

Unable to work out whether 'old boy' was a class insult or a friendly dialect greeting, Leo was relieved to see that Justin had not taken offence. Instead he asked politely, 'Is that all the sailors do?'

'I cudden say, reelly. Though when convoys pass, the navy goes with 'em for their safety. Don' want no U-boats, or E-boats to sink 'em, see.'

Leaving the beach for the woods, Justin was preoccupied. 'They know more than they're saying.'

'Why think 'ee that, ol' boy?' asked Leo.

'Because, toe-rag, the sailors who landed from that gunboat were young. But the men on the patrol boats near my aunt's village are as old as the Home Guard.' Leo said nothing as he dragged his bicycle out of the bushes beside the track. The flowers his bike had been lying on looked like white bluebells but stank of garlic – ideal for apple-pie beds. 'What do *you* think?' demanded Justin.

'The sailors near your aunt could be unusually old for patrol boats, and the ones down here could be the normal age.' The boys pushed their bicycles up the hill in silence until Leo snapped, 'Okay. They really may be doing something hush-hush, but why get steamed up about it?'

'Because finding out is more bloody interesting than catching shrimps.'

'More bloody worrying, too.' Leo pulled a face. There was probably no mystery at all, but that wasn't going to stop Justin trying to solve it. Not now his mind was made up.

The moment Leo saw his mother sitting at the writing table in the drawing room, he thought she looked tired and depressed. He had always considered her better looking than the mothers of other boys, but today her beauty had a set and faded look, like a dried flower's. He went across and kissed her on the cheek, making her smile.

'Say, what is this, sweetheart? Nothing wrong?'

He realised his affectionate gesture had seemed odd, because he'd been spending no time with her. Guilt made him want to say he was sorry; but how could he without seeming dishonest?

'You looked sad, mum, that's all,' he mumbled.

She pushed away the list she had been making and closed her eyes for a moment. 'Dad's strained his leg. He's lying down right now.'

'Is it bad?'

'The old problem.'

Leo sensed that his mother was desperate but wanted to hide this from him. Around his father's left knee joint, some of the muscle had turned to bone during his year in hospital, and, although some of this unwanted bone had been removed in an operation, the whole joint was inclined to puff up if he walked too far. Unfortunately, 'too far' was not always the same distance. The condition was called 'myositis ossificans', which Leo remembered because his father had written a short verse about it with some very clever rhymes that he had now forgotten.

'Poor dad,' sighed Leo.

'He should *not* have climbed so many stiles. Did you and Justin have a good day?' Without waiting for Leo to give more than a very brief reply, she walked to the door. 'I have to go get a doctor's note for painkillers.'

When his mother had gone, Leo crossed to the French windows. Justin was in the garden with the air gun he had persuaded his idiotic aunt to give him for his birthday. As Leo watched, Justin shot at something in the pear tree, then ran across to search among the daffodils. Leo went out and saw his friend hold up a sparrow and blow into its breast feathers as if to revive it. Then he tossed the light limp little corpse into a redcurrant bush.

'I'm going to sit with my dad,' Leo announced, turning his back on Justin.

The walls in Peter's bedroom were flaking in places, showing a dirty bronze-coloured paint beneath the present dreary green. His father was lying on his bed, fully dressed, looking through a sheaf of papers covered with mathematical calculations.

'Bad luck, dad.'

'I was a fool to overdo it.'

'I could bring a book in here if you want to go on working.'

'That'd be nice. I've almost finished this stuff.'

When Leo returned with a copy of *The Thirty-Nine Steps*, his father looked up. 'Everything all right, old chap?'

'We saw an MGB in the river. Is it a spy ship?'

'Most unlikely. It's a shame poor old Justin needs to escape the whole time.' Peter smiled at Leo. 'What's your book?' Leo held it up. 'John Buchan? That old stuff! I'm no pundit, Leo, but adventure novels aren't rated highly by people in the know.'

'It's exciting. What's wrong with that?'

Peter glanced heavenwards. 'Does it have intellectual or *moral* excitement?'

'It's jolly moral, dad. Hannay's trying to foil a plot against this country.'

'That's not quite what I was driving at. If he could only save his country by sacrificing his girl's life, then he'd face an interesting moral choice.'

'Interesting?' gasped Leo. 'Don't you mean sad?'

'But is a sad book a bad one?'

'Do *you* like being upset, dad?'

'Of course not, but we're supposed to respond to sad events in books and plays in a special way which . . .' He broke off and smiled helplessly. 'Look old chap, literature isn't really my subject.'

Leo's irritation with his father never lasted long. Dad was a hero to lie flat on his back for days without whining. Not that dad himself believed in heroes. He thought people couldn't do good things *just* for the sake of other people. Instead they were always trying to appear in a good light. Leo didn't agree with this. Dad wasn't being brave to make people admire him. He was behaving well so he wouldn't upset his family.

Andrea had telephoned the doctor and was on her way to collect Peter's prescription from the surgery. After a short drive, she arrived at a large stone house standing in a garden incongruously containing Scotch pines and palms. Entering the panelled hall, which smelled of furniture polish with an underlying hint of drugs, Andrea saw a glamorous blonde woman of about her own age cross from one doorway to another, and then suddenly turn in her direction.

'I've come for my husband's prescription,' said Andrea. 'His name's Pauling.'

'Don't look at me. I'm not the doctor's secretary.' The woman's ladylike indignation at having been taken for a secretary struck Andrea as hilarious.

'I'm so sorry. Is his secretary available?' she asked, with exaggerated humility.

'No, but don't worry, I'll find the damned thing.'

The sudden change of tone from imperiousness to matter of fact good humour was too much for Andrea, who let out a strangled laugh. The woman grinned at her as if to say, 'Fooled you, properly, didn't I?' Andrea followed her strange guide through a waiting room into a small office, where the prescription was quickly found. The woman glanced at it and whistled. 'Powerful stuff. Why does he need it?'

'His leg's bad. He had polio.'

Andrea was struck by her guide's extraordinarily carefully made up face, which would not have looked out of place in Bond Street, but seemed strange above a highnecked wool sweater and riding breeches. She looked again at the prescription before handing it over.

'So you're staying in that funny little place outside Trevean Barton.'

'I like it.'

'Very poky, isn't it?'

'Not at all.'

'Oh, I'm probably thinking of somewhere else.' She thrust out a hand. 'I'm Sally Lowther – the doctor's wife, in case you hadn't guessed.'

'Andrea Pauling,' replied Andrea.

Sally's eyebrows were dark in contrast to her natural looking blonde hair; and because her left brow arched slightly higher than the right, she seemed to be appraising the world with wry amusement. Suddenly she frowned.

'Is your husband a bore about his leg?'

'Is that really your business?'

'Of course it isn't. I'm afraid I'm terribly prejudiced against

37

sick people. They're so selfish. My husband never gets a moment's peace, even at night.'

'That's a shame.'

'*He* doesn't think so. Only me. He loves them all, the sicker the better.' Sally looked at her watch and then back at Andrea. 'Do you play tennis, Mrs Pauling?'

'Not to boast of.'

'Your husband's game's about the same?'

'He doesn't play.'

'Jesus! His leg!' Sally emitted a theatrical groan. 'Silly me. Never mind, unattached women can be very useful as partners. You must come round next time I have people over for a game.'

'I'm only here for the month.'

Sally's brow arched even higher. 'A whole month in the sticks. Gosh!' She smiled conspiratorially. 'I'll have to see it's not too dull for you.'

'You will?' asked Andrea, baffled.

Sally laughed ruefully. 'I'd like to rephrase that. It's we locals who have a dull time, hence all the chasing after exotic newcomers.' She smiled bravely. 'My husband's always busy.'

'Mine too,' murmured Andrea, before she knew whether she wanted to exchange confidences. 'But he's doing worthwhile work.'

'There!' cried Sally. 'So's mine. I guessed we had things in common.' She moved towards the door. 'I'd love to natter, but I must fly. Actually, I must see a man who must fly.' She laughed rather edgily. 'I'll ring you.'

As Sally hurried away, Andrea was left standing in the hall beside an elephant's foot containing several odd golf clubs and umbrellas.

Before arriving in Cornwall, Andrea had expected to be spending most of her time with Peter and the boys, so she had been keen to find a servant in order to have more liberty. But with

Peter in bed for a week at least, and the boys choosing to be out together from dawn to dusk, she doubted whether she really needed help. What the hell. Why should she cook and shop and clean the house if there was a local girl, eager to earn money?

Sitting in a meticulously kept cottage in the village, Andrea listened to its owner's account of her daughter's skills.

''Tis like this, madam, Rose can do nothin' in the way of fancy cooking. She's a clean girl, mind, and only needs experience to get a position that's not temp'rary.'

Minutes later, Andrea found herself in the street, having agreed, without having met Rose or asked for references, to become her stepping stone to better employment – if only for a month. Andrea's next task took her on a short drive to the Polwherne River.

Below her, green water beckoned through gaps in the trees and a long thatched building sprawled along a shingle beach. A stone tower sprouted a flag pole. This being the sailing club, Andrea had imagined flags being flown and cannons fired as races started – until she spotted a notice: RACING SUSPENDED FOR THE DURATION OF HOSTILITIES.

The place seemed deserted until a pale thin man drifted up from the slipway. He was the club's 'Hon. Secretary', and, when questioned, explained that the person who sometimes gave sailing lessons had joined the navy. He could show her the boats the club hired out. These small craft were kept in an enclosure with others, many upside down or tilted on their sides.

Her guide paused beside a rain-filled dinghy. 'She's nice and stable. Beamy, you see.' Andrea thought the boat looked very small. 'They'll need to be on their toes. April's always windy.'

'The boat might overturn?'

'The air in the foredeck locker will keep her afloat, if she does.'

'If they remember to close the locker door.'

'Very true,' he laughed. 'I'll help them put the sails up,

first time out. Oars and sails have to be locked up after-wards.' Andrea looked puzzled. 'In case the invader comes,' he explained, starting to cough. 'Gas,' he gasped, 'in the last one.'

A gust of wind set the halyards of the boats slapping freneti-cally against their masts. On the far bank, a heron raised a lazy wing to the squall and let itself be lifted upwards.

Entering the house, Andrea imagined Leo and Justin applauding her good news. The only voice that greeted her was Peter's.

'The boys are out.'

Andrea was surprised to see him on a sofa with both feet on the ground. 'Why aren't you resting your leg?'

'They rang from the dockyard.' Peter's voice was theatrically doom laden. 'The wave tests have thrown up a new problem.'

'They want you down there, don't they?'

'If I'd ever thought this might happen, I wouldn't have prom-ised you anything. You understand that, don't you, Andrea?'

'Did you tell them you can't walk?' She found it hard to keep her voice steady.

'They've got wheelchairs down there.'

'And morphine shots?' She moved closer. 'Why should you go? They don't give a damn about your health.'

'I'll be fine.'

'When are you leaving?'

'About an hour.'

'Jesus! That's really considerate of them.'

'It's pretty urgent, Andrea.'

'If I had to choose between a successful commando raid and you not wrecking your leg, I'd save your leg for sure.'

He said gently, 'There's a whole team of people waiting for me down there.'

'How long will they need you?'

'As long as it takes to find a way to stop lorries swinging when it's rough.'

'I really thought it would be different this time.'

'Me too.' Peter was looking at her with sincere regret.

She touched his hand for a moment. 'You have to do it, Peter.'

'At least I'll be coming home alive.'

Through the window behind Peter's head, Andrea saw a strange looking girl enter the garden. She had long frizzy hair and stood rubbing one foot against the other, as if too nervous to approach any further. In one hand she held a small cardboard suitcase. It took Andrea several seconds to relate this untidy person to the woman in the spotless cottage. But who else could the girl be but her daughter. Andrea hurried from the room in order to keep to herself the existence of this new arrival until Peter had departed.

Several minutes after Peter's shiny faced Wren driver had helped him into the car, Andrea headed for the kitchen, meaning to tell Rose that she could leave the room now. But just then the telephone rang.

'Is that Mrs Pauling?'

'Yes.'

'Sally Lowther here. I was wondering if you were at a loose end?'

'Ends don't come looser.'

'Want to go somewhere jolly?'

'I have to stay home with my son and his friend.'

'Your husband won't be out, surely?'

Before realising it, Andrea had made up her mind. 'He is already, but I have a maid. Will you come by for me?'

'About seven-thirty?'

'Fine.'

Only when Andrea had hung up did she realise that she had not asked where they would be going. Luckily, she had a dark green dress, which was fine for cocktail parties, and in the country would do for a smarter occasion. Deciding not to put the bathroom geyser to the test at short notice, Andrea went to see Rose and asked her to heat some water on the stove and bring a jug to her bedroom.

Watching the girl walk with slow deliberation to the wash-stand and pour the steaming water into the china bowl, Andrea was relieved to see such care and method.

A slight breeze came in from the garden, making Andrea's skin tingle pleasantly as she washed her face and arms. Rose was watching closely as Andrea bent over the basin in her brassiere and slip. At just the right moment, the girl squeezed water over her employer's neck and shoulders with a sponge. When Andrea reached behind her for a towel, Rose was ready to press it into her hands.

Andrea patted her face with the towel. 'That's better.' She shook out her hair, and then slipped into her elegant little cocktail dress. As Rose continued watching her, Andrea was disconcerted to notice that the girl's clothes were inexpertly home-made.

'Zip me up, please.' Andrea smiled at Rose. 'You might think it silly of me to ask, but can you follow a printed recipe?'

Rose nodded eagerly. 'I can do that, an' I can make bread, an' pasties.'

Rose's skills extended from cookery to caring for her sister's three sons. Andrea was in front of the mirror putting on lipstick when she saw Leo enter the room behind her.

'Dad's not in his bedroom.' The boy sounded both scared and accusing, almost as if he suspected that *she* might be to blame for his father's disappearance.

'He's at the dockyard.'

'He can hardly walk, mum. Why didn't you stop him?'

'You *know* he's impossible to stop.'

Leo suddenly seemed to take in that his mother was dressing for some social occasion. 'You're going out.'

Andrea felt herself blush. 'You didn't miss me all day, so why be upset now?'

'Because dad's going to hurt his leg really badly.' Andrea feared he might cry.

'He's the one who's decided, so you mustn't feel bad, sweet-heart. Rose will get your supper.'

'I haven't even met her.'

'You'll like her.' Andrea noticed that Leo's socks and sandals were soaking wet.

'Why not go change out of your wet things?' she said cheerily, determined not to let him make her feel bad about going out.

He left the room and returned a few minutes later, wearing dry shoes and flourishing a sheet of paper.

'Dad left this on my bed. He says he had to go.'

'Does he say anything else?'

'He's going to make something special with Justin and me next week.' His lips began to tremble.

'What's wrong, Leo?'

'I'm the only one who cares about his inventions.'

'The navy cares.'

Whenever Leo enthused about his father's inventions – recently his new totalisator for Sandown Park, and a gadget enabling laundries to price washing by volume rather than weight – Andrea longed to tell Leo they were nonsense. But they were fiendishly ingenious. I suppose I can't love Peter, she told herself, trying to deny the thought, even as it formed.

Leo was looking tragic. 'Do they have doctors at the docks?'

'Lots. He'll be fine.'

Leo came across to the dressing table and glanced at his mother's dress as if he hated it. 'Where are you going, mum?'

'Out some place. With a doctor's wife, actually.' Leo was still looking at her with hostility. Was it possible he disapproved of her going out alone? She grinned at him. 'Hey, darling. I have a really nice surprise for you.'

'You've found a boat?' He clutched her hand.

'A sailing one. Quite small.' Incredible that his irritation could vanish so quickly.

'Gaff-rigged or Bermudan?'

'Would I know stuff like that?'

'Can I go out in her tomorrow?'

'Of course you can.'

He danced around her and then sped up to Justin's room to break the news.

The two boys were in Justin's attic when Andrea called up to them to say that she was leaving. They looked down from the dormer as a woman in a short camel-hair coat and a shimmery dress opened the passenger door of a green Sunbeam-Talbot. Then she said something inaudible that made Andrea laugh.

Justin looked at Leo in the steady unblinking way that meant he was thinking up something scathing to say. He looked down at the departing car.

'I'd say that female in the sandy coat looked rather tarty.'

Leo had not noticed anything special about her, and was unsure what 'tarty' was exactly. 'Why did she look tarty?'

'Her face. My mother does hers the same, and nobody can say *she* isn't tarty.' Justin's dark eyes were probing again. 'Do you reckon your parents still do it?'

Leo felt his heart thumping hard. 'It's none of your beeswax.'

'Do they sleep in one bed at home?'

'Yes.'

'Mine, too, but it didn't mean much.'

'But my parents love each other,' said Leo, hearing his voice go quavery and breathless.

'Don't get your knickers in a twist. They may do it lots for all I know. Your dad's leg is what made me wonder. That's all.'

Leo's face felt very hot. He both wanted to hit Justin and to ask what he meant. But he knew he couldn't ask questions without seeming childish. The father of a boy called Wilkes had lost a leg in the Great War and had managed to have three children after that; so why, wondered Leo, had Justin hinted that *his* father's bad leg was stopping him 'doing it'. A woman who loved a man already would love him more if he became lame. Two years ago, when Leo had been ten, his mother had asked him if he would like to know where babies came from, but he had said he knew. A friend had told him the man put his seed in the woman's mouth and the baby came out of her navel months later. But Justin had said this was rot. In fact the man's seed came out of his cock when he put it in the woman's hairy bottom. There had been a joke going around Leo's old school about a little girl asking her father about the funny thing between his legs. 'What is it, daddy?' And daddy had been embarrassed. 'It's a carrot.' Then she had asked her mother about the hairy thing inside her pants. 'It's a garden, dear.' The little girl had returned to her father and asked whether he would like to plant his carrot in 'mummy's garden'. There had been another joke, which Leo had not found funny, about a man and a woman getting stuck together and being prized apart in hospital. But both jokes told him that, as usual, Justin was probably right.

Justin flopped back on his bed and grinned to himself. 'Guess what I'm doing tonight?'

'What?'

'I'm going to find out if anyone guards those boats at night.'

Leo could hear some kind of bird chirping in the garden. He felt slightly sick. 'If there are no guards, what will you do?'

'Swim out and get on board.'

'What if you're spotted?'

'I'll climb on from the side that isn't facing the shore.' He sat up. 'I've planned it all. Every detail. Are you coming?'

'I don't think so.'

'Yellow-belly.'

'The current may be too strong for you.'

'I'll swim back if it is.'

'You may be swept away.'

'You're scared,' sneered Justin.

Leo recognised the stubborn look which usually heralded one of Justin's crazy ventures. 'I'm not a good swimmer. You know that,' said Leo.

Justin examined a scab on his knee, testing the edges to see if it would lift. 'Make up your mind later.'

They went down to the dining room and sat facing one another across the round table. As Rose came in with the soup, Justin sniggered without being able to stop. When she had returned to the kitchen, Leo whispered fiercely, 'She'll leave if you're not careful.'

'Her hair,' gasped Justin, 'it's just like Struwwelpeter's.' He took a sip of soup. 'Mmm, not bad.' He bit into his bread. 'Want to know something really tasty? Country girls show their bottoms for money.'

Leo's mouth was full of soup, most of which spurted onto the table. 'They're religious here,' he spluttered.

'How do you know?'

'Mum told me.'

While Rose was removing their soup plates, Justin turned to her casually, 'Do you go to church?'

'Round 'ere we go to chapel. Would 'ee like to come with me Sunday?'

Justin looked around, as if eager to escape. Leo kicked him under the table. Rose was still waiting for an answer, her eyes wide and eager.

'All right, I'll come,' muttered Justin, staring at the table.

'Ha, ha, ha, clever dick,' Leo flung at Justin as soon as Rose had gone out again. 'I bet she was making a fool of you and doesn't really go to chapel.'

'We'll see.'

They had gone first to a thatched pub beside a creek and Andrea had drunk gin and Sally whisky. There had been old-fashioned brass ships' navigation lamps on the walls and photographs of Edwardian lifeboatmen standing beside their antiquated sailing lifeboats, and the ceiling had been stained a deep nicotine brown.

Leaving for their next port of call, Sally said, 'Being an American, I expect you just lurved the Fisherman's Rest. Pub snobs adore it.'

'Pub snobs can keep it.'

'I'll have you know they play a very special kind of cribbage there with ancient shark's teeth counters.'

'You're kidding.'

'Listen, lady, I'm the native round here, and you're the visitor. You like my American accent?'

'It stinks.'

Andrea could not work out whether it was the double gin she had just tossed back or Sally's peculiar influence that accounted for her failure, until now, to ask where they were going. She certainly did not often carry on wisecracking conversations with women she hardly knew; but, for some reason – possibly the absence of Peter and Leo – an irresponsible lightheartedness kept bubbling up inside her. Why shouldn't she enjoy herself?

Back in the Sunbeam-Talbot, she decided to take a grip on the evening. 'You haven't told me where we're going.'

'You didn't ask,' said Sally, despatching another tight bend with steely competence. 'But since you've asked now, we're going to Elspeth's.'

'A restaurant?'

'A club owned by a gem of a widow. Her husband went down with his ship, so she bought Ferndene Park as his memorial. It's really for naval officers, but pilots can join. Even brown jobs.'

'Farmers?'

'Soldiers. You must know that. Light me a ciggy, will you?' Sally rummaged around until Andrea snatched her bag away from her for safety's sake and extracted a silver case and gold lighter.

'Thanks,' said Sally, exhaling twin tusks of smoke as Andrea lit her cigarette.

'Why do you like Elspeth's?' asked Andrea, wondering how much Sally had drunk before collecting her.

'It's great because the top brass don't go there, and all the service people are young.' Without warning, Sally swung the car into a narrow driveway.

Tall rhododendrons brushed the sides of the car until the drive opened out into a wide carriage sweep. The house was late Victorian baronial and covered in Virginia creeper. Suddenly, Andrea felt as nervous as she had, years ago, when taken to country clubs by her father's rich patients.

'What's this club for?' she murmured.

'To give officers a relaxing time.'

Inside, there was a lot of dark panelling and plenty of chintz-covered sofas and armchairs. A brass telescope on a stand and several marine paintings contributed a vaguely nautical feel, although there were also a number of flower prints and an oil of ballet dancers. About a dozen officers were sitting around chatting to about half that number of women, most of whom appeared to be in their late thirties or early forties.

'Come and meet the girls,' said Sally, just as one of 'the girls' was homing in on Andrea.

'Three cheers, a new face! And who are *you*, dear?'

'She's my new pal,' cried Sally. 'Andrea, say "how do" to Elspeth.'

Elspeth was wearing a black satin bow in her hair and a lace collar that hid her throat. Andrea guessed that her real age was forty-five, though she looked considerably younger. The youngest of the men appeared to be under twenty and was wearing a naval uniform with magenta patches on his lapels. Andrea was taken round and introduced to everyone, though several minutes later she could not connect more than one or two names with their owners. Most of 'the girls', she learned, lived within a radius of fifteen miles and were either widows, spinsters, or had husbands serving at sea. Andrea supposed that the virtual absence of young females was because most would inevitably be in the services and stationed far away from rural backwaters.

Sally returned from the bar with a gin for Andrea. 'Come with me,' she commanded, 'and meet James the Divine.' Andrea allowed herself to be led across the room towards a young man in RAF uniform standing by the window. She had sensed, despite the jocular introduction – and even before Sally had slipped an arm through his – that she was in love with this man, who looked incredibly young, with his dark curly hair, peachlike skin and long lashes. He blushed when Sally murmured, 'James flies Hurricanes and is terribly brave.'

'Darling, I wish you wouldn't say things like that,' he muttered.

'Why not?'

'Because you know I'm like all the rest.'

'What are *they* like?' asked Andrea softly.

He twisted the stem of his wine glass between finger and thumb. 'Scared witless but making out they're not.'

Sally's exalted eyebrow shot up further. 'Jamie, that definitely won't impress my chum.'

Andrea found it disconcerting that Sally was clearly so confident that she would not disapprove of her for having a young lover. Never having met Sally's husband, she couldn't feel sorry for him, except in an abstract way; but it crossed her mind that some of the people present would be his patients. As a doctor's daughter, Andrea found this possibility depressing.

A sallow, fine-featured naval officer came up. 'Sallikins, you can't go on hogging this gorgeous redhead.'

Sally made the introduction and Andrea exchanged stilted small talk with the officer, answering questions such as, why was she in the area, was she married, and did she have children? And her replies did not even slightly dampen the man's interest in her. 'Aren't you going to ask about me?' he murmured, soon volunteering that he was a bachelor, and then, drawling like a matinée idol, 'I'm serving in a very fast and menacing ship, Mrs Pauling. I might have to put to sea at any moment.'

'And what might you be expected to do then?'

'I can't possibly tell you that.'

Since Andrea had already been told by Sally that all the naval people present were serving in coastal forces, she guessed that this man's duties were confined to rescuing ditched airmen and looking for submarines in places where he was most unlikely to find them. Soon after accompanying him to the buffet table, she tried to give him the slip by visiting the ladies, but he was waiting for her outside, and asked her sneeringly why America was 'still sitting on its fanny'. She was tempted to say, 'Because Englishmen like you aren't worth getting excited about', but instead murmured something about President Roosevelt's problems, before walking away.

During the next hour, two other officers – one in the RAF and one in the army – talked to her in a sociable, ordinary way, making her feel that the club was not just a place for sexual assignations as she had started to suspect.

Next to approach her was a sandy-haired naval officer called Tony Cassilis, who had been talking intently to James and Sally as if he knew them well. Because Tony showed no inclination to flirt and had a reassuringly diffident manner, Andrea felt safe to ask him why he thought a complete stranger should have been more eager to make advances as soon as he'd learned she had a husband.

Tony gazed at her sagely. 'Officers prefer their affairs to be with other men's wives simply because they won't be asked to marry them or father a child. And most of these wives are delighted their lovers never get serious.'

'Wives never run off with their lovers?' she asked with a raised brow.

'The balloon goes up now and then,' he conceded.

Andrea frowned. 'What would happen to Sally if her balloon went up?'

'God knows. Her old man's a damned cold fish. Maybe he knows already. Don't get me wrong though. I think he's a terrific doctor. I'd rather go to him than to our naval MO.'

Someone put a record on the radiogram, and several couples began dancing to the song 'Heaven'. A tall man came in from the hall wearing a shabby duffel coat over a white rollneck sweater. There was a sudden turning of heads in his direction and the very young officer with the patches on his lapels hurried over to greet the new arrival with sycophantic enthusiasm. But he remained motionless, listening to the music, his memorable face conveying neither disapproval nor pleasure. Andrea was struck by some inner quality that she could not quite grasp. His interest in the room and its occupants seemed only a matter of form, as if his mind were wholly occupied elsewhere.

Above the words of the song, Andrea heard the man in the white sweater demand, 'Where's my Jimmy?'

'Oh God,' groaned Tony.

'Who *is* his Jimmy?' Andrea asked.

'I'm his sodding Jimmy,' groaned Cassilis.

'But you're called Tony.'

'"Jimmy the One" is naval slang for the first lieutenant of a ship.' He ran a hand through his hair as if involuntarily preparing himself for something. 'Over here, skip,' he called out, waving eagerly despite his earlier irritation.

'Skip's' dark hair looked as if it had been blown back by a stiff breeze, which was strange since Andrea could not remember any wind to speak of when she had arrived. Perhaps he had brushed it back, just before entering.

Tony said, 'Mrs Pauling, I'd like you to meet Lieutenant Commander Harrington.'

As Andrea shook hands with Harrington, his fingers felt surprisingly cold. This poised, weary looking man glanced at her briefly as he was told her name, and then murmured to

51

Cassilis, 'I'm sorry, Tony, I must have a word alone with you.'

Even while telling herself she didn't care, Andrea felt vexed. To be talking to the two most interesting looking men in the room one moment and the next to see them eager to get away was not a cheering experience.

'Maybe we'll meet again,' said Cassilis, draining his glass and thumping it down on a table.

'Maybe we will,' said Andrea, puzzled by his gloomy tone. True to form, Harrington said not a word to her before hurrying to the door.

Sally had spotted the two men abandoning Andrea and joined her immediately after their departure. James was no longer in tow.

Sally asked, 'What did you make of Tony?'

'I liked him.'

'Elspeth worships the ground he treads on.'

'Does he repay the compliment?'

'You bet.' Sally moved closer. 'What was your impression of mournful Mike Harrington?' To Andrea's surprise she rolled her eyes like the swooning heroine of a silent film.

'He's handsome. Maybe a bit pleased with himself. But I only saw him for a few seconds.

'If you'd seen him for a few hours it wouldn't have helped.'

'I don't care about him, Sally.'

'Just as well. He's still in love with his wife.'

'Good for him.'

'You think so? She ditched him a year ago. Plenty of gals have made eyes at him, without a dicky bird of interest for their pains.' Sally took a pensive drag at her cigarette.

Behind her, through the window, Andrea heard the sound of an engine starting up. She turned, and, lifting the edge of the blackout, saw Mike Harrington, with Tony crouched behind, speeding away on a motorbike. So *that* was why Harrington's hair had been windswept and his hands so cold. She was aware of Sally standing right beside her, also watching, but with a glumness and anxiety that astonished her. Could James be second best to one of these men? Having seen Sally look at her airman so dotingly, Andrea could not believe this.

'What's wrong?' she asked.

'I was thinking of James, and what he'll be doing later tonight.'

'Tell me,' murmured Andrea.

'U-boats surface after dark to charge their batteries, so James and his mates go up with searchlights and bombard them with R/Ps, whatever they are.' Andrea felt dumb not to have realised till now that Sally's brashness was a defence against anxiety.

'What will Mike and Tony be doing tonight?' she asked, trying to sound casual.

'Nothing dangerous. Searching foreign looking trawlers in case they're carrying spies. That sort of thing.' Sally took Andrea's arm and said firmly, 'Come on, let's play billiards and forget the lousy war.'

Andrea disengaged herself. 'They *are* in coastal forces, aren't they?'

'Of course they are, lucky devils.'

Walking to the billiard table, Andrea saw Elspeth emerging from a room marked 'Private'. She had been crying. Could Elspeth have thought that Tony had spent too much time talking to her, wondered Andrea. But when she mentioned this possibility to Sally, she shook her head dismissively.

After being told the rules of billiards, Andrea remarked, tongue in cheek, that all her previous knowledge of the game had been gleaned from a few remarks in *The Cherry Orchard*. From this it had soon emerged that she was a teacher of literature. 'And piano, too,' she admitted.

'Well, I'll be jiggered,' muttered Sally, 'I'd never have guessed you were a schoolmistress.'

Since Sally had plainly thought her a kindred spirit before knowing what she did for a living, Andrea wondered whether this revelation would change everything. She guessed it wouldn't. But after a very onesided game of billiards, Sally suggested leaving.

During the journey home, Sally seemed depressed. 'I shouldn't have brought you,' she muttered, accelerating out of the drive.

'Because I'm a schoolmistress?'

'You probably think I'm a slut.'

'Of course I don't.'

'Most people do who know about James. The Cornish are low church moralists. Even the local pillars are hypocrites.'

'The war must have opened their eyes.'

'If it has, most don't let on. You'd be amazed how often I'm told that Ferndene's a sink of iniquity. There's a creepy mural in the church, called "Souls in Purgatory". I know for a fact that the vicar's bitchy wife thinks I should be roasting there.' She laughed mirthlessly as they sped along between black hedgerows, guided by the pencil thin beams of her masked headlamps. 'I'll tell you what *is* sinful: being forced to go on living with a man you're sick of.' The wind poured through the open windows making Sally's hair fly. 'Jesus, was I glad when the war came along, with loads of new excuses for getting out of the house: Red Cross, evacuees, entertaining pilots. Blimey, they were sad when they arrived. Most had lost friends, and were scared stupid on their own account. So I cheered them up with the odd peck on the cheek.' She changed gear for a corner. 'Some wanted more than that, so I thought what the hell. They might be dead tomorrow. And that was incredibly arousing: the thought that every fuck might be the last. Then I met James and fell head over heels, so I stopped seeing all the rest. And now I'm terrified all the bloody time in case he's killed.'

'Does your husband know about him?'

'He suspects. But he's got his work, and he's got our son. They're all he really cares about.'

'Where is your son?'

54

'Staying with a school friend till next week. Mark's sixteen and wonderful in spite of it.'

'Don't you miss him when he's away at school?'

'I did when he was little. But now I'm thankful he's not around to cramp my style.' She turned to Andrea and grinned in the darkness. 'Aren't you sometimes secretly pleased your lad's miles away?'

Andrea looked out at the passing trees. 'Never. I often wish I could care a lot less.'

Sally touched her arm. 'I love the way you don't get prim with me even when you don't see eye to eye. If only more people were like you down here. I could cope with a scandal myself, but Mark would hate it. As the doctor's wife I'm meant to set an example to the lower orders. The irony is that Mark'll soon be grown up and gone, and I'll probably lose James by not going off with him now.'

Andrea felt a lurch of panic. She'd thought herself quite different from 'good time' Sally – in some ways she didn't even like her – but their situations were disturbingly similar: both having husbands whose work mattered more to them than anything except their sons. Fellow-feeling swamped Andrea as they sped towards the river.

The water was black as ink as they crossed the bridge over Polwherne Creek. Across it, the road sloped upwards and the trees thinned to reveal a panoramic view of the estuary. Sally stopped the car and they gazed in silence at the bar of moonlight stretching across the sea.

At first all they could hear was the tick-tick of the cooling engine and the gentle whispering of oak leaves overhead. Faintly at first, a new sound became audible: a low droning that grew louder. Instinctively, Andrea reached for Sally's hand. Two fighters dipped down out of the darkness and swept seawards, leaving the estuary behind.

Leo woke with a start. Someone was speaking to him.

'I'm off now.'

Justin's face loomed darkly in front of him. Leo glanced at his luminous watch. The hands pointed to quarter past one.

'Can't you forget about going?' he faltered.

'Course not, espèce d'idiot, fou.' French was Justin's best subject.

'You're the one who's fou,' muttered Leo. 'I'll tell my mother if you're not back by four. I ought to tell her now.'

'Stop moaning and come too.'

'No thanks. What'll you say if mum catches you pushing a bike through the hall?'

'That I'm sleepwalking.'

'Ha, ha.'

'Anyway it won't happen. She went to bed half an hour ago. Ta-ta for now.'

Leo watched Justin tiptoe down the garden path with his bicycle and then disappear from view into the lane. He felt relieved and ashamed at the same time, and wished he had Justin's courage; but he sensed that, if he did, he might also suffer from Justin's moods. He lay down and tried to sleep but whenever he closed his eyes he imagined Justin swimming and getting cramp. Instead, he forced himself to visualise Justin walking back over the rocks on the shore where they had first seen the naval ships. Again and again he told himself that his friend's swim was over and that he was coming home. But though Leo's waking dream was remarkably real in every detail, he wasn't fooled by it.

Being realistic, Leo knew there was little chance that his friend would be back until four or four-thirty. So when he looked out at the garden, where the leaves of a large tree were moving like a shoal of grey-green fish in the moonlight, he did not really imagine he would see Justin creeping through the gate. After all he had only been gone an hour, but fear was already tightening its grip on his mind, making him long to look out every minute or two. A desire to defecate sent him hurrying to the lavatory. 'I'll be blamed,' he thought, imagining the worst as he sat on the lavatory. 'I said nothing when a few words to mum could have saved Justin's life and now he's drowned and nothing can bring him back.' Soon after Leo returned to bed, his heart leapt at the sound of the latch on the garden gate. He raced to the window. Justin was pushing his bike up the path.

'Tell me everything,' begged Leo, dragging Justin into his room.

'There's nothing to tell.' Justin sat on the edge of Leo's bed and smiled to himself as if enjoying a private joke. 'The gunboat wasn't there. Only the minesweeper and the MTB. No sign of the small boats either.'

'Maybe they're anchored somewhere else.'

'Why would they be?' Justin sounded put out.

Leo said reasonably, 'Their engines might need repairing in a yard.'

'Not three at a time.'

Justin's certainty irritated Leo. 'Oh, I forgot. They were away on a secret mission.'

'I won't give up, whatever you think.'

Leo said flatly, 'You'll go out night after night, and sleep in the day?'

'That's right.'

When Justin was up in his attic, Leo could hear him moving about the room, taking off his shoes, and finally getting into bed. Leo had hoped that the whole mad adventure would be over in a day or two, and that then they would be able to enjoy a normal holiday; but now it was obvious it wasn't going to stop. At least not until Justin could manage to climb aboard a vessel and see for himself. Till then, there would be more sleepless nights and hours of waiting.

CHAPTER 4

A ndrea had been wondering what account of her evening to give to Leo and was relieved, in the event, not to be asked to give any. At breakfast, both boys seemed preoccupied with their boiled eggs – rare delicacies at the best of times – but they became more animated on being told that they could go sailing later that morning.

'I'll take you in the car,' offered Andrea.

'Can't we go by bike? It's all downhill,' said Leo.

Andrea couldn't tell whether her son's coldness of the previous evening had lasted through the night. She said, 'You must both wear life jackets.'

'Aye aye, cap'n,' giggled Leo, unexpectedly kissing his mother.

Suddenly both boys were laughing helplessly, for no reason she could fathom. When they had gone, Andrea contemplated driving to the hill behind the club to see how they were doing. But the idea of spying on them was repugnant: having hired the dinghy, she would trust them.

While Rose was piling the breakfast things onto a tray, she hummed quietly to herself, taking occasional glances at Andrea. 'Where did 'ee go weth doctor's wife, ma'am?'

'An officers' club.' The girl picked up the tray smartly. 'What's wrong, Rose?'

'I cudden say, reelly.'

In view of Sally Lowther's warning about local prejudices, Andrea let Rose leave the room without pressing her to elaborate. To avoid being the subject of local tittle-tattle, she would have to be careful. Recalling Sally's remarks about the vicar's wife, Andrea decided with time on her hands to look at the purgatorial fresco. Though an agnostic, she enjoyed churches, especially for oddities like lepers' squints and misericords. Why not for a vision of hell?

On entering St Peter's, she walked past the Boy Scouts' banners and the neat piles of prayer books. A monument near the font caught her eye. '*Here lyeth interred the body of Mary relict of Henry de Roos, Gent. A lady who gave constant heed to her husband through ten years of his patient affliction, and uncomplainingly returned to God ten of her twelve children, and was yet an example in virtue and piety . . .*' Mary was surely the creation of a professional writer of epitaphs.

The Judgement Day mural extended in patchy fragments above two arches in the nave. A line of men and women was being poked and prodded into a fire by a posse of pitchfork-wielding devils. The sinners' naked bodies were white and bulbous, as if the women were pregnant.

To the right of the chancel arch stood a piano, presumably for use when the organ was out of commission. Andrea tried some notes and found that it was not badly out of tune. She was playing the opening bars of a Beethoven sonata when a woman emerged from a door to the right of the altar. Andrea stopped in mid-phrase.

'So beautiful. I hope you don't mind my asking whether you're a professional?' The woman was carrying a brass flower vase and a jug containing water. She wore a baggy green housecoat over her clothes.

'I'm a teacher.'

'We rarely hear good music down here. Are you visiting or staying longer?'

Andrea told her she would be returning to Oxford at the end of the month. The woman moved closer. She had a clever face with inquisitive eyes. 'My dear, if it's any interest to you, the local school has a piano, paid for by an appeal – it's much better than this poor creature. I'm sure the headmistress would be delighted if you would play to the children. They break up next week, like all the state schools.'

'I can't promise, but I'll try.'

'Splendid. Just tell her Mrs Jefferies suggested it. My husband's the chairman of the governors, *ex officio*. He's the vicar you see. And your name . . . ?'

Andrea introduced herself and they shook hands. Had this quietly spoken woman really had the nerve to rebuke Sally for her way of life? As Andrea was leaving the church, she spotted a rusty metal object fixed onto a pillar, and described beneath as '*A Gudgeon from the wreck of HMS Anson, in which perished 208 souls on 14th May 1784.*' The way in which Leo popped into her thoughts like a surfacing cork made her wonder whether she ought to drive to the sailing club after all.

An easterly wind was blowing directly upstream from the sea, giving the boys a hard time as they tacked to the naval flotilla's anchorage. But Leo still enjoyed hearing the strange plopping noises inside the centre-plate casing. With the boat heeling steeply, he asked Justin to sit up on the gunwale, which he did grudgingly.

Shortly before his father had fallen ill, Leo had been taken sailing by him, and, though only nine at the time, had learned a great deal. But it was one thing to know the theory and quite another to carry it out in practice. Crucially, Leo did not know how the boat should 'feel'. So, a vital consideration, such as how far he could safely allow her to heel over before spilling wind or heading up, worried him whenever they were tacking.

While Leo was puzzling over what to do, Justin trailed his fingers in the water as if bored to death. This added insult to injury, since Leo was already irritated with him for insisting that they look at the warships. Leo would himself have preferred to land on a beach and laze about.

'Ready about!' shouted Leo, pushing the tiller across, but neglecting to say, 'Lee 'o!', since this traditional nautical announcement had already caused Justin too much amusement. 'Leo says "Leo" because he loves his name. Leo says "Leo" because he's fou.'

On the new tack, they would surely manage to get round the next tree-covered point. Then they would be able to see whatever beastly grey ships were behind it, and then, with luck, forget the navy for the rest of their sail.

'The gunboat's back again,' cried Justin triumphantly. 'It must have done something in the night.'

'A big job?' suggested Leo. 'Yuk!'

'God, you're an infant.'

'You too. I'm going to go about before we reach them.'

'No,' screeched Justin. 'I want to get as close as we can.'

'No point. I can see from here that the two smaller boats aren't there.' Leo grinned. 'Maybe *they* did a big job too, and are going to do another tonight.' Justin gave him one of his pitying looks. Leo said briskly, 'All right, ready about.' But before he could push the tiller across, Justin had grabbed his hand.

'We're going closer.'

As they struggled together, the mainsheet slipped from Leo's hand, causing the dinghy to lose momentum and start drifting with the tide onto the gunboat's buoy. 'Let go of me,' pleaded Leo, still struggling.

They hit the metal cylinder with a dull clang that must have been heard all over the ship. Justin grabbed the ring on the buoy to stop them bumping along the gunboat's side, but his fingers lost their grip.

A sailor appeared on the foredeck high above them and shouted, 'Fend off, you sprogs!'

Another leant down with a boathook and jabbed at them at intervals until they had slipped astern. Even when they were well clear, Leo wanted to scream his anger and humiliation at Justin. 'What idiots we looked.'

'Who cares? I spotted the perfect place to get aboard.'

'That little ladder thing? They won't leave that out at night.'

'We'll see.'

'*I* jolly well *won't* see,' cried Leo.

Lacking the heart to go on sailing, Leo headed for the club. He was distressed that the boat hook had dented the dinghy's gunwale, splintering the wood.

'Let me have a go at steering,' demanded Justin. With the wind behind them, they were going much faster, without heeling.

Leo stared up at the mainsail, as if he had not heard the request. He was trying to remember what his father had told him about avoiding gybes. Push the tiller away from you, or pull it towards you? Towards you, he decided.

'Heads,' screamed Leo, as the boom crashed across, narrowly missing Justin's head but striking him on the shoulder.

'You need bloody well teaching,' screamed Justin, rubbing his upper arm. When Leo had apologised Justin rapidly recovered his composure. 'Those sailors looked shocked as hell to see us so close to them.' He laughed loudly at the memory. 'I'm bloody glad we came.'

Leo managed a wan smile.

At the sailing club, Andrea found that the boys had not yet returned. On leaving the village, she had spotted the school and, remembering her open invitation, returned there to kill time. Entering the yard, she saw an attractive bell tower and a mock Gothic door marked 'Infants'. In the tall schoolroom was a motley gathering of girls and boys, many in old boots and ragged stockings, with the big boys crammed into desks designed for much smaller children. On the wall behind the teacher's desk was a map of the world – Mercator's projection – in which Britain was placed in the centre, and the red imperial parts looked much larger than they really were.

The teacher on duty was a neatly dressed young woman with curly hair and an openwork jumper, revealing disconcerting flesh-coloured shades of silk in the gaps. Moments after mentioning Mrs Jefferies' suggestion that she play to the children, Andrea was led to the piano – not a new one, as she had expected, but a reconditioned Broadwood upright. She had thought of playing from memory a few of Schumann's *Kinderszenen*, but, seeing so many children of four and five gazing up at her, and noticing that many older ones fidgeted all the time, she asked to see any music that might be kept in the classroom.

Andrea's programme finally included, 'Early One Morning', 'Billy Boy' and 'Yankee Doodle'. The children were not given songbooks, so Andrea invited them to sing along if they knew the words. Several tried bravely, but fell silent on realising how few others were singing. Afterwards, several girls begged Andrea to come again. The school's second teacher, who had always played the piano for them, had recently joined the ATS. One boy, who resembled Leo in his sweetest incarnation, fetched a banana from his desk. Was it, Andrea wondered, a bribe to lure her back?

'Want a 'nanee do 'ee?' he asked, shyly proffering this all but unobtainable piece of fruit.

Andrea looked to Miss Lawrence for guidance. 'Should I?'

'Don't worry. Michael's father's in the merchant navy and often gets them.'

'Thank you *very* much,' she said bending down and giving Michael a hug.

As Andrea closed the lid on the keyboard, a thickset boy kicked her benefactor. The headmistress caught the offender by the ear, and with commendable dexterity whacked him behind his knees with a ruler. 'Bullies must be beaten,' she sighed.

Before Andrea departed, Nancy Lawrence pressed a large key and a smaller one into her hand. 'You're welcome to play the piano, any day, after school. In the holidays too.'

'That's wonderful,' murmured Andrea, touched by the offer.

'Come again before term ends. The children love new faces. They went wild over the naval officers who came last week.' She smiled radiantly. 'On Tuesday we're being shown over one of their ships. Have you ever met any of our coastal forces people, Mrs Pauling?'

'Very briefly.'

'Such kind and courteous men.'

'I'm sure,' murmured Andrea.

By the time Andrea returned to the sailing club, the boys had landed and cycled away. She found the secretary bent over paperwork in the office.

'How did they get along?'

'Made an awful hash of landing, poor chaps. Tore the pintles out of the rudder as they ran in on the hard.'

'I wish someone could teach them.'

'I'll ask around.'

'I'd really appreciate that.'

Back at the house, Andrea waited for Leo to tell her about the rudder, but sensed that something else was bothering him more. So, to avoid pressing him, she recounted how she had played for the village children, and produced the banana.

'I say, mum, where did you get *that*?'

'From a boy in school.'

'Give us a bite, *please*.'

'Maybe.'

Instead of pleading with her, Leo looked worried again. At last he said, 'Justin asked Rose something rude.'

65

'What was that?'

Leo blushed fiercely as he gazed through the glass doors into the garden. 'He asked to see her bottom for ten bob.'

Andrea laughed before she could stop herself. 'I never expected *that*,' she gasped. 'What did she say?'

'She was hopping mad.'

'I'm not surprised. It really isn't at all funny.'

'Then why did you laugh, mum?'

'The shock. I'll have to talk with her I guess.'

'I bet she wasn't shocked really. Justin said she's sly.'

'She had every right to be mad at him.'

During the silence that followed, Andrea did not like the way Leo was studying her. She sensed that he was trying to sound casual as he asked, 'Who was the woman who came for you yesterday?'

'Sally Lowther. She's the doctor's wife.'

'She looked tarty.'

Andrea felt her cheeks burn. 'Did Justin say that?'

'He could have.'

'Mrs Lowther uses a lot of make-up, but that doesn't make her anything bad.'

'Justin's mother wears loads.'

Andrea moved towards him and said firmly, 'Listen, sweetheart, sometimes unhappy people like to make other people sad, too. It makes them feel better. So don't listen if Justin tries to make you worried about the people I see.'

'Okay.'

'Was it for a bet, what he said to Rose?'

'Nope.'

'Why did he take such a stupid risk?'

'He likes to. Anyway he knows someone who got a woman to show him her things that way.'

'I'm pretty darn sure the boy who told him was lying.' Andrea sat down beside her son. He had not changed his sailing clothes, and there were saltwater stains on his shorts right up to his groin. She said gently, 'Justin's a mixed-up kid. Remember that. So what happened to the rudder?'

'I couldn't pull it up in time. There's a pin that fits in the top and stops you getting out the tiller. I yanked hard, but it wouldn't budge.' He pulled a face. 'I think we should have gone head to wind at the last moment.' She stood up and tossed him the banana. His smile faded. 'It's a bit green, mum.'

'Then let it ripen.'

If only Leo had never met Justin, thought Andrea, as she went in search of Rose. The kitchen was empty but the scullery door was open. What the hell did one say to a respectable domestic who had been treated by a twelve-year-old boy as if she were a serving wench during the ancien régime? As Rose came in from the scullery, Andrea stared at the chopped vegetables on the table.

'I am really so sorry my son's friend insulted you.'

'Don' 'ee worry. I told 'im plenty.'

'I'm glad you did.'

'He won't try messin' again.'

'Did you hit him?' asked Andrea uneasily.

'I said there's nothin' Satan won't do to 'im now. So he got frighted and ran up over the fields.'

And what could she say to that, wondered Andrea. Hardly rebuke the girl for involving the powers of darkness in a prank. Andrea murmured, 'I hope his rudeness can be forgotten now.'

Feeling anxious in case Justin had been badly scared, Andrea wished she had told Rose about his father's death. Back in the sitting room, she found Leo taking tiny nibbles from his unripe banana.

'Was Justin upset by Rose?' she asked him.

'Nope. He faked being scared.'

'You're sure?'

'She's a religious maniac, mum.'

'Maniacs can be kind of scary.'

Leo said sharply, 'Justin is never scared.'

Andrea raised conciliatory hands. 'Leo, dearest, Justin pre-
tends nothing hurts him, but that's because he's been hurt more
than we can imagine.'

'I think I know him by now.'

'Then tell me what he truly cares about?'

Leo tossed away the banana skin. 'You really want to know?
He thinks the navy's ships in the river are hush-hush boats and he
wants to snoop around inside one. *That's* what he cares about.'

Andrea smiled happily. 'But that's marvellous. The kids from
the village school are going aboard a ship next week. I'll ask the
headmistress to let you and Justin go along too.'

Leo jumped up, white-faced. 'You musn't. He'd kill me for
telling you his plan.'

Andrea was appalled. 'He'd injure you?'

'No, no. He'd say he couldn't trust me, *ever*; that I'd betrayed
him; wasn't his friend.'

Andrea's patience gave way. 'I could call his aunt right now,
and she'd want him sent home for insulting Rose.'

'Don't call her.' He was breathless with horror.

'You have better friends, I know you do.'

'He can't go home.'

'Would he bully you at school?'

'I can't explain.'

She touched his hand gently. 'Leo, if I call his aunt, he won't
know you spoke with me first. Let's do it now. He's wrecking
your holiday.'

Leo drew himself up. 'He can't go.'

'Why not?'

'Because,' shouted Leo, 'his dad's face was burned right off
before he hit the ground.'

When her son had left the room, Andrea sat down heavily
on the lumpy sofa and stared at some discoloured wax fruit on
the table in the window. Talking to Justin about Rose seemed
suddenly less urgent.

*   *   *

Justin crept into Leo's room soon after midnight, leaving him in no doubt, from the moment his eyes opened, that this was to be the night of the crucial attempt. At once, Leo knew he would not be able to endure another night lying in bed waiting for Justin. It would be easier to share the danger with him than stay behind. As Leo got up and slipped out of his pyjamas, Justin silently applauded him.

'Put on your dark blue aertex.' Leo did as commanded and then held up his white plimsolls. 'Don't worry,' soothed Justin, 'you can rub mud on them later. Shove your swimming trunks in here.' He patted a canvas beach bag. 'Wear long socks or you'll get scratched.'

'What about a torch?' asked Leo, searching for socks.

'Got my school one here, but we may not use it.'

A square of moonlight on the linoleum told Leo why. As he put on his socks, he said, 'Mum says some village kids will be shown over one of the ships soon.'

Justin seemed shaken, but only for a moment. 'That'll be the MTB or minesweeper.' His conviction grated with Leo.

'Could be the MGB,' he objected.

'Look, who cares?' snapped Justin. 'I'm only interested in the small boats.'

'Why?'

'They spend more time away from their moorings than the rest. I've bloody told you that, Leo.'

As they crept past his mother's door, Leo felt a pang of guilt. By going with Justin, he was deceiving her. But at least with the two of them together one would be able to raise the alarm for the other in an emergency. And Justin's plan seemed likely to keep them out of trouble, since they would creep down to the ships through the woods, instead of approaching in the open, along Porthbeer beach.

Speeding towards the river, Leo felt an unexpected surge of happiness. Earlier he had been worried about cycling without lights, but his eyes had quickly grown accustomed to the darkness. If he could only be told that their mission would not after all involve plunging into black and icy water, he would enjoy every minute. But fear nagged constantly.

'What will you say if we're caught?' he asked Justin as he pedalled beside him.

'We won't be caught.' The wind flung Justin's words away so that they were hard to hear.

'But we *must* know what to say.'

'It's a dare. We'll say that.'

The tarmac glowed palely in the moonlight as it wound snakelike between black woods on either side. Bats swooped across the road, making the boys duck and swerve. After riding for ten minutes, they freewheeled to a halt at a point which Justin declared was due north of the spot where he wanted to hit the river. Leaving their bicycles, they walked towards a tangle of trees and undergrowth. In the profounder darkness of the wood, Leo blundered into hollies and brambles. The pain of his scratches hardly troubled him. They were closer to the river now, and panic fluttered in his chest. A long way off, he heard what he thought was a farm dog barking.

'A fox,' whispered Justin authoritatively. Whenever a twig cracked, Leo froze, to Justin's amusement. 'We could knock down a tree and no one would hear.' They moved across a clearing overgrown with straggling elders and stumbled into the bed of a stream.

'All we do now is follow it,' said Justin, as if he had meant all along to arrive at this spot.

The stones underfoot were jagged and the bottom often dropped into deep hollows. At times their progress exhausted them as much as if they'd been running. Searching out safe shallows by the bank they were obliged to push aside brambles that arched across the stream.

On the beach at last, Leo was thankful to find the tide out. The distance to the ships would be shorter now than at high water. Pulling on their trunks, the boys kept on their shirts in case their pale skin was visible in the dark. Because the ships were half a mile downstream, they crept along at the top of the beach for what felt like ages to Leo.

To their left, the water was coal black except where small waves reflected ribbons of moonlight. In silhouette, the ships looked dark and threatening. Leo's queasiness was growing worse. The furthest he had swum in his life had been six lengths of the swimming pool at his old school, a distance which would just about take him to the nearest of the ships.

'What are we meant to look for on board?' he whispered.

'Anything unusual.'

'Like what?'

'If I knew *exactly*, we wouldn't be looking.'

They had left their shoes with their clothes and the shingle was already hurting Leo's feet. He was glad when they moved onto soft mud, until he felt it oozing between his toes. They struggled not to laugh as their feet made lewd squelching noises as they walked along.

The shingle spit from which they chose to swim shelved steeply into the water, forcing them to dig in their heels to stop themselves falling in with a splash.

Justin whispered, 'Can you see the trawlers?'

'Aren't they the smaller ones with the sentry boxes on top?'

'The boxes are their wheelhouses. You swim to the nearest. I'll try the other.'

Even now, Leo could not believe what he was about to do. He should come clean at once and tell Justin it was too risky for a poor swimmer like himself; but even as they entered the water he could not bring himself to utter. The water was cold enough to make his legs ache painfully, though seconds after he started swimming the pain vanished. With each stroke, he saw sparks of phosphorescence flicker around his hands. The ships looked deserted, so he doubted whether any sailors were keeping watch. Though he supposed their blackout could be faultless.

Every few strokes, Leo told himself he would give up and swim back to the shore the moment he felt tired. But he swam on, even when his fingers were numb and he had pins and needles up his arms. When reaching the buoy of his trawler, he rested for several minutes, clinging to its ring.

From the land this small ship had seemed to lie very low in the water. Close to, the sides rose high above him, as daunting as an overhanging shelf of rock. There was a wooden ridge that ran round the boat about four feet above the water, so he hoped to pull himself up onto it, if he could find a rope fender. He was swimming towards the stern, looking, when he heard something that made him gulp in water. Men were talking behind the timbers of the hull. Terrified, he launched himself towards the beach.

With the tide in his favour, Leo was soon swept upstream beyond the spit where he and Justin had first entered the water. He landed in watery mud on the far side of a low reef. Stumbling back towards his clothes over barnacle-covered rocks, his whole body was wracked by uncontrollable shivering. He knew he had to struggle on without resting until he could put on his dry jersey.

As Leo reached his clothes, angry shouts echoed from the moorings. He heard a splash, as if someone had jumped into the water from the deck of one of the ships. Seconds later, there was a squealing noise and a heavy smack, which reverberated across the river. A ship's boat had been lowered fast and hit the water. A searchlight on the MGB's bridge stabbed the darkness, its beam swivelling from side to side. Leo didn't know whether to stay or escape. If Justin had been caught, the sailors might bully him into admitting he hadn't been alone.

Leo waited for ten minutes before accepting that Justin would not be returning. Then he dragged his aching limbs up the beach. Too cold and distraught to brave the woods without help from Justin's torch, he allowed its beam to lead him swiftly to the stream. Driven by acute anxiety for his friend, he found his way to the road in half the time it had taken them to reach the river.

Andrea sat up in bed, averting her eyes as she switched on her bedside light. Blinking, she saw her son standing near the door.

'What's wrong, Leo?'

She listened with a sick feeling in her stomach as he stammered out a fantastic tale about swimming to different naval ships – he and his trouble-making friend.

'Where's Justin?'

'Under arrest, most likely. They caught him.'

Wanting to hug and kiss her son because he had not drowned himself, she also wanted to shake him. 'How could you do anything so downright crazy? You could have gotten in trouble in the water and died.'

'He was going anyway. So I had to go.'

'You should have told me. You're almost thirteen, Leo. Not six.' She started to dress rapidly, not even bothering to tell him to wait outside. 'How come you're sure he's okay?'

'The sailors launched a boat for him.'

'You saw them do that?'

'I heard it.'

'Maybe they launched the boat to go ashore. Maybe they never saw him.'

Leo started to make small snuffling noises. 'He's a really good swimmer. Really he is.'

Andrea fastened her skirt. 'We'd better go find him.' She had a vague memory of having seen a house outside Porthbeer with the navy's flag flying outside. She picked up her handbag and ran downstairs. 'Don't delay me, Leo.' In the dining room, she downed a mouthful of neat whisky from the bottle. Just then, she heard an automobile stop in the lane.

She opened the door. A sailor was leading Justin up the path. The boy was wrapped in a grey blanket and was barefoot. He no longer looked cocky, just scared and rather pathetic. As soon as she had ushered them into the sitting room, the sailor cleared his throat.

'I'm Petty Officer Lee, madam. Sorry to call at this hour, but this young gent was caught trespassing on one of HM's ships.'

The man's uniform was not quite the same as the officers' at the club. When he removed his hat, she saw that he was older than she'd thought – about forty. Out of the corner of her eye, Andrea saw that Leo looked almost as scared as his friend.

'Come and sit down, Justin,' she said, gently steering him to the sofa and then sitting with her arm through his. 'I don't imagine he did any harm,' she remarked coldly to the petty officer.

'I wouldn't know about that, madam. It's up to Captain Borden and Lieutenant Commander Harrington to decide whether to call in the police.'

'To arrest a boy of twelve?' she gasped. Leo began coughing as if to drown her words.

'Best ask the officers, madam. They're expecting you both at ten.'

'Where?'

'The Polwherne Hotel – it's naval property now. On the right as you leave Porthbeer on the Tregwidden road.'

'What if we stay home?'

The petty officer lowered his voice. 'I'd be sweet as sugar if I was you, madam. For the kid's sake.' He winked at her, and then turned to Justin. 'Just answer their questions, lad, and you'll be fine.'

Andrea said sharply, 'He looks like a spy, does he?'

The man's friendliness did not waver. 'Let's leave all that to the officers.'

'It was a prank for Chrissakes.'

'Leave it, mum,' whispered Leo.

'I'll be getting back to bed, madam, if you don't mind. G'dnight boys.'

After closing the door behind him, Andrea felt faint with anger. Why this stupid pretence that something awful had been done? It was cruel and pointless. Justin still seemed on the verge of tears.

'Don't be a ninny,' she murmured. 'What can they do?'

'I dunno.'

'Not a thing.' She smiled at them both, but their faces remained glum and chastened. She kissed Leo, and gave Justin a hug, which he did not resist. 'Don't worry, Justin. What you need right now is a hot bath. Leave those sailors to me.'

CHAPTER 5

When Rose brought in eggs and bacon for breakfast, Andrea dutifully oohed and aahed for the second day running, implying how lucky they were to have gained unrationed access to farm produce. The girl accepted this tribute in silence, making sure her employer noticed when she stared pointedly at Justin – though whether this was because he was wearing his school suit, or because Rose still had a grievance against him, Andrea couldn't tell.

'Why do 'ee wear Sunday best on Friday?' the girl demanded, as she passed behind Justin's chair.

'He's visiting some officers,' said Andrea brightly, as if this was a rare privilege.

'I'm getting a medal,' added Justin.

'Don' 'ee go tellin' fibs. I waked up and saw 'ee come home like a drowned rat.' She leant forward and snatched away his empty plate.

On the way to Porthbeer Justin remained very quiet, staring out at the hedgerows as if in a trance. As Andrea tried to think of something comforting to say, she noticed how tight his suit jacket was. Feeling tearful on his behalf, she said, 'Don't let them get to you.'

'I won't be cheeky, if that's your worry.'

'It would also be smart to promise you'll never go near those ships again.'

'I promise.'

'Promise to *them*, Justin, not me.'

'Okay, Mrs Pauling.'

'Okay, *Andrea*.'

Her spirits plunged as she became aware of the great effort Justin was making to seem unafraid. She said gently, 'You don't have to pretend to be so gutsy, you know.'

He seemed puzzled. 'You think I should make out I'm scared when they ask their questions?'

'Showing respect will do fine. What I meant was you can share your feelings with me if it helps you.'

Justin did not reply but gazed intently into the woods on his side of the car. Suddenly he cried, 'Stop here. Now!'

Andrea did as commanded and watched in astonishment as he disappeared between the trees. Just as she was beginning to think he had run away, he reappeared, pushing the bicycle she had lent him. Together they slid its muddy wheels into the car's trunk. As he sat beside her again, she was dismayed to see tears spilling down his cheeks.

'Hey, don't do that,' she soothed. 'What's wrong, honey?' He pointed to his grey trousers where the bicycle's chain had left an oily mark. His earlier calmness made this sudden breakdown over a minor misfortune seem more shocking to her. Of course today of all days he would have wanted to look his best, and now he couldn't. She gave him a handkerchief from her bag and he dabbed at his eyes before handing it back. 'No, keep it,' she insisted, 'for luck.'

He surprised her with a wobbly smile. 'Thanks,' and after a brief pause, 'Andrea.'

The Polwherne Hotel already looked a little down at heel, with the paint peeling from the drainpipes and window-frames and grass growing on the tennis courts. When Andrea had given her name to the sentry at the gate, he picked up a primitive looking telephone and rang through to the house.

Permission granted, they drove in, parked beside some Nissen

huts and then walked round to the front. On a tall flagstaff with
a crosstrees, a white ensign was flapping loudly, casting a
moving shadow on the lawn beside the river. A long way out
on the shimmering water – or so it seemed to Andrea – were
some grey ships and a couple of others painted in patches of
greys, browns and blues.

'Did you swim to one of those?' gasped Andrea.

'To that one.' He indicated a small ship, further away than
the rest.

'That's amazing, Justin,' she murmured, meaning it.

'Thanks.' To her relief he grinned at her but almost immediately his face resumed its strained expression.

It was a sunny morning and seagulls were wheeling and
screeching overhead, their breast feathers looking improb-
ably white. A naval motor boat, manned by two Wrens in
bell-bottom trousers, tied up at a small pontoon and landed a
red-faced officer. Let's hope *he* won't be seeing us, she thought,
on entering the house.

Although painted signs bore witness to the house's former
use – Reception, Tudor Bar, Reynolds Room, whatever that
might have been – all vestiges of comfort had gone with the
long vanished carpets and furniture. To protect the panelling,
whole walls had been covered in brown hardboard, an ideal
surface for the notices which proliferated.

'Ugh! Just like school,' muttered Justin.

A sailor wearing white gaiters and a matching belt ushered
them along a corridor to a room facing the front lawn. A
photograph of the King in naval uniform hung on an otherwise
empty wall behind a table. A blackboard, with rows of chairs
facing it, reinforced Justin's earlier comparison.

The sailor said briskly, 'Wait here, please,' and went out.

As Andrea sat down she wished she had worn a different
suit. Her cream-coloured wool which she had chosen for its
youthfulness now seemed *too* young with its knee-length skirt
and short jacket. She placed her handbag over her knees,

thinking, as she did, that she would have been less likely to be patronised if she had worn a more matronly outfit. The man who had brought Justin home had said they would be seeing a Captain Borden, whom Andrea had never met, and Lieutenant Commander Harrington, whom she had. She imagined Borden would be older than Harrington, whose age she guessed to be about the same as hers, though possibly he was younger. She remembered his cold hands and Sally's remarks about his indifference to admirers. Something else had remained with her since their brief meeting at Elspeth's: a suspicion that his inscrutable good looks masked an iron will responsible for his elevation above more relaxed contemporaries such as Tony Cassilis.

This impression seemed to be confirmed as he entered the room and ignored her in favour of a grey-haired companion whom she now recognised as the officer she had seen stepping onto the pontoon. Harrington turned his handsome face towards her at last.

'Mrs Pauling, let me introduce Captain Borden, our senior naval officer on the river.' He smiled at his superior and nodded in Justin's direction. 'And that, sir, is Mrs Pauling's alarmingly aquatic son.'

Andrea said sharply, 'Justin is my son's friend.'

'No offence meant, madam,' muttered Captain Borden, seating himself next to Harrington on the opposite side of the table. 'I understand you took great exception to the boy being ticked off by Petty Officer Lee.'

'He was making way too much fuss over a silly prank.'

Borden stared back at her stolidly. 'You think so.' The deep creases on either side of his high-bridged nose gave him a sneering expression. 'You think trespassing on naval property in wartime is something to be laughed about?'

Andrea sat up very straight. 'Captain Borden, I did *not* say that.'

Harrington cupped his chin in a hand, and, to Andrea's

surprise, smiled encouragingly. 'Go ahead, Mrs Pauling, and tell us exactly what you think about Justin's escapade.'

'My son was there, too. It was just a boys' dare to swim out to the boats.'

Borden suddenly barked out, 'Tell me, boy, did your friend get on board too?'

'No, sir. He's a bad swimmer.'

Captain Borden's skin was sunburned and blotched with large freckles. In Andrea's eyes, he looked self-important and peevish in his creased uniform with its rows of medal ribbons. 'But you're a good swimmer, eh, Justin?'

'I'm better than him.'

'So why didn't you decide to win your bet by swimming across the river? You wouldn't have failed.'

Andrea looked anxiously at Justin, but he said calmly, 'It'd have been less fun, sir.'

'Why's that, boy?'

'No chance of being caught.'

'I see.' Borden shifted his heavy body on his small chair. 'So you were happy to play silly buggers with the navy for a bit of excitement. Too bad if you'd banged your head when you jumped over the side, or if one of our ratings had been drowned going in after you.'

'They launched a boat, sir.'

'In the middle of the night, just for you.'

'I promise I'll never do it again.'

Afraid that Justin was about to cry, Andrea felt suddenly distraught. 'That's enough, captain.'

'Why's that, madam?'

'Because he's said he's sorry.' Borden's exasperation with her for intervening made her angry. 'So he saw inside a patrol boat. Is that such a big deal?'

Harrington faced her with an affability she decided was bogus. 'In the navy we tend to think that even humble gunboats and armed trawlers shouldn't be treated like public property.'

'Damn right,' agreed Borden. 'Minor warships are bloody well invaluable. Who else looks after our coastal convoys and protects our fishermen from E-boats? Nobody.'

Andrea inclined her head. 'Captain Borden, I didn't question their value, only your sense of proportion.' While Borden's face went a deeper shade of red, Harrington seemed to have trouble keeping a straight face. Andrea feared he was laughing at her. 'If he'd gotten aboard a new submarine or a secret airplane, I'd be on my knees to you. But all he did was climb onto a dirty old . . .'

'That will do, madam,' thundered Borden. He gestured to Justin to leave his chair and come closer. The boy did not look at Andrea before obeying. 'You listen to me, young man. If I hear you've been within a thousand yards of one of His Majesty's ships, I'll have you in police custody within the hour. You and your friend almost rammed HMS *Stork* the other day. Why was that?'

'It was a mistake,' quavered Justin. 'My friend's no good at sailing.'

'Just tell him from me to stay away, will you?'

'Yes, sir.'

'Or you'll both find yourselves in police cells.'

'Yes, sir,' faltered Justin.

Borden pushed back his chair and rose. 'I hope your mother won't tell you it doesn't matter, because it most certainly does.' He thrust out his jaw. 'Just remember that.'

'You *know* I'm not his mother,' cried Andrea, addressing Borden's back as he turned to leave. The moment Justin began to sniffle she realised she should not have corrected the man. Her remark would have seemed a rejection to Justin. To make up for it she hugged him and then he really started to sob. Until then, the whole scene had been poignantly reminiscent of that famous painting of the brave and lonely boy being questioned: *When Did You Last See Your Father?* Not that a gruff old salt and a stereotypical stiff upper-lipped young officer could be expected to be touched by anything so vulgarly sentimental.

While trying to comfort Justin, Andrea started to feel let down by Leo. It was too bad of him not to have told her about the sailing incident. Though even if the boys had actually hit the side of a warship, that couldn't excuse Borden for having spoken to Justin like a criminal – particularly after he had apologised.

Though Borden had departed, Harrington lingered, leaning elegantly against the door frame. Tall, slim, clean-shaven, with brown eyes and dark hair, his whole body conveyed arrogant English sang-froid. She hated his indifference to Justin's tears. The great value of Justin's father's former duties compared with the insignificant work Harrington and his colleagues were doing made her ache with resentment.

Andrea said dryly, 'I suppose I should thank you for not bullying Justin, too.'

He looked past her towards the window. 'I don't disagree with what Captain Borden said.'

'Do you ever?'

'Almost daily.' His eyes met hers with a candour that confused her. 'Blast, I shouldn't have said that.'

'Do I look the type to tell him?'

'Of course not.' He laughed loudly, once more confounding her earlier assumptions. 'But that's not the point really,' he added, becoming solemn again.

'I get it,' she said sharply, 'loyalty, no matter why. Well, since I won't be telling any tales, may I ask a favour?' He nodded eager agreement, making her feel guilty, but only for a moment. 'Tell Captain Borden that Justin's father was a pilot who risked his life every day till he died, unlike some officers.'

Harrington neither avoided her eyes nor attempted to contradict her. He simply retreated a step as she pushed Justin past him. They were well ahead by the time he came after them. 'I'm so damned sorry, Justin,' she heard him call out.

Expecting Harrington to follow, Andrea wondered what she would say. But when she and Justin reached the main hallway, the corridor behind them was empty.

Justin cried some more in the car and begged her not to tell Leo he had been upset. Andrea reluctantly agreed.

'It's because you mentioned my dad. I was all right until you did.'

She wished she could believe him but she couldn't. Her thoughtless remark about not being his mother had left him vulnerable to self-pity, that deadly foe of all stoics. When he admitted how surprised he had been that she had stuck up for him, Andrea was mortified. She knew she deserved to feel bad. She had wanted to be rid of him almost since the start of the holiday.

Outside the dining room, Leo caught hold of his mother's arm.

'Stay here,' he hissed. 'Were they beastly to him?'

'They were.'

'Did he blub?'

'Not once.'

'What did I tell you,' said Leo gloomily. 'He's just not human.'

'But sweetheart, he feels a lot without ever showing it. I *know* he's sensitive.'

'Oh, mum, you don't at all.' She tried to keep hold of him, but he pulled away and went into the sitting room. She followed him and he surprised her by smiling happily. 'Dad 'phoned soon after you left. He's coming home at the end of the week. Isn't that ripping, mum. He had a huge row with the dockyard people because he wanted to take everything to bits just before the bigwigs came.'

Andrea could well imagine the arguments. 'What happened in the end?'

'The admiral-superintendent locked him out of the yard.'

'My God! You're sure?'

'Of course. Dad told me. The funny thing is the admiral was right and dad was wrong. His road worked perfectly at the trials.' He flung himself down on the sofa next to her. 'Isn't that wizard, mum. Aren't you proud?'

'Proud of what?' asked Justin, coming in.

'Of you,' sang out Andrea, frowning at Leo.

'She thought you'd crack but you didn't,' improvised Leo, without any trace of a smirk. 'And this is my good news: dad's coming back and he'll be making things with us.'

To Andrea's relief, Justin said, 'That's good,' and looked as if he meant it. Then he shrieked, 'I can't wear these things another minute.' He was struggling out of his school suit as he left the room.

Two days before Peter was due to return, Sally telephoned and suggested another visit to Elspeth's. Since Andrea wanted to tell her about her naval interview she agreed to meet her there. In fact, she would not get a chance to speak to Sally for more than an hour after arriving. On Wednesdays and Saturdays Elspeth engaged a pianist, but today the usual man had failed to turn up, so Sally had told everyone that her friend Andrea was a piano teacher, and a good sport, and would be sure to stand in.

'How can I?' demanded Andrea while listening to some young men in the next door room singing in tuneless falsetto voices about the wife of a pork butcher.

> 'All day my husband stuffs sausages, sausages,
> And at night he comes home and stuffs me.'

'You think there's sheet music for *this*?' laughed Andrea.

'Don't worry,' said Sally, 'they'll get fed up soon. Everyone prefers singing proper songs with a pianist.' And, after two more obscene ditties, they did indeed fall silent.

Elspeth handed Andrea a Cole Porter songbook, the music

for Rodgers' and Hart's 'Dancing On The Ceiling', and some homegrown favourites such as 'The White Cliffs Of Dover'. Not knowing what to expect Andrea felt apprehensive, but she had often been obliged to sight-read when accompanying singing classes at school, so she launched into the first Cole Porter with a show of confidence. It happened to be 'Let's Do It', which, she now realised, provided a sort of link with earlier subject-matter.

After a hesitant start, about half a dozen passable singers of both sexes joined in and were soon craning over her shoulder, doing their best to read and sing the words. So by the time they reached 'Even highly educated fleas do it', there was plenty of noise and hilarity reverberating around the piano. 'I've Got You Under My Skin' went better for Andrea, with fewer fluffs and wrong notes, and she was pleased to see several couples dancing, including Sally and James.

While she was playing, Mike Harrington and Tony Cassilis arrived, but neither came across to sing, though Andrea was sure both had seen her at the piano. Although by then she had drunk two highballs, she felt hurt. She had obviously been ruder to Harrington than she had intended. She couldn't go over to him to make amends because people around the piano were clamouring for her to play 'There'll Always Be An England'.

After an emotional rendition had come to an end, Sally pushed her way through the knot of singers to plant a smacking kiss on her friend's cheek.

'It was so damned good of you to step in.'

Andrea said, 'I'd like to talk to you, without James, if possible.'

Seated together on a small sofa in a corner of the main sitting room, Andrea told Sally about Captain Borden's treatment of Justin, and Mike Harrington's support for his boss. 'It was really horrible the way they treated the poor boy. All he'd done was swim out to one of their boats. When Borden left, Commander

Harrington was a lot nicer. In fact, I may have been a bit hard on him.'

Sally looked at her with a sad but sympathetic smile. 'Darling, can't you guess why they were so stern?'

A presentiment made Andrea hesitate to answer. What had Leo said about Justin's suspicions? 'You'd better fill me in,' she murmured.

Sally moved closer. 'All this is fearfully hush-hush, so not a word to your boys. Borden's just a figurehead. It's Mike and Tony who go off on missions with different crews. Until a while back, they used to land commandos on the French coast, and bring them back after blowing up power stations, lock gates, or whatever. Recently, Mike's been taking agents across to Brittany.'

Though horribly embarrassed, Andrea found herself laughing at the sheer scale of her misconception. 'Is that *all* he does?'

'He brings back airmen shot down over France.' Sally smiled, consolingly.

Andrea gazed at her grey silk-stockinged knees and hardly saw them. How grotesque her scornful attitude must have seemed to Harrington. What the hell should she say to him now? Could she even admit that she knew the truth? Possibly not.

She leaned towards Sally. 'How did you find out what they were really doing?'

'My husband knows a couple of surgeons in Falmouth. About six weeks ago, one of them couldn't resist telling him that Mike's ships had been strafed by Messerschmitts on the way back from Brittany. There were French civilians among the dead and wounded, and a few of our airmen.'

'Terrible,' murmured Andrea.

'One ship caught fire and sank.'

Andrea's throat tightened, recalling Sally's sadness as she had watched Mike and Tony roar away into the night. At last Andrea knew why Elspeth had been weeping on the same evening. Andrea covered her face with her hands until she was sure she wasn't going to cry.

'My husband would kill me if he thought I'd told anyone. I'm a bloody fool really. Imagine what would happen if the Krauts were ever ready and waiting when Mike's boys turned up on the other side.'

'I'll keep quiet.'

After Andrea had returned to the piano to play some more songs, Mike Harrington still showed no inclination to come and talk to her between songs. Several times she saw him glance in her direction and this made her feel worse. When he and Tony left together, Andrea consoled herself with the thought that there would be better, less crowded occasions on which she could apologise to him.

It only occurred to her while driving home that he might be dead before she had another chance.

With songs churning in her head for hours, Andrea found sleep impossible and she was obliged to read until one in the morning. Not long after switching off her bedside light, she heard a motorbike growl by on the road at the end of the lane, and, shortly afterwards, two cars speeding after it. Of course there would have to be a number of motorbike owners in the area, and the one she had just heard might belong to any of them. But once the image of Mike Harrington, crouched forward on his bike, had formed in her mind, she could not dispel it.

The following morning she went down to Porthbeer, telling herself that her only concern was to buy fish on the quay when the fishing boats came in. Yet driving into the little port she knew she was really going there so that she could walk along the beach and see whether the naval ships were on their moorings.

She bought a monkfish, two mackerel and a pollock while the gulls swooped and dived into the harbour behind her. It was surprising how little she was asked to pay, but, even as she was chatting to the fisherman, she was eager to be on the move.

The bay curved along a shingle beach to a promontory of black rocks. Andrea had not thought to wear boots and very soon her shoes were sinking into the wet sand between the stones. The day was overcast, and, while there had been little wind up at Trevean Barton, there was plenty down here. As she reached the rocky point, a fierce gust made her pull her cardigan protectively around herself. The usual blue of the estuary had changed to slate grey.

When she had stood beside Justin on the lawn, before he'd been questioned, Andrea had seen six or seven vessels in a group. Raising a hand to stop her hair blowing into her eyes, she now saw only three boats anchored out there. At once she felt uneasy. The missing ships might be patrolling along the coast, so it was stupid to jump to conclusions. But she jumped anyway: the ships would have reached France under cover of darkness and would be lying up in a Breton cove until it was time for them to carry out their mission.

On returning to the house, Andrea was mildly surprised to find the boys at home. They were playing a board game called L'Attaque, and facing one another from behind opposing cardboard armies. Occasionally a major, brigadier, or sapper would be pushed forward, great vigilance being exercised in case either player attempted to peer around the cards on their flimsy metal stands. The game looked incredibly old-fashioned. Eager to find out whether the missing ships were moored higher up the river, Andrea came up behind Leo and asked him sweetly when he intended to take her sailing.

'How about tomorrow?' she cajoled.

'Isn't dad back then?'

'Not till late evening.'

'The rudder may not be fixed yet, mum.'

'If it is, you'll take me?'

Without lifting his eyes from the board, Justin muttered, 'Don't be mean, Leo.'

'All right then,' said Leo graciously. 'You can come.'

Andrea telephoned Sally during the afternoon, hoping to find out from her whether anyone was likely to know when Mike Harrington would be back. After a knowing pause, Sally said, 'Darling, I suppose you *might* learn something at Elspeth's this evening.'

'Should I ask Elspeth herself?'

'If she's alone. But what's the rush? I'd calm down if I were you.'

Andrea was outraged. 'You'd calm down, would you, if you'd told Mike Harrington he was a coward?'

'We all make mistakes,' said Sally sanctimoniously.

When she had hung up, Andrea suddenly remembered that Peter would be back by eight or nine, so going to Elspeth's was out of the question.

A windy overcast morning, and Andrea was standing up to her knees in freezing water, on the sailing club's broad concrete slipway. Under Leo's instruction, she was holding the boat so that its sails could not fill with wind. The admiring looks she had attracted while playing at Elspeth's seemed like a dream. Today, life was certainly back to normal. But despite her freezing feet and legs, she was glad to have this chance to find out more.

Over a thick blue sweater Andrea wore a life jacket – a cumbersome orange creation made of stitched sausage-like panels, stuffed with something called kapok.

'It only keeps you afloat for six hours,' Leo warned her. 'Then glug, glug.'

'You reckon anyone would live that long in water this cold?' snapped Justin, who had just dipped in a toe.

Moments after scrambling into the boat, Andrea was ordered to hold the rusty lever that let down the centre-plate.

'We're not going yet, mother!' yelled Leo, as she used all her weight to budge it.

Out in the main channel, with everything apparently under control, Leo asked Andrea if she knew what 'beating' meant.

'It's what we're doing now.'

'It's also what happens on Wednesdays at school,' remarked Justin, as if the memory pleased him. Did Leo also like to recall pain and hardship? Looking at him, smiling as he balanced precariously on the gunwale, she rather feared he might.

Ahead, the river narrowed to a fork, where a wooded creek entered on the right. As they came level with this inlet, the wind hit them with unexpected force. Without waiting to be asked, Justin clambered up beside Leo on the gunwale and Andrea joined him. Even while the boat was heeling right over, she looked around, hoping to spot naval vessels at anchor. But there were no boats of any description on this stretch of the river.

In lulls when it was not gusting, the background wind seemed to have become stronger. Worryingly, Leo seemed unsure whether to keep his sail pulled in or released as angry squalls raced towards them. Left to his own devices, Justin was allowing his smaller sail to flap noisily most of the time, which Andrea knew could not be right. When renewed gusts forced the boat onto its side, Leo's only response was to try to lean out further. Since water was already slopping over the lower gunwale, plainly no amount of weight was going to keep them upright on its own.

'Darling, it could be a good idea to steer into the wind,' advised Andrea, as a surge of water poured in.

'If I do that, I might go about without meaning to,' quavered Leo, plainly demoralised by her anxiety. Andrea reckoned that if the wind didn't funnel out of another creek, they might yet stay upright. Since all the locker doors were closed, they'd float if they tipped over. Too conscious of Leo's agitation to respond to the mysterious beauty of the river, Andrea knew she would not be sorry when this sailing trip was over.

They had just passed a well-made stone quay with a grassy top when Justin pointed. Andrea clutched his arm. A grey ship was coming downstream, just where the river divided in two.

She smiled ecstatically at Justin. 'Is that the one you got on board?'

'It could be.'

'Where did it come from?' asked Leo.

Justin was staring up river. 'Out of a creek. We'd have seen it earlier otherwise.'

'I think there's a creek right there,' said Andrea, shielding her eyes.

Recently, Leo had been paying more attention to keeping upright than to sailing close to the wind, but when he saw the trawler he pulled in his sail as tightly as he could and told Justin to do the same.

'Steam gives way to sail,' he told his mother, steering straight for the warship. 'I'll show them we can't be shoved around like last time. They did actual damage to our boat, mum.'

'Maybe they did, Leo, but Justin promised not to go near any navy ship.'

'We'll go about before we get too close. I bet they won't dare hold their course.'

With the sails filling well, and everyone sitting on the gunwale, the dinghy was gathering speed, slapping into the waves with brisk thuds.

'This is spiffing,' shrilled Leo, with a tremor in his voice.

'Sweetheart,' urged Andrea, 'You *must* turn around now.' Leo's knees were shaking and not just, she guessed, with physical strain. He was clearly desperate to impress Justin.

'We'll just make it,' boasted Leo.

Fifteen yards from the foaming bows of the trawler, with collision moments away, Andrea tried to wrench the tiller from Leo's hand. But he clung on so tightly that she could not take it from him.

Summoning up all her classroom authority, she roared, 'Do it now!'

Leo seemed incapable of action, gazing ahead as if mesmerised. Andrea reached again for the tiller just as the air was shaken by three peremptory blasts from the ship's hooter. Within yards of the trawler's overhanging bow, Leo lost his nerve and put the helm over without a word of warning. Justin was late clambering across and failed to free the jib sheets, which tripped Andrea, sending her sprawling across the centre-plate casing.

The boat lost the wind completely under the trawler's side and lay wallowing next to her, sails flapping, as the larger vessel slipped by. As the dinghy cleared the trawler's stern, a savage squall hit her. Totally unprepared, Leo clung to the mainsheet and watched in amazement as a wall of green water swept over the gunwale.

As the boat capsized, Andrea got a foot on the now horizontal mast and sprang onto the rising gunwale a split second before it plunged towards the water. As if on a pivoting seesaw, she flung herself forward and grabbed at the planks of the hull. Climbing this ladder of ridges like a squirrel in a wheel, she was awed to see the centre-plate rise up in front of her, like Excalibur. As the boat settled, Andrea grasped the vertical plate and twisted round to see what had happened to the boys. Justin was in the water, swimming towards her, and Leo was nowhere to be seen. As she opened her mouth to scream, he bobbed up from under the sail. Though grateful to be pulled onto the hull, both boys were appalled that Andrea had kept dry. Shivering and gasping, they glanced at one another and then looked away, too embarrassed by their predicament to want to share it.

On the upturned hull, the three of them watched in silence as the trawler's stern grew smaller. Andrea fancied she knew exactly what the boys were feeling. Because it would be humiliating to be rescued by the Royal Navy, they dreaded seeing the trawler turn back.

'She's slowing down,' groaned Leo.

Seconds later a small motorboat was swung out from the trawler's stern. Fighting an urge to look for make-up in her canvas bag, Andrea patted her windswept hair. At least her slacks were not clinging wetly to her hips and bottom.

'Oh God,' gasped Justin. 'It's *him*. What can I say? He's going to kill me for coming so close.'

Recognising Lieutenant Commander Harrington at almost the same moment, Andrea soothed, 'Don't worry, I'll deal with him.'

'Silly idiot,' Justin hissed at Leo from between chattering teeth.

Harrington was accompanied by two ratings, one standing beside him in the stern steering the launch, another in the bow armed with a boathook with which he fished up the dinghy's painter. When he had secured it, the other rating brought the side of the motorboat up against the stern of the dinghy so that Andrea and the two boys could crawl along the upturned hull to their rescuers' craft without falling into the water again.

As Andrea stepped into the motorboat, Harrington bowed respectfully. 'I do believe you're dry as a bone, Mrs Pauling.' He added *sotto voce*, 'Plays the piano *and* walks on water.'

'I'm sorry,' blurted out Justin.

Harrington looked down at him gravely. 'I can't *keep* pulling you out of the drink, you know.' He tossed him a blanket, and one of the sailors gave one to Leo.

'It was my fault, sir,' mouthed Leo, shivering so much that he was scarcely comprehensible. 'I thought I could get across your bows.'

'Well don't be such a daft little beggar again.' Harrington's tone was severe enough to frighten Leo, but he was smiling kindly when he turned to Justin. 'Have *you* tried helming?'

'Nobody's ever taught me.'

'You couldn't do any worse than your friend. I'll try and find someone to teach you. Where are you staying?'

'Prospect House, Trevean Barton,' Justin told him.

'But only till the twenty-fifth,' put in Andrea.

'I need lessons, too,' murmured Leo.

Although Andrea normally thought that headgear, worn tipped back, looked silly, she was puzzled to find herself thinking that Harrington's officer's hat was elegantly raffish worn that way. Even in a grubby white sweater and a blue jacket without any badges of rank, his appearance struck her as workmanlike and attractive. While he steered the boat very slowly ahead, the two sailors moved to the bows where they raised the sailing boat's mast from the water. Having righted the dinghy, they began baling with a couple of buckets until one of them was able to get aboard and lower the sails.

'You can empty her properly on the sailing club's slip,' Harrington told Leo. 'We're only taking out enough to be able to tow her.'

'Aren't we going aboard the big boat?' asked Justin plaintively.

'Ask me that again, and I'll think you capsized just to get taken on board.'

With the two sailors back aboard the motorboat, Harrington opened the throttle. He was standing looking straight ahead with the tiller in his hand. And because she was sitting nearby, Andrea could not help looking up in order to speak to him.

'I feel very bad about what I said to you that time.'

'Sorry?' He raised a hand to his ear.

The engine was making so much noise that she had to move very close to him in order to be heard without shouting. 'I feel bad because I disparaged your work.'

'Join the club.'

'My husband's been working in the naval dockyard.'

'In what capacity?'

'Designing a . . .'

He threw up his hands before clasping the tiller again. 'You mustn't tell me.' He was smiling, but she knew he was serious.

His face was very brown and she noticed a network of fine lines around his eyes as if they were often screwed up staring into the distance – as he was doing now.

'Someone mentioned what your work was.'

'Who did?'

'A man in the dockyard.'

'Your husband reported this person, I hope?'

'I'll ask him. Commander, will you please accept my apologies for what I said.'

'Best forget it.'

His attitude stung Andrea. 'You're rejecting my apology?'

'I didn't say that.' He kept looking ahead. 'Of course I accept.'

'Thank you.'

After that he remained silent. Remembering Sally's warning about security, Andrea feared he was worrying about the indiscreet dockyard worker she had invented. But as they approached the slipway, he cut the throttle right back and said, 'I liked the way you stood up for Justin the other day.'

When one of the sailors had untied the dinghy's painter and grounded her on the hard, the other rating helped Andrea and the boys ashore.

'Keep out of trouble,' Harrington shouted above the noise of the engine.

As the launch surged seawards he waved and the boys waved back. An arrowhead of foam fanned from the bows, spreading lace-ribbons far astern. Out on the river, Andrea saw the trawler slowly approaching her buoy. There were now as many ships at the anchorage as there had been four days ago, yet Andrea did not experience the sense of relief she had expected. Within a week or two these ships would sail and the hateful waiting would begin again.

CHAPTER 6

O n the first morning after his return, Peter enjoyed having
breakfast in bed, while Leo sprawled across the quilt at
his feet and Andrea chatted to them from the window seat. The
past few days had been extraordinarily tense for Peter but the
modifications to the bridge had finally been successful, and now
he could think of nothing more enjoyable than relaxing with
his wife and entertaining the boys. When he suggested another
coastal walk to Andrea, and she declined to accompany him,
Peter assumed that she must still think him partly to blame
for his recent absence. Otherwise she would not be denying
him the pleasure of winning back the leisure activity they had
enjoyed most before his illness. But though it was unfair of
her, Peter had no intention of sulking. In any case what could
he say that he hadn't said before? The work in Falmouth had
been urgent and unavoidable, and for him to apologise for it
would be absurd. He had hated going and had made this clear
at the time. To remind Andrea now would be to treat her like
a child. As Peter came downstairs, his wife took herself off to
another room, so he assumed she would prefer him to devote
the morning to the boys.

There was a stream at the far end of the garden and he led
them there first. Peering from the dining room window, Andrea
could see her husband, with his two Wellington-booted acolytes

at his side, splashing along in the streambed looking important, as men often did when engaged in some joint venture involving planning. When they returned to the house, Leo and Justin busied themselves with fret saws, cutting out two large circles of plywood from opposite sides of a tea chest which Peter had found in the garage. He also produced a rusty bicycle wheel and a number of empty cocoa tins, and then tantalised the boys by not explaining exactly how they would fit together. Although Andrea knew just how marvellous he was with children – setting them guessing and then sharing their excitement as their deductions brought them closer to his intentions – today, because he hadn't said anything to show that he regretted having been away, she could not enjoy watching him with the boys. His suggestion of a walk had also amazed her. How could he have imagined that she would want to repeat the experience of their abortive attempt to reach the headland?

Because it was Saturday, the village school would be empty so Andrea decided to use her borrowed keys for the first time. She would play the school piano until lunch.

She had feared it might be depressing to enter the school when it was silent and empty, but when she actually unlocked the mock Gothic door and went in the children's paintings immediately cheered her. Mercifully, the joys of fiddling around with cogwheels and copper wire had not yet claimed them.

Andrea unlocked the piano and started to play. The need to think of anything except the music slipped from her shoulders like an unwanted coat.

While he and Justin were cutting the cocoa tins in half and bolting them together with Meccano, Leo felt hurt that his friend seemed so uninvolved in what they were doing. He had often been distant and secretive at school but this was little comfort. Earlier in the morning, Justin had announced, out of the blue, that when he had climbed aboard the naval trawler he had found fishing nets and floats.

'Why would stuff like that be on a warship?' he had asked Leo, unaware that it had been unfriendly of him to keep this information to himself for a week.

'Maybe the navy found the nets in the sea. Fishing boats lose them in storms sometimes.'

'That's possible,' Justin conceded, making it clear to Leo that he thought Harrington's people had bought the nets for their own purposes.

'Why do *you* think they have nets, Justin?'

'I dunno yet.'

And that had been all he had been prepared to say. The worst thing about having Justin to stay, thought Leo, was being obliged to admit that part of the reason for being his friend had been because other boys had been impressed.

As soon as his father had made a drawing of the half cocoa tins bolted together in a circle and mounted on the bicycle axle between the plywood circles, Leo wanted to cheer. It was easy to imagine the wheel turning the moment a regular flow of water began filling each cocoa tin in turn.

'Of course we'll have to dam the stream,' said Peter, 'or this will be useless.' He waved his drawing at the boys and limped away to look for some bricks to form the base of a dam.

Justin was frowning. 'Isn't he taking a lot of trouble to make a waterwheel? What will it *do*, anyway?'

'Turn, of course.'

'I realised *that*.'

Suddenly, Leo was close to tears. 'We're bloody lucky my dad wants to do this with us.'

'I never said we weren't.'

Remembering how pleased Justin had been when Harrington had been nice to him, Leo felt angrier. Just because he wore a uniform and ordered sailors about, it didn't make him important. One inventor could do more to win the war than shiploads of naval nobodies. Leo decided to join his father in the stream.

'Is your leg okay?' the boy asked anxiously, as Peter struggled to empty a barrow full of earth in front of a row of bricks. He had got mud on his tweed jacket and on his face, too. As the contents of his barrow splashed into the water, his trousers were soaked.

'My leg's fine. How's the wheel coming along?'

'Justin's moaning about it.'

Peter chuckled to himself. 'We'll surprise him yet.'

'Will we surprise mum, too?'

'God knows.' Peter looked more closely at Leo. 'Anything wrong, old chap?'

Leo shook his head and promptly started to sniffle. 'I missed you, dad.'

'I missed you too, old man.'

Pressing his cheek against his father's chest, Leo felt sad that his mother was not around to see how their project was progressing. Since the car had gone, she must have gone off somewhere on her own.

'Will you be able to stay a week now?' Leo knew he sounded pathetic.

'Let's hope so.' Peter drew Leo closer. 'You know I'd stay longer if I could.'

'Why can't someone else do your work for a week?'

'They just can't, I'm afraid. But I've got something exciting to tell you. I think we'll be able to come back here for the summer holidays.' Peter frowned. 'Better keep it under your hat till I've told your mother.'

'Mum's the word.'

After leaving the school, Andrea drove into Porthbeer for lunch and ate a crab sandwich at the Fisherman's Rest. She had not been back there since dropping in with Sally on the way to Elspeth's. Then, with her friend beside her, she had not felt self-conscious about sitting among so many men. Today she was struck by the strong smell of fish on their clothes, and by

the raw redness of their skin. Sitting only feet away, she could
scarcely understand a word they said. Afterwards, she walked
along the shingle and listened to the sigh of each withdrawing
wave and the clatter of submerged stones. She stopped before
reaching the rocks and felt pleased with herself for being able
to resist her desire to walk on and count the ships.

When she returned to the house, Peter was standing in the
middle of the lawn, holding up two lengths of electrical wire.
She moved a little closer, remaining partially hidden under a
canopy of apple blossom.

'Over here you two,' Peter was shouting. The boys approached
eagerly from the direction of the garage. Andrea moved closer
and heard Peter say, 'Justin, I'd like you to join these up for
me.' Justin then did something to the wires, while Leo watched.
Suddenly, her son looked up and saw her. Andrea waved and
crossed the lawn. Peter was smiling happily. 'Darling, what
perfect timing. We're just about to follow the wire up to
Justin's room.'

'I can come, too?' She sounded surprised to be admitted to
this male mystery.

'Be our guest,' replied Peter.

In fact he remained in the hall while everyone else climbed
the stairs. On the table by Justin's bed was a small light bulb
mounted on a piece of wood. The light it cast, though flickering,
was continuous. Justin looked at Leo in astonishment and then
back at the bulb.

'Is it being lit the way I think it is?' He sounded dazed and
strangely humble.

'Sure it is,' cried Leo, cavorting round him.

Justin let out his breath with a whooshing noise. 'Your dad's
damned clever, you know that.'

Downstairs, Peter clapped a hand on both boys' shoulders.
'Pretty impressive, eh? Better come and see the electric generator
your waterwheel's working. Had to keep it under wraps or I'd
have given the game away.'

So they trooped over to the stream to gaze on their triumph, with Andrea following. And there it was, the clumsy looking wheel they had constructed turning freely on the bicycle axle – the cocoa tins being filled, one after the other, by a steady trickle from the overflow channel of a crudely made dam. Five hours of purposeful messing about and Peter was as happy as both the boys.

Basking in everyone's good opinion, Peter took Andrea's arm as they walked back to the house. 'I think I'll soon be working on a project that'll bring me back to Falmouth in the summer.'

Andrea asked quietly, 'Have you told Leo?'

'Yes, but nothing definite.'

'You shouldn't have told him before me. Don't you see that, Peter? It's so disrespectful. Maybe I wouldn't have minded coming back for the summer holidays, but I should have had the chance to discuss it with you first.'

His crestfallen face made her think of a misunderstood child. Knowing she would lose her temper if asked to spell out why the holiday hadn't been perfect for her, she hurried into the house. As she entered the hall, Rose emerged from the kitchen and handed her an envelope.

'Letter for 'ee.'

'Who brought it, Rose?'

'A sailor; not one of them officers.'

Andrea went into the sitting room and read her letter. Lieutenant Commander Harrington had written saying he had failed to find anyone suitable to give the boys sailing lessons, so he himself would teach them, provided they didn't mind falling in with last minute arrangements. 'Can we leave it that I will telephone them on any morning when I have an hour or two? I'm sure it won't always suit them, but sometimes they won't have made other plans.'

As she finished reading, Andrea thought how absurd it was that she'd ever thought him insensitive. His generosity with his free time was most unusual. At least she would be able to ask him to lunch after he had taken them on the water. Only when she recalled the explanation she had given him for knowing his real duties did her depression return. She was going to have to confess to Peter that she had said that *he* had passed on to her a dockyard worker's indiscretion about Harrington's work. Otherwise Peter would be in for one hell of a shock if Harrington asked him to his face whether all the workmen in the dockyard were blabberers.

They were going to bed when she eventually told Peter that Harrington had offered the boys sailing lessons. Then she made her confession. Her timing was poor, since Peter was tired. He was also breathless, having just taken off his trousers – a troublesome procedure involving balancing on one foot while trying to shake the garment off his unbending leg.

As Andrea finished speaking, Peter sank back onto the bed and said despondently, 'I still can't understand why you couldn't have told him that the doctor's wife was your source.'

'She asked me not to.'

He shook his head sadly. 'But my dear Andrea, by attributing the leak to me and some nameless dockyard fitter, you've given him the impression that there's virtually no security down there. If Harrington insists on an investigation, he'd be a hundred per cent right.'

While conceding that Peter had good reason to be annoyed, Andrea found his 'more in sorrow than in anger' tone needlessly humiliating. 'Okay, I guess I've made a big mistake,' she admitted breezily. 'So I'll see him and fix things.'

Later, when Peter moved towards her in bed, making clear what he wanted, Andrea didn't feel able to refuse him. To give him another opportunity to look misunderstood and long-suffering was absolutely out of the question.

CHAPTER 7

'How can we catch a fish without a rod?' asked Leo as he and Justin trailed after Rose.

'Don' 'ee worry 'bout that, my dear,' she said, looking back at them as they pedalled after her – or, more accurately, as *Leo* pedalled after her. Justin was sitting in idleness behind him, perched on the saddlebag bracket. Rose's offer to take them fishing had surprised Leo, considering how angry she had been with Justin for the past few days. But maybe mum had told her about 'the poor boy's loss'.

After scrambling over numerous hedges, the boys found the river disappointingly narrow, little more than a brook, and hemmed in by alders and willows. At any rate it was shallow enough to wade across and quite fast-flowing. As Rose strode ahead, she looked odder than ever in her wrinkled brown stockings and long black dress. On the riverbank she took off her rose-trimmed hat, and, lying on the grass, pulled up her sleeves. She gestured to them to do the same.

'You mean we'll catch a fish in our hands?' gulped Leo.

'I don' know what you'll do, boy, but I'll tickle 'em with mine.'

'Won't they bite us?' asked Justin.

'Course they won'. Them never bin frighted by gentle hands. Hands ain't like a hook in the jaw.'

Following her example, the boys lay down and, reaching cautiously with their fingers, began to feel under the bank, which, to their surprise, went back almost a foot among the tree roots. Keeping their hands open and very still, as Rose had told them, they waited. Apparently, the fish would not swim away even when they stroked them, provided their hand movements were smooth and slow.

'What will they think our hands *are*?' asked Justin.

'Sticks or tobs.'

'Tobs?'

'Lumps of earth.'

When Leo touched his first fish he was too excited to speak. The electric thrill of it was like nothing he had ever experienced.

'I'm touching one,' he whispered at last. 'What do I do?'

'Thumbs behind his head and fingers under. Then hold 'im tight and lift.'

As Leo raised his hands above the surface, the fish struggled so fiercely that he lost his grip and it slipped between his fingers. He made a desperate last attempt to catch it one-handed as it shot into the air but the next moment it hit the water and swam away, leaving only a trace of slime on his fingers.

Minutes later, Rose caught a trout and made it look insultingly easy to hold him until she knocked his head on a stone. Nor did Justin muff his chance when it came soon afterwards.

But nothing destroyed Leo's recollections of the moment when his hands had first closed around that sinuous living thing – not even Justin's triumphant whoops as a small spotted fish lay flapping at his feet.

'Who is it?' called Peter from their bedroom. His leg was bad again after all the dam-making and messing about with the waterwheel.

'It's for me,' Andrea shouted back from the hall, covering the receiver with the palm of a hand. Mike Harrington was offering to take the boys sailing at noon and Andrea could not think what to say to him. They had gone somewhere with the maid, she explained, and might not be back in time. 'I guess another day might be better,' she added, allowing her voice to tail off uncertainly. A strange panic gripped her. What if he never called again, either because this conversation discouraged him, or because he was killed; how would she feel? Terrible. For the boys? No, for herself. She really needed to be nice to him after getting him so wrong.

His disembodied voice was saying, 'Why don't I drop by anyway, and if they turn up that's fine, but if they don't, it won't be the end of the world.'

'You may be wasting your time. But if you don't mind the risk . . .'

'That won't kill me,' he said with a rueful laugh, and she understood at once what he meant. Other risks he had to take were the kind that really might kill him. 'I'll see you soon,' she heard him say, and then a click. Slowly, she replaced the receiver.

So what to do? Change her clothes? She had looked like a windswept Campfire Girl on top of the upturned boat. But she really shouldn't get too excited about the way she looked. He was just a young man in the navy – about four years her junior – about whom she knew nothing, except that his work was dangerous enough to make her feel anxious on his behalf. Anyone knowing what he did would feel the same. She decided not to change her clothes, though she did revive her make-up.

Harrington parked at the end of the lane, so she did not see him until he had almost reached the door.

'Any sign of them?' Mike Harrington asked cheerfully. He was dressed in a pair of old flannels and a thick blue sweater that made him look less willowy than she remembered.

'No sign yet. I'm really so sorry.'

'Not your fault.'

'Come on in.'

He sat facing her in an armchair with his back to the French windows and remarked, after a silence, 'I meant to tell you something at Elspeth's that time.' He said this almost humbly. After the tense atmosphere of their earlier meetings, she was completely unprepared for the change of tone. If it heralded some kind of romantic admission (and what else could explain his suffering smile) what would she say? As his expression changed to open admiration, her heart began to thump. He said quietly, 'Because I can't play an instrument myself, I suppose I'm overly impressed by people who can. But you caught the fizz and sparkle of that music perfectly.'

Andrea laughed more loudly than she had intended. She felt relieved and yet disappointed, too. 'Why didn't you come over and tell me? Musicians love compliments.'

'Tony and I were rather down in the dumps.'

'I'm sorry to hear that.' And she really was. There was something dreadfully poignant about his tired handsome face. Nothing pretty or boyish about him. In fact he rather reminded her of an ageing leading man: his forehead lined, cheeks starting to redden a little under his tan, hair receding slightly – making him appear to be in his mid-thirties, though, actually, she was sure he was younger. She tried to imagine his looks before the war: heartstopping, she guessed. Anxiety could be cruel. It probably also explained the remoteness she sometimes sensed beneath his easy manner.

His present silence was like that, disturbing because unexpected. Maybe this was the moment to make her own confession. 'Oh dear,' she said, 'this is kind of embarrassing, but I have to do it sometime. I told you something pretty dumb in the boat.'

'I don't remember anything like that.'

'I said my husband told me about your work but, really, Mrs Lowther did.'

'Did she say you weren't to tell me she'd spilled the beans?'

'Yes. I promised.'

'Did she say who'd told *her*?'

'Her husband. And he'd gotten it from a surgeon in Falmouth.'

'That makes sense.' His face relaxed and he smiled at her with unembarrassed satisfaction. 'Frankly, I'm not sorry you found out.'

'You're not?'

'Because now you know the truth, you won't think I'm a complete waster.' His happy smile bemused her. Was he really thrilled that she might think better of him? If Sally was right, and Mike still loved his faithless wife, he was only playing games.

She asked sharply, 'Why do you give a damn what I think?'

He ran a hand through his wavy black hair. 'Because you know how to ask terrifying questions like that.'

'Which you're too scared to answer? Don't tell me.'

'I will tell you,' he murmured, his expression suddenly matching the seriousness of hers, 'because it's true.'

The door was open. Thinking of Peter lying in bed upstairs, Andrea got up and closed it. Returning to the sofa, she said more gently, 'Local heroes don't scare that easily.'

'I'm not a hero, local or otherwise.'

'Boy, do I smell false modesty!'

'It's not false.' His brown eyes met hers so candidly that she felt sorry she'd been sceptical. He said gently, 'Want to know why?'

'Sure.'

'I'm often in danger; that's not in question. But it doesn't make me a hero – not like the agents I take to France. When they risk their lives, it's their own free decision to do it. Because they're completely alone, nobody would have a clue if they made up an excuse for failing to keep a rendezvous. For me, it's quite different. Every moment of the Channel crossing I'm surrounded by people who look up to me and expect me to behave well. So turning back isn't an option. Bravery doesn't come into it.'

Andrea shook her head doggedly. 'I bet there are times when you can turn back without getting blamed.'

'Sometimes I *do* turn back. Like when we've been seen by enemy spotter planes. But *even then*, if my orders are to collect agents from a beach, I'll probably risk carrying on.' He grinned at her knowingly. '*You* think that's because I'm the local hero? Think again. It's because if I fail to show up, they'll be shot, along with the locals who helped them. And if that ever happens, I won't be able to look Tony in the eye, or any of my crew. That's why I do the decent thing, week after bloody week.'

'Why did you tell me this?'

'You don't remember? He looked genuinely astonished. 'You said I wasn't the kind of man to be afraid of a woman.'

'I did?' she echoed.

'That's right. So I needed to prove you wrong.'

Just then, before she could ask him why, she heard the boys' shrill voices in the lane. Mike heard them too and looked at his watch.

'If we're on the water for an hour,' he said, 'we won't be back much before two.'

'I'll serve lunch later.'

'Are you sure that's convenient?'

'Would you rather not come?'

He gazed at Andrea with a gentle smile. 'I think you know the answer.'

When Mike and the boys had gone, Andrea went over their conversation in her mind and felt the same mixture of fear and elation she had known while it had been going on. Could she have imagined the intense, almost beseeching way he had sometimes looked at her? The adolescent nature of her own feelings suddenly overwhelmed her. I'm thirty-five, married, with a son who needs me. How could I endure the lies of an affair, the feigned indifference in public, while actually longing to kiss and touch?

In the past, whenever she had fantasised about falling in love – and she had done this quite often when neglected by Peter – Andrea's greatest hope had been that the unknown man's thoughts would mirror and complement her own. She had certainly never dreamed that she might one day be drawn to someone whose mind was a mystery to her, and to whom she was attracted mainly for physical reasons. Until meeting Mike, Andrea would sooner have imagined herself intimately involved with a conscientious objector than with an officer, even a volunteer naval reserve one.

When Peter had been in hospital recovering, a friend with a warped sense of humour had shocked Andrea by giving him a novel about a French businessman crippled by *myelite* whose wife had promptly begun a passionate affair with a tennis professional whom she happened to meet on the beach at Juan-les-Pins. Her choice of an athlete's body had added to her husband's misery. It occurred to Andrea that the real-life wife of a crippled non-combatant scientist would cause only slightly less hostility if falling for a fit and youthful serving officer. What kind of woman would do that? Only the empty kind that loved magazine romances in which crisp bemedalled uniforms made a girl's knees tremble. So was there no morally acceptable course for such a wife to take if she needed love? Yes, indeed. She should leave her husband for a man even more damaged. The magazines knew the sort: a blinded officer with half a face.

Despite the painful stiffness of his leg, Peter was determined to come down and meet Mike. He was delighted to learn from Andrea that she had already come clean on the subject of how she had heard about the local flotilla's French missions.

'Damned shame we can't grill Harrington about his near scrapes, but *pas devant les enfants* and all that,' muttered Peter as Andrea helped him tie his shoe laces. 'To be honest, I'm damned envious of him.'

111

'For his better chances of dying?' suggested Andrea, squinting up at him as she fastened his final lace.

'Be honest, Andrea. Women are just as fascinated by soldiers and warfare as men are.'

'Not this woman.' The words were out before she could even blush. Not that he was looking at her any more. Now, he was trying to choose a necktie.

'Think of Spain, Andrea. We both know several wives of pacifist dons who . . .'

'We know *one* wife, Peter.'

'Okay, one wife, who definitely misbehaved with her husband's pupil as soon as he'd volunteered – and another wife who may have done.'

'Wasn't that left-wing solidarity?'

'It was women being driven crazy by male self-sacrifice.'

'Is *that* why you envy Harrington?'

'Don't be silly.' Peter chose a bow tie, and began to knot it. 'I wouldn't want to admit this to Leo – so don't give me away – but those little warships are something special. The camaraderie of their crews; their sleek lines and speed. Imagine roaring home successful at dawn, your signal mast shot away, decks full of bullet holes.'

'Like your crew?'

He gave her two claps of silent applause. 'Oh very well, I *know* I've been indoctrinated. But it's pure hypocrisy to deny the lure of it.' He pulled a face. 'Though that's what I did with Leo – denied it. Well, I've had time, plenty of time, to think.' He sighed heavily. 'Believe me, my sweet, doing important work like mine is *not* everything.' He adjusted his tie and stared at his reflection in the small dressing mirror. 'Given the life he leads, it's really jolly decent of Harrington to devote his spare time to the boys.' He combed his hair thoughtfully. 'I wonder what he did for a living in civvy street.'

'Something frivolous and selfish, I hope,' said Andrea, finding

Peter's sudden enthusiasm for Mike embarrassing and unwelcome. 'Too much dash and heroics can soften the brain.'

Peter chuckled to himself. 'For God's sake, don't tell *him* that. Rumour has it that he's just won the DSO.'

'Doesn't he wear it?'

'And give the whole game away? Tsk, tsk.' Andrea watched her husband limp to the bedroom door, where he paused and sniffed appreciatively. 'Mmm! That smells delicious. I must be one of the few men alive who actually likes kedgeree.'

'Let's hope Commander Harrington is another.'

'My liking for it even survived the terrible stuff they passed off for the real thing at school.'

'Perhaps his school was better.'

'In terms of cookery, quite possibly,' conceded Peter, whose loyalty to Uppingham amused Andrea, not because she knew much about the precedence of English public schools, but because the intricate web of trivial distinctions which differentiated these extraordinarily similar institutions for their alumni had always struck her as humorous. Given the universal awfulness of most English food, the quality of a school's kitchens probably conferred kudos in inverse proportion to their merits. It was strange to think that, though she had been living in England for a decade, she had made little progress in the art of placing Englishmen in whatever positions in the class hierarchy their socially aware countrymen would instantly pigeonhole them. Mike Harrington was a case in point. His accent, an occasional diphthong apart, was very like Peter's – but whether this reflected badly on one, both, or neither, she could not tell.

The round table in the dining room was small but just large enough for them all to squeeze around. The boys were euphoric after their sail, and Mike Harrington was generous with his praise for their 'hard work'. Andrea was immediately struck by the way Justin looked at him – attentively and without any of the reserve he displayed when talking to Peter. The boy

113

wouldn't like him, would he, unless Mike was a sympathetic person?

While they were drinking Rose's vegetable soup, Justin begged Mike to tell them about fighting in MGBs.

'It might bore everyone else.'

'No, it won't,' exploded Leo.

So Mike gave a deliberately vague account of the cat and mouse tactics employed against E-boats in the North Sea. If the navigator's calculations for direction and speed were even fractionally wrong, the enemy's boats would be missed by many miles. When the boys had finally stopped pestering him to describe being hit by bombs, Peter said quietly that he was working on a weapon that would make air attacks on small warships much less likely.

'Tell us about it, dad,' cried Leo.

'Of course I can't. But I do promise Mike will be pleased when he gets one.'

'How soon will that be?' asked Mike, smiling.

'A couple of months if you're lucky.'

While they were all eating their kedgeree with differing degrees of enthusiasm, Peter asked Mike how he had first become involved with coastal forces.

'I was teaching at King's, London, but when war broke out I joined the Crown Film Unit. One of my first jobs was to make a short film about the motor torpedo boats at Great Yarmouth. I was hooked from the moment I went out in one.'

Peter said, 'I've often wondered what they ask on their selection boards?'

'Nothing too esoteric.'

Peter laughed. 'Stuff like, do you know about navigation?'

'Exactly. I said yes, but they weren't impressed. So I said I'd rowed for my college – which was a lie – but as soon as I'd said it, they took an immense shine to me. One of them held up a large optician's card. "Can you see those colours?"

"Would they be green, blue and red, sir?" "Good man. You're definitely officer material."'

'A triumph for informal selection,' choked Peter, with his mouth full of food.

'Disgraceful,' said Andrea lightly, still surprised by Peter's obvious liking for Mike.

'You're right, Mrs Pauling, I'm still ashamed of myself. But joking apart,' continued Mike, 'these people choose trawlermen and tug skippers, as well as bogus oarsmen.'

While Rose was offering second helpings, which only Peter accepted, he asked Mike what he had taught at London University.

'Classics,' Mike announced, plainly enjoying Peter's amazement. 'My father worked for a Midlands metal-bashing company and never stopped enthusing about gaskets, so I opted for an ivory tower existence, naturally.'

Peter seemed puzzled. 'I'm pretty sure my boy will do something in the same line as me when he grows up.'

'But not what I do,' said Andrea. 'I'm a teacher, too.'

'At a school for girls,' said Leo, in a tone Andrea found hurtful.

'You'll grow to like them some day,' Mike told him. And Andrea felt grateful for this gentle put down. She prayed that Peter would not treat Mike to one of his well-rehearsed dismissals of the humanities as unfit for serious study. Whenever she recalled occasions on which Peter had jovially commiserated with arts dons at Oxford, because "they had so little to be clever about in comparison with their scientific colleagues", she could hardly believe he could have been so insulting to them and to her. Yet Peter would not have seen it that way. He thought people ought to face the truth, particularly when it was what they didn't wish to hear.

Rose was clearing away their plates when Peter asked Mike how his teaching had been changed by the development of psychoanalysis.

'Not a lot,' he replied, evidently unaware that Peter was in earnest.

Peter seemed amazed. 'Really? Though the people in Greek drama now seem ludicrously unconvincing?'

Mike seemed more amused than angry. 'Would you enjoy a modern play that sounded like an analyst's case notes?'

'He doesn't enjoy plays, period,' said Andrea.

Peter looked heavenwards, as if seeking divine vindication. 'That's not fair, dearest. I often find them highly entertaining.'

'Oh yes. Like you find ITMA entertaining.'

'Really, Andrea.' He smiled reassuringly at Mike. 'Don't listen to her. In point of fact I have considerable respect for several ancient Greeks.'

'I'd be intrigued to know their names,' remarked Mike, evidently suspecting that Peter was mocking him.

'Thales of Miletus for a start. Don't look so bored, Leo. One day in the sixth century BC, Thales asked a hell of a good question, "Of what is the Universe composed?" and answered, "Of water."'

'But that's wrong, dad.'

'Agreed. But it was still remarkably farsighted to deduce that some form of homogeneous matter underlay everything.' He turned from Leo to Mike. 'So why the hell did the Greeks base their principal art form on pessimism, rather than on scientific optimism?'

'Tragedy isn't all pessimistic,' said Andrea trying to sound authoritative.

Peter forked in a final mouthful of kedgeree and spluttered, 'You wouldn't by any chance be referring to that Greek nonsense about purging one's emotions?'

'Nonsense is a bit strong,' said Mike, as if encouraging an intelligent but wayward pupil. 'Though I don't buy *catharsis* either.'

Peter rubbed his hands. 'Then you'll agree with me that the

Greeks only invented tragedy because they loved seeing blood everywhere.'

Mike inclined his head donnishly. 'An interesting slant on Aristotle's *Poetics*.'

'Don't josh him,' warned Andrea. 'He won't see the joke and will only think he's gotten the better of you.'

Mike smiled at her. 'All right, to be more serious, I like tragedy because it tells me that human beings can sometimes be greater than their fate.'

Peter sucked in his cheeks. 'Greatness, nobility ... bah ... just whistling in the wind. If Freud's right about our fundamental drives being instinctive, a man can't be blamed for doing wrong, or praised for doing right. So where does that put the Tragic Hero, Commander?'

'In the theatre. Where else?' For the first time, Mike looked a little rattled. 'In ancient Chinese drama, a man with a white face was good, and one with a red face was bad. If they could swallow that, I can accept a bit of *hamartia* and *hubris*.'

Rose placed two bowls in front of Andrea. 'Stewed apple and blancmange, madam.'

Andrea thanked her effusively. 'Any orders?' She looked round the table expectantly.

'One day we'll have a real discussion,' Peter promised Mike, evidently rather pleased with their conversation.

'Not when I'm around,' whispered Justin, earning himself a fierce stare from Mike, followed by a discreet wink.

Looking at the smiling naval officer across the table, Andrea had no idea whether he had been offended by Peter. Could his remarkable good nature have been genuine? And if so, why? Because he truly liked Peter – as many people did – or because an affair with a wife was always easier when the husband liked the lover?

Before Mike Harrington left, Justin made him promise to take him and Leo out again before the weekend. Andrea

117

found it touching that the boy was confident Mike would agree.

It had started to rain while they had been eating but this did not stop Andrea walking with Harrington to his car.

'I thought you were awfully restrained with Peter.'

'I didn't try to be.' He smiled wanly. 'When my own life became dramatic, I stopped caring so much about Greek plays.'

'You're making fun of me.'

'Only a little.'

'I can't figure out whether that's worse than a lot.'

They walked in silence through the gate and into the lane. The rain was coming down harder, making dark marks on her turquoise blouse. He said gently, 'I'll be away for a few days from this evening. I couldn't tell Justin. So please think of something to say if he asks why I didn't ring.'

'It's good of you to think of his feelings.'

'I don't see much of my own son.' He raised his hands and let them fall. 'I'll tell you about him some day, but not now.'

'Are you still afraid?' she forced herself to ask as they reached the automobile. She could hear the rain pattering down on the roof. The vehicle was old and blue, with RN painted on what he called the bonnet and she the hood.

'You mean afraid of you?'

'You said it, not me.'

'I did.' He opened the driver's door but did not get in. 'Can I be honest with you? For months now, I haven't been leading any kind of life – just staggering from one day to another. But it can't go on.' He got into the car and left the door open. 'I can't let it. Do you understand?'

'Not really.'

'Get in out of the rain.' He pushed open the passenger's door for her. She heard Leo calling her from the house.

'Another time,' she murmured, but Mike looked so disappointed that she changed her mind and slid in beside him.

He said rapidly, without looking at her, 'I was talking to

118

Tony the other day about what might make life better for men like us. Not wealth, he said. We wouldn't be needing money if our luck ran out. Not success, because one needs time to enjoy it.' His eyes fixed upon hers, and, though he was smiling, she sensed that he was nervous. 'What makes all the difference, according to Tony, is having someone who says he's the bee's knees. Death's no problem now, he tells me.'

'Do you still love your wife?'

He shook his head vehemently. 'After our bust-up, I didn't look around for anyone else either. I thought I wouldn't be able to cope with my job if I had a second disaster on the romantic front. Now I feel much more robust.'

Andrea reached out to him and placed a hand on his. The moment had come – he had shown his wounded heart to her; explained. 'When will you be back?' she asked, in a strangely stilted and high-pitched voice.

'Sunday morning. Why do you ask?'

'I'd like to see you, of course.' She could feel the blood rushing to her cheeks.

'I'll need to sleep for a couple of hours when we get in. So I'll ring you late afternoon.' Suddenly he laughed edgily. 'What a hole you're in. You had to say what you did.'

'Really, I didn't.'

'Not even out of pity for a departing matelot?' She could hear the pained anxiety in his voice.

She let out her breath. 'Pity doesn't figure at all.' The next moment he leaned across and kissed her on her half-open lips. Too flustered to resist or join in, she let it happen. He drew back and gazed at her.

'You look lovely with the rain in your hair.'

'It looks nice in yours, too.'

'Let's hope it rains some more.'

'Keep safe,' she whispered as she got out. Her legs shook as she stood up. But she did not dare stay a moment longer, although she could hardly drag herself away. Instead she hurried home along the dripping lane, knowing she would suffer until he returned, and that when he came back she would not see him enough. Tears leaked from her eyes and merged invisibly with the falling rain.

CHAPTER 8

A freighter had run aground in the night and Peter suggested driving up onto the headland beyond Bolidden Quarry so that Leo and Justin could watch tugs from Falmouth trying to save her. But when Andrea drove them onto the cliffs above the stranded vessel, attempts to float her off had been abandoned until the next high tide. However, they did see the Porthbeer lifeboat take off most of the crewmen, leaving behind only a skeleton crew.

Soon after breakfast, Andrea had been amazed to see her husband come in from the lane with a small posy of violets he had picked for her. Each flower could only have been gathered with pain. Taking the violets from him, her confused feelings about Mike had overwhelmed her. Tears had sprung into her eyes as she had stammered incoherent thanks.

As they sat in the car eating sandwiches, Peter was dismayed to hear the whine of aircraft out at sea. Moments later, the thump of exploding bombs reached them. On the horizon, a slanting column of black smoke began to bend in the wind until it was lying parallel with the water. Three black gnats appeared above the skyline. The whine of engines increased in volume to a drone.

'German bombers,' gasped Justin, shielding his eyes.

'Better get moving,' said Peter, guessing these planes had just attacked a convoy and would now be eager to discard their remaining bombs. A solitary car would not be worth hitting, but the nearby quarry's trolley-ways would be.

While Peter limped after everyone, Andrea led the way to a rocky depression surrounded by clumps of golden gorse. But once there, they remained standing, eyes still riveted to the three crooked little planes – more like wasps now than gnats.

'They're Junkers 88s,' announced Justin, and at that moment Andrea could clearly see the black crosses on their wings. The noise of their engines had risen to a roar that became a shriek as the leading plane swooped down, turning his belly briefly towards the cliffs.

'That's torn it,' muttered Peter. 'He's attacking the freighter.'

Like eggs squeezed from the abdomen of a blowfly, a few black dots detached themselves from the plane's underside and hurtled seawards. Two fountains of water sprung up close to the ship. A third bomb buried itself in a field two hundred yards from where they were sheltering. As clods of earth rained down, the four of them flung themselves on their faces. Peter prayed that a fourth bomb was not on its way. He was still waiting in agony as the next bomber went into its screeching dive.

'Aargh!' groaned Leo. 'They got me.'

'Don't joke,' reproved Andrea.

She had rested her forehead on the ground for a moment and something was sticking to her skin. She raised a hand and brushed off some moist rabbit droppings. Her smile was brief. What a fool she'd been not to figure out that a helpless ship would attract enemy aircraft.

The next bombs landed in the sea. The third Junkers started its descent, and, though no one saw the bomb strike the ship, they certainly heard it detonate. Only when the sound of the bombers' engines had become very faint did Andrea let the boys stand up. By then, the freighter was on fire from stem to stern.

'There's a man in the bows,' screeched Leo, just before the pin-sized crewman leapt into the sea. Peter thought he saw another tiny figure on a ladder by the bridge but the smoke was very thick and the next moment there was an explosion and the whole bridge was engulfed in flames. Had anyone else seen this second crewman die?

If either boy had, Peter didn't expect Andrea to forgive him in a hurry. Even before this morning she had seemed alarmingly tense. The night before she hadn't wanted to make love, but had submitted to him. So to thank her for putting his pleasure before her own wishes, he had picked some violets. Her strange response had not reassured him.

Now there were more aircraft in the sky. Two silver planes were closing with the bombers ten miles out to sea. The German planes seemed slow and cumbersome as these new arrivals attacked in turn, diving from above with machine guns rattling, leaving vapour trails in the sky. Nobody spoke as one of the Junkers disintegrated, its fuselage tearing apart like tissue paper. One wing flew off sideways, quite slowly, while the engine plummeted seawards like a huge bomb.

'Poor devils,' murmured Peter.

'Another's on fire,' cried Leo, as smoke billowed from the entrails of this second victim of the British fighters. The plane lost height before managing to climb again. It was still airborne as it disappeared over the horizon, pursued by both Hurricanes. Two minutes later the fighters were back again but something was wrong with one of them. It was coming down in a slow glide, its propeller scarcely turning. A cloud of burning fluid trailed behind. Bale out, Peter willed the pilot, bale out. But the cockpit remained closed as the plane tilted into a steep dive. When the Hurricane hit the water, Justin ran off blindly across the heather. At the spot where the plane had sunk, a patch of oil stained the water. Too stunned to move at first, Andrea sprang to life and raced in pursuit.

'That was the last thing that poor boy should have seen,'

123

groaned Peter, knowing the kind of trouble he would be in when Andrea returned.

'What about me?' sniffed Leo.

'Did *your* father die in a plane?' demanded Peter.

'I'm sorry, dad,' said Leo, feeling a great sob swell in his throat.

Peter hugged his son tightly as he began to shake. 'Bloody bad luck we were here when it happened.'

Justin had run on past a 'Danger' sign into the abandoned part of the quarry. Breathing hard, Andrea paused where the ground began to fall away. Ahead of her was a gigantic circular hole, large enough to accommodate the Albert Hall. A series of sloping terraces ran round the quarry's sides and on one of these she spotted Justin. He was sitting on the very edge, legs thrust out into space. She approached slowly, in order not to shock him, and sat down several paces away. Far below them, the sea was visible through a wide gap that had been blasted over the years into the side of the headland.

'You okay now?' she asked softly.

'It wasn't the plane,' he blurted out after a silence.

'No?'

'Maybe a bit. It was mainly the ship.'

She moved closer and slid an arm round him. 'Tell me, sweetheart.'

'I thought of Mike.'

A lump formed in Andrea's throat. 'Because he didn't call about taking you sailing?' Justin nodded, fighting back tears. Andrea's eyes were also filling. 'I should have told you. I'm really sorry. He *did* call. He had to go on a training exercise.'

'He was really nice to me when we went out that time.'

'I can imagine.'

'I did everything right for him. That's really odd for me.' Justin managed a twisted smile.

'You'll see him again real soon.'

'If they kill him like my dad, I'll . . .' He raised his hands to his face and stayed hunched and very still.

'He'll be just fine, honey. His work isn't dangerous.' The boy did not answer but sat swinging his feet back and forth over the drop. 'Let's walk down,' she suggested.

The bottom of the quarry was overgrown with brambles that had almost engulfed a rusting winch and the twin boilers of a large ship. Andrea guessed that these had been salvaged from a wreck; but, after what Justin had just witnessed, she did not say so. Justin, however, seemed to enjoy poking around these maritime relics and was clearly frustrated not to be able to hack his way through the undergrowth to explore an entire steel deckhouse complete with portholes.

Sitting in the car, Leo and Peter had the satisfaction of seeing the lifeboat nose in right under the cliff. The man who had plunged into the sea had evidently managed to swim to the rocks, because when the lifeboat returned to view a man was in the cockpit, swathed in blankets. The hull of the freighter was still burning and listing.

'I'd hate to be a sailor,' murmured Leo, gazing at the doomed vessel. He suddenly seemed chastened. 'I wish Commander Harrington liked me as much as he likes Justin.'

'He's probably nice to Justin because of his father.'

Just then the burning freighter seized their attention by sinking with a boiling hiss. Strange burping noises could be heard as huge bubbles broke the surface.

When Andrea and Justin came in sight, they were smiling and swinging their arms. Justin was soon enthusing about 'the amazing quarry we discovered'. His grief seemed forgotten. Peter could have hugged him. Andrea would not now accuse him of causing the boy lasting upset.

'You missed seeing the ship sink,' Leo told Justin, wondering why his mother was staring at him. 'What's wrong with saying that, mother?'

'Nothing,' she replied briskly, trying to convey that more

bad news might make his friend rush off again. Leo wasn't even convinced that Justin's rapid exit had been genuine. He suspected a performance aimed at winning his mother's sympathy. The way he was smiling at her now, she might almost be his own mum. She seemed to like it. When Justin tried hard with anyone, he usually got what he wanted.

In the car on the way to Trevean Barton Leo imagined himself back at school, telling Justin that he couldn't come to Cornwall in the summer holidays. Justin begged, but Leo did not change his mind. This imaginary scene gave Leo pleasure, but also made him feel a little ashamed.

On Saturday morning Andrea went to the shops with Rose. The village grocer's had two long mahogany counters: one for butter, ham, bacon and lard, the other for tea, coffee and porridge oats. Even in wartime every purchase was wrapped in white sugar paper and skilfully parcelled up by a boy who did nothing else. As Andrea and Rose were leaving, they were stopped by a grey-haired, beady-eyed woman whom Andrea recognised.

'A little bird told me you *did* go and play to the children,' said the vicar's wife, smiling brightly at Andrea from behind pink-framed spectacles. 'So kind of you.'

'I enjoyed myself.'

'Their teacher was delighted. But you're a teacher yourself, I'm told. Perhaps you'd care to come along this evening to our little First Aid class in the village hall?'

'I'll try, Mrs Jefferies.'

'Splendid.' The vicar's wife lowered her voice conspiratorially, 'There are know-it-alls who say it couldn't matter less if villagers learn to tie tourniquets or not. It's not like London, they say. Well, a bomb fell in Polruan last night and a man bled to death.' Rose took a few steps towards the door. 'I hope you'll come too, Rose.'

'I don' know 'bout that, ma'am.'

Mrs Jefferies turned back to Andrea. 'Some officers' wives will be there. One came down from London this morning – a Mrs Harrington. Such a pretty woman. And only yesterday Mrs Henderson promised she'd ... Are you all right, Mrs Pauling?'

Dizzy with shock, Andrea managed to ask, 'Do naval wives live with their husbands when they're on dry land?'

'Some do; others would like to, but can't.'

'Is Mrs Harrington one of those?'

Mrs Jefferies' face suddenly became bland and inscrutable. 'If you come along, you can ask her yourself.'

'Of course I can't.' Andrea was relieved to hear herself laughing very naturally. 'I was only nosy because Mrs Harrington's husband was very good to my son's friend.'

Mrs Jefferies pursed her narrow lips and then relaxed them as if she had just applied lipstick. 'In that case, there's no harm in telling you the gossip. They separated, and now, rumour has it, she wants to be taken back. A happy story for once.'

As Andrea and Rose walked back to the house with their parcels, Rose muttered, 'Thinks there's nothin' she don' know, does rector's wife.'

Somehow, Andrea managed to conceal the misery she was feeling, though she hardly saw the Temperance Reading Room, or the rabbits hanging in the butcher's shop. It was as if the glass shield of indifference that had kept her safe for years had finally been shattered. A man had thrust his hand through the glass and touched her.

As she walked, Andrea railed at romantic love for forcing her into a role she wouldn't normally have looked at: the neglected wife craving affection from the brave but vulnerable fighting man. Her style was love against the grain. Love for the scientist whose views were nothing like her own. To fall for a man who shared her interests, and was handsome and clever, was to put social externals first – when the accepted wisdom, at least for intellectuals, was that only the primitive, the inarticulate and unsophisticated was authentic. Well, too bad. No gamekeeper, criminal, or jazz trumpeter would do; only Mike; intelligent, brave, and probably tragic, Mike.

And Peter had nagged *him* about tragedy! Andrea had once been told by her headmistress that 'tragic' was not a word to be used for describing sad or disastrous events in life, only those in art. To speak of accidental deaths as tragedies was to be guilty of 'a vulgar solecism'. Maybe Mike would be amused, if he came back safely, and didn't fling himself into his wife's arms.

Even before she entered the village hall, Andrea could hear Mrs Jefferies' thin, commanding voice, 'Come and be splinted for a Colles fracture. Do I have a volunteer? Thank you. Over here, please.'

Andrea had imagined that the occasion would be a throw-back to Edwardian days, with nobody being thought to be able to do anything unless the gentry were gracious enough to show them how. In fact the scene Andrea met was much more democratic. People of all classes were at work on one another without receiving instruction from anyone. The room echoed with curses as tourniquets were applied and fingernails pinched to see if blood flow had been stopped. Improvised splints were causing widespread discomfort as umbrellas and lumpy walking sticks were bound to 'broken' limbs.

Looking around for Mike's wife, Andrea felt her heart accelerate. She still scarcely understood why she needed to see her, and yet she did. Andrea imagined she would be in her late twenties or early thirties, attractive, well-dressed. Two women looked possible candidates. If Sally was here, *she* would know her. But Sally had not come, and was not likely to, given her dislike of the vicar's wife. Yet just as she was about to give up and leave, Andrea saw Miss Lawrence, the schoolmistress, and questioned her.

'Mrs Harrington? She's over there – the dark-haired woman with the doctor.'

'He's in the brown suit?'

'That's our Dr Lowther.' Andrea was aware of a balding, pleasant looking man, but only for the brief moment before her eyes were drawn to the figure beside him. Mrs Harrington was not younger than she was, as Andrea had imagined, but older. She could easily have stepped from the pages of *Tatler*: the silver fox fur, the beautifully cut coat and stylish soft hat.

Miss Lawrence whispered, 'Mrs Harrington came to our prize-giving with the commander.'

Mrs Jefferies bore down on them. For some reason she had a large 'M' written on her forehead in indelible pencil. 'I've been given morphine,' she explained, touching her brow, 'so I mustn't be given any more.' She laughed quietly. 'Moderation's my motto. We'll be breaking for tea and biscuits soon. You can meet Mrs Harrington then.'

'Please don't go to any trouble, I'm . . .'

But by now the doctor was coming in her direction, still talking to Mike's wife. He said to Andrea, 'You must be Sally's American friend. I'm afraid I can't remember your name. I'm John Lowther, by the way.'

After introductions had been made, and the doctor had promised the vicar's wife that he would speak about burns after tea, Mrs Harrington, whose christian name was Venetia, said, 'If there's one medical word I can't stand, it's *crepitus*.'

'The condition's worse than the word,' suggested the doctor, smiling at Andrea, who did not know what it meant. As if suspecting this, he added, 'There must be worse noises than the jarring of broken bones.'

'Do you think so?' laughed Andrea.

Venetia said in her low sweet voice, 'Be honest, John, if a bomb fell on this village, wouldn't these people run a mile rather than cope with the terrible injuries?'

'I think they'd cope pretty well.'

Across the room, someone said, 'Before giving artificial

respiration to an unconscious man, you must pull out his tongue so he doesn't swallow it.'

Mrs Harrington turned her heavy lidded eyes on Andrea. 'So you're a friend of the famously tactless Sally.' Andrea could not help smiling. 'Your wife is *such* good fun, John. I love Sal dearly, despite all her *faux pas*. She's the one person who kept me sane last winter.'

'Are you still down here a lot?' asked Andrea, in terror of her reply, yet managing to sound only mildly interested.

'Depends what you mean by a lot. I'm here now, as you see,' said Mrs Harrington in a decisive tone that seemed to close the subject. Andrea tried to imagine her being loving to Mike and failed. Although the woman's lips were full and soft and her eyes darkly expressive, there was a brittleness about her that seemed designed to keep people at arm's length. Then, moments later, Venetia let slip something which Andrea had wanted to know. 'Please get Sally to ring me, John. I'm not at Polwherne in the naval wifery, but staying in the new funk hole at Bonallack. She might find some of the guests amusing – a couple of BBC types, an American oil man, and me till Tuesday.'

'Of course I'll tell her,' said the doctor, with a strained little smile which Venetia Harrington appeared not to notice.

When she had gone, John Lowther guided Andrea towards the tea urn. 'Sally needs all the friends she can find at present.'

'What's happened?'

He looked away for a moment, towards three women practising resuscitation in a tangled heap near the tea urn; then he said quietly, 'Just come and see her when you can. I can't say more than that now.'

Andrea reached the door as Dr Lowther started to explain why medical experts were now saying that burns should not be smeared with jelly. Mrs Jefferies bustled up to her. 'I do apologise, Mrs Pauling, but I quite forgot to ask whether you could play the organ for us on an important occasion. Our Miss Edgelow is getting too old to be reliable.' Mrs Jefferies moved her face close to Andrea's ear. 'The navy retrieved the body of an RAF pilot this morning.'

Andrea shivered. 'Was his name James?'

'James Hawnby. You knew him?'

'Only by sight.'

'My husband should have been the one to invite you to play at the funeral, but he's down at the cottage hospital with a German survivor. Eighteen years old and both legs amputated.'

'I'll play,' whispered Andrea before hurrying out, past the Sunday school books and chairs, into the village street.

CHAPTER 9

On Sunday morning – not long after telling Rose he wouldn't go to chapel with her – Justin announced to Leo that he wanted to visit the creek from which the trawler had emerged.

'We may find out why I saw fishing nets when I got on board.'

An easterly wind had been blowing all morning, so they were able to run all the way up river to the mouth of the creek without tacking. The tiller vibrated in Leo's hand and the boat's bow surged exhilaratingly. Justin had refused to reveal exactly what they would be looking for in the inlet but Leo had not made an issue of it. He was intensely curious to learn what his friend had found out, and didn't intend to give him any excuse for keeping things to himself.

'Your mum was jolly depressed this morning,' said Justin, gazing not at Leo but at a man digging for lugworms on the riverbank. When Leo said nothing, Justin added, 'It's because Mike isn't back.'

'Why should she be worried? He's only on a training exercise.'

'She doesn't believe that.'

'How do you know?' demanded Leo.

'Because she drove down to the river early this morning.'

133

'So?'

'So she saw the trawlers weren't there.'

'Pull the jib across. It'll fill better on the other side,' said Leo, and waited until Justin had done this. 'Mum happens to be depressed because she knew the pilot who died yesterday. She's playing the organ at his funeral.'

Justin whistled softly. 'If she isn't worried about Mike she should be.'

'You never say why.'

'Don't rush me.'

Since the tide was low, and still falling, they dispensed with their sails and started to row after entering the creek. Soon the inlet narrowed, dwindling within minutes to a thin central channel that twisted in serpentine-fashion between high mudbanks.

'We should be keeping a lookout,' said Justin.

'For what?'

'Clues, of course.'

Justin's solemn expression annoyed Leo. He might almost be a commando, the way he was looking from side to side. On the shimmering mudbanks, numerous birds were feeding. Leo wished his father was here. He would note the colours and markings of lots of these birds so he could identify them later. One solitary white wader stood taller than the rest, and had a strange bill – long and yellow at the tip. There was no other bird like him, either among the gulls or ducks. Did birds ever feel lonely, Leo wondered. If they did, this tall white specimen certainly would, like being the only European in a Chinese town.

When the channel had become shallow enough for them to feel the bottom with the blades of their oars, Leo stopped rowing. 'We'll get stuck for hours if we go any further.'

'Let's leave the boat here and wade,' said Justin.

'We might sink up to our waists.'

'Let's test it.' Justin stood and jabbed his oar down into the mud. He pulled it up and showed Leo several inches of mud on the blade.

'It's still going to be risky to wade,' said Leo, thrusting down his own oar to see whether Justin's experiment could be repeated. Finding it could, he rolled up his shorts and, grasping the boathook, slipped into the water. The mud on the oar had smelled like rotting leaf mould. He could feel this muck squishing about in his plimsolls as he waded to the bows to throw out the anchor.

As they splashed upstream, they were unnerved by the mournful calls of birds and the isolation of the creek. From time to time, Leo thrust the boathook into the mudbanks on either side. The pole always sank in about a foot or so. Both boys wondered how they could possibly cross the mud to reach the creek's shoreline. Leo stopped wading.

'How the hell did that trawler come in here?'

'At high water. You saw it come out.'

Leo raised his eyebrows. 'So it just chugged up here and chugged out again? Funny thing to do.'

Justin pointed to the thick oak woods. 'They come here so nobody can see what they're doing.'

'Which is? Oh sorry . . .' Leo pretended to peer through an invisible magnifying glass. 'Got to find those clues.' Justin stared ahead, ignoring him. Suddenly he let out a whoop.

'Look!'

A fallen tree jutted out from the bank as far as the channel. They would be able to reach the shore by clambering along this bridge. High above the mud, balancing on the trunk, Leo pretended to stagger. 'How'd you get me out if I went splat?'

'I'd leave you to drown.'

They were soon on dry land, walking among oaks and hollies. 'Okay,' demanded Leo, 'if the trawler came up here, why didn't it fall over at low tide?'

'They propped it on planks.'

'Shouldn't we find them?'

'I'm looking.'

'What else should I look for, clever clogs?'

Without speaking, Justin went down on his knees and pulled a used pot of grey paint from the undergrowth. He held it up like a lump of gold. 'Fantastic!'

Leo wanted to fling it into the creek. Why would the navy go to the trouble of bringing a trawler here, just to paint it grey, when they could do that anywhere? If the solution was so bloody obvious, why couldn't he see it?

'Give me that,' cried Justin, pulling the boathook out of Leo's hand and beginning to poke and hack at the brambles.

Leo stalked ahead between the twisted trees that marked the margins of the creek. Here, the oaks were producing catkins earlier than those deep in the wood. Scientists noticed things like that. Justin might think *he* was observant, but he wasn't at all. In the open again, Leo looked across the mud. The dinghy appeared to be exactly where they had left it – probably aground by now. If they spent too much time here, they'd be stuck for hours.

Leo walked along the belt of shingle at the edge of the creek. In front of him on the shore lay a stout piece of timber, about six feet long. Close by were a couple more. Whether they'd been washed up or tossed here by people, he had no idea; but something about their appearance made him stare. All of them had traces of mud at one end or the other. On two, there were splatters of blue paint as well as grey. The third merely had grey brush marks. Looking more carefully, Leo noticed a few spots of brown paint, too. These brown marks were less numerous. He turned. Behind him, Justin was looking at the planks, wide-eyed.

'Blimey!' gasped Justin. 'We've found them. They're what they prop the ships up with.'

Leo asked hesitantly, 'Do they paint on these colours to make their ships look like fishing boats?'

'They do, they do,' shrieked Justin, capering about. 'But you didn't see blue and brown boats in Porthbeer harbour.' Leo frowned in puzzlement. 'Why didn't you?' roared Justin, circling Leo as if he was a totem pole.

'Because . . .,' faltered Leo.

'Say it,' shouted Justin. He picked up one of the props and brandished it.

Leo hung his head. 'I suppose because blue and brown are fishing colours in Brittany.'

'They cross the Channel looking like French fishing boats. That's why I saw nets on board.'

Leo couldn't bring himself to look at Justin. He'd been wrong all along and hadn't kept his doubts to himself. In fact he'd deserved to be kept in the dark. A most unexpected sob broke from Justin and Leo began to babble apologies.

'Stop!' spluttered Justin. 'They must go dressed as fishermen. That's terrible! Don't you see?' Leo shook his head. 'It's their clothes, silly.' Justin covered his face. 'People without uniforms are shot as spies.'

'He's too clever to get caught,' soothed Leo.

Justin handed Leo the prop he had been carrying and pulled himself up onto the tree that bridged the mud. He looked down sadly at Leo. 'Mike's still not back from France.'

Leo was too dazed by their discovery to listen any more. He imagined sailors covering up the French colours with grey naval paint, so the trawler would cause no comment in the river. Then, when the boats were due to return to France, the grey would be replaced by brown and blue. French names and fishing numbers would be painted on, too. Though Justin was still tearful, Leo felt elated. Dad would have to admit they'd found out something he didn't know.

Leo jumped down from the tree into the channel and suddenly stopped dead. Mike really could be shot. 'Summarily executed' was how books on spying described it. The Germans would probably torture him to make him give away the names of the French people he was meeting. Then he'd be tied to a post and blindfolded. Leo felt the kind of shivers he had last experienced when waiting to be caned.

Peter went out into the lane. There were no bicycles propped against the hedge, so the boys had not yet returned from their sail. Since Andrea was out, too, Peter began to pack to avoid being in a rush later in the evening. He found it very touching that Leo hated to see him go back to Falmouth, but this didn't ease Peter's depression as he collected up his socks and handkerchiefs. Andrea had given no sign that *she* regretted his departure. Her detachment contrasted strangely with her distress before his last return to the dockyard. He was the uncommunicative one, she had always told him, unable or unwilling to express his feelings. Yet now she would herself sit for long periods saying nothing, and offering no explanation even when asked why she seemed sad or preoccupied. 'I'm thinking,' she would say; or, 'Do I keep asking what's on your mind?'

Her refusal to go out walking with him had spoken to Peter more clearly than words. Physical things – walking, tennis and cycling – had become all-important to their relationship after Andrea had stopped asking him about his work. Until this holiday, Peter had managed to persuade himself that polio hadn't destroyed the few activities they'd still shared. But now he knew better. He didn't intend to make airy promises to Andrea before he left, but by the time he saw her again Peter was determined to have acquired whatever medical certificates might be needed to extract from the Admiralty a new deal on health grounds. Unless he saw Andrea more often, their marriage would end. To prevent this happening, he would resign if need be.

Peter was still folding shirts and ruminating as he heard a motorbike in the lane. When he reached the window, he saw that Mike Harrington had dismounted and was striding up the path. Rose was showing the naval officer into the sitting room by the time Peter reached the hall.

Mike turned and said cheerfully to Peter, 'Thought I'd drop by and see if the boys would like a sailing lesson.'

'They're on the water already.'

'Good for them. I'll call back another time.'

Mike was wearing a leather sheepskin-lined jacket similar to those favoured by RAF pilots. He delved into an inner pocket and produced a bottle of wine.

'Since you and your wife are in the know, I thought I'd give you a couple of bottles. The other one's still on the bike.'

'Very good of you.'

'I get given plenty.'

Looking at Mike's smiling face, Peter was surprised to find himself feeling a little brighter. Here was a man able to be cheerful and think of others though he might be dead in a month. So buck up. Though envying Mike his physical fitness and the excitement of his work, he liked him, too. Not many men would think of doing favours for a couple of boys, just after returning from a mission. Peter might have suspected a homosexual interest but Harrington didn't fit that picture – though appearances could be misleading.

Peter clapped his hands heartily, as if this was his usual style, and said, 'I know the sun isn't anywhere near the yardarm, but what about a spot of wine?'

'The wine's yours.'

Peter went out and returned with a corkscrew and two glasses. While drawing the cork, he asked Mike about his motorbike and learned that it was a Velocette similar to the machine that won the Manx TT in '39. After sipping the wine appreciatively, he questioned Mike about the engines of his trawlers and was impressed to learn that he had bullied the navy into installing twin 500 hp Hall Scott engines like the ones used in the fastest MTBs.

Peter grinned widely. 'Must be quite a sight, a fishing boat ripping along at twenty-five knots.'

'Dead right,' laughed Mike. 'So we cross at night and slow right down when we're five miles from home.'

Peter calculated that Mike was about thirty, almost ten years younger than him; yet age was not such a straightforward indicator of experience. Much of adult life involved endless repetition, except for people like Mike who rarely knew two weeks alike. Did this age them more quickly? Maybe not, since childhood was also full of new experiences, and this was what made a child's life so vivid. A broken toy or cancelled treat was terrible for a child because he thought the loss could never be put right. Like children, Mike and his men lived with losses. Longing to have a serious discussion, Peter felt he didn't know Mike well enough to demand the honesty required to make such a conversation worthwhile. Being with Mike made Peter wonder what his own life would have been if he had not contracted polio. Such speculation caused him no resentment. Was that because he could live more adventurously through Mike? It embarrassed Peter to suspect that this was true.

The boys arrived without either man hearing them. The instantaneous delight on Justin's face as he saw Mike touched Peter. Leo also seemed pleased, but in a more reserved way.

'Vroom! Vroom! Will you take us on your Velocette?' cried Justin.

'I haven't got a helmet for you.'

'Do *you* wear one?'

'Not always. But that's different,' insisted Mike with a smile.

'Why?'

'Because I'm not a minor.'

'If you crashed and died your loss to England would be a zillion times worse than a schoolboy's.'

'Your mother might disagree.' Mike turned to Peter. 'My God! Does he press *you* like this?'

Peter smiled back. 'I haven't got a motorbike.'

140

'I'd better get rid of it! You know I came to take you two sailing?'

Justin came and sat next to him. 'Do you know the creek beyond Grove Point?' asked the boy, looking closely at Mike, who merely nodded. 'That's where we went.'

'French wine,' said Leo, peering at the label on the bottle. '1940.'

Mike nodded briskly, no longer amused. 'A friend brought it back from Dunkirk.'

After a silence, Justin said breathlessly to Mike, 'We found the props you use when you paint on the French colours.'

Mike snapped, 'You should have done what Captain Borden said, Justin. What my flotilla does is my business.'

'D'you think I'd ever tell anyone?' gulped Justin.

'You made a promise and you broke it.'

Without speaking, Justin jumped up and ran out. Peter said urgently to Mike, 'That was pretty hard on him. You're his idol, you know. Finding out couldn't have been easy.'

'What do you suggest, professor?' Mike's tone was exasperated but remorseful, too.

'You should talk to him.'

'I guess you're right. Oh hell!'

When Mike had gone, Leo burst out angrily, 'He was horrible.'

Peter drank more wine. 'Our secret service sends agents to France.'

'I know that. I'm not stupid, dad.'

'Do you also know that the Germans send spies over here – wearing English clothes and speaking perfect English? Maybe there's one in this village.'

Leo said fiercely, 'No spy's going to hear me give anyone away.'

'But you might tell other boys, and they might blab all over the place. There are hundreds of lives at stake. Mike has every reason to be worried.'

'How did you and mum find out?'

'Mum was told by the doctor's wife, who'd heard from her husband. That's how secrets spread.'

Leo had gone very white. 'Would Mike be shot if he's captured?'

'It's pointless to speculate.'

'It isn't, dad.'

'It is,' said Peter, closing his eyes.

Just then, Justin came in holding Mike's hand. Almost at once, Justin launched into one of his self-confident, searching questions. How could Mike and his sailors stop the paint looking new and giving the game away?

'Good question,' murmured Peter.

'But easy to answer,' remarked Mike. 'We throw iron filings onto the paint while it's still wet, and then hose it down with salt water. A couple of hours later, the rust marks look as if they've been there for months.'

'That's really clever,' remarked Leo.

'We do our best.'

'Hey! What's this?' Peter was startled to hear his wife's voice. 'Drinking in the afternoon?'

Andrea came up behind her husband, kissed him lightly on the temple and gazed at Mike as if at a mythical creature. 'I thought you were some place else, Commander.'

Mike looked resigned. 'Everyone in this room knows where, so don't be coy about naming it.'

'I'll be as coy as I like.'

'Mike kindly gave us this wine,' said Peter, filling his glass and handing it to Andrea. She looked particularly pretty in a striped sweater and faded blue slacks. He tried to imagine that his own destination was Brittany, and immediately he felt great tenderness for Andrea. Facing the possibility of never seeing her again, he would insist they were left alone together so they could make love. Surely she would feel an answering tenderness. It came to Peter that the significance of adventure lay not in the thing itself but in the value it gave to the time before and after. Odd that he'd never thought of this before.

Justin came in from the garden holding a paint-spotted baulk of timber. He held it up for Mike's inspection. 'One look and everything was clear to me.'

Peter tried to think of a day when he too had discovered something that had changed everything. Not any of his scientific inventions; only meeting Andrea.

Mike took the plank from Justin. 'I think I should have this. I'll send someone for it.'

Andrea went out into the lane with Mike, just ahead of Peter, who wanted to take a closer look at Mike's bike. He was surprised to hear her ask Mike something about his wife. He hadn't realised the man was married. 'Is she enjoying her vacation?' Andrea ended lamely.

'God knows,' said Mike. 'She came down here to talk about our divorce.'

Andrea stammered a confused apology: she'd had no idea his marriage was over, blah, blah. Peter felt embarrassed for her. She wasn't a village gossip but that's what it had sounded like.

'Small places are the devil for rumours,' grumbled Mike, tilting his bike and flicking up the stand.

As Mike slung his leg over the machine, Andrea said, 'Next time, why not call up before you come for the boys?'

'Righto.' He held out a hand to Peter. 'See you soon, prof.'

'I'm afraid I'm off to Falmouth this evening. We'll meet on my return.'

Mike took another bottle of wine from a compartment under the pillion and gave it to Andrea before kick-starting his machine and roaring away. Standing beside her husband in the lane, Andrea smiled at him – quite sadly, he thought, but that seemed better than not at all.

CHAPTER 10

After his father had been driven away, Leo thumped upstairs to his room in an ostentatiously unhappy way. From the sitting room, Andrea could hear faint snatches of song – Rose was crooning to herself while ironing sheets. Too tense to read, Andrea turned off the standard lamp and gazed out across the rough lawn to where the candles on the large horse chestnut glowed serenely in the deepening gloom.

How in hell's name had Mike been so calm? In the half-light, Andrea's eyes took in the pale buff wallpaper, the dull green Wedgwood china on the mantelpiece, a Bartolozzi print by the door – what a bland and passionless setting for her longings. If Peter hadn't followed them into the lane, Mike would have told her when to meet him, and she would not be in suspense now. How would she endure it if days were to pass and she heard nothing from him?

'You're sitting in the dark.' Andrea jumped at the sound of Justin's voice. He had come in so quietly that she had not heard him until he was almost behind her.

'Don't *you* ever like being alone?'

'Only to ambush someone.'

He switched on the ugly lamp beside her chair. 'Guess what Mike told me?'

'I can't,' she murmured, suddenly gripped by the absurd

145

notion that Mike might have told Justin about his love for her.

'He said when he gets leave he'll come and see me at school.'

'That's really nice of him.'

'It's not really,' objected Justin, 'it's because he likes me and *wants* to come.'

'It's still nice,' she insisted.

'He can't see his own boy, so I'm the next best thing.'

'His wife won't let him see his son? That's awful, Justin.'

'He's getting divorced just so she'll have to.'

Andrea was shocked. 'Mike told you he's getting divorced just so he can see his son some more?'

'Yup.'

The alarming possibility that Mike was divorcing, while still loving Venetia, slid snake-like into Andrea's breast. The telephone rang as Justin was leaving, placing him almost beside the instrument at this crucial moment. Andrea snatched the receiver from him, only to hear Sally's voice.

'Andrea, dear, I'm telling all my friends not to speak to me at the funeral. I know I'll howl if they do. Smile at me if you must, but not one word, please.'

Since Andrea had not yet learned from the vicar what music she was to play, she had managed to avoid worrying about the funeral although it was only two days away. Sally's call forced her to imagine how it might be. John Lowther would probably drag himself to church, so people would think he'd forgiven his wife. Thinking about John made Andrea feel sorry for Peter, but not sorry enough to want to put off Mike.

By eleven that evening, Andrea was telling herself that Mike wasn't going to call till morning. But just as she was getting into bed, the telephone rang. To reach it first, she ran downstairs in her nightdress.

'Andrea?'

'Mike?' Feigned surprise in her voice.

146

'Are you alone?'

'Yes.'

'You're whispering.'

She giggled. 'You'd be whispering, too, if you had two juvenile detectives breathing down your neck, and a maid who catches fish in her hands.'

'When can we meet?'

'Tomorrow.'

'I can't manage that. What about the day after?'

'I'm playing at the pilot's funeral.'

'That's fine. I hope to be there. Perhaps we shouldn't leave together. What about going straight through the graveyard afterwards, and past the Great War cross. Then keep going till you find a lane on the right just after the butcher's and the baker's.'

'And the candlestick maker's?'

'Just the first two.'

'I guess it'll have to do.'

She heard him laugh a little uneasily. 'But you'll be waiting?'

'Of course I will,' she replied, amazed with herself for being flippant when she was overwhelmed with happiness. His acknowledgement that they ought not to be seen together was the sign she had longed for. A sense of the inevitable made her head swim. From the lane, he would take her to a place where they could be alone – and after that, what would be would be. On her way upstairs, she met Justin leaving the bathroom.

'Was that the telephone?' he asked.

'No, it was the fire department.'

'Was it Mike?' His tone was magnificently matter of fact.

'No, it was not,' she said emphatically, already wishing she hadn't lied. But, despite his tender age, Justin really rattled her. How many times must he have seen his mother talking with the men who later became her lovers? Enough to have

147

made him expert at reading the signs: their lowered voices and their looks; lustful expectation in the air like an intimate scent. Andrea vowed in future never to run to get the telephone, nor to sit in the dark.

So that she would have no doubts about where she would be meeting Mike, Andrea walked to his chosen lane before the service. As she entered the church, the vicar and his verger were putting in place tall trestles for the coffin to rest upon. As Andrea came closer, the vicar smiled approvingly, 'I'm so glad you're not wearing a hat with a brim, Mrs Pauling. Miss Edgelow's headgear once touched the candles lighting her music. She was lucky to escape with only minor burns.'

For the past two years, Andrea had been the organist at her girls' annual carol service in an Oxford church; but, until now, she had never played a country organ powered by a human 'blower'. Today, the pumping of air would be done by the verger, who came and sat next to her, placing himself, rather eerily, behind a red curtain. If he were to stop working the lever, a discordant wail would soon dwindle to a squawk. For her own part, Andrea knew all the chosen hymns pretty well, and had practised, on the school piano, the uplifting Buxtehude prelude selected by the vicar for the entrance of the coffin. With her back to the gathering mourners, Andrea could see them reflected in the mirror above her keyboard. When Sally and her husband entered together, the glass distanced Andrea a little from their pain.

Before the arrival of his coffin, she pictured James Hawnby as she had first seen him at Elspeth's, with his girlish complexion and his nervous manner. Recalling this, she feared Mike's calmness could only be a brave pretence. Andrea had doubted whether she would be able to recognise him in her small mirror, but, since he swept in at the centre of a tight-knit group of naval officers, she had no trouble. A dozen or so RAF pilots had entered just before him and were filing into pews near the chancel arch. It struck her as typical of Mike to choose to sit near the back, a position which the air force 'heroes' would probably consider good enough for members of an unglamorous coastal patrol.

Obliged to give all her attention to the tricky toccata-like passages in the Buxtehude, Andrea glanced up at her mirror once only, just as the choir entered the nave, leading in the coffin. As the final notes died away, the vicar's voice boomed out, 'I am the resurrection and the life, saith the Lord: he that believeth in me, though he were dead, yet shall he live . . .'

When she was not playing, Andrea's eye was caught by isolated details: a shaft of magenta light shining through a stained-glass saint; the glowing sanctuary lamp. The hymns moved Andrea more than anything, especially when James's comrades-in-arms carried out his coffin to Bunyan's 'He Who Would Valiant Be'.

She did not leave the church until almost everyone had gone. In the graveyard, she paused behind an eighteenth-century box tomb and was sad to see Sally standing well away from the graveside, presumably out of deference to her husband's feelings. Sally's face wore its usual emotionless mask of make-up. Mike and Tony Cassilis stood by an ancient yew. One day, they too might be buried here, if their bodies were ever recovered from the sea.

Soon after the coffin had been lowered, and the last prayers spoken, someone tapped Andrea on the shoulder.

'Thank you for your lovely playing,' murmured Mrs Jefferies through her veil. 'One can only hope the Almighty will look down kindly on the poor young man.'

'You surely can't think He won't.'

'I don't consider adultery a peccadillo, my dear.'

Andrea walked away, repelled. Without meaning to, she caught up with Sally and her husband at the lych gate. Having promised she wouldn't speak to her, Andrea took her arm instead.

'At least he was happy on the day he died,' sniffed Sally. 'He knew he was loved.' She clamped a handkerchief over her mouth to stop any sound emerging. Dr Lowther stared intently at the path.

'Let's talk tomorrow,' murmured Andrea, not trying to follow them. Instead, breathing abnormally fast, she retraced her steps across the graveyard, past the Great War cross. Soon she was passing the bakery and the butcher's on the corner.

Mike was not in the lane, but his motorbike was, propped under some flowering lilac. She thought how strange it was to be embarking on an affair wearing a dark coat and skirt. Stranger still to have little idea what *his* expectations were. Looking at his motorbike, she felt confused. Would she ride away on *this*, in a long skirt?

He came round the corner with his hat in his hand, looking formal and out of place in this rural lane.

'Not a lot of fun,' Mike declared, adding with a grin, 'except for your contribution, and the little fellow's next to you.'

'I'll tell him.'

'He'll be thrilled.' Mike walked to his machine. 'Ever been on one of these?'

'So often they bore me dreadfully,' she drawled, like an English debutante. Then, in her normal voice, 'Never in my life.'

'Don't do that! For a moment you sounded like my wife.' He touched the handles under the pillion. 'Grab hold of these.'

'I'll have to pull my skirt up.'

'Go on then. The road'll be empty.'

'Where are we going?'

'A little place I know.'

'Is it fearfully squalid?' she simpered, as if a character from *Mrs Miniver*.

'Fearfully,' he simpered back.

'I'll close my eyes.'

'And think of England?'

'To my last breath.'

They were laughing quite spontaneously as Andrea struggled to get a leg over the pillion seat without pulling her skirt up round her waist. Since Mike's back was to her, she didn't feel embarrassed when the wind blew around her stocking tops and step-ins. The engine roared beneath them as trees and hedges blurred by. They plunged down a hill, and through a shallow ford at its foot. Andrea was intoxicated to lean, as he did, into each bend and to feel no fear.

Views of the estuary glimpsed through gates told her they were descending to the water long before they reached a secluded cottage in a cove. The house looked empty but not derelict, since the pittosporum hedge had been cut back.

The silence after Mike cut the engine echoed in her head until she heard the soft thud of waves on the beach. He led her to the door and she was fleetingly aware of diamond-paned windows and lead drainpipes.

'We bring our agents here before embarking them,' he said, ushering her inside.

'How many return?'

'Some. I don't know how many.'

Suddenly the house seemed melancholy – a last sight of England for a doomed group of men and women. The sitting room smelled musty and the walls were spotted with damp. On a round table some magazines were scattered, as if tossed aside by departing agents. She picked up a novel – *The Remembered Kiss* by Ruby M. Ayres. Would anyone want to read such stuff when facing a terrifying future? But would they want to read *The Brothers Karamazov* or extracts from the great philosophers? On a sideboard were packs of cards and various board games.

'How long do they stay here?' she asked, looking around at worn sofas and hideous floral curtains.

'A couple of days; sometimes only hours.'

'Then what happens to them?'

'Since you know the main story, I can't see that a few minor details will hurt. We whizz them from the beach to a gunboat which puts to sea. A couple of miles out, they're transferred to one of Justin's painted trawlers.' He looked at her with concern. 'Please don't feel too sad about them. The risks they take are no worse than fighter pilots face.'

She smiled back at him. 'And that's comforting on a day like this?'

'For us sailors it is.' He moved to the door. 'I thought we'd have lunch here.'

'You've brought a man to cook?' She was horrified.

'Christ no. Wait here till I fetch a few things.'

After he'd left the room, Andrea felt confused. Why was he fussing about food? He ought to be in here still, talking, if not yet kissing her. Perhaps he was nervous. They'd only had the one kiss. Remembering it made her feel shaky. To stop herself feeling worse, she tried leafing through a copy of *Woman's World*. There were articles on make-up ('Beauty is your Duty') and keeping up morale ('Beating those Black-out Blues'), and one called 'Rebuilding Marriages', with a sub-heading in a panel:

```
'The woman who lets her husband down.
This problem is frankly discussed by
Leonora Eyles, who comes across her
far too often.'
```

Andrea read: 'What untold harm a foolish, unthinking woman can do with a scrap of paper, a pen and ink. So *don't* tell him about your affair. Tear up your selfish confession and wait till the war's over, when his mind will be at his disposal, not taken up by the business of fighting for life.'

When Mike returned, he was carrying a tray loaded with Brie and Camembert, presumably fresh from France, and also with bread and fruit and wine. He put down their lunch on the table and stood gazing at her.

'How shall we do this, Andrea?' The directness of the question surprised her. He noticed this, and said softly, 'I meant do you want lunch now or later?'

'I'd like a glass of water and then I'd like you to sit right here.'

He brought some water for her and watched as she drank. Then he took the glass away and sat beside her. She said quietly, 'You haven't kissed me.'

'It's nice to have everything still ahead of one.'

'Not forever,' she whispered, lifting his hand and drawing his fingers lightly across her lips.

'My darling, God knows how I've left you alone till now.' Slipping an arm round her shoulders, he kissed her neck. As his lips touched her skin, a marvellous feeling of warmth and wellbeing flowed through her. He was stroking her knee through her funereal skirt which was slipping back and forth over her silk stockings. How beautiful his hands were.

She inclined her neck so he would kiss her there again and murmured, 'Oh Mike, I want you so very much.'

'I want you, too,' he said, tilting his head so that their mouths met easily.

'When did it start for you?' she asked after a long kiss.

'When you and Justin came that day.'

'You didn't show it.'

'I couldn't. It was a nightmare for me. And you were so shamingly dignified. I felt a monster.'

'Darling, you weren't at all. Well, maybe a little.'

He grinned ruefully. 'A little monster.'

'That's right,' she said, refusing to smile and break her mood. Instead she began to kiss him with slow sideways movements, longing all the time to press her body against his. As he touched her breasts, all her senses seemed to be waiting there. 'Does this house run to a bed?' she sighed.

'To ten at least.'

'Choose for the both of us.'

'I'm afraid they're all single. Like I wish you were.'

They clung together on the stairs, breathless, bumping against one another, stopping to kiss on the landing. She could feel him trembling as his cheek touched hers. There were dead flies on the window ledges and the wallpaper was peeling with the damp, but everything felt right for her, except that she was crying.

'What's wrong?' he asked, kissing away her tears.

'Can't you tell I'm happy?'

'I'll know in future,' he said, smiling.

After they had made love, she lay with her head on his chest, breathing hard, her skin looking very pale against his. He had come too soon, and had tried to go on for her sake, until she had helped him out by pretending. Another few seconds and she would have reached her own climax. Unlike the calculated physicality of her sexual relations with Peter, Mike had hardly needed to touch her.

After a while, he said softly, 'let's hope I do better next time.'

'You did fine.'

And later he really did; and they slept in one another's arms in their narrow bed.

Andrea woke with a start and looked at her watch. Almost two hours had passed. Soon the boys would be wondering where she was. She lay back and closed her eyes against the world.

He said sleepily, 'Isn't it marvellous to laze afterwards?'

'It's heaven,' she agreed, knowing she would have to get up soon but not wanting to end his peace and happiness.

He propped his head on a hand and gazed at her. 'I could look at you for ever and still keep saying soft things like that.'

Feeling the same way herself, she stared back, thinking him perfect, from the slight scar above his right eye to the soles of his feet. She hugged him to her, loving his body's firmness. 'I have to go soon,' she sighed.

They both got up. As he dressed, even his slight self-consciousness at being watched delighted her. Every damned thing he did seemed beautiful: running a hand through his hair, turning his head, stepping into his pants. As Mike put on his jacket she pointed to a medal ribbon. 'I thought you couldn't wear those.'

'That one's different.'

'How come?'

'I got it before I came here.'

'What did you do?'

'We killed some Germans who weren't expecting us. I promise you don't want to know more.' He buttoned his shirt in silence.

Andrea stepped into her skirt. 'You're not mad at me for asking?'

'Not at all. If anyone had tipped off the Krauts ahead of our visit, *we'd* have been dead meat, not them.' He put on his jacket, leaving it undone. 'Luckily, my present orders are to avoid the Boche like the plague.'

She felt her eyes smarting. 'Please be *very, very* obedient.'

'I will. Don't worry.'

He walked across to the window and looked down at the beach and the estuary beyond. It was still sunny, with high clouds casting ragged shadows on the sea. 'This may surprise you,' he said, turning to her, 'but I really don't expect to be killed. Whenever we've been attacked by aircraft, it's always been down to some decision I took earlier.'

'Like what?'

'Not to delay our return till after dark. Or to go back twice to the same rendezvous. I only take risks in exceptional circumstances.'

It touched her that he should be trying to give her peace of mind by pretending to control his destiny. 'When do you go over there again?' she murmured.

'Too soon.' He took her by the arm. 'Let's eat something.'

155

As he cut bread and cheese for her and pulled the cork from the wine bottle, she was surprised to think that they had made love only an hour ago. Mike looked so elegantly composed, she could hardly credit he had just been in her body, though the evidence was still wet between her thighs. Time was gliding along in such a pleasant, almost somnambulistic way, that its true speed was impossible to judge. Feeling so close to Mike, it was odd to think how little she knew of his past – not even how he'd become interested in the subject he taught. So how had his interest in Classics started?

'The usual sort of thing ... homosexual master takes a few boys to Greece, and though they don't play ball with him his passion for Socrates and company seduces them anyway.'

'How come you like talking to my philistine husband?' She looked at him through sceptically narrowed eyes.

'Admiration. You forget my dad wanted me to be an engineer.'

She smiled knowingly. 'Guilt plays no part?'

'A small one.' She kept smiling. 'All right, quite a big one. Another drink?'

She let him pour more wine into her glass. 'Maybe I'm naïve, but I feel kind of rotten when I see you being all friendly to him.'

Mike had just taken a mouthful of cheese, so his words came out indistinctly, 'But darling, you can't want to rouse the poor chap's suspicions. Why upset him? Nicer for everyone if he's happy to see me around.'

'I guess.'

After they had eaten, Mike told Andrea that they would not be able to use the house in future. A full-time caretaker would be taking up residence over the weekend. Andrea mentioned her possession of a key to the village school.

He laughed delightedly. 'I'm still eager to learn.'

Because it would be hard to explain daytime absences to her

boys, they agreed to meet at the school after midnight two days hence. Mike suggested arriving on bicycles, since they would be quieter and easier to hide than cars or motorbikes when left outside.

'Have you done all this before?' she asked neutrally, feeling anxious inside.

'I had a couple of brief walk-outs after Venetia shoved off. Neither lasted long.'

'Why did Venetia leave you? Oh Mike, I shouldn't have asked.'

'It's all right. She found Cambridge too provincial, and me too poor. I was paid more in London but it wasn't enough. Luckily, my successor's loaded. He's also on the fringes of national politics; just what she wanted.'

'Is he in the services, her new guy?'

'He's something nice and safe in Beaverbrook's ministry. Venetia would never fall for anyone who might be killed. I don't blame her really.'

'I do.'

Mike considered for a moment. 'You've persuaded me.'

Because Andrea could see how moved he was by her loyalty, her eyes began to fill. Disapproving of adultery in principle, in practice she found her feelings extraordinarily pure and righteous. Because Mike might die at any time, how could she be blamed for wanting to repair the injury inflicted by his wife?

When he kissed her again, it was different from earlier kisses – intimate, possessive, grateful – a kiss between acknowledged lovers. She thought of the bombs hurtling down on the freighter and could hardly bear to look at Mike. This must be what living with danger did to people – allowed them fragments of forgetfulness before returning them to terror. What use could wit or courage be when bombs rained down? Mike's mind, his elegance, his smile would not even be ashes after such an inferno. Oh God, let nothing happen to him. His thoughts had also darkened. Without her noticing, his expression had become sad and self-absorbed.

'Darling,' she cried, folding him in her arms. 'You make me so happy.' And as she said this, the haunted look left his face, and, for that moment, he seemed carefree again.

CHAPTER 11

Having feared a grilling, Andrea was thankful when Leo showed little interest in where she had been. Predictably, he asked why she had not come back for lunch but then he accepted, without question, her banal explanation: that she had needed to be alone after the funeral. Andrea had never before lied to him about anything of consequence.

On her return, the two friends had been playing L'Attaque with the grim hostility that enslaved them whenever they embarked on this archaic game. In his head, Leo was probably commanding a real army, not several rows of crinkled cardboard. Wanting so much to understand her son better, it consoled Andrea to believe that the failure wasn't hers alone. Leo could never tell when he hurt her, failing, as most children did, to appreciate the reality of a parent's private thoughts and feelings.

She herself had been no better as a girl, thinking her father a model of maturity – the hospital chief, devoted to family and patients. Yet within months of his wife's death, Andrea's faultless daddy had married a much younger woman, one who wore Indian bangles and thought herself an artist. For years her father had been bored to death by his bridge-playing wife with her three-cornered hats and love of Republican meetings. And for years Andrea had failed to notice.

Before coming to Cornwall, Andrea's fondest hope had been to win back Leo's trust, in the relaxed atmosphere of the countryside. Now, her need to conceal her most important thoughts had made success unlikely. Ironically, the boy she was starting to understand was the one she'd blamed for alienating Leo. But Justin, unlike her own son, had revealed his need to be loved.

That afternoon, Sally called up to suggest getting together. Andrea could not tell from her disembodied voice whether she would be distraught or stoical when they met. And even when Andrea found her sitting stiffly on a horsehair settee in the private bar of the Anchor Hotel, she could not guess at her mood.

'Sorry I couldn't invite you *chez moi*, darling, but I'm turning over a new leaf.'

Andrea looked at her open-mouthed. 'I've become an unsuitable friend?'

'A scarlet woman, no less. Not that anyone knows except me.'

'I never told you a single thing, Sally.'

Sally inclined her head. 'Remember that time when you rang to ask if I knew when Mike Harrington was back from France? Don't fuss, dear heart. Your secret's safe with me.'

'My secret?'

'We're big girls, Andrea. Don't be a silly prune.'

Andrea couldn't help smiling. 'No prunes, I promise.'

'I'll buy you a gin.'

When Sally returned with two glasses, her sprightliness had vanished and she looked depressed.

'I love him, Sally. You're right.'

'As always,' she growled, taking a large gulp of gin. 'I'm afraid I was being serious about not seeing you. I'm out on my ear next time. So I've got to be good.'

'Will that be easy?'

'With James dead and buried? Jesus Christ!'

'I wasn't thinking. I'm really sorry, Sally.'

'Don't go on. Things could be worse. John's a good man. Frankly, love's a luxury at my age.' Sally raised her glass. Well, bottoms up!' She downed the rest of her gin in one swallow. 'If I were you, Andrea, I'd make the most of Mike while he's still around. The only thing I regret is not making love to James more often.' She made no sound as tears flowed down her cheeks, cutting channels through her make-up.

'Will I see you at Elspeth's?' asked Andrea.

Sally shook her head. 'I can't risk going there. John's only agreed not to tell our son about my goings-on if I stay away. I couldn't bear to be hated by him.'

'He might not react like that at all.'

'Darling, he thinks the sun shines out of his father's bottom.' Sally stood up and managed a stiff little smile. 'Maybe Leo wouldn't mind, but my Mark jolly well would.'

Shaken by her friend's words, Andrea tried not to imagine Leo's righteous anger on his father's behalf. Sally said sadly, 'It's been fun knowing you.'

Andrea found a pencil in her bag, and, tearing a page from her diary, scribbled down some figures. 'This is my Oxford number. Come see me.' Sally took the paper without comment.

They said goodbye in the village street outside the Methodist Chapel with the words EBENEZER, BETHEL written across the cracked yellow stucco over its door. In a God-fearing community no doctor would be able to afford to keep a wife who became a scandalous figure, and so many eyes and ears would be eager to detect the signs of transgression.

On parting from Sally, Andrea drove to the school on the pretext of practising on the piano, the real reason for her visit being to take sheets and blankets. On an earlier occasion, she had noticed numerous small cushions in the younger children's reading corner. Piled together, these would make a mattress of sorts. In broad daylight, with the children's paintings on

161

the walls, and with shells and fossils on every surface, she found it hard to imagine lying on the floor with Mike. But at night these incongruous details would fade away, leaving their improvised bed as the undisputed hub of their universe. 'This bed thy centre is, these walls thy sphere.' For days, Andrea had been attributing her own tastes and likings to Mike, and not just John Donne's poetry. Years ago, when discussing romantic love with Peter, he had quoted Freud on narcissism, claiming that lovers invariably overestimated their beloveds, since their own personalities benefited by the association. But what was wrong with overestimating, when it was so magical to value another human being highly? Nothing at all, she told herself, as she took her contraceptive cap from its box and went to the bathroom.

By the time she left the house, having satisfied herself that the boys were asleep, it had started to rain. This bothered Andrea, not because she minded getting wet but because she had decided to say, if Leo found her bed empty, that she had been unable to sleep and had gone for a walk to relax herself. This would hardly sound convincing with rain teeming down, but she had already decided not to take the car, since it might have wakened the boys.

When she was almost ready to leave, Andrea found that the saddle of the bicycle which Justin used was several inches too low for her. So for ten minutes at least she crept about with a torch until at last she found a spanner. On the road she was filled with a wonderful sense of freedom. Everything seemed remarkable: the rain, the velvet blackness of the sky, the wind in the telephone wires, a badger lolloping across the road.

As she reached the school and dismounted, Mike stepped out from a wedge of darkness under the playground wall. They moved together like swimmers through the rain. He was wearing a black oilskin that made him feel bulky as they kissed. His hair was plastered down, like hers.

'I'm so wet,' she laughed. 'Let's hope I haven't lost the key.'

As she held it up for his inspection, there was a break in the clouds and the yard was bathed in moonlight. Inside the deserted classroom, the face of the clock gleamed white and the narrow ecclesiastical windows cast pale fingers across the floor.

With the aid of a torch, Andrea fetched the sheets and blankets from the raffia cupboard where she had hidden them. Then they heaped up the cushions.

Though Andrea most certainly did not want to think about Peter at this moment, she could not help but notice the difference between her husband's and her lover's bodies. When Mike had undressed and was walking towards her through shafts of moonlight, the sight of his narrow hips and waist and his long legs was so strikingly unlike Peter's shape that she could only stare. Hastening to undress as well, she quickly unbuttoned her dress and unhooked her brassiere.

'You're so beautiful,' he murmured, kissing her breasts.

'I'm so cold, too,' she whispered, slipping her underskirt and step-ins over her hips in a single movement. He held her tightly and she could feel his penis against her stomach, growing in little pulses.

'Should I wear something?' he asked.

'I've seen to it.'

She kissed him on the lips, a long, open-mouthed kiss. The tension was building so rapidly for her that she felt faint. Mike dropped to his knees, and she to hers, their lips briefly separating before joining again; his hands were moving over her, searching, stroking. Tension gripped her more tightly. As she felt the length of his body pressing down on hers, she was amazed to find herself ready. And as he moved on her, the little cushions slid from under her hips. Yet she was scarcely aware of the floor beneath the sheet. All she knew was how easily they moved together, and how right it felt. She cried out as he entered her, and heard him gasp her name.

163

'Don't leave me yet,' she sighed afterwards, holding him back.

When she let him move, relief and triumph shone from his face. Supporting himself on his elbows, he gazed down at her adoringly. Later, he asked how old she'd been when she'd had her first lover? Sixteen, she told him. Not that she'd chosen to be seduced early. Her father had forbidden her twenty-one-year-old boyfriend from coming to the house, or taking her tea dancing, to the movies, or even for a sundae. So they'd spent hours together in his blue Jordan roadster, as far away as Westchester and Long Island – any place, outside of Baltimore, where they wouldn't be seen by friends of her parents – and the rest had followed, more or less naturally.

Mike chuckled to himself. 'So you had your first affair in a car, thanks to dad.'

'You could say that.'

'I wish we had more light,' he murmured. 'I can't see the colour of your hair.'

'I guess we could risk candlelight next time.' At the very moment of saying 'next time' she suffered a deep stab of panic about the future.

Until then, the moonlight had seemed kindly. Now it seemed to fall with cold impartiality on mathematical tables, on children's paintings, and on her lover's naked body. Andrea heard the clock ticking, quite loudly, amazed she'd not been aware of it when they first came in.

Since any loss of consciousness would be a loss of her time with him, she resolved to remain awake, even after Mike fell asleep. Soon afterwards, he flung his head to one side as if to escape a blow and shouted indistinct words. Andrea kissed him on the shoulder and watched his face relax again. When the same thing happened half an hour later, and his body tensed, as if he would run somewhere if he could, she woke him.

'It's all right. You're here with me.' And she held him.

'Bad dreams,' he muttered. 'We all have them.'

'What happened in yours?'

'Our engines failed when we needed them most.' He covered his face. 'I'm sorry.'

'Will your next trip be difficult?'

'No worse than usual.'

She kissed his frowning forehead. 'Would it help to talk?'

'It's part of my life that has to stay separate. I couldn't bear you to regret our time together.'

'How could I regret doing this?'

He stroked her hair and murmured, 'We none of us happen again. This is it, *now*. Even in peacetime, life's a gift that can be taken back.'

'I can't bear you to say that.'

'You *can* bear it. I know you can.'

'How do you know?'

'It's simple.' He smiled mysteriously. 'Together we're invincible. Sorry; that sounds too naval: Indomitable, Invincible, Implacable.'

'I'll try and be all those.'

'You're crying.' Deep dismay in his voice.

'I shouldn't be, since I'm sure you'll be around till the war ends.' She looked into his eyes. 'Darling, I want to make some kind of promise for the future.'

He placed his cheek against hers. 'You're so sweet, Andrea. But you mustn't wreck your marriage for a bad risk like me.'

She said urgently, 'Mike, I won't do anything right away. But if we're still lovers in the summer, I'd like to tell Peter and Leo about us then. I would hate to go on hiding things forever.'

'Just for now we're fine,' he said gently. 'Friday's as far ahead as I can think.' Although he said this gently, he had ignored her pledge, and Andrea was hurt. Was he scared of commitment? Or had losses at sea made him dread feeling too much?

Towards three o'clock they made love again. Then, as the dawn chorus was starting, they dressed and prepared to leave. After Andrea had concealed their sheets and blankets, they followed the beam of her torch. In the yard, a smudge of yellow light glowed behind the trees. Mike stood close to Andrea as she locked the door behind them.

She turned to him, distressed to realise she'd forgotten to ask a favour she'd meant to mention earlier. She frowned. 'I know Leo can be kind of grouchy; but if you could be specially nice to him when you come over, I'd really appreciate it, Mike.'

'Of course I will.'

'Can we meet Tuesday, before you go?'

'I'd love to, but I'll be awake most of the next night, so I ought to sleep the one before.'

'Of course you must.'

They embraced for several minutes under the carved 'Infants' sign before he walked her to her bike. As Andrea pedalled away, the moon was a pale disc and birds were singing everywhere.

CHAPTER 12

'Can I have a tail and a paw to keep?' asked Justin. The two rabbits which Rose was skinning on the kitchen table looked pink and purple and shockingly naked as she stripped away their fur.

Rose glanced at the boy suspiciously. 'Why do 'ee be wanting they?'

'Witch doctors have paws and stuff.'

'Don't let him have them,' urged Leo, rolling his eyes as if to indicate that Justin was crazy. 'Anyway, witch doctors don't have paws, they have claws.'

'A fat lot you know,' muttered Justin.

'I don't hold with no spells,' Rose told Justin fiercely. 'And don't 'ee go thinkin' they won't stink without preservin'.'

Even when Justin promised to keep them outside in the garden, Rose still refused to listen. But her expression softened slightly as she took in his disappointment. 'Tell you what tho', my dearie, ef you want to go catchin' lil crabs, I'll give 'ee bacon rind for your lines. You can catch 'em by the ol' harbour wall.'

Justin accepted some rind with a bad grace, and then said sharply, 'I've a bone to pick with you, Rose. You should have asked before borrowing my bike.'

'*I* didn' take it.'

'Someone did; after supper or in the night.'

'Stole it?'

'Borrowed. I told you that.'

'''Twasn' me, stupid.'

'You could have used it to go and see a boyfriend in another village.' Justin was blushing with irritation and embarrassment.

'Well I don' have a boyfriend or a man friend, you cheeky pup.'

'Maybe a witch took the bike,' suggested Leo.

'Witch doctor, more like,' said Rose.

Justin did not stay to hear more but stalked out of the room, slamming the door.

'Did *you* play a joke on 'im?' asked Rose, smiling mischievously and looking very pretty, thought Leo, despite her funny old-fashioned bonnet and long dress.

'Of course not. I could play a better joke than that, if I wanted,' he declared grandly.

Rose let out a peal of laughter. 'He didn' half get angry though.'

Rather flattered by her amusement, Leo felt confident enough to tell her that she need not expect him to eat her rabbit stew unless she cut the meat off the bones.

'This time, I'll do it. And ef you keep playin' jokes, you won't need to be frighted of no bones again.'

'He can be a dratted nuisance sometimes,' muttered Leo, having just realised that Justin had said something extremely worrying.

On entering the garden, Leo was surprised to see his friend clapping his hands to chase off some cackling jackdaws, apparently robbing a nest in the elm. To see Justin – the killer of sparrows – helping other small birds surprised Leo, but not enough to divert him from the question that was making his heart thump. He walked across to Justin, and asked straight out, 'What makes you think someone borrowed your bike?'

Justin seemed to be about to speak, but then lowered his eyes
and kicked at the dying foliage of some daffodils. 'I only said it
to annoy Rose.'

'You *invented* it?' cried Leo.

'Are you deaf. I said, Y-E-S. Comprendo?'

Leo followed Justin almost to the house as he strode away,
but then decided against arguing with him. He didn't believe
what Justin had just said, but there were still too many days
left of the holidays to risk a big row.

Andrea woke and immediately closed her eyes again, cocooning
herself in the warmth of recollected pleasure. But almost at once
she stirred and sat up. Oh God! Sunlight was stabbing through
the gap in the curtains, casting a bright rectangle on the faded
rug by her bed. She had set her alarm for eight and had gone
back to sleep again, seconds after stopping it. Dazed with lack of
sleep, she swung her legs to the floor. If she dressed at once, the
boys might never know that she had slept in. On several other
mornings she had eaten breakfast before them, so, today, if she
could slip out into the lane without being seen, and then return,
they would think she had been awake for hours. She struggled
into a sweater and a pair of slacks, and was brushing her hair
when she remembered something. What a fool she'd been not
to lower the bicycle seat before going to bed.

From the stairs she saw the machine resting against the wall.
Had it been moved a few feet down the hall since she'd placed
it there before dawn? Impossible to say. At night everything
looked different. To get the spanner was the work of moments;
but where were Leo and Justin right now? She could hear Rose
moving about in the kitchen. What could she say to explain
herself if any of them saw her tinkering with the saddle? No
excuses came to mind. But what the hell; it had to be done. Her
hands remained impressively steady as she made the adjustment
and pressed down the saddle, fixing it in about a minute. How
could she have neglected to do the one thing that mattered? She

169

replaced the spanner in the tool box, and stood for moment in dazed self-reproach. At that moment the boys came in from the garden.

'Are you guys going any place this morning?' she asked, hoping to pre-empt speculation about where she had been while they'd been eating breakfast.

'We're going to catch crabs in the harbour,' said Leo, as if announcing an impossibly boring activity.

'Aren't they caught in pots?' asked Andrea pleasantly.

'We're only after the small ones that hang out under stones.'

'And eat rotten fish and rubbish in the harbour,' added Justin.

'*Chacun à son goût*,' laughed Andrea, following them out into the lane with their bicycles. As Justin swung his leg over the saddle and mounted, she saw his look of amazement. Oh Jesus, he'd already noticed that the seat had been raised. Her surreptitious readjustment would only have emphasised the significance of his discovery. She waited, desparingly, for him to denounce her. But, after glancing at her for a moment, he looked away. He knows, she thought. He knows.

CHAPTER 13

Until they cleared the Lizard, conditions had been ideal, with pale unbroken cloud concealing them from enemy aircaft and a choppy sea preventing the formation of a long and easily spotted wash. But below the headland, Mike could already make out, through his binoculars, a line of jagged peaks with breaking crests, and, above them, darker clouds rolling in from the west like damp ink stains seeping across the sky. Though reckoning the forecast of Force 5, gusting 6, would prove an underestimation, he was eager not to reduce speed before nightfall. So *Luciole* was throbbing along at almost twenty knots as she reached the top of the first big swell. She hung suspended for a moment at the crest, her screw out of the water and racing, before she hurtled down the wave's smooth slope. Mike's stomach was left behind long before the fishing boat's bow hit the hollow of the wave. Out on the narrow bridge in front of the wheelhouse, wearing a Breton fisherman's canvas smock rather than an oilskin, Mike saw the green and white curtain tumbling downwards. Soaked and spitting out salt water, he shook his hair like a dog, swearing aloud as a cold trickle reached his boots via the small of his back and his trouser legs.

Tony Cassilis grinned at him as he burst into the wheel-house.

'Bad luck, skip.'

'Better take this sea more on our beam, Number One,' said Mike, trying not to sound reproachful, since he had not seen the wave coming either.

'Starboard 5,' Cassilis grunted to the coxswain.

'Starboard 5, sir.'

Tony studied the swinging compass. 'Steer 170.'

'Course 170, sir.'

Looking at his imperturbable first lieutenant, Mike knew that, despite appearances, Tony would already be worried about the conditions they might face when making their rendez-vous. After all, *he* would be the officer going ashore in the dory to contact the four agents and eighteen airmen, now supposedly waiting on a small island to the west of L'Aber Wrac'h inlet. If Mike's navigating officer could manage to find Le Petit Tuyau – a twisting and extremely narrow channel fringed by submerged rocks – they could anchor in the lee of Beguen Island, enabling Tony to steer for the beach without fear of his dory being swamped by breakers.

Luciole was not really large enough to carry back to England a party of more than twenty people in rough weather. In any case, her dory and smaller pram dinghy could, between them, only accommodate seven passengers at a time, necessitating four journeys to the beach and back if the whole party were to be embarked. For this reason, an MGB was keeping station a few cables to starboard. To start with, the gunboat would remain five miles offshore, while *Luciole* – less likely, in her Breton colours, to attract German interest – would go in close to locate the escapers. A signal on the secure S-phone radio link would then summon the gunboat and her launch to collect the airmen, while *Luciole* took on board the agents. Without the darkness, the blacked out buoys, the enemy forts, and the reef-strewn approaches, the plan would have been almost straightforward.

As always at the start of a mission, Mike turned his back on all predictions. Instead, during successive crossings he strove to empty his mind and enter a state of impersonal watchfulness. From this mental sanctuary, only a change in the engines' rhythm, an unexplained light or shape, could rouse him to action. But, as dusk fell – and the two Beaufighters that had given daylight air cover flew northwards – Mike's anxieties about Andrea denied him his usual inner calm. By offering to tell her son about them in the summer, she would only have meant to prove the strength of her love. But since his own future was so uncertain, her pledge merely reminded him of this.

Living from day to day was the best Mike could manage, and what was wrong with that? Thoughts of the moonlit school room and the touch of her pale smooth body made him feel weak with happiness, even standing in the cramped wheelhouse with the bulky coxswain by his side and the smell of bilge water in his nostrils.

Two months earlier, Mike had brought back his first boat-load of airmen from France. As British raids on the U-boat pens at Lorient intensified, more and more bombers were shot down over Brittany. Soon Mike's rescue missions doubled. The ramifications were endless, and not just for him. Local farmers were stretched to the limit concealing these dangerous airborne guests from the Gestapo. Agents and resistance groups suffered from increased German vigilance. And when life became more hazardous for returning agents, it became more hazardous for Mike. For everyone's sake, the airmen had to be rescued as quickly as possible. The more they were ferried about from barn to barn, the greater the chances of a dropped cap or brass button betraying them. And if that happened, their rescuers could easily sail into a storm of gunfire on the rendezvous beach.

At the back of the wheelhouse, Mike pulled back the curtain concealing his navigator's fat but neurotically restless figure. Over the chart table a bulb burned almost as dimly as the glow from the helmsman's compass. As usual, Tom Bruce had prepared a graph of the heights above or below water of the major rocks on their track at different times. In a few hours, when Mike saw white foam boiling close to the ship's hull, he would put his trust in his navigator, unless Pierre Norbert became hysterical. In which case Tom, who was on excellent terms with the Breton, would still demand angrily of Mike whether he preferred the opinions of 'an ignorant French fisherman' to those of a man who had been navigating officer on a destroyer.

Shortly before midnight, the bridge lookout thrust his head round the wheelhouse door.

'Light flashing Red 30, sir.'

Mike noted down a bearing and handed it back to Tom, who replied, almost without hesitation, 'Ile Corce lighthouse.'

Everyone in the wheelhouse was now keeping an eye out to starboard, knowing very well that the Germans only permitted lighthouses to function when they had a convoy on the move.

'Why not take a rest?' Mike murmured to Tony, who would be leaving within the hour.

'I'd rather not.'

Mike understood his feelings. Commanding *Luciole*'s two small boats demanded not only good judgement but a liberal helping of luck. The two men ventured onto the bridge and saw the swell racing along an outlying reef like a white sea snake. 'You'll be fine behind Beguen Island,' insisted Mike.

Tony shrugged. 'If our party-goers actually turn out to be there.'

'They'll be on Runiou if they're not.'

'That's a great comfort,' remarked Tony drily.

Mike did not answer. He knew as well as Tony that there were three German blockhouses guarding the foreshore opposite Runiou, and that the tide-race between the two islands frightened even local fishermen. Though Tony would be taking a compass (inside a condom to keep it dry) and a waxed chart, these would be useless in the dark, with rain squalls reducing visibility to a few yards. Even with the help of night glasses, the two men could barely make out the coast.

The agreed signal from the airmen and agents would be a blue light, spelling out the letter 'R' in morse. Though whether, in the heat of the moment, the correct signal would be given – and whether an incorrect one should actually be ignored – were matters which would soon be out of the hands of those left behind on the trawler.

Not trusting his echo-sounder, Mike ordered a seaman into the bows with a sounding line. The depth was three fathoms as they turned south-east of Beguen with both engines reduced to 600 rpm. The message relayed from the bows, seconds later, was two fathoms.

'Slow ahead both,' Mike cried into the engine room voicepipe.

The next depth from the leadsman was one and a half fathoms. On a falling tide they could go no further; Tony would not be sheltered by the mass of Beguen after all.

'Stop both engines,' ordered Mike and then, after the answering clangs, 'Let go.'

As the anchor slipped away silently on its coir-grass rope, Tom clamped the rubber-cupped earphones of the hydrophone to his head and listened. Suddenly, his expression changed.

'Fast-moving diesels to the north-west,' he sighed, handing Mike the earphones.

Mike listened with a sick feeling in his stomach. 'Uneven beat,' he muttered. 'Must be two or more.'

'I guess they're the outer screen of a convoy,' said Tony. 'The one they lit the lighthouse for.' Neither he nor anyone else wanted to admit the possibility that these E-boats might be operating alone. If they were, they were probably already homing in on the MGB. When Tony left the bridge to join his waiting boat crews, Mike continued listening, hoping in vain to hear the deeper sounds of a convoy. A blazing burst of starshell, out to sea, ended his hopes. When Mike relinquished the headphones he could hear with his own ears the unmistakable mutter

175

of distant E-boats. A moment later, gunfire echoed beyond the islands: a cacophony of six-pounders, 20-mm Oerlikons and Lewis guns. Even if the MGB was lucky enough to give the E-boats the slip, she would almost certainly be damaged and therefore unable to do anything further on this mission. *Luciole* would be on her own then, and every man on board was praying that the E-boats' commanders would not start searching for companion vessels.

As a large searchlight swept the sea north-east of Beguen, Tony reappeared wearing a naval cap and a uniform coat under his life jacket. It consoled Mike to know that, if caught, members of his boat crews would not be executed, this fate being reserved for everyone on the trawler in their fishermen's clothing. Yet their French identity had to be kept up at all costs. If an E-boat challenged *Luciole* while her boats were ashore, Pierre would shout back in French, claiming to have lost touch with other fishing boats due to mechanical trouble. The searchlight was still moving, illuminating rocks and islands.

'Better wait and see what the Germans do at Penhir Fort,' Mike told Tony. This blockhouse had a field of fire commanding the channel behind Beguen, and was armed with a 76-mm cannon.

After five minutes, the firing at sea stuttered to a halt, and no sound came from the blockhouse. The fainter hydrophone noise suggested the E-boats were moving away to the north. Whether they had sunk the MGB or were still pursuing it, Mike had no means of knowing, since his R/T operator was getting nothing on the S-phone link. Ten minutes later the searchlight went out and Mike ordered the boats to be launched.

When they were lowered there were no words of farewell. Silence on deck was a firm rule, with all lights banned, including cigarettes. Steep waves were piling up as the tide flowed out past Beguen and met a freshening wind. Mike smiled down at Tony in the dory, then waved to Petty Officer Ginnery in the dinghy. Tony was taking two ratings as oarsmen, and had a leading seaman in the bows, clutching a sub-machine-gun. In the smaller boat, two oarsmen completed Ginnery's crew. The rowlocks had been oiled and muffled, and both boats moved away silently.

However many missions Mike went on, it never got any easier waiting for his boats to return. The longer the wait, the worse the strain. The absence of pounding feet on the decks and the unfamiliar silence in galley and engine room always got on his nerves. Staring landwards, he glimpsed heavy vehicles crawling along the coast road and prayed that enemy troops were not gathering.

Fear licked at *Luciole*'s hull and rolled under her like an evil reptile. Everyone on board knew that their lives were in the hands of the landing party. If *they* could manage to avoid detection, no searchlight would snap into revealing brilliance; no bursts of tracer rip across the water, leaving *Luciole*'s decks running like a butcher's counter. Everything depended on those few men out there in the darkness.

When the boats came in sight again, they were tiny specks, low in the water, battling a wind that moaned in the trawler's rigging and flung spray from the caps of the waves. For an age, the two dots appeared to make no progress, but the last of the tide was still with them and they came on steadily. As they bumped alongside at last, the oarsmen sagged forward, exhausted. Tony had managed to cram into the dory five unshaven men wearing odd remnants of flying kit, bizarrely augmented with berets and filthy overcoats. Several carried the forks and baskets which had helped to disguise them as seaweed gatherers. In the dinghy sat three of the four agents looking more shaken and emotional than the airmen, who, by now, were cheerfully climbing the scramble nets onto the trawler's afterdeck.

'No talking till you're below,' mouthed Mike in a stage whisper. The way these men thought themselves safe now that they were in the hands of the navy both touched and irritated him. Their relief was wholly understandable; but, since they must have been told that the wind was blowing straight towards German gun emplacements, their chattering was absurdly irresponsible.

Before rowing away again to pick up more airmen, Tony chose fresh oarsmen for both his boats.

'Wind's getting up,' said Mike, leaning out above Tony's bobbing dory, wishing he knew how to convey his affection without making the moment harder.

'Crikey! Is it really?' muttered Tony.

'The tide turns in half an hour, so don't expect any help from that quarter after that.'

'We'll do what we can, skip.'

They were both speaking in forced whispers. Mike said, 'Have you considered putting four oarsmen in the dory and towing the dinghy?'

'She'd swing too much in this wind.'

Mike nodded. 'You may be right. Where are the rest of the grey jobs?'

'On bloody Runiou, worse luck.'

'Turn back at once if your rowers are tiring. That's an order.'

'Sir!' A hand raised in mock salute.

Mike ignored this. 'Bloody well come back, okay, and don't take all night about it.'

For the next half-hour, Mike was crushed by pessimistic presentiments. But, to his joy, the boats returned only a little more slowly than on the first trip, having taken full advantage of the slack before the tide turned. All the agents were now on the trawler, and half the airmen. They agreed to return one more time.

At three in the morning, Mike was still waiting for the boats to reappear, and blaming himself bitterly for having let Tony go again. He stood alone just aft of the galley, leaning against one of the gallows on which trawl nets were suspended when not

178

in use. With his binoculars fixed on the strait between Beguen and Runiou, it scared him to see no trace of either boat. Squalls were tossing up larger waves, forcing him to consider starting an engine to take the strain off his coir-grass anchor line. If it came to this, he would certainly regret not having used a heavy anchor chain. It would be horribly ironic to have avoided a few seconds of metallic rattling only to find himself dependent on a noisy engine for several hours.

A translucent glow was lighting the eastern horizon by the time Mike finally spotted his boats. Both vessels were side by side, and, through his glasses, he saw a man being transferred from the dinghy to the dory. He lowered his binoculars sadly. Tony had decided to sacrifice the larger boat to give the smaller a better chance of returning. Already perilously low in the water, the dory, with Tony aboard, was blown back behind Pen ar Guarc'h reef towards the dunes. The water there was too shallow for Mike to risk bringing *Luciole* in to assist them. He could have wept with frustration. If Tony and his sailors were not drowned, or shot, or taken prisoner, they would have to be rescued within the next ten days, along with the remaining airmen.

Waves were breaking over the dinghy, but somehow she kept inching closer to *Luciole*. What this effort was costing the oarsmen Mike tried not to imagine. Sensing that the little boat was wavering, he ran to the wheelhouse where he gave the order to start both engines and weigh anchor.

By the time the men on *Luciole*'s foredeck could throw a line to the dinghy, she was sinking. Mike broke his rule of silence and used the ship's tannoy to order every sailor out on deck to pull the men up the nets, and hoist the waterlogged vessel aboard. If that dinghy sank here, she would probably be washed ashore, handing the Germans evidence of the navy's visit, and advance notice of their inevitable return. The dory ought not to pose the same problem, since Tony would bury her in the dunes if he could stay long enough on the beach. After the engagement with the gunboat, the Germans would be searching every beach and cove for evidence of a landing.

Dreading the interview he would soon be having with Tony's grief-stricken Elspeth, Mike gave his orders to the helmsman almost absentmindedly as *Luciole* entered Le Petit Tuyau. Imagining the woman's angry tears, he felt almost relaxed about the possibility of meeting E-boats beyond the rocks. But bowel-loosening fear soon reasserted itself. Nothing could rival the fear of imminent death.

Soon after dawn, the protective cloud layer blew away, but the sky remained as empty of danger as the sea. And when *Luciole*'s air escort joined her seventy miles south of the Lizard, only the irrepressible vomiting of several airmen was spoiling the celebratory mood below decks.

Mike walked into the Polwherne Hotel shortly before eleven in the morning, after a night entirely without sleep. He felt like a diver in an invisible diving suit, weighted down and distanced from the world around him. As he was sitting in his office, waiting to give Captain Borden a preliminary report, he slipped into a deep sleep that ended abruptly when his telephone rang. The Wren operator was telling him she had a Dr Pauling on the line.

'Do you want to speak to him, sir?'

Mike couldn't think who the hell this doctor was, until, like the flash of a 6-inch gun, the answer scorched his mind.

'Put him through,' he sighed, not wanting to speak to Andrea's husband but knowing he would not sleep unless he did.

'That you, Harrington?'

'Speaking.'

'I'm back in the village this evening, so what about coming over for a spot of lunch tomorrow?'

'If Mrs Pauling doesn't mind.'

'Why on earth should she?'

'Well, if you both want me . . .'

'Right then. That's settled.' A slight pause. 'I was thinking that the boys might find it amusing if you could bring over a bosun's chair. We could rig it up between a couple of trees in the garden.'

'I'll see what I can do.'

'Noon tomorrow.'

'Fine.'

Mike pounded both his fists on his desk like a child in a rage. Not because he still did not know whether the MGB had limped into another port, and not because Tony might be lying dead on the sand with the waves breaking over him. No, he was distraught because Andrea's husband was coming home today, stopping her getting away tonight to make love to him. Mike rested his forehead against the table and groaned.

'Cheer up, man.' Sitting up sharply, he saw Borden's red face looking down. 'Behold the bearer of good news. The gunboat crawled into Dartmouth an hour ago. Three wounded, and their launch shot to matchwood. That's why they shoved off.' Since there was only one chair in the room, and Mike was sitting on it, Borden parked his large bottom on the table. 'No news of the chaps you left behind. Sorry about that; but it's early days.'

Mike looked past Borden's broad back at the dirty window. The wind had dropped and the sun was stretching a net of filigree silver across the river's gently ruffled surface. If only things could have been like this a few hours ago. Instead, Tony was missing. And all because I didn't stop that disastrous final trip. Fool, fool, fool. Mike shut his eyes, and saw, as clearly as if witnessing it, a group of Germans gawping at the stern of the dory as it protruded, coyly, from a dune. Won't the bastards give us hell when we come back. You bet they will.

When Borden had shambled out, Mike picked up the telephone and asked the girl to get him Andrea's number. He hoped she would answer, but if she didn't he wouldn't let it worry him. He heard Leo's voice.

'Hello, Leo. Mike here. Your dad's asked me to lunch tomorrow.'

'He's not here.' Curt, matter of fact. Suspicious? Probably not.

'Can I speak to your mother?'

The receiver was thumped down on the table, the noise hurting Mike's head. 'Mum, mum, MUM!' he heard the boy yelling, and then as an afterthought, 'Telephone! TELEPHONE! It's the commander.'

He heard footsteps, another voice, possibly Justin's, then hers. His anger of moments earlier vanished as he heard her say his name. For a second he imagined himself telling her about Tony, and the pain reached him for the first time. His throat became tight.

'I've just got in.'

'That's wonderful, Mike.'

'Can you get to the school this afternoon?'

'That sounds interesting.' He guessed at once that the boys were still in the room.

'What about four o'clock?'

'I wouldn't say that exactly.'

'Three?'

'Yes.' A short pause. 'Till lunch tomorrow then.'

The need for deception suddenly struck him as silly and wearisome. Maybe he should have encouraged her to tell Leo and Peter about him. After all, she'd been the one to suggest it. If she didn't mind risking her marriage for a man who might be dead in a fortnight, why should he keep warning her that he was 'a bad risk'? The harsh fact was that, if the dory had been found, his next mission would probably be his last. Why not see her every day till he sailed, instead of once or twice? Who needed her more than he did? Her grumpy son? Her gullible husband? Of course not. His head felt incredibly thick and heavy but he knew he wouldn't sleep for hours now. Maybe start his report.

To Deputy Director, Operations Division (Irregular)

Sir, I have the honour to submit the following report on 'Operation Moses' which was carried out on the night and early morning of . . .

Two hours later he was on his motorbike driving to Elspeth's, rehearsing what to say. 'He'll be back in a week and none the worse for his ordeal.' Would she believe this? Possibly. But there was no question of telling her what he really thought.

And this was how he lived now, always making things easier for other people but never for himself.

CHAPTER 14

The moment Andrea had closed the heavy wooden door behind them, she and Mike clung together and kissed as if they had been apart for years. His face was grey with tiredness, and she was both proud and touched that he should have wanted to see her without sleeping first. He was unshaven, and, because she smelled whisky on his breath, she was afraid his mission had failed.

'Was everything okay?'

'No, but it's fine now.' His dark-shadowed eyes expressed strained dignity and a hint of shame. He went on ahead of her into the sunlit schoolroom. 'I've just been explaining to Elspeth how I managed to mislay her dearest Tony.'

'How horrible for you.'

Mike made an impatient clicking sound. 'Not so nice for Tony either.' He let himself slip down onto a child's chair. 'Elspeth was *simply marvellous* in that specially guilt-inducing British way. Oh God, I shouldn't say that. Last week, she'd fixed an informal tennis tournament for tomorrow afternoon, and of course the show must go on. It's at lunch-time tomorrow.' He held his head in his hands for a moment. 'It gets worse. Elspeth was going to play with Tony as her doubles partner, so she's asked me to step in.'

'So we won't see you tomorrow?'

'Hang on. Elspeth refuses to play doubles with anyone but Tony, so she got me to say I'd play in his place, with my own partner.' He smiled at her. 'Will you be my partner?'

'You know I will.'

'Your husband can come and watch – what am I saying – and Leo and Justin can be ball boys, if they like.'

'They'll like, I'm sure.'

'And Peter?'

'I never can tell what he'll enjoy.'

'Okay, he's a maybe, but you and the boys are definites. Please don't tell them about Tony. Officially he's sick, not missing.'

Andrea frowned. 'Will Elspeth play along with that?'

'Elspeth knows lax security won't help us get him back. So she'll keep smiling, or die in the attempt.'

Mike stood up abruptly and walked towards the stove. As his smile collapsed, naked misery transformed his face. Moved by her memory of the two friends roaring into the night on Mike's motorbike, Andrea reproved herself for remembering so little of her only conversation with Tony.

Mike murmured tenderly, 'How long can you stay?'

'A half-hour.' Mike seemed to sag as if winded, making her feel terrible. 'I'm sorry, sweetheart. Justin knows I took his bike that time. So I need to be careful.'

Mike said curtly, 'Boys think grown-ups do all manner of daft things. Cycling at night probably won't worry him.'

'Oh Mike, it was raining,' she objected. 'Justin's a hell of a smart kid. When you called me late that time, he asked if it was you, as if he knew.'

'Even if he does – why should he tell anyone? He likes us both. I've promised to visit his school. In a funny kind of way we're the parents he'd love to have.'

'Mike, you were the one who said I shouldn't take risks with my marriage – not yet, anyway.'

'You're right,' he admitted sadly and looked away. 'When does Peter go back to Falmouth?'

'Monday. He's going to London this time.'

'Can you be with me all night Monday and Tuesday?' His humility made her want to weep.

'Yes, yes. You know I will.'

As he embraced her thankfully, she sensed he needed her more than he had before. Otherwise she might have suggested less risky options: an hour or two together instead of two whole nights. But believing him truly in fear for his life, she would not burden him with her own fears, though these had grown worse since Sally had said *her* son would hate her if he ever found out. And Leo was more attached to his father than Andrea could imagine any other boy on earth being. At times recently, she had seen an unrelenting, almost accusing look in his eyes. And he didn't know anything yet. So, if he ever did, how would they manage to live under the same roof? Mike was hugging her so tightly that she could feel the seams of his blue battledress jacket through her linen dress. Though the day was warm, she shivered. Ten days from now Mike could be dead, and Leo living with his father.

To escape such thoughts, she said more solemnly than she intended, 'I didn't bring my racquet to Cornwall.'

'Hell's bells, Andrea! The things you worry about! Elspeth has racquets galore.'

It had been sunny when they arrived, but now a few raindrops flicked across the tall windows and gusts rattled the frames. Andrea could think of nothing to say as Mike examined some little balloons painted onto large cards pinned to the wall.

'I get it,' he declared. 'One gets a different coloured balloon for every maths table mastered. Competition starts early, even in the backwoods.' He returned to her side. 'What trinkets do your girls get for good work?'

'Aside from merit marks? Knowing they've pleased me.'

'Lucky girls.' His dark eyes sought hers without amusement.

She kissed him softly on the lips and murmured, 'You please me all the time. I really hate having to go now. What time do we meet at Elspeth's?'

'About one. She's doing a sort of picnic.'

As they were leaving, Mike paused to look at some of the younger children's drawings – people with stick-like arms and legs, lollipop trees, suns with spiky rays.

He said wryly, almost to himself, 'Funny how special our childhoods seem, when really they're just like everyone else's.'

They walked out into the school yard in silence. The flurries of rain had stopped and for a moment the sky was blue. Walking along the road, away from the village to where Andrea had left her car, they passed some tumbledown cowsheds and a filthy pond.

His fingers tightened on her arm. 'Just for these few days,' he said, 'please could you not sleep with your husband?'

She nearly told him it wouldn't mean anything if she did, but, instead, she squeezed his hand and whispered, 'I haven't wanted him for years.'

'That isn't a proper answer. Imagine I was going home to my wife as soon as I left you. How would *you* feel, Andrea?'

'Terrible,' she admitted, embracing him. 'Forgive me. He won't come near me, I swear.'

'I hate being so bloody weak,' he groaned, as they reached the place where he had left his motorbike.

'If I had to do what you do, I'd be weeping all the time.' He kissed her gratefully. 'Shall we go back to the school?' she asked, suddenly desperate to make up for having disappointed him.

He shook his head and smiled. 'I can wait.'

Driving away between wet hawthorn hedges that sparkled in the sun, she wished she had given in to him twenty minutes ago. Considering the strain he was under, he had been entitled to expect her to take a sizeable risk for him.

*   *   *

After his mother had gone out, Leo had spent a happy hour, one that would have been happier still if Justin had been somewhere else. They had both accepted the challenge set by Rose to straighten her crinkly hair, and, although wetting it and rolling it in curlers, they had achieved only a very transitory flatness. After coming to terms with failure, they had been reasonably content to let her teach them how to make bread.

A few days ago, Leo had been told by Justin that men and women put their tongues in each other's mouths when they kissed. Leo had looked at his own in the mirror and had thought it looked disgusting, with a thin whitish coating that must be covered in germs and microscopic bits of food. The thought that Rose might welcome such a thing in her mouth horrified him. As for the noises which Justin claimed that women made when they were in bed with men – he was sure this couldn't be true.

When Andrea suddenly appeared and wanted to know why Rose's hair looked so strange, Leo felt irritated. Why did his mother have to make Rose feel bad about amusing him and Justin? Apparently because they might have been 'taking advantage of her' because she was a servant. His mother said this to them during tea.

'I'm not saying she doesn't want you around. Only that you shouldn't assume she does.'

His mother was wearing a pale green dress, with squares of a thready material that pulled it in tight round her waist. It made her look girlish, and rather busty, in a way Leo disliked, though from the way Justin glanced at her he supposed it might suit her. He suspected that Justin had started drinking tea rather than orange squash in order to impress her. Anyway, there was no way *he* would pretend to be grown up for anyone.

Putting down her cup, his mother smiled at him. 'We've been invited over for tennis at a country club. Isn't that swell.'

'We don't play much at St Bede's,' Leo remarked quietly, aware that his mother knew this.

189

'That's not a problem. You can be ball boys.' Her enthusiasm grated with him. Ball boys ran about all afternoon and were cursed and shouted at. He stared unhappily at the remains of one of Rose's scones on his plate.

Justin took a sip of tea and asked politely, 'Who'll be playing?'

'People we don't know, mostly. But Mike Harrington should be there.'

Leo saw how pleased Justin was and pushed back his chair. 'I don't think I'll come.'

Andrea said sweetly, 'Dad'll be home tomorrow and he'll want to cheer me on.'

'Don't be such a spoilsport,' cried Justin, as Leo left the room.

Outside in the hall, Leo began to cry. He had wanted a family holiday with just his parents; what he had instead was a holiday in which other people made all the plans, while Justin sucked up to his mother, and his father was usually away, and this 'frightfully decent' but really rather pushy officer came round every other day – making it obvious how much more he liked Justin, and then dragged them off for tennis. 'Oh good shot, sir,' everyone would say, including mum. Leo felt sick to think of Mike hitting winners. Dad surely wouldn't want to come and see lots of sporty people leaping about; but because he was so jolly good natured and doted on mum, he'd be bound to tag along. And then to cap it all he was going back to the Admiralty laboratories in London for the rest of the holiday.

The first people Andrea saw on arriving at Ferndene Park were Dr Lowther and Sally, getting out of her Sunbeam-Talbot. John Lowther looked much older. Without his usual baggy tweeds, his stomach could be seen, rolling over the waistband of a pair of white flannels that might have fitted a decade earlier. With Peter limping beside her and the boys running on ahead, Andrea wished she could forget about her friend's dead pilot and stop imagining that Sally disliked her for still possessing a living, breathing lover.

'They're over there,' called out Justin, pointing.

Across a patchy lawn, Andrea saw two rust-coloured clay courts beside a walled vegetable garden. While Justin swung his arms cheerfully, Leo seemed to be having trouble dragging himself over the grass. He had only consented to come after some spirited arm-twisting from his father. Already, they could hear a hubbub of chatter, as if at a cocktail party. Right beside the courts, a small group of men and women were standing huddled together against the wind. Wondering whether Mike was among them, Andrea felt a nervous fluttering in her stomach.

Magnificent in a double row of pearls and swinging furs, Elspeth burst from the midst of a gaggle of players to welcome them. Andrea felt like applauding the bravery of her performance.

'Greetings to our bushy-tailed ball boys! So nice to see you all. Since you won't be playing, Mr Pauling, perhaps you'd like to umpire our final?'

To Andrea's surprise, Peter seemed to consider the offer quite seriously for a moment or two, before politely declining. He let himself down, gingerly, into a deckchair.

A cool easterly wind robbed the fitful sunlight of warmth. Looking at the other women with their short tennis skirts and mottled legs, Andrea was not sorry that, with her own tennis skirt in Oxford, she had been obliged to wear slacks. She worried a little about her hair. Mike had never seen it tied back in a band. Nor did she relish the idea of getting red as a beet.

Seeing her lover coming towards her in white flannels and a sweater with a striped V-neck, she thought how handsome and athletic he looked. Incredibly, she hadn't asked him how well he played. Though he looked the perfect tennis champion, it would be a bore if he turned out to be one. Andrea hated games of

191

mixed doubles in which the men darted around, denying their female partners the chance to lose (or win) more than a small proportion of the points.

As Elspeth announced the pairings, and who would be playing against whom, there were loud complaints and pleas. 'Oh, Elspeth, *please* don't make me play Prue Millington-Harris' was the most common. She was rumoured to be the best player on the courts.

Elspeth dismissed these jitterers with a wave. 'I'm giving her John Lowther as her partner, so that'll even things out.'

A few minutes later, Mike and Andrea walked on court to play Sally Lowther and Mark, her teenage son. Andrea found it an added strain to have to treat Sally like a distant acquaintance. Justin appeared and asked Mike if he could be ball boy for this game.

'Of course you can,' said Mike, patting him on the back.

Sally smiled suavely at Andrea. 'You'd better watch out, Yankee, Mark plays for the Malvern First Six.'

'Second Six, mother.'

'For God's sake, darling! Psychology!'

Since Andrea played quite frequently with the girls at her school – but never with other adults because of Peter's leg – she had no idea how she would shape up today. While she was unscrewing the press from Elspeth's racquet, she heard a commotion behind the court. Leo's anguished face was pressed against the wire. Andrea hurried to him.

'Mum, Justin was a total pig to me when I said I wanted to be your ball boy for this game. Can you put him right?'

'I can't argue about anything right now, sweetheart. You be my ball boy next time I play.'

He said quite loudly, 'The people on the other court are blotto. Looks like they've been plastered for hours.'

'Then they won't notice if you're slow.'

'Who said I am?' His freckled face gazed back resentfully.

'Oh all right . . . inexperienced. Darling, I can't change things now.'

'Thanks a lot.'

Justin had been leaning against one of the net posts, as if indifferent to what was being decided, so Andrea was disturbed to see the look of joy that lit his face as Leo walked away.

Even while they were knocking up, Justin showed what a remarkably efficient supplier of tennis balls he was. Never for a moment did she or Mike have to wait. By contrast, Sally's son, Mark, often had to stoop or leap awkwardly for the balls Justin flung his way. Sally herself fared only marginally better. Touched by Justin's partisanship, Andrea said nothing. Before they started playing in earnest, Mike had a word with him about the need to be more sporting.

Almost from the moment they began their first and only set, Andrea played far above what she thought of as her normal form. Freed from the need to direct easy shots to her girls, so that even the no-hopers could return them, she found herself hitting with the same pinpoint accuracy but with a power that surprised her. Mike's admiring looks embarrassed her at first, but, as game followed game, she began to enjoy his praise as her natural due.

'So dreary,' muttered Sally to her son, 'most Americans start tennis lessons when they're two or three.'

Sally played a stately game, with solid ground strokes, but showing no inclination to run for the ball. Consequently, she missed most of her volleys. Her son played better at the net, but was reluctant to poach on his mother's side of the court and so lost numerous points he would easily have won had he not been inhibited by his fear of offending her.

Occasionally, Andrea poached from Mike, which always made him laugh. In fact he was a stylish, though erratic player, who mixed plenty of double faults with good serves and tended to smash balls out on points when a drop shot would have been best. Yet as the game went on, he played with more control, and as his shots improved, Andrea had trouble stopping herself from kissing him passionately, when he won a fiercely contested point. As it was, they only ever touched fingers very briefly, when handing over a ball – a most infrequent event, given Justin's prowess as a ball boy.

Once, while changing ends, Andrea heard one of the officers on the next court shout at Leo, before serving, 'Balls come in pairs, lad, so where's my second?' Though the man had obviously meant to be funny, Leo plainly longed to sink beneath the court's dusty surface.

Quite often, Andrea saw Peter applauding Mike's shots, and again found herself wishing that he had not taken such a liking to him. It would also have been easier on her conscience if Peter had argued against coming here, or had at least complained because Mike had broken his promise to bring ropes and pulleys to the house for the boys' scientific amusement. But though Peter had mentioned this earlier arrangement to Andrea before being told about the tennis, he had shown no irritation at all when the change of plan had been presented as a *fait accompli*.

After their easy victory, Andrea left the court with Mike and chatted amiably with Peter, whose praise for her playing struck her as disingenuous. He could easily have suggested she continue to play with other people after he had ceased to be able to partner her himself, but he had never said anything of the sort. So Andrea had virtually given up the game, except when coaching girls.

Andrea's and Mike's next match was against Miss Millington-Harris. But since Elspeth had paired this former county player with Dr Lowther, whose game was extremely rusty, points could easily be won by returning exclusively to him. As soon as Mike and Andrea had discovered the doctor's weak backhand, they exploited it ruthlessly. Starved of the ball, Miss Millington-Harris was soon making increasingly desperate interceptions at full stretch.

'Show some sportsmanship,' screeched Sally, appalled by the sorry figure her husband was cutting.

'Pah! We play to win,' laughed Mike, sending a tantalising lob looping over the tip of the doctor's racquet.

Soon after Sally's interjection, Andrea began to take on Miss Millington-Harris directly, finding, to her amazement, that she won as many points as she lost.

After a string of archaic oaths, the champion was heard to mutter, 'Dashed impossible to play against a rotten length.'

During this game, Leo acted as their ball boy without causing any annoyance, but without matching Justin's seamless delivery. As soon as the game ended, he congratulated his mother and said that, since he and Justin had now ball-boyed once each for her, they ought to toss for who was given the final. Knowing that Justin deserved to be chosen on merit, Andrea was trying to think how to disappoint her son without upsetting him too much, when Mike came over.

'Look, old chap, no offence meant, but Justin's so dashed good, you two ought to do the job together.'

'What if I want to toss up instead?' A smudge of the reddish dust from the court was streaked across the boy's forehead.

'That wouldn't be fair on Justin,' replied Mike in a firm but friendly voice.

'Why should *you* decide? We're not your sailors.' Leo was almost too breathless to get his words out.

'What's gotten into you, Leo?' cried Andrea, horrified by her son's hostility.

Leo went on in a quavering voice, 'Justin's so quick and clever, but I'm so clumsy, aren't I, mum?' He turned to Mike tearfully. 'I wouldn't ball-boy with your little pet if you begged me.'

'What side of the bed did he get out of?' exclaimed Mike, as Leo stumbled away.

Andrea watched Peter lever himself out of his garden chair and stagger towards them.

'My God, what's up with Leo?'

Andrea studied the grass. 'He won't let Justin ball-boy with him in the final.'

Peter frowned. 'Not like him at all. I bet he and Justin have fallen out over something else.'

'Seemed like a fit of jealousy to me,' murmured Mike.

'But why?' ruminated Peter. 'Leo shouldn't be jealous of Justin . . . if anything, it should be the other way round.'

Mike was about to mention the way the boys competed for his attention but thought better of it.

Over by the table where Elspeth was serving drinks, Andrea saw Leo say something to Justin. She could not hear his words, but they froze Justin where he stood. By the time Andrea reached the spot, Leo was walking towards the house and Justin was trying not to sob. Andrea put an arm round him.

'What's wrong, honey?'

Tears were trembling on the boy's long lashes. 'I can't come back in August. Leo just told me.'

'I don't know if we'll do that ourselves.'

'I won't see Mike any more.' Justin's voice was very small and frail.

'Sure you will.'

'Maybe he'll come to Yorkshire once or twice. Then finito.'

'Hey, nothing's decided,' she soothed, shaken by his distress, and feeling furious with Leo.

Suddenly he could not hold back his tears. 'It's no good,' he sobbed, 'Leo won't change his mind.'

'He might if I twist his arm.'

But, ten minutes later, as Andrea stepped out onto the court for the final, she doubted whether she would be able to change her son's mind. Indeed it would be wrong to try to force him to.

As she and Mike were struggling and failing to overwhelm a tall RAF officer and his well-built wife, it bothered Andrea that Leo had not returned to help Justin with the balls. His absence seemed to underscore his determination to stick with his decision. Perhaps Justin was aware of this. At any rate his face was heartbreakingly sad as he moved about the court.

'What the hell's the matter with Justin?' muttered Mike, while they were changing ends.

'Tell you later.'

It must be whatever her introverted son had said, thought Mike. And, very likely, the boy's remarks also explained Andrea's mysterious loss of form. Though not addicted to winning, in the present circumstances Mike definitely wanted to. Having always considered Wing Commander Bertie Harrison a pompous fool, it offended him to be facing defeat at his and his wife's pudgy hands. As if he had fallen from a sunlit cloud, Mike suddenly understood how insubstantial his illusion of brilliance had been. To win points now, he found himself obliged to do something he loathed: volley from right under Andrea's nose and whip these stolen balls at Jane Harrison's sturdy legs. But such tactics only stemmed the tide for a few games.

As Andrea thwacked another half-volley into the net, Mike took twisted consolation from observing Peter's pain as his wife's game fell apart. The man could have been forgiven if he'd resented Andrea's success in the earlier sets. After all, *he* would never play again. But no matter – while Andrea's racquet had been magically putting away ball after ball, Peter's face had been transfigured. Still more surprising to Mike had been the scientist's keen enjoyment of *his* best shots. Was there even something nostalgic about this appreciation, as if Peter were watching Andrea and *himself* playing together before illness had struck him down? Certainly – when the match had been lost, and the posturing wing commander was boasting that there had only been 'one or two moments' when he'd feared he might lose – Peter commiserated most sympathetically with Mike.

'Don't you have something nice to say to me, too?' muttered Andrea, as she sank down into a chair. Mike thought how radiant she looked with a bloom of colour in her cheeks and her red-gold hair falling free.

'Maybe it was just one game too many for you,' suggested Peter kindly. 'You were fantastic till then, my love.'

Seeing them together, as an obviously married couple, Mike felt as if the ground had opened under him. If he failed to come back from France, they would simply stay together and carry on with their lives. Andrea would weep for a while, and would admit to their affair, promising that it would never happen again. Peter would forgive her, of course. With a wife like Andrea, what else could he be expected to do? Her grief would encourage him to forgive her very quickly. But that had always been the way things were likely to work out, when statistical probability finally had its way with him. His eyes were still fixed upon Andrea as a light hand touched his arm.

'Bad luck about losing.'

Mike swung round and saw Justin pulling an exaggeratedly despondent face. He smiled. 'As the poet said, what matters is not the winning, but playing the game.'

'It's still nice to win.'

'I'm afraid so.' Mike put a hand on Justin's shoulder and guided him away from Andrea and Peter. 'You're upset.'

Justin picked up Mike's racquet and started rolling a ball back and forth across the strings. 'I won't see you in the summer.'

'Why's that?'

'Leo won't ask me here again.'

'You may be wrong about that. In any case, I may not still be stationed here.' He paused. 'In fact I may not even be around.' The ball fell from the racquet, but Justin replaced it. 'I'm really sorry, Justin, but that needed saying.'

'As if I didn't know.'

'Of course you did. You're a sensitive person, and that's why I'd really hate it if you felt lousy for a long time. Will you promise to get back to normal quite soon afterwards.'

'What if I can't?'

'You must try.'

'Why?' The question flicked out bitterly.

Mike said very quietly, 'Because it's what I want, and because you owe yourself something a lot better than the grief you've been through.' The boy was still rolling the ball round inside the rim of the racquet. 'Okay, sermon over. Believe me, I'm not planning to pop my clogs just yet.'

Justin looked at Mike solemnly for a moment. 'Wouldn't someone have to pop them *for* you?'

'You're right.' Mike was surprised to see Justin smiling. Somehow he managed to smile back as the boy tossed aside the racquet and hugged him.

Leo and Justin were washing and getting ready for bed.

'Funny the way tennis court dirt sticks between your toes,' said Leo, rubbing at it with a finger.

Justin watched him without speaking. His heart was hammering and he longed to scream his hatred. Instead he sat on the side of the bath next to the geyser, which reminded him of a ship's boiler. He no longer knew why he had liked Leo. He hadn't backed him up one bit when he'd been trying to find out about the trawlers – the opposite really. His feet were too long and thin for his size and his freckles had all joined up across his face making his eyelashes and eyebrows look peculiarly white. In Kenya, Justin had once seen an albino and had been shocked by the strange pink blotchiness of the child's skin, and by his white eyebrows. At school, saying someone looked as bad as that would usually make him cry. Sometimes Justin had made himself think of his father's charred flesh, before saying the cruellest thing he could think of to whoever crossed his path. Why should they get off scot-free, without a day's unhappiness?

'Why did you upset your mum before that game?'

Leo was cleaning his teeth and went on scrubbing until

199

spitting noisily. 'You were the one who looked like a sick cow before the game. *You* upset her, not me.'

'I could make you cry for days.' For a moment Justin was not sure he had spoken. He had certainly been *thinking* this. But the way Leo's toothbrush hovered in the air put the matter beyond doubt. At last Leo put it down, and swilled his mouth.

'You don't scare me.'

Justin knocked the geyser with a clenched fist as if intending violence. Then he said suavely, 'You know I said my bike had been borrowed in the night.'

'You said you'd lied.'

'Well, it *was* borrowed.'

Leo started for the door, but Justin stuck out a leg to stop him. 'I want to go to bed,' Leo complained.

Justin held him around the waist. 'Your mother took it.'

'Oh ha, ha. You didn't see it taken, so how do you know?'

'The saddle was a different height in the morning.'

'Maybe it slipped.'

'Slipped higher, I don't think! Anyway she lowered it just before we went crabbing.'

'You saw her?' The sharpness of the question did not deceive Justin; Leo was challenging him, yet he was also terrified. Justin knew that to admit he hadn't seen anything would be to lose all advantage.

'Yes, I saw.'

'You're lying.' Leo pushed him so hard that he fell back into the bath tub.

Rubbing his head where he had bumped it, the pain goaded Justin. 'She's in love with Mike,' he screeched.

Leo glared at him from the doorway, his eyes wide and staring. 'When I tell mum, she'll chuck you out of the house.'

Justin pulled himself up out of the bath. 'I wouldn't tell her anything if I was in your boots. She'll tell your father if you do. Then there'll be a huge row and maybe they'll split up.'

200

'They bloody won't, you rotten liar.' Though Leo was trembling, his voice was steady. 'You just want me to keep my gob shut so your precious Mike doesn't get to know what a lying pig you are.'

'He may be grateful to me for telling.'

For a moment Justin managed to believe this, but the seriousness of what he had done was finally sinking in. Mike might be furious with him. Maybe he only liked Andrea a lot, but didn't love her. Yet it *must* go further. He remembered his own mother in love: much more lively than usual, then gazing into space and smiling to herself for no reason, just like Andrea. But the clincher had been taking that bike in the middle of the night. If she'd only been going for a ride, she wouldn't have changed back the saddle so slyly. She *must* have met someone.

Leo was still standing quivering in the doorway. Fearing that he would suddenly rush at him, fists flailing, Justin snatched up the lavatory brush as a defensive weapon. Seeing him do this, Leo let out a stifled cry and ran from the room.

The following morning, Leo got up early though he had hardly slept. He meant to catch his father alone and tell him what Justin had said. But his mother chose this morning to give his father breakfast in bed, it being Peter's last day before leaving for London. And because she then chose to sit with Peter while he ate, Leo lost his chance of being alone with his father. Sitting in the dining room a little later, he felt thankful, on reflection, that he hadn't been able to blurt out everything. Imagine, if he had, how awful it would have been if Justin had been lying, and dad had actually been taken in by the lie. Believing he had narrowly escaped a disaster, Leo swore to himself that he would continue to hold back, although his longing to scream at his mother was almost beyond resisting. Recalling what Justin had said about careless talk causing separations, Leo wondered whether it would be foolish to tell his father *at any stage*, even if Justin's bombshell turned out to be true. Perhaps he should work on his mother instead. Could he even make her feel guilty enough to give Mike up? Yet being direct with her could easily go wrong. She might turn round and say, 'You're right. I do love Mike. In fact I love him more than your father and I want to be with him always.'

And then what? Panic seized him. Leo was eating toast and marmalade, and some sour-tasting bits came up into his mouth, though he managed to swallow them again. He imagined living somewhere with his father, like a bigger version of his shed-like workshop in Oxford. Really it would be more like living alone, since dad would go on working day and night. Leo's throat felt tight and choky. How often would he get to see his mother? Probably not at all if Mike was around. A few months ago he would have found it impossible to imagine such a thing. But that had been before Andrea had let him be sent to St Bede's. Now he knew he would go on living whatever happened.

When his mother came into the room, he could not look at her. He imagined her letting Mike put his tongue in her mouth, and wanted to get up and hit her. He knew she was wearing her stripy sweater, which made her bosom seem to stick out, because he could see it reflected in the polished surface of the table.

She said, 'I gave dad his coffee in bed so you and I could talk.'

Leo felt scared. Was she about to say she'd decided to go away? To end the awful silence, he asked in a chirpier tone than he had intended, 'Where's Justin? Did he have breakfast in bed, too?

'He ate early. Now what's this stuff about him going to his aunt? He says he's leaving because you're so mean to him. He's even 'phoned her for Chrissakes.'

'I only said I didn't want him in the summer.'

'You must have said more.'

Leo pushed back his chair so violently it hit the sideboard. 'I didn't.'

202

He saw how flushed she had become – always a sign of rage, rather than embarrassment, with mum. 'Am I dumb or something?' she demanded, shaking her head. 'Your friend has a great time at tennis and the very next day he wants to quit. I want to know how come?'

'Why not ask him,' shouted Leo. 'I bet you'd rather *I* pushed off instead. Everything's my fault, isn't it? Never his.'

Andrea's attitude softened perceptibly. 'Be fair, sweetheart, and stop acting as if I'm a mind-reader. Unless you tell me, I won't *know* what he's done.'

'Ruined my holiday, that's what,' cried Leo, and rushed from the room.

Justin had walked along the beach and over the rocks until he reached the pontoon at the back of naval headquarters. But now that all he had to do was climb some stone steps and cross a lawn, his courage failed him. He knew he should warn Mike about what he had told Leo. If he didn't, Mike could be confronted out of the blue by Leo or Peter, with no time to think. And then, if Mike found out who had told them, he would never want to speak to the traitor again. So really there was no choice but to confess, and hope to be forgiven.

To start with, walking along the beach, Justin had tried to persuade himself that Mike would be secretly delighted if Peter found out without being told by him. He himself was probably too soft-hearted to do the deed. But this line of reasoning didn't convince Justin for long. He knew for a fact that two of the men who had slept with his mother had told his father straight out what they'd been doing with her. But really their situation had been different from Mike's; *they* hadn't been about to get themselves killed. So maybe Mike *wouldn't* be delighted that someone had ratted. Instead, he might feel very angry indeed. After all, there wouldn't be much point upsetting Leo and Peter if he wasn't going to be around for long. And this thought really upset Justin – things were bad enough for Mike already, without having to deal with such nasty problems just when he was planning his missions.

The tide was out, and, though part of the pontoon was still afloat, the mud stretched out on both sides, almost to the end. As Justin stepped onto one of the wooden platforms, a mass of wading birds rose from the weed-covered flats like a small snowstorm against the dark woods on the far shore. The day was overcast and out in the estuary the sea looked a dull greeny grey.

He meant to lose no time in walking the few paces that would take him to where the stone steps began, but he found he could not make himself move at all. It would be almost five minutes before he could drag his feet to the top. Almost as he stepped onto the lawn he was stopped by a sailor, a large man with three red stripes on his arm below crossed anchors.

'You boy! Looking for someone?'

'Lieutenant Commander Harrington.'

The petty officer led Justin past a sentry in white gaiters outside the main door and into the echoing hallway which Justin remembered from his first visit, those sad signs – Tudor Bar, Reception, Games Room – summoning up days when families would have come for their holidays. He was directed to a chair and the sailor spoke briefly to a Wren sitting at a table on the far side of the room. She made a telephone call, though whether it was to do with him Justin did not know.

He had decided that Mike would not come and see him before lunch, and this enabled him to relax a little, rather like a patient relieved to be waiting well down in the queue for the dentist. But then, Mike suddenly appeared from a doorway opposite. Perhaps because he was in uniform, Justin felt ill at ease. He had intruded into Mike's world and felt unwelcome. He looked down at the damaged parquet floor, rather than meet Mike's gaze.

'I came to tell you I'm going tomorrow.'

'Why so soon?'

204

The moment to be honest had arrived already. Justin opened his mouth. 'You know when Leo was so grumpy yesterday, he said things which made me angry, too. So I said something I didn't mean to, but which I couldn't stop because . . .' He paused, imagining how the kindly attentive expression on Mike's face would suddenly be replaced by one of disbelief and anger.

Mike was waiting, his expression becoming slightly less patient. At last he cleared his throat. 'Look, Justin, I'm always glad to see you, but I'm jolly busy this morning.' He smiled briskly. 'I'll try and say a proper goodbye tomorrow. Let's walk to the gate, shall we.'

Justin let himself be led out onto the gravel. He was not going to say anything now. He wasn't brave enough. So Leo would tell his father, who would come and shout at Mike. Or Leo would attack his mother, who would be sure to tell Mike what Leo had said, and how he had come to know it. Either way, Justin was sure that Mike would never want to see him again. Before they reached the sentry's hut at the gate, Justin's eyes were filling with tears, and he could not have spoken even if he had known what to say. The weight of Mike's hand on his shoulder only made him feel worse. Two ratings marched in at the gate and saluted Mike as they went past.

'Come on, Justin,' soothed Mike. 'Nobody's indispensable. Not me, and certainly not Leo. You can stand on your own feet already. So don't forget it.' Not trusting himself to speak, Justin nodded. 'See you in Yorkshire.'

'See you,' gasped Justin, already moving away, knowing that he had let Mike down and would never be able to put it right.

CHAPTER 15

When Peter and Justin left for the station early on Monday morning, with Andrea driving, Leo wished he could face going with them to say goodbye to his father on the platform, but he could not bear to sit in the same car as Justin. Before his mother closed her door, she looked back at him, as if, thought Leo, he had just plunged a knife into Justin's gizzard, and the blade was still dripping in his hand. Yet only a week ago *she* had been the one who'd wanted Justin's aunt to remove him for what he'd said to Rose. And who had stood up for Justin then? Only little me, sighed Leo.

Although he had not started on his father yet, Leo meant to work on him till he agreed to come back to live all the time in Oxford. That way, his parents wouldn't keep on drifting apart. Somehow, Leo had resisted the huge temptation to weep all over mum and beg her to stop seeing Mike. Mercifully, now that his longing to do this wasn't so powerful, he knew he could manage to keep his mouth shut, at least till he had found out more. Justin's warning that he would hurt his father most of all, by blabbing out everything, still haunted Leo. Thinking about his dad upset him badly: especially remembering his friendly smile as he sat sipping wine with Mike, and how he'd cheered when Mike won points in the tennis. Considering dad couldn't hit a single ball, that had been amazing of him. So what an idiot he was going to feel if he ever found out what Mike had been up to all along. Luckily, dad wouldn't have to know anything, if mum could be stopped.

Leo paced about in the sitting room trying to work out how to make her see what a brute she was being. Dad had once said that moral choices were the most important ones – maybe he hadn't quite said that, since he'd been talking about books – but Leo reckoned he at last understood what his father had meant. Right and wrong choices *did* matter most.

Since he absolutely had to to come up with a plan, Leo began to feel frightened when nothing came to mind. He had been getting along so badly with mum recently that he couldn't imagine things ever getting better. So what could he say, when she finally breezed in and dropped her car keys beside her handbag on the table? She was never going to believe that Justin had nagged him into doing exactly what he wanted every damned day of the holiday. She liked Justin because Mike doted on him. Even dad seemed to have taken a special shine to him. A fog of hopelessness enveloped Leo. Perhaps things had gone too far for him to change them. His parents would split up and he would lose his home. If Mike came through the war, he would adopt Justin and marry Andrea. Leo flung himself onto the sofa and beat his fists against its lumpy seat.

Time had passed – ten minutes or thirty, he scarcely cared how many. He leapt up as if a change of position might ease his misery. His eye lighted upon the black lacquer cabinet in the corner. Inside it there were glasses, a decanter of sherry and a whisky bottle. So why not do as grown-ups did to cheer themselves when they couldn't cope? Mum didn't drink often, but when Justin had not come back from the boat that night even she had gulped down Scotch. He opened the cabinet door and poured himself some whisky. What a stink! Like a girl jumping in a swimming pool he held his nose and tipped his head right back with the glass clamped to his mouth. Choking and spluttering, he staggered to a chair. How *could* people drink such stuff? *Nobody* could like it. Mercifully, he'd managed to swallow most without gagging. So how long till he felt better? Justin would have known to the nearest minute, bloody know-it-all. At school he'd once said that by tossing back different sorts of drink one after the other, the drinker got even drunker. Leo splashed sherry onto what was left of the whisky.

After a few gulps, a pleasant warm feeling began to spread upwards from his stomach. His problems seemed already to be dwindling. The thought of Justin having Andrea for his mother no longer hurt so much.

He said out loud, articulating carefully, as if testing an idea, 'Au contraire, amigo, my mum never touches men in or out of uniform. And no naval pig gets in her poke. Never.' He began to pace about, stumbling over the rug and falling, without hurting himself.

'Blinking, stinking,' he confided to the lacquer cabinet. 'One for the road? Don't mind if I do.' He raised his glass and poured an inch of sherry first, and then an inch of whisky. The whole operation took longer than he had expected. 'Down the hatch, bottoms up,' he muttered. Even as this new drink was coursing down his throat, he began to feel thick-headed and a little wobbly. He was surprised to see Rose staring at him from the doorway. How long had she been there?

'Naval pigs! Bottoms up! That's a tidy mouthful, Master Leo.'

For a moment, Leo felt unpleasantly dizzy, but as he focused on Rose the feeling passed. 'Wha's wrong with bottoms up?'

'You shouldn' be drinkin' at your age, that's what's wrong.'

'Would 'ee like a drink, ol' gal?' Leo gestured gallantly towards the cabinet. 'Just a jotto blotto,' he admitted gravely, turning much faster than he had intended and spilling his drink on the table. He pulled out a grubby handkerchief and rubbed at the wet wood, making the table tilt and the waxed fruit slip away towards the edge. Rose sprang forward and caught the glass dome.

Leo watched her disapprovingly. 'Steady on, sweetheart. Gin or sherry?' She was looking at him with a mixture of dismay and hilarity. 'What's wrong with bottoms up?' he demanded, irritated by her superior smile. Suddenly Leo strongly suspected she *had* shown Justin her bottom, and he'd only pretended she hadn't. Bloody little liar. 'Did you show him yours?' he cried.

Her cheeks reddened, though Leo did not notice. 'Don' 'ee go askin' such a thing.'

'Girls *do* show their things, so don't say they don't.' For some reason, his mood had changed from anger to tearfulness.

'Tisn't true 'less they be tarts,' reproved Rose.

He closed his eyes for a moment and the room seemed to roll sideways like a ship at sea. 'Ordinary girls do it, too,' he insisted, his voice coming out shaky and very faint. He wondered what bits of herself his mother might have shown to Mike already. The room was trembling at the edges now, even though Leo's eyes were wide open. He felt horribly sick.

'I think my mum's been . . .' he began, but could not finish. Instead, he shook his head slowly and started to cry. Rose came and gave him a comforting hug. He was aware of the soft feeling of her breasts under her cotton dress, but he didn't enjoy the sensation. The room was spinning now, and, suddenly, he knew he was going to vomit. Just in time, he turned his head away, but a hot cascade still splattered Rose's lace-up shoes.

Leo woke in bed soon after the church clock struck two in the afternoon. His eyeballs were aching and his mouth felt dry and furry. He blushed fiercely at the memory of Rose undressing him and helping him into his pyjamas. She had promised not to tell his mother why he'd been sick. And since he had not been disturbed, he presumed Rose had kept her word. Mum must surely have got back from the station some time ago.

On being greeted by Rose, Andrea was alarmed to hear that Leo had been unwell. But when she saw that the girl was not worried she experienced a deep glow of relief, and not only because he would be fine. At the station, she had learned something that had left her in need of a quiet time.

As they had been waiting for the train, Peter had gone into the gents, and Justin had moved right up close to her, looking even more determined than usual.

'Will you swear to tell me if Mike is killed.' The calm, adult way he said this shocked and moved her. He had accepted that Mike might die and was already living with the possibility. And he *knew* that she meant to follow Mike's fortunes come what may.

'We're not staying here a lot longer,' she had told him, avoiding his gaze.

He said with a hint of reproach, 'I know he'll make sure another officer tells you.'

'I'm sorry, Justin, of course I'll let you know.' She wanted to admit to him that she loved Mike, because Justin loved him, too, but she couldn't say it.

Because Justin had seemed to be in complete control of himself, Andrea was shaken when he lifted his hands to his face to hide tears. At last he gasped out words that she could scarcely imagine she was hearing.

'I told Leo about you and Mike.'

'Did *what*?' she gasped, eyes on the small doorway, where Peter would soon reappear.

'I'm really sorry. I lost my temper. I didn't mean to tell him, I swear I didn't.'

Andrea did not permit herself to look at him directly in case she showed her anger and lost the chance to ask the questions she needed to. In his pink school blazer, he looked too youthful to have dealt her this unexpected blow. With her eyes fixed on the slug-like heraldic creature on his breast pocket, Andrea asked as calmly as she could, 'Did Leo believe what you told him?'

'I don't think so.'

'But you're not sure?'

'I am pretty much.'

'Any special reason?'

He shrugged. 'Just the way he was. I know him well – that's it, mainly.'

Justin looked so guilty and woebegone that she could not help saying, 'I'm glad you told me.'

'I couldn't just go and leave you in the dark.' He stood head bowed: a picture of contrition.

She might have said something mildly comforting, if, at that moment, Peter had not stepped into the archway of the gents, like a mechanical saint bustling into view to the chimes of a cathedral clock.

When her husband came closer, Andrea saw several dark spots on his trousers. Because he needed both hands to undo his buttons, she knew he always found it hard to keep his balance in public lavatories, unless lucky enough to encounter a stall-like urinal to hold onto. Andrea watched him smile sympathetically at Justin, having noticed the boy's unhappy expression.

'Come on, old chap,' he urged, patting him on the back. 'Leaving Cornwall isn't the end of the world, you know.'

Over her husband's shoulder, Andrea had seen a young soldier and his girl embracing, their mouths glued together as they concluded a long farewell. From beyond the latticed footbridge came a loud screeching as the engine's brakes were engaged. In another moment, Andrea would have to say goodbye to Peter. She knew this, and dreaded kissing him with Justin looking on, knowing what the boy would be thinking. But what else could she do, as the train juddered to a halt and Peter thrust forward his familiar, trusting face?

Switching her gaze from the rose-patterned bedroom wallpaper to her son's pale face, Andrea had no idea what he was thinking. He'd been moody so often this vacation that his present glumness didn't prove a thing. Andrea practised an everyday smile – nothing too fulsome. He was sitting up in bed, a book of puzzles propped on his knees.

Her smile slipped when she took in how frail he looked. 'My, you do look green, darling.'

She sat down on the bed beside him. So many thousands of times they had sat together like this, happily. Yet this might be the day on which things changed forever.

'Was it a bad egg?'

'I just felt sick . . . and was.' Exasperation creased his smooth forehead, as if he had expected her to fuss and was not pleased to be proved right.

As he looked down again at his book, deeper furrows marked his brow. Would he frown a lot when he was a man? Hoping he wouldn't, she successfully fought a desire to whisper something tender and said breezily, 'I've been wanting to go sailing one more time.'

'I only went out in that beastly boat to please Justin.'

'You never enjoyed it?' She tried not to sound shocked.

'Not really.'

'Not everyone gets rescued by the navy.' Andrea smiled at him, hoping to get him to admit that, along with his painful memories, he also had some amusing ones.

He said mournfully, 'I was always scared I might need rescuing.'

'Maybe it's not too late to have more lessons now.' How had she dared suggest it? But how else could she find out whether he believed Justin's tale?

'With the commander?' Leo sounded unenthusiastic rather than outraged.

'Sure.' She hesitated, but only for a moment. 'If he has the time, you should go.'

Leo stared at his book without speaking. Andrea could feel her heart thumping. His next response would surely reveal what he knew.

'Okay,' he said, not even looking up from his book.

'Okay, what?'

'I'll have a lesson with him.' Matter of fact, unemotional; even bored.

So it was all right, wasn't it? If he'd suspected anything he would *never* have agreed to see Mike again. Faint with relief, Andrea wanted to hug Leo, but her worries wouldn't go away so easily. If Justin had told him about the bike's saddle, what must Leo have thought? Details like that couldn't simply be ignored. And Justin *must* have served up a few facts to lend credibility to his tale-telling. So if Leo did have suspicions, and wasn't going to say anything to her, maybe he wouldn't be able to hold back when seeing Mike. Until he had gone out for that sailing lesson, Andrea knew she could take nothing for granted.

When she had become resigned to her son's continuing concentration on his book, Leo unexpectedly fixed her with steely attention.

'Did he blub at the station?'

'Justin or dad?' she asked, smiling.

'Dad doesn't cry.'

'Justin was upset. You know it, Leo.'

'Do you like him because his dad died and his mum's a tart?'

'Because I'm sorry for him? Maybe a little.'

'But mainly because he's such a perfect little sweetie. I know what you really mean, mum.'

To stop him goading her, Andrea stood up to go and said lightly, 'Shout if you want to eat something. Some crackers, maybe?'

Downstairs again, she let her breath out in a long sigh. Was Leo's anger due to jealousy of Justin, or because he believed the boy's revelation about her? Maybe he didn't know what to think. For a moment Andrea wanted to run upstairs to reassure him. But how could she, while still meaning to spend the night with Mike? She would hurt him badly if she cancelled. But what if Leo saw her leave the house in the night? He might

214

tell his father he didn't want to go on living with her. Keep calm, Andrea. Until Mike takes Leo sailing, the balancing act must go on.

'I could use a highball,' she thought. Holding up the whisky bottle it seemed lighter. The level of the sherry was definitely lower. But if Rose had been drinking at her expense, Andrea didn't care. Highball in hand, she called Mike and told him she had to meet him right away.

CHAPTER 16

Looking at the boy as he gazed angelically at the bellying mainsail, Mike was disconcerted to feel such dislike. Yesterday, because the little sod had apparently treated his mother even more churlishly than at the tennis, Andrea had rung up to say she couldn't spend the whole night at the school after all. Mike was also upset with her for assuming that Leo must have believed Justin's vindictive tittle-tattle, especially since, according to her own account, Justin had thought Leo *hadn't* been convinced. During a snatched half-hour together, Andrea had wept before telling Mike that she hated herself for breaking her promise. Then she had begged him to be understanding. He had certainly tried to be, though his concern for what was going on under Leo's reddish thatch was limited to the effect it was likely to have on his chances for seeing Andrea. Yet this one consideration *did* make Leo's thoughts very important to him.

'When he's out on the river for his lesson with you,' Andrea had told Mike, 'he'll be sure to spill the whole thing. He won't be able to hold back. I know it. And then we'll know what to do.'

Yet here was Leo, *out on the river*, and, for the past hour, far from *spilling* anything, he'd hardly said a word.

Even as Mike was explaining, in a relaxed and friendly way,

217

why it was sensible for the helmsman and his crew to move their weight aft when running, he felt twinges of resentment towards his pupil. Mike was sure that Leo had provoked Justin to make his disastrous disclosure.

If Andrea was right, and Leo openly accused him while they were sailing, Mike meant to protest his innocence. He didn't *want* to lie to the boy but felt he had no choice. Andrea would definitely desert him if she ever thought Leo knew enough to persuade Peter to leave her and take him too.

Leo looked so young and inexperienced holding the tiller, that, even now, Mike found it hard to credit that this twelve-year-old boy might have the power to stop him being close to Andrea ever again. But by convincing her that he believed what Justin had told him, Leo could quite easily achieve this. It was strange he hadn't told her already, but presumably he had his reasons. Boys sent away to school at an early age were often capable of forming elaborate secret plans.

A gull swooped down, briefly regarding Mike with its round, expressionless eye, before soaring away across the dinghy's lace-like wake. On this overcast day, he and Leo were sailing past a beach which curved, like a white apple paring, under the shadow of a granite cliff. Framing this cove were twin reefs which jutted seawards, tilted into layered ridges at some remote period during the earth's cooling.

'Like to go ashore?' Mike pointed.

'I *thought* I was having a sailing lesson.'

Mike nodded cheerful assent. 'That's why I want you to practise getting the main down fast, and landing under jib alone.'

After they had beached the dinghy, Leo flipped stones into the sea while Mike pulled the boat up on his own. Leo waited for Mike to sit down first, and then sat several yards away from him on the sand.

'When did I catch the plague?' Mike asked affably.

'I think you know that.'

Mike made a show of thinking deeply. 'Was it when you realised I liked your friend?'

Leo jumped up angrily. 'Just leave my family alone.'

Mike gazed up at him quizzically. 'Justin's not family, is he?'

Leo's eyes narrowed. 'My *mother* bloody well is.'

'I can't believe you're saying this, Leo. What reason have you got?'

'Justin *saw* you and her.'

'Saw what, precisely?' Mike managed to make his voice quietly menacing.

Leo hesitated for a moment, blushing fiercely. 'He saw you stick your tongue in her mouth.'

Mike could not help laughing. Nervous astonishment mainly; but the effect of his amusement was splendidly insouciant. 'You really believe that?' he chuckled.

Enraged at being patronised, Leo hissed, 'For your information, Justin followed her on my bike when she took his.'

Though shaken, Mike said calmly, 'When did he tell you this?'

'What does it jolly well matter?'

'If he told you *after* you'd refused to invite him for the summer, it matters a lot.' Mike stood up so he would be the one looking down. 'Justin wanted to punish you, so he lied. His own mother walked out on him, so he knows the kind of fib that really hurts.'

Leo cried out, 'He wouldn't have lied about mum putting the saddle lower.'

'When did he say he first noticed that?'

'I don't know and I don't care,' replied the boy, enunciating very clearly.

'That's silly of you, Leo. If it was supposed to be several days ago, it's very curious he didn't tell you then. Don't you find it odd he only "remembered" when he was angry with you?'

'He wouldn't make up that stuff about the saddle.'

'You think he couldn't invent a clever thing like that? I thought we all knew how clever Justin is.'

Several sleek round waves had swished onto the sand before Leo turned and fixed Mike with his blue-grey eyes. 'Do you swear on your honour that Justin was lying.'

'Of course he was.'

'But do you swear?'

'If it makes you any happier, sure I do.'

At the end of the longer of the two reefs, a cormorant was twisting his neck to preen his tailfeathers. Mike was about to draw Leo's attention to the bird when he heard a scraping sound behind him. The boy was already pushing the dinghy into the water.

'Home, James,' murmured Mike, as he gave the boat a powerful shove. There was something magnificently dismissive about Leo's haste to be gone. Is it because he knows I lied? Mike dismissed the idea. Leo would never have asked him to swear to anything if he'd been sure of his facts.

Sorry to have lied 'on his honour', it occurred to Mike that 'honour' was probably a concept which Leo's father would dismiss as quaint pre-Freudian self-deception. Perhaps there was something to be said for a coldly scientific view of human pretentions. Indeed, for most people, morality was what circumstances made it – only a handful were naturally virtuous. And I, it seems, am not among them, since I would lie repeatedly to keep Andrea's love.

'Yes,' Mike would say to her, 'Leo *did* mention Justin's story, though he didn't seem impressed by it. And, frankly, he was even less impressed after our chat.' So unless Leo himself contradicted this anodyne version of events – which didn't seem likely, given his earlier reticence – Andrea would surely feel relaxed enough about her son to risk spending part of the next two nights away from home.

The line to take with Leo now would be to treat him as if nothing untoward had been said. So, seeing salt stains on

Leo's shorts, Mike told him that in Brittany any man caught by the Germans with similar marks on his clothes would be interrogated and shot, unless able to explain himself.

On Leo's return from his sailing lesson, his mother asked him whether he had 'gotten the impression he was improving'.

'Improving? The commander? No, he's still a smooth clever-clogs,' he replied, noting the disapproving compression of his mother's lips.

'Did you talk sailing all the time?'

'Sometimes he boasted about his work.'

'Oh, Leo! He never did when he was visiting here.'

'He knew dad wouldn't have swallowed it.'

Andrea held up her hands. 'Stop joshing me, Leo.'

She was laughing, falsely he thought, as she went out to talk to Rose. Later, she told Leo she was going to practise the piano for an hour or two at the school.

Since Rose was busy doing the washing, Leo felt safe to look for Mike Harrington's love letters. All lovers wrote them, and ladies never threw them away, he had read in a women's magazine. Since *he* would never hide anything secret of his own in his bedroom, Leo decided his mother's bedroom could wait. Instead, he started searching in the dining room, looking under the box containing place mats and the wooden cutlery tray in the top right-hand drawer of the sideboard, before removing the napkins and napkin rings, and grovelling under the table to see if a letter had been pinned there.

He himself would probably tape something of the sort behind a picture, so he tilted all of them away from the wall, peering behind without dislodging the cords from the hooks. Nothing. In the drawing room it was the same story behind the pictures, so he lifted cushions and rugs, and then looked into vases, and inside the drinks cabinet. But again, failure. The kitchen and the scullery were out, since his mother would have known Rose would find anything hidden there.

In the bedroom, Leo felt embarrassed to be looking through his mother's things, especially her underwear, but what else could he do? There was an all-in-one garment not unlike the Berlei 'controlette' recently advertised in the *Daily Mail* with the heading 'Figure Precautions' instead of 'Air Raid Precautions', and a picture of two girls, one a search-light girl in a bulky coat, the other beside her wearing nothing but the undergarment. Though he didn't seek them out, sometimes, when looking at such ads, they gave Leo a warm feeling in his penis that made him want to rub it.

Most of his mother's stuff was lighter and made of pink or black silk. He held up petticoats, step-ins and camiknickers for brief inspection, fascinated by the feel of them and by their unfamiliarity. Girdles and garter-belts left him briefly forgetful of the task in hand. But soon he was searching again, under sweaters and carefully folded blouses, beneath silk stockings and coarser oatmeal-coloured ones, and even among her shoes at the bottom of the wardrobe.

He found her jewel case on top of the wardrobe but neither inside it nor anywhere else could he lay his hand on a letter. He looked blankly at her silver-backed brushes and the mess of spilled powder on the dressing table, but no new hiding places occurred to him. Nothing was pinned behind the mirror. Nothing was in the pocket of her bathrobe, as she insisted on calling her dressing gown. He slipped a hand under the mattress as far as he could push it. Then at last, under the bed, Leo found something: a small square cardboard box, which he feared might be nothing important. There was a picture on the lid of an odd, dome-shaped thing, not unlike a sliced section of an inflated fooball bladder.

'Lambert's "Wife's Friend" Dutch Pessary' was printed under the picture, and below that a manufacturer's address, 60, Queen's Road, London, E.8.. A dictionary would tell him what a pessary was, but he feared there wasn't one in the house. He lifted the lid and was disappointed to find the box empty, except for some tissue paper smelling of talcum powder. Inside the lid, there was a printed drawing of a woman in an odd hunched-up posture, and under her were several paragraphs of print.

'In order to place the Dutch pessary in position, squat on your heels with your knees bent and feet apart. Holding the pessary in the palm of your left hand in such a way that the dome is pointing upwards, pinch the rim – now lying in contact with your palm – between the thumb and forefinger of the right hand, and introduce the pessary into your vagina.'

Leo had sensed that this pessary thing was a very private item, more than likely to do with a woman's health. The instructions seemed to confirm this. He knew from dirty jokes, and from the big dictionary at home, that a woman's vagina was her hole where men pushed in their cocks and where babies came out, but that *didn't* tell him why the dome thing should be put up there too. Since it wasn't in its box, his mother might have to wear it inside herself all day. Perhaps, like false teeth, it was only taken out at night. Leo put the box back under the bed and wondered why she had concealed it there. Perhaps to stop him seeing the picture of the squatting lady, though it was really only a diagram, and didn't show anything interesting because the woman's hand was in the way. But if he had to push something into *his* bottom every day, he knew he would definitely keep its box in a secret place. On leaving the bedroom, he began to fear that his mother might be seriously ill. His anxiety was bad enough to persuade him to ask Rose.

She was not in the kitchen, but he saw her as soon as he went outside, over by the apple trees, hanging wet sheets on the line. After helping with the pegs, he delivered a line he had rehearsed in his head while crossing the grass.

223

'Please don't think I'm being rude to ask, but do ladies wear Dutch pessaries when there's something wrong with their stomachs?'

Rose burst out laughing. 'It's to *stop* somethin' bein' wrong with their stomachs.'

Leo knew he was blushing again. For a moment he was close to tears. But then he rallied. 'What's so funny about stopping being ill?'

'Pessaries don' stop illness, my dearie. They stop babies. Don' 'ee worry. I didn' know nothin' 'bout it neether, till doctor told my sister when she married, and she told me.'

He swallowed hard. 'Women only wear them before . . . ?'

'Before they go with a man. And they gotta keep it in for a fair while after.'

'How long?' Leo managed to gasp.

'I don' know reely. A few hours maybe. Long 'nuff for his seeds to die.'

Wanting to be alone again, Leo mumbled, 'You won't tell mother I asked?'

She grinned appealingly. 'Not if 'ee tell Rose why 'ee wants to know.'

'I can't,' he muttered. 'I'm really grateful you talked to me. But *please* don't tell.'

She caught him by the sleeve of his jersey and whispered, 'Are you a bad boy, Master Leo? Drinkin' and buyin' Dutch caps for your girl!' She laughed shrilly.

'I haven't got a girl,' he screeched, trying to pull away from her, but feeling her lips planted playfully on his neck before he could.

'I could ask 'ee to do anything, couldn' I?'

Her cheeks were flushed with the effort of hanging onto him, and Leo's heart was hammering. 'Stop fooling,' he shouted, before darting away towards the house with her laughter in his ears.

Before his mother came home from her 'practising', which

had started to sound horribly bogus, Leo had an idea which made him cheer out loud. The box could have been under the bed for months, and might have nothing at all to do with his mother. The house had been rented out for ages. What a fool not to think of this. So the fact that the dome thing hadn't been in the box probably wasn't important after all. Really, there was no reason to be suspicious. Unless, of course, he looked inside the box tomorrow and found the pessary had returned. But at present Leo was so relieved he couldn't believe such a thing possible.

Downstairs again, he thought of all the rude things he'd said to the commander, and felt dreadfully embarrassed. Mike would be sure to tell Andrea, who would be furious. Leo knew he'd offended her enough already over Justin, and was depressed to reflect that he'd given her a whole new reason to be angry. In most ways though, Leo was glad that Mike's arguments had made him doubt Justin's story – just as his own failure to find love letters made him do. But Leo still detested Mike's confident manner and dreaded having to apologise to him, as he supposed he would have to.

Just as Leo was allowing himself to become miserable over the prospect of grovelling to Mike, he suddenly realised what a prize fathead he was. The one thing he wanted, above all others, was for his mother *not* to be involved with Mike, and for her to love his father again. And dad's prospects looked a lot brighter than a few hours ago.

Andrea was running her fingers through the hairs on her lover's chest and thinking how amazing it was that they had made love only minutes after meeting, when there had been so much she had wanted to ask him. But that must be what happens, she thought, when two people have spent days imagining their bodies entwined and have then been obliged to wait at the last moment. It was two in the morning and she and Mike were lying together on the cushions in the schoolroom. His eyes were closed and there was a smile on his lips.

'I can't imagine what you said to Leo,' she murmured, 'but he was really friendly this evening for the first time in a whole week.'

'I gave him a new perspective on things.'

She snuggled up to him, and said in what he imagined was a Southern drawl, 'Michael Harrington, did you lie to my sweet baby?'

'Ma'am, I can't deny it,' he groaned, turning away from the light of the single candle they had allowed themselves.

'Mike, I'm really glad you did,' she whispered in her ordinary voice.

He rolled over to face her, with a martyred smile. 'If the wages of sin are what they used to be, I'll burn.'

'For one white lie?'

'That's *all* it is?' he asked weakly, running a hand down her stomach and letting it rest between her thighs. He sighed deeply. 'At least I didn't rape you. I expect you teach your girls to loathe the Lovelaces of literature.'

Andrea looked at him in amazement. 'You think I'd study *Clarissa* with them? I want to keep my job.'

'But the rapist paid with his life,' he soothed. 'What could be nicer than that?'

She moved her lips closer to his ear, 'A happy ending, dear heart.'

Mike pulled away from her. 'Dear God, Andrea, don't *say* things like that.'

'Oh, Mike.' She hugged him tightly as if to protect his body against all dangers. 'I'm awfully sorry.'

'Things could be worse. In the Middle Ages, I'd be in church at this moment doing some eve of battle grovelling, instead of sinning some more with you.'

'You don't think of it like that, do you?'

'Oh, Andrea,' he soothed, 'being with you is like taking

great gulps of life, one hundred per cent proof. I'm totally intoxicated.'

She sat up so that she could see his whole face. 'You still look awfully sad, my sweet.'

He stared into the pitch-darkness near the stove and said quietly, 'It must have occurred to you that if I'd failed with Leo, you wouldn't be here now.'

'But you *didn't* fail, and he's fine.'

'Till he finds out I lied to him.'

Andrea leaned across Mike so that her breasts pressed down on his chest. 'Can't we forget him till then?'

'Dearest Andrea, *you* were the one who didn't want to do that.'

'I guess you were more sensible.' She kissed his shoulder. 'Honey, please don't spoil things.'

'I won't . . . unless my luck runs out.' He moved as if to slip out from under her and she freed him at once. Then, as he groped around for his pants, she watched him lovingly in the flickering light.

'Don't go now.' She held out her arms, distressed to see him leaving sooner than he needed to. 'Please come back here.' He paused a moment before sitting beside her again. 'Mike, I admire you so much for setting Leo's mind at rest. I didn't thank you enough. Can you forgive me?' She sat up and kissed his lips, at the same time gently drawing him down into a recumbent position. A little later, she murmured, 'Maybe we could try again?'

'Darling, I'd love to if I thought I could,' he murmured, slipping down onto the cushions with her.

She closed her eyes and kissed Mike's mouth very softly. Whatever happened she must never lose him. She mustn't lose Leo either, but definitely not her lover: her dearest Mike, whom she adored for himself, and because she couldn't help it; and because his looks were the answer to a prayer (his feet and wrists included), and because one day he would talk to her

227

about literature – squashing Peter's view of it as a by-product of man's need to create illusions rather than face life as it was. With Mike, reality was fine.

She had been fondling and caressing for some time without any serious expectation of success when suddenly she felt a change.

'God's balls!' gasped Mike. 'Lazarus rises!'

Leo had not anticipated thinking about Justin after he had gone, but, being unable to decide what to do, he found himself wondering what Justin would have suggested. Probably he would have wanted to watch the sailors painting the trawlers. To do this, it would be necessary to get up several hours before dawn and cycle to the woods above the creek in order to reach the mud, and then get home again before Andrea and Rose had got up. Could he face it? Not the whole thing, but going to see if they were moored on the river would be an easy start.

It was a morning of gusting rain and fast moving clouds, with squalls whipping between the boats in Porthbeer harbour. Oblivious to the wind, a boy wearing a lopsided straw hat crammed down on his head was standing up in a rowing boat, propelling it with a single oar towards a moored fishing vessel. He was working this oar back and forth over the stern with wiggling movements like a fish might make with its tail. It struck Leo that this boy, who looked about his own age, already knew what he would do when grown up, and would probably never leave the village. God knows what I'll be doing, or where I'll be living even next year.

As Leo walked along the beach looking down at gulls' feathers and bits of cork and driftwood, he realised he didn't want to stay in Cornwall any more. Maybe he would suggest leaving when he and his mother were having lunch. He had been trying not to think about her, because he knew he ought to look inside that cardboard box. It would still be empty, he was sure; but he still had to look.

He clambered onto the rocks where he and Justin had often stood. Neither of the navy's trawlers was on its moorings. Because Mike was still around, the boats could not be in France. Leo was not immediately seized by the idea of scrambling through the woods to investigate, but when he imagined himself feet away from men doing the painting he found he was trembling. Imagine it! Being close enough to leave a note pinned to the hull – or better still below decks – 'Leave her alone or else, Commander.'

Leo tried to imagine what would happen after the painting was done. The fishing boats would stay hidden in the creek – presumably guarded night and day – until their crews came to take them downriver to load them with ammunition. If the painters were still working today, the trawlers might possibly be ready to sail tonight, but more likely tomorrow. The temptation to go now, and peer through the trees at what was going on, was too much for him. He had over three hours till one o'clock.

Leo arrived back at the house exhausted, ten minutes before lunch was due. Rose was in the kitchen trimming fat off some cold meat, and Leo got her to pour him a glass of water. He gulped it deeply before asking where his mother was.

'Don' ask me 'zactly where she is, dearie. She says to tell 'ee she'll be home directly.'

Because he knew that, when Rose said 'directly', it meant anything from a few seconds to twenty minutes or more, Leo decided to slip up to his mother's room at once. On the stairs his heart began to thump so hard he found it hard to catch his breath. Once in the room, he rushed to the bed and thrust his hand under it, exactly where he had first discovered the box. Nothing. He moved his hand rapidly from side to side, but still found nothing. He lay down flat and looked under the bed properly. The box had vanished. Could his mother have thrown it away because it wasn't hers? There was a bedside table with a marble top and several drawers beneath. He opened them rapidly, and, still not finding the box, searched the drawers in the dressing table, again without success. Recalling where she had hidden her jewel case, he dragged a chair across and stood on it to look behind the wooden rim above the wardrobe.

As he raised his face above the cornice, he saw the cardboard box just inches away. Without getting down from the chair, he reached out and opened it, trembling as he did so. A grey rubbery thing regarded him like a large blind eye. He pressed it down with a finger and raised his hand quickly since it felt slightly clammy. The thing resumed its shape at once. A little talcum powder was left adhering to Leo's finger. Too shocked to know what to do or think, he shut the lid, replaced the box, and fled from the room as soon as he had jumped down from the chair.

After delaying lunch for almost an hour, Andrea decided to eat without Leo. He had seemed reassuringly cheerful earlier in the day, so she was shaken that he should have quit without a word just before a meal. Rose said she had seen him in the house at ten minutes of one. So why had he dashed out again?

By two, she was alarmed as well as angry. On the principle that she usually felt better doing something, she went up to Leo's room, just to be sure he wasn't in there, sulking. The room was empty and no more untidy than usual. On entering her own bedroom moments later, she was shocked to see, beside the tall clothes closet, the chair which she normally used when making up her face at the dressing table. Could she have carelessly forgotten to replace it, after hiding her contraceptive cap? Very likely – unless Rose had been prying. But, if she had, would she have left behind such obvious evidence of her presence as a misplaced chair? No chance. So Leo might have come in. But why would he have been searching her room in the first place? Boys his age often stole from their mother's bags, but hers was never hidden away. The only plausible explanation was that she herself had left the chair where she had found it. Before returning it to its usual place, she got up to check that the box was still in its place. To her relief, it was.

Downstairs in the living room, she decided to call Mike to ask his advice. She was pleasantly surprised to be put through immediately. Expecting him to come up with some soothing explanation for Leo's strange behaviour, Andrea was alarmed to detect anxiety in his voice. Mike promised to come over as soon as he could get away – within the hour, he hoped.

After a brief silence, he said, 'Maybe you should 'phone the sailing club to see if his dinghy's on the hard.'

'But where might he have gone to?'

'Probably nowhere at all. But let's take no chances. If the boat's gone, I'll find it as soon as I can. Could be sensible to check whether he's taken any money. Maybe he's taken off to see his father.'

'Don't scare me, Mike.'

'Look, he'll probably come waltzing home in five minutes flat. But there's no harm being a step ahead.'

Afterwards, Andrea did not feel strong enough to search Leo's things. His father often gave him small extra sums in addition to the half-crown he received each fortnight. So, even supposing she found Leo's purse or billfold, she would still have no idea how much he had with him. Nor had he ever kept a diary. She hated to think that when he had seemed happy earlier in the day he might instead have been desperate. That was certainly what Mike had implied. She realised how despairing she would be feeling if he hadn't agreed to come right over. Just hearing his voice had calmed her. It was awful to be burdening him with her problems on the eve of his departure for France, but she didn't seem able to help herself.

CHAPTER 17

Leo's disillusion was wild and tearful, yet with his misery came moments of relief, even of euphoria. He knew the worst about his mother, and couldn't be hurt by anything else she did. His course was simple now: to take revenge on Mike Harrington. He imagined Mike's face turning brick-red, as every officer in the briefing room learned what their admired commander had been doing to a wife and mother.

The wind hummed in the spokes of Leo's bicycle wheels and buffeted him as he swept out from between tall hedgerows onto the coast road above Porthbeer. He was an arrow of fate aimed at Harrington's hard heart, so he lowered his head over the handlebars to make himself more arrow-like. The sailors on duty in the entrance hall would try to stop him, but he would dart past into the room where Mike was spouting. But here there was a problem. How would he know which room to head for? If he guessed wrong, he would be caught and thrown out. But if he snooped outside, he would certainly be spotted.

Leo had been pedalling ferociously, but now slowed down and even freewheeled for a while. Perhaps he ought to hide in bushes near the gate and spring out when Mike was leaving. Yet this might not be for hours, and Mike might leave alone – and then there would be no chance of shaming him.

By the time Leo reached the bridge at the head of Porthbeer

Creek, his confidence was draining away. A worse problem had occurred to him. If Mike simply laughed, and said, 'Don't be ridiculous', what could he shout back? 'My mum shoves a rubber thing in her hole before she sees you'?

But even then the great pig might deny it all. 'Watch it, laddie. You can't go spreading lies, you know.'

And people might believe Mike. Leo braked sharply just after the bridge. They might even think some other man was stuffing his thing in her. Dipping his wick, Justin had called it once.

Sitting in the grass by the roadside, Leo suddenly felt sick. It was bad enough thinking of her in bed with dad, but it was hugely worse imagining her doing it with other men. In fact it made Leo's cheeks burn though no one was looking. With his head right down in the grass he saw a black beetle blundering from blade to blade like an explorer in a tropical jungle. It was incredibly black and shiny, with iridescent patches on its lacquered wing cases. Maybe he should take encouragement from seeing this heroic insect battling on regardless, though often tumbling down – like Robert the Bruce having his spirits lifted by the spider. But in his case, not even an army of plucky insects would be able to get him back on his bike to go after Mike Harrington.

Leo closed his eyes and saw the redness in his lids as he faced the sky. If there was that much blood in those flaps of skin, imagine crashing his bike – there'd be gallons of gore on the road. Oh God, if only he could forget everything, for a while, and doze in the grass like he sometimes did while waiting to go in to bat. At school his ability to do this made people think him a cool customer.

Shrill voices distracted him. They seemed to be coming closer. Leo clambered onto the parapet of the bridge and saw some boys running along the bank. One of them was holding something under his jacket. The river was narrow and fast-flowing between the piers of the bridge, its brown and peaty water flecked with foam. As the boy opened his jacket, a marmalade cat poked out its head and miaowed. The moment the animal was held up, Leo screamed. Several boys looked around uneasily. But the moment they realised it was just another boy, they took no further notice. Without more ado, the cat was flung out from the bank, high above the stream. With a terrified yowl, it hit the water. Leo screamed again as its head bobbed up several times, before disappearing.

One of the boys shouted up at Leo, 'Wanna go in too, do 'ee?'

'You shouldn't have done that,' cried Leo.

Laughter greeted his words, leaving him gasping, as if he'd been hit low while boxing.

'Should've knawed better 'n that, should we?' The tone of this larger boy was heavily sarcastic.

'I say, you chaps, let's drag the river,' mocked another.

Leo did not realise a stick had been hurled in his direction until he heard it clatter down on the road behind him. Several of the yobs were clambering up the slope just below the bridge. Convinced they really meant to throw him in the water, Leo ran towards his bike. Ashamed to be running away, he began pedalling uphill towards the Polwherne Hotel. If he couldn't save a cat from some village oiks, how was he going to get the better of a man like Harrington?

He was passing fields and hedgerows again. Cows stared at him over a gate and he screamed at them, 'I'm going to show him. I bloody am.' But it was bosh, and even the Guernseys seemed to know it. The only thing that kept him pedalling was his memory of his father's stupid niceness to Mike. It made Leo want to cry and punch the air at the same time.

Some distance from the crown of the hill, Leo had to get off and push. Some sort of bird of prey was peering down at him from the top of a telegraph pole, but he never managed a second look to identify it. At that moment he heard a motorbike and the bird took wing.

Unable to see over the rise ahead, Leo couldn't be sure it was *him*, but already his heart was racing. The engine noise was louder now, though muffled by the rushing of his blood. Who else, down here, owned a powerful motorbike? Leo stopped pushing his bike, and stood still, eyes fixed on the square of blue between the hedgerows.

As machine and rider burst upwards into the empty space, they seemed to hang in the air, so fast were they travelling. But Leo hadn't a moment's doubt – the flying jacket, the make of motorbike, the absence of a helmet – it was *him* for sure. Fury made his legs tremble. He swore but made no sound. Suddenly his whole body responded with pent-up violence. Though his cycle was between his legs and facing uphill, he managed to wrench the handlebars sideways and literally flung himself into Mike's path. Tyres screamed and smoked and a chalky face blurred past him like a shooting star. The Velocette ripped into the verge, missing Leo by inches, tearing up clods and hurtling on downhill in a careering skid. Mike regained control, a split second too late to avoid clipping the bank. He spun round so fast, Leo wasn't sure if he hit the gate, going backwards or sideways, or even whether he was upright at the time.

The splintering crash of timber, the bellowing of cattle, and the eery absence of engine noise a second later left Leo standing frozen, as if his joints had fused. His mouth was dry and he retched without being sick.

I've killed him. Jesus Christ! Someone may drive past at any minute. His own position and the twisting skid mark on the road would tell them everything. Knowing he should rush to offer first aid, Leo couldn't even look in that direction. In a moment of blind rage he'd wanted to kill his enemy. Not any more. Now all he wanted was to avoid detection. Even as he pushed his bike over the brow of the hill and pedalled away, Leo was telling himself he would go back when he felt calmer. He'd meant Mike no harm. Really he hadn't.

He imagined his mother weeping at the funeral. She would pretend she was grieving for an ordinary friend, and dad would be fooled. 'Why the hell did you stop in a place like that, Leo? Slap in the middle of the road. You *must* have heard his engine.'

Leo pictured his mother. At this moment she'd probably be reading a book or chatting with Rose – a day like any other. In the Polwherne Hotel the naval bods would be carrying on as usual, too.

By now, Leo was cycling past the woods which he and Justin had stumbled through on their way to the river. Dismounting, he wheeled his bicycle between the trees. He would wait here among the oaks and hollies for an hour or two – long enough for a passer-by to see the smashed gate and enter the field. The cows would have strayed onto the road and the farmer would be called. If Mike was dead, or badly injured, he would be found and taken away. Leo couldn't decide how soon to go home. In case Mike had survived, it might be safer to return at once and tell mum it had all been Mike's fault. 'He was going so fast I could hardly see him. Damned near killed me.'

Even if Mike gave his version later, mum wouldn't know which was true. So why go back to the field at all? To see if it looked as if Mike had bought it. If the Velocette was a blood-stained heap of scrap, Leo reckoned he'd be better off saying nothing to his mother. But how could he be sure he was a goner, even if the bike was a write-off? Sometimes people survived really dreadful accidents. Around him, the earth was carpeted with bluebells, but he was too jittery to notice. Suddenly he knew he didn't want Mike to be dead. What made him want to vomit was not knowing if he was. A new thought tormented him. If Mike had continued straight on, instead of veering, he would have hit the cycle's front wheel and brushed it aside without harming himself. Instinct made him swerve like that. It wasn't to save me. Pure instinct. He didn't give me a thought. But what if the opposite was true? Alone among the bluebells, Leo started to scream.

Leo was cycling again, as fast as he knew how, scraping

his legs as the grocer's van whizzed by, forcing him into the hedgerow. But now he *had* to know Mike's fate. He imagined him lying bleeding and couldn't bear it another minute. Thank God the van driver had come past that broken gate. If a body had been lying there, he would have stopped for sure. Yet by the time Leo approached the field, he didn't know what to expect. Mike's body could have been flung behind the bank.

Leo tiptoed through the space where the gate had been. Bits of broken wood were scattered in front of him. On the far side of the meadow, a farmer and his dog were driving fawn-coloured cows into another field. Nearer to hand, Leo saw a beast lying motionless on its side. One of its legs was twisted oddly. On coming closer, he noticed a bleeding hole in its head as if it had been shot. The Velocette was propped against the bank near the shattered gate. Apart from a torn front tyre, not a lot seemed wrong with it – nothing obvious anyway, except for a few dents and scratches. He knelt to take a better look. No blood anywhere. Maybe the front wheel was a little bent, but it was hard to be sure without getting it to turn. But Mike was going to be all right. Leo's chest swelled. He wanted to pray to God, which he hardly ever did. In fact he didn't do it now either, because already Mike could be walking into Trevean Barton, or have reached the telephone box in Porthbeer.

Must tell it my way first, thought Leo, running to his bike. Now he was sure Mike was alive, he no longer felt bad about planning to tell lies to get the better of him. Mike had lied, too.

At first overjoyed to see her son, Andrea was soon regarding him with bafflement. Leo had just told her, stammering with rage, that Mike's motorbike had missed him by inches and had sped on by.

'But, sweetheart, he couldn't have seen you.'

'Yes, he did, mother.'

'Though he was driving so fast?'

'He saw me.'

Dazed by his anger, Andrea murmured, 'I guess he stopped someplace along the lane?'

'I didn't hang around to look.'

'Why was that?'

'He could have been mad at me.'

Andrea shook her head as if to clear it. 'After driving too fast, *he* would be mad at *you*?' From the beginning she had suspected that events might not have been as Leo had described them and now she felt certain.

As if sensing her doubts, Leo muttered grudgingly, 'I may have been a few feet out from the side of the road.'

'But he was still driving too fast?'

'Lots too fast. He must have had a hell of a shock when he saw me trying to scram.'

'But I'm sure he was relieved.'

Leo hung his head. 'I think I moved the wrong way, mum. I didn't have time to think.'

Fear clawed at the pit of her stomach. 'He wasn't hurt, was he? Look at me, Leo. He didn't fall off?'

His eyes would not meet hers. 'No.'

'How do you know if you didn't hang around?' She knew her voice had risen sharply but could not help it.

'I saw he'd made it round the corner.' Oh God, thought Andrea, Mike would have been on his way to see me when this happened. To her amazement Leo cried angrily, 'I got a worse shock than him. He shouldn't zoom along country lanes at ninety mph scaring the daylights out of people.'

'All right, darling,' she mumured, feeling too sick and anxious to continue the conversation. The only important thing now was to get to the telephone before him when Mike called.

They met on the headland at the mouth of the estuary, Mike having arrived in the automobile in which she had first kissed him – the one with RN painted on the hood in chipped white letters. It was late afternoon but the sun had not quite lost its warmth. Across the wind-flattened grass, banks of rose-pink thrift fluttered bravely. The headland was known locally as the Beacon after one of the many bonfires, warning of the Spanish Armada's approach, which had been lit there, another interesting local fact that Andrea had never managed to share with the boys.

They had left their automobiles on a farm track and walked down, hand in hand, onto the flat-topped bluff. Mike's left hand was bandaged. Not a deep cut, he'd told her on the telephone. There were dark circles under his eyes and he was tense and restless. She wanted to hold him but knew he was angry.

'He's a lying little toad,' had been Mike's first reaction when she'd relayed what Leo had said. But Andrea had found it impossible to believe that the boy had deliberately pushed himself into Mike's path. She still couldn't accept it.

Mike turned to her with a tight little smile. 'Funny to think I'd be dead now if I'd hit a gatepost instead of a nice fat cow.' As if his back was hurting, Mike eased himself onto the grass. 'Let's hope I've not used up all my luck for the month.'

'Maybe you won't need any for a while.'

He lay back and gazed up at the sky. 'I looked at myself in the mirror this morning, and I could have sworn I wasn't there. I'd left hours ago.'

'What time *will* you be out there?' she asked, glancing at the ocean beyond the reef.

'Just before midnight.'

'It's awful I didn't ask before, but is Tony safe, and the others?'

'I've heard no names – just numbers of "parcels" to be collected. He's fine I expect, though his boat's been found. So there's a hell of a kerfuffle going on. The Boches are sending direction-finding vans all over the place and closing harbours.'

'Can't you delay your mission, Mike?' Her tone was scared, almost imploring.

'Not a chance. The BBC messages have gone out.'

The wind was blowing back his hair, making him look as he had on the day she'd first seen him at Elspeth's. Fighting back tears, Andrea fumbled in her bag. 'Take this with you, darling.' She handed him a length of green ribbon. 'I wore it when we played tennis.'

He raised the hair-ribbon to his lips. 'Ivanhoe before the tournament. I'd tie it to my breastplate, if fake fishermen wore them.'

'You sound so bitter.'

'And that's surprising?' He fixed her with sad, indignant eyes. 'Quite apart from what I'll be going through in the next few hours, don't you think I've good reason to feel a little miffed? Your twelve-year-old son tried to kill me. Really did his best. And what do you say to me on the 'phone?'

'He panicked, darling. He chose the wrong way.'

'I was there, Andrea. He had plenty of time to avoid me. He's found out about us. Must have.'

'It's possible.'

He leaned across and clasped her hand. '*It happened*, and it changes everything. If I come back alive, we can't have a repeat of today.'

'I know.'

'Either we'll have to part, or you'll have to tell your family about me and face the music.'

Andrea felt she was being rushed into deciding something tremendously important without being given time to think. Yet she couldn't bring herself to argue. If she never saw him again, what would she think of herself for making their last meeting wretched?

'It's hard, of course it is,' he said, relenting. 'I hoped it wouldn't come to this; but since we love each other, we'll get through it somehow. Unless you tell them, something worse will happen.' His brown eyes held hers. 'Do it for Leo, too.'

'I will, after you're back.'

He noted her qualification and smiled. 'Thank you, my darling.'

'You do still love me?' She was scared that Leo's behaviour had done lasting damage to his feelings for her.

He squeezed her hand. 'You know I do. Let's forget the little beast for five minutes. It's bad enough going through the sailor's umpteenth plucky farewell like a cut-price Noël Coward.'

'I guess we five-and-ten Greer Garsons feel kind of helpless, too.'

Mike stared out to sea for a long time. 'Suppose it's this time tomorrow and there's still no sign of me. Will you come back here, and stay for a while?'

'Darling, of course I will.'

She hugged him to her, very tightly, as if some great wind was tearing him away.

CHAPTER 18

When Andrea entered the living room, Leo and Rose were sitting together listening to the news on the radio. Mostly it was the same old story: more night raids on London, British withdrawal from Greece continuing, and yet another setback in North Africa. As soon as she had sunk into an armchair, Andrea knew she would be unable to sit still. Because Mike would not be on his way to France for many hours, it distressed her to imagine him still at the Polwherne Hotel, and therefore within reach. But if she *did* call him, would he even be able to spare the time to talk?

As Leo turned off the radio, Rose jumped up, gabbling about a pan on the stove. The sight of the two of them together had surprised Andrea, but with Leo so young what could be the harm in it? He would have wanted to hear the news because his father was in London – not that many details of individual raids were given over the air.

'What did dad say in his letter?' he asked, sitting on the arm of her chair, effectively trapping her. She must have looked at him blankly because he went on, 'I saw it in the hall this morning.'

Since Andrea had skimmed through the letter, she remembered its contents only sketchily. 'He's been out of London,' she said, trying, for Leo's sake, to sound interested in his father's movements. He stared back at her, worried.

'I think he's working on triggering devices for bombs. Mainly delayed action.'

'He told you that?' she asked shakily.

'No. I saw a drawing in his room.'

Andrea said gently, 'I can't imagine he'll be asked to defuse anything.'

'I suppose not.' Leo smiled gratefully. Andrea was immensely relieved that he seemed happy to talk to her. Certainly Leo would not be beside her now if he had found new evidence of an affair – and without such evidence he would never have attempted to harm Mike, deliberately.

Not long after supper Leo went up to his bedroom, saying he wanted to write to his father.

'I'll send dad your love,' he promised, after kissing her goodnight, the first time for several weeks.

'Thanks,' she murmured, wishing he had decided to stay a little longer. But it was wonderful he had talked at all, and this was what she would tell Mike, in twelve hours' time, God willing. Yet in her heart she knew he would not be pleased. Mike had wanted an excuse to bring matters to a head, and, disliking Leo, would not want her relations with her son to become close again.

With this difference of opinion looming, and Mike on a mission, too, Andrea was thankful to have in her possession a bottle of the sedatives which Peter's Oxford doctor had prescribed for him. Two of these small white tablets would guarantee oblivion until seven or eight in the morning, and by then there should only be a few more hours to wait.

When Andrea passed her son's door, shortly after nine, and saw that his light was out, she went to bed. A half-hour later she took her pills and was soon dreaming that she was with Leo and Mike as they drifted down the river in an elegant white sail boat. Though she hugged Mike from time to time, Leo didn't mind.

As Leo crept through the woods, doing his best not to step on twigs or scrape his shins, the whisky bottle in his string-bag slapped comfortingly against his leg. Straining his eyes in the darkness, he expected at any moment to see the mudflats shining between the trees like dirty silver. The tide was coming in, but, having studied the published table, Leo reckoned there would not be enough water in the creek to float the trawlers off until after eleven. This left him just over an hour.

Even in daytime, these woods were dim and shadowy. Hazels grew thickly between the oaks, vying to force their leaves skywards through the dense canopy. On this moonless night, the darkness seemed to press in on Leo almost like blindness as he passed beneath thick evergreen trees. At times he flicked on his torch for a few seconds, rather than lose all sense of direction – though he knew that by doing this he was not allowing his eyes to get used to the darkness.

Nearer to the creek, the soil resembled garden leaf mould and muffled his footfalls. He rubbed the dark mulch onto his legs and face as night camouflage. Wearing dark blue shorts and a matching sweater, he felt all but invisible. The creaking and sighing of the trees increased his confidence, since his steps would be hard to hear. Considering how panic-stricken he'd been during his earlier escapade with Justin, it was a welcome surprise, on this occasion, to feel calmer.

The woods thinned out near the head of the creek where the ground sloped steeply to a narrow stream. Leo slid down on his bottom and then waded across, placing his feet gingerly. The sound of the flowing water made him want to pee, which he paused to do, before emptying the stream water out of his sandals. The creek itself lay ahead of him across an open tract of moss and reeds. Judging by the vegetation, the tide never reached this level, so he still had no idea how much water would be under the boats by the time he reached them. Retreating to the treeline, he moved along, parallel with the creek.

When he first caught sight of the trawlers, they looked small and insignificant, dwarfed on both sides of the water by tall

black trees. His heart began to race. Would he really have the
courage to go through with it? He sat for a moment on a
fallen tree and drank some watered down whisky from his
bottle. He felt a shiver of pride, recalling how brilliantly he
had acted with his mother. She wouldn't have imagined in a
million years that he'd been planning something. Nor would
she have had the faintest clue that he had found her rubber
thing. Unless his nerve failed, everything would be different
in future.

From Leo's present viewpoint, he could not tell whether or
not either ship was joined to the bank by a gangplank. But
seeing a lamplit tent, he guessed they must be. With the tide
already halfway up the timber props, the sailors under canvas
could hardly be expected to wade through mud and water to
get aboard. As Leo crept towards the creek, an unexpected gust
of wind dabbed his cheek. Away from the trees, the darkness
seemed to pale a little. He lowered himself to the ground and
crawled through the grass. From the bank itself, he could see
water glinting in the central channel. A powerful smell of mud
and seaweed filled his nostrils, laced with a faint savour of
fresh paint.

After one more swallow of whisky, he abandoned the bottle.
After ensuring that his empty pickle jar could not knock against
his water flask, he thrust several damp rags into his pockets.
Then, grasping a long snaky root, he let himself slip below
the level of the bank. His cautious and distressingly squelchy
progress along the foreshore had begun.

CHAPTER 19

When Mike had been an undergraduate, he had sometimes discussed ideas such as whether reality was experienced in consciousness or in things, and then had tried to work out how, in either case, he could live his life with the greatest intensity. Or was real vividness and edge only possible in art? A decade later, looking out for enemy aircraft over the Channel, he knew that the most intense experiences available to any man were not chosen or sought out, but were flung at him.

Entering the cramped wheelhouse from the bridge, Mike grinned at Pierre Norbert, his Breton coxswain. The Frenchman always wore a dirty old guernsey which he swore had given him the luck to survive as long as he had. The spokes of the wheel had worn a large hole in the wool where his paunch touched it, but this, he said, only gave the garment greater *efficacité*. Standing beside Norbert was Martin Cleeves, a young sub-lieutenant, who made no secret of his admiration for Mike. Prematurely balding, gentle, serious-minded, Cleeves was also athletic and had been a keen yachtsman before joining the Royal Naval Volunteer Reserve. As a first lieutenant, he was not a patch on Tony Cassilis, who had never been an admirer of anyone. But since every commander was compelled to act a part, Martin's high expectations of him did not dismay Mike. They might even drag from him a bravura impersonation of

247

relaxed self-control. He'd heard it said that a man draws his own portrait through his actions. But this was wrong. In life most men tried to resemble the person they wanted to be, rather than the one they actually were.

Mike took up his binoculars again and swept the horizon. The clouds were breaking up. Already visibility was disconcertingly good. The wind was also dropping and Mike feared that, further inshore, they might experience the peculiar kind of calm that made even a muffled exhaust echo for miles. Smooth water would also mean phosphorescence. Yet, regardless of such facts, even the meek Martin Cleeves was trying hard not to show excitement. Mike was excited, too – as a gambler might be excited, imagining a winning streak. How magnificent if, against all odds, he could bring everyone home alive.

The rendezvous would not be Beguen Island, where the Germans had found Tony's boat, but a place about ten miles to the east. Not that today's chosen beach would be risk-free, since it was overlooked, at a distance, by a German gun emplacement. According to Naval Intelligence, the Germans would not expect the English to be such fools as to land under their noses. Instead their patrols would be scouring coves where there were no fixed defences. And this was what Mike tried to believe, as *Luciole* and her sister ship, *Volonté*, sighted the village near Pointe de Beniguet.

Soon after four in the morning, Mike raised his binoculars, and, from three thousand yards, peered at the grey-black houses behind the harbour wall before examining the dunes that stretched for a mile and a half, almost to the blockhouse on the headland's tip. He gave the order for navigation lights to be lit in the manner of local fishing boats, and supervised the raising of sails. With their engines shut down, the two trawlers moved silently across the bay in a moderate offshore breeze. With petrol severely rationed in France, local fishing vessels used their sails more often than their engines. Mike liked to look authentic, though the lack of speed worried him.

As the rust-red lugsails filled, Mike sent his starboard look-out, Able Seaman Peters, aft with orders to the men by the gallows to drop a couple of weighted drogues to simulate nets being towed. As usual Peters struggled not to salute him. Though dressed as fishermen, he and the other three-badge ABs could not shake off their habitual deference to officers.

Luciole's crew swung out the dory, ready for launching, and Mike watched the same preparations being made on *Volonté*. His second trawler was commanded by a recent arrival at Polwherne, Lieutenant Philip Evenshaw. Perpetually smiling as Evenshaw was, and too manically energetic ever to make a relaxing companion, Mike wished that Tony Cassilis was out there in Evenshaw's place. He said a silent prayer that Tony was waiting in the dunes at this moment along with all the airmen.

As they sailed sedately across the bay, Mike tried not to imagine starshell erupting from the blockhouse, illuminating every winch, spar and barrel. The beach at low tide stretched in front of the dunes for at least two hundred yards, and men crossing it would be visible against the pale sand, even if no lights were fired by the enemy.

Mike planned to anchor at the habour end of the dunes, keeping as far as possible from the blockhouse, preferring to increase the risk of being observed from the village. A moment later he regretted his decision. A match flared on the harbour wall and faded, as if cupped in someone's palms. Was he a sentry? They couldn't be that unlucky. But who else would be lighting a cigarette at four in the morning? A married man creeping home after meeting his mistress? Knowing he could do nothing, Mike forced himself to guess what the darkened shops might be: *Epicerie, Bar Tabac, Boulangerie*.

As the boats were made ready for lowering, Able Seaman Peters came panting up the bridge ladder in a distressed state.

'A stowaway,' he gasped. 'I just found him.'

Mike stormed into the wheelhouse and faced Martin Cleeves. 'You reported the ship ready to sail, Number One.'

'Yes, sir.'

'She wasn't bloody well ready. There's a bloody stranger on board.'

'But I searched the ship with Chief Petty Officer Simms. I can't understand it.' Cleeves cast his eyes around, as if they might miraculously alight upon some clue explaining the mystery.

Mike's fists were clenched and he was breathing fast. He pulled Able Seaman Peters in through the door. 'Tell Mr Cleeves where he was hiding.'

'Under them new bunks across the stern, sir.'

'Why the hell wasn't he spotted?'

Cleeves took a step forward. 'B-b-because it's used as a glory hole. The ratings stuff all their spare clothes and kit bags in there.' He retreated again behind Norbert's bulk. 'I've seen boxes of tinned food there, life jackets, even some . . .'

Mike silenced him with a wave before turning back to Peters. 'I trust you placed him in custody?'

'Locked in the fish-hold, sir.'

'How old would you say he is?' murmured Mike, already knowing.

'Just a young lad, sir. Scared silly, I'd say.'

Wanting to sink to his knees and moan aloud, Mike was saved by the sound of an aircraft. Only one 'young lad' in Cornwall would have known where *Luciole* was likely to be on the day before sailing. As the aircraft roar grew louder, Mike tilted his binoculars skywards.

A Heinkel 111 was passing half a mile to seaward, looking very black and angular against the paler sky. Flying high and straight, it showed no interest in them – though since trawlers were meant to fish in a single fleet at night, it was possible they might be reported. Moments ago, this plane's appearance would have depressed Mike dreadfully, now it merely added to the sense of doom oppressing him. Yet he was a little comforted to reflect that the whole operation had been planned in such exhaustive detail that, even if he fell overboard and sank without a trace, everything would go ahead quite satisfactorily without him.

He said quietly to Cleeves, 'I want to drop our hook in three cables on this course. Buck up, Martin, and forget the bloody stowaway.'

After watching *Luciole*'s two boats being rowed away towards the beach, where they caught up with the two from *Volonté*, Mike hurried across the raised deck between the engine room and the fo'c'sle. 'Forgetting the stowaway' was not an option open to *him*. He lifted a tarpaulin stretched over some hatches and found the handles. The fish-hold proper no longer existed, having been divided into an Asdic cabinet, two cabins for petty officers, and a magazine for the ship's concealed Lewis guns and .5 Colts. Mike lifted the hatch-cover and felt for the ladder with his feet.

With amazing insensitivity, Peters had locked the boy in with the ammunition, not that Mike really blamed him. He had other reasons for shaking with anger as he released the bolt.

'Pleased with yourself?' he demanded, surprised by the calm sound of his own voice. Leo stared back with a mixture of pride and terror, as Mike had guessed he would. He bent closer, the better to see him in the dim light. 'We've just been spotted by a Heinkel. D'you know what that means?'

'I don't care.'

'Your mother's life'll be wrecked if you're killed.'

'I care heaps more about my father.'

'He'll be thrilled, will he, if you vanish into thin air?'

'I posted him a letter.'

'Perhaps he'll frame it, if you're blown to bits.'

'You can't leave me in here with this stuff.' Leo glanced anxiously at the ammunition boxes.

251

'I can do any bloody thing I like.' Mike placed a hand on the door.

'Please.' Leo's eyes were wide with fear. Over his head was a stanchion that took the weight of the deck, and the steel plates reinforcing it. A single red bulb hung from a flex twisted round a ventilation pipe. Even in the half-light, the boy's resemblance to his mother tormented Mike: the almost feminine shape of his eyes and lips, his soft pale skin. If anything happened to him, Andrea would blame herself forever – and blame me, too, he thought. The extraordinary callousness of the boy's stunt made Mike catch his breath.

'Why did you do this?' he whispered thickly.

'You know why.'

'I *don't know why*,' shouted Mike, starting to close the door.

Leo blurted out, 'To stop you doing it to her, of course.'

'It? *It*!' snapped Mike. 'I love her, you dirty-minded little beast.'

'My dad loves her more.'

'You really think so?' Mike smiled, though he wanted to scream.

'Why else would I be here?' shouted the boy, as if the words had been ripped from him.

Mike said nothing. Leo's sincerity had sneaked under his defences. So it *hadn't* been revenge on his mother. He'd done it for his father; risked his life for him. Poor brave little bugger. Mike placed a hand on his shoulder.

'I'll take you back to where you were, if you promise not to move from there.' Leo nodded assent. 'There are life jackets under those bunks, so put one on, please.' He pushed Leo towards the ladder. 'Go up and I'll follow. Do you need to visit the heads?'

'I brought a jar for that.'

Mike could not help grinning for a moment. 'What else did you bring?'

'Water, and some rags to wipe away my muddy footprints.'

'Very considerate.'

'It was so you wouldn't see them.'

'I did realise that.' They paused outside the galley, before descending again. Mike said quietly, 'You won't be the first boy we've brought back.' He had wanted to reassure him, but Leo was clearly crestfallen.

'I *must* be the first.'

'We brought back a French agent with his whole family, including his *petit fils* and *petites filles*.' Mike grinned at him. 'Sorry, old chap. Better get below.'

Back on the bridge again, Mike could see the four boats pulled up on the beach, and, through his binoculars, the tracks of the crewmen who had gone in search of the escapers. Just one alert sentry in that German blockhouse and they could all be blown apart within minutes in a blaze of pyrotechnics to shame Brock's display after Henley Regatta. And poor Andrea would be sleeping peacefully all the while, her hair spread across her pillow like a golden fan. Even on waking she would be unaware of anything amiss. Very likely she would only know that her life had changed forever, when Peter 'phoned with news of Leo's letter.

The sands were still empty – so what the hell was taking the wretched airmen so long to emerge? And where were Tony and the ratings who'd been in the dory with him? Somewhere behind the dunes, a dog was barking. Surely the whole party must be closer than that by now? If only he could risk signalling with an Aldis lamp. The aimless splashings and lappings of the sea against the hull, when *Luciole* was at anchor, always reminded Mike of how long it would take, from the moment when he gave the order to ring on the engines, before she could reach her top speed.

He stared at the beach and willed a line of hurrying men to appear. For them a moment of wild emotion, the end of their long ordeal in sight, but the worst dangers only yards ahead. Very likely, they had aroused suspicion locally – incongruous figures, creeping down country lanes and over fields. So when they left the dunes, and went on without one scrap of cover, a searchlight could pick them out like a spot in the theatre. German inactivity, as every one of them must know, could indicate a waiting game, with the deadliest hand held back till last. How hard it must be for those who'd almost escaped before, or, like Tony, should never have been there at all. Wives were waiting; children, parents, lovers, friends, an invisible company many times larger than the number soon to cross the sands. And how much did Mike care about them, now that Leo was here?

A fragment of Euripides ran through his mind: 'Love does not vex the man who begs his bread.' But it certainly vexed the man who might be held responsible for the death of his mistress's child. Had love ever survived such a thing? The wages of sin, he thought, remembering his conversation with Andrea. If he came back alive, bringing the boy's dead body – what then? Suicide in the Roman manner? Maybe Peter ought to kill him instead – better tragic irony – slain by the man with no time for Greek theatricals. A smile still lingered on Mike's lips as the first airman ran onto the beach.

The ragged figure stopped in its tracks, and almost overbalanced; then he saw the boats and started running again. Others stumbled after him, like faltering runners in a marathon, almost too exhausted to breast the tape. Next came a slower group with a woman in it. And, after an interval, two men half-lifting, half-dragging a third. One of these supporting figures resembled Tony in height and build, but Mike could not be sure it was him. No longer aware of his own problems, Mike wanted to cheer. He swung his glasses round to study the blockhouse and was shocked to see a square of yellow light. A casemate had been opened and a man was outlined in the aperture.

Scarcely able to breathe, Mike waited. He was determined to do nothing until absolutely sure they had been seen. Almost a minute passed, and then, from the black headland, a dazzling white flare shot skywards followed by others. On the beach, the tiny figures clambering into the boats were lit as clearly as in sunlight.

'Ring on both engines,' Mike roared into the wheelhouse. 'We'll weigh anchor before the boats reach us, so get some way on by then. All right, Martin?'

'Straight at 'em till we turn,' confirmed Cleeves.

Cleeves pressed the buzzer for action stations, and men began snatching up steel helmets and running to their places. As Peters pulled off the oildrum lid concealing one of the twin stripped Lewis guns, the counterweighted barrels sprang up into the firing position. Mike watched sadly. Firing against 88-mm cannon behind concrete defences was a waste of time and ammunition.

'Out scramble nets,' he shouted, as he ran aft, with a helmet in one hand and a megaphone in the other.

CPO Simms was craning over the stern, waiting for the boats. 'Don't even try to hoist them in,' Mike told him, before going below.

'Leo,' he called softly. The boy came out slowly from under the bunks.

'Will they get us?'

'I hope not.' The boy's lips were stretched tight and his whole body shook. The portholes flickered as more flares went up. 'Just stay here, okay?' Mike held out the helmet. 'Stick this on your nut and lie flat. If you smell smoke, or she starts to list, come up at once. I won't forget you.'

On deck, Mike was relieved to see that all the boats had left the beach. Why was it taking the Germans so long to use their guns? They couldn't have failed to see the men on the sands and grasp what was happening. As more starshells were flung up into the sky, the dying ones spiralled seawards, leaving long trails of smoke.

The blockhouse opened fire on *Volonté* first, with two

pounder shells mostly, and lighter stuff, judging by the absence of large water spouts, and by the way the sea looked pitted, as if someone had shaken a sieve of gravel over it. It overjoyed him to think that the larger guns were probably fixed in a wide arc seawards, unable to swivel back to bear on the beach. The first shots aimed at *Luciole* burst astern of her and about six metres above the water.

'Faster,' Mike shouted to the rowers, who were already slowing. The thought of shells ripping through *Luciole*'s flimsy hull made his stomach plunge. The half-inch steel plates fitted inside her bulwarks at the bow and stern would offer some protection against cannon-shell splinters but none to anything larger. He thought of the Germans, safe behind their steel gun-shields, and felt sick with envy.

In the wheelhouse he opened the medical chest with his navigating officer, Tom Bruce. After handing him a morphia syringe, he placed a couple in his own pockets, meaning to give one to Simms, who had served in the sick bay of a corvette. What a luxury it would be to have a proper MO. From the bridge, he hurried down to help the rowers and their passengers clamber up the scramble nets. The oarsmen's faces shone with sweat. They and their companions were scared and very quiet. The enemy's gunners were sending streams of red and white tracer down both sides of the boat, hitting and sinking the empty dory.

Luciole was moving forwards slowly, heading straight for the battery to narrow the target she presented. From outside on the bridge, Mike heard Cleeves ring for full speed. Then Norbert spun the wheel. As the trawler settled on her new course away from the headland, her bows lifted to the thrust of her propellers. Never designed for powerful engines, *Luciole*'s timbers shook and juddered as broad curls of spray flew up from her forefoot. Behind her counter, a plume of phosphorescence gushed like a magic fountain.

The bellies of the clouds were already turning luminous when

Mike was given a list of the names of all those who had been rescued. Tony Cassilis had not been picked up by *Volonté* either. Laughter and singing was coming up through all the hatches. Mike thought of Elspeth and her club, and the many times he and Tony had gone there. He remembered Tony's fondness for one particular song from *Funny Face*. 'He dances overhead / On the ceiling near my bed . . .' 'Overhead' was the only place he would ever be able to imagine him in future.

A lookout shouted, 'Aircraft bearing Green five oh.'

Two planes were sweeping in low over the sea. The sound of *Luciole*'s engines had masked their approach. Running to the bridge, Mike collided with a sailor carrying a tray of hot tea. He arrived at the bridge ladder as Cleeves announced over the loudspeakers, 'Aircraft bearing Green six oh. Take cover. Take cover.'

The alarm bell started to ring though most of the crew were already at their stations. The aircraft were Me 109s, their distinctive fuselages spotted with brown and green camouflage paint.

Again Cleeves's breathless voice, 'Starboard Lewis gun and Colts – aircraft bearing Green eight oh, angle of sight oh five, coming left to right.' The roar as they screamed down at mast height obliterated every other sound, so that Cleeves's shout of 'Open fire!' scarcely registered as a whisper, though amplified by the speakers. But the men at the .5 Colts in the forward deck ponds, and Able Seaman Peters at the Lewis gun, had not needed to be told. They were firing wildly, swivelling their guns after the planes.

Mike's eyes followed the aircraft as they strafed *Volonté*, starting a fire near her galley that snaked across her stern. If the same thing happened to *Luciole*, Leo's quarters would be a deathtrap. Immediately beneath him, Mike saw Able Seaman Peters lying by his Lewis gun. A lump of flesh had been torn out of the seaman's neck, exposing his windpipe. Incredibly he was still conscious and seemingly in little pain. As Mike reached him, Peters tipped forward and died. In the deck ponds one of the two gunners had been hit by the storm of cannon-shell splinters that had scorched the foredeck.

The fire on *Volonté* had forced her to reduce speed to a few knots. Mike expected the German pilots to concentrate on her before dealing with *Luciole*. He didn't like to admit it, but he was relieved to have no choice. His clear duty was to leave *Volonté* to her fate, having signalled her position to the Admiralty. The worst thing to do would be to stay and lose both ships.

Hurrying into the wheelhouse, he announced, 'I'll take her now, Martin.' Through his glasses he could see the two specks approaching, this time from the port side, aiming to attack both ships on the same run.

The bridge lookout shouted, 'Aircraft bearing Red one hundred.'

With studied calm, Mike spoke into the microphone, 'Stand by on deck, stand by for manoeuvring.' Then he snapped at Norbert, 'Hard a'starb'd. Far as you dare.' The noise of the swooping planes became an obliterating howl. 'More helm, Pierre. Put on more,' cried Mike, though the ship was already heeling steeply into the turn. 'Port guns let 'em have it,' he roared into the microphone, as the gunners desperately tried to keep their feet on the sloping deck. He saw the Lewis gun's tracer spitting into the sea, and was dimly aware that the sky was spotted with black and white woolly balls.

The inner and outer casing of the wheelhouse had been filled with cement reinforcement, but this did not hinder the two cannon-shells that entered through the windows. One missed everyone; the second passed through Tom Bruce's skull, splattering the navigator's brain onto the walls and roof, before smashing its way out in a shower of steel splinters that blinded the bridge lookout and tore into Martin Cleeves's shoulder, spinning him round in a balletic whirl of arms and legs. Mike found himself on his knees seeing through a film of redness.

When his eyes cleared, he raised a hand to his head and felt warm stickiness – whether his own blood, or someone else's, he couldn't be sure. Pierre Norbert towered above him, hands still on the wheel, with his lucky guernsey pressed hard against the spokes.

Rose woke a few minutes before six, half an hour earlier than usual, but, being unable to get back to sleep again, she dressed and crept to the bathroom. She urinated, omitting to empty the cistern afterwards in case she woke her employer. After pulling up her heavily darned brown stockings, she went to the window. Outside, the day looked grey and misty with a hint of drizzle in the air. She carried her shoes as she tiptoed downstairs. In the hall, she paused and looked about.

There was no sign of Leo's bike. Funny. She could have sworn it'd been there the night before. She opened the hall door and looked out. The machine wasn't leaning against the hedge either, and it wasn't in the garden, so far as she could see. Out on the dew-wet lawn, she looked up at Leo's window. The curtains had not been drawn the night before. Though the mist was as soft as on a mild summer morning, she was shivering.

Alarmed, but curious, she crept into the house and climbed the stairs. Such a puzzling little chap. Quieter and better mannered than the one who'd left. Weirder, too. Nice to his mother one day, mean as Old Nick the next. Rose had thought him hoity-toity till she'd caught him with the whisky bottle; but, after that, he'd been nice as pie. It was odd with a young boy to feel he liked her almost as a man might.

Leo's door squeaked as she pushed it open. The bed had something in it. Even from the door, Rose was not fooled. She pulled back the blankets and saw a rolled-up counterpane and several sweaters in a pillowcase. She wasn't exactly scared on his account, but it was strange him running off, specially since he'd seemed happy the night before.

Outside, Rose looked closely at the path. If he'd left after dawn, his bike's wheels ought to have left marks on the paving stones. There was still some drizzle on them from the night. But she couldn't see a single tyre track.

When she knocked on Andrea's door, she felt suddenly unsure. The atmosphere in the house had been awful lately.

'Mrs Pauling,' she breathed softly; and, when Andrea didn't move, she squeezed her arm and called her name loudly. Andrea covered her face with her hands and groaned as if she hadn't slept for a week. That was how she looked, too, when she opened her eyes.

'What's time?' she mumbled.

'It'll be half-six directly.'

'Jesus Christ, Rose.'

'Can't help that, Mrs Pauling. Leo's not home. Been gone half the night.'

Mrs Pauling rolled over and sat up with a great effort. 'His bike?'

'Gone with 'im.'

Andrea gave a faint cry and her hands rose to her mouth, but she did not stay motionless for long. The next moment she was patting her cheeks to wake herself, and swinging her feet to the floor. Forgetting there was another person in the room, she stumbled to the chair where she had laid her clothes the night before, and in a single movement drew her nightdress over her head. Rose looked away as Andrea stood naked for a moment, before pulling on her clothes with feverish speed.

'Mrs Pauling,' Rose called out, as Andrea ran to the garage. 'Should 'ee go drivin' directly? Why don' 'ee wait a bit?'

But Andrea did not even glance at her. Instead she flung open the garage doors, as if something terrible would happen unless she could get there to stop it. She certainly drove that way, her little Standard screeching out into the lane like a crook's car in a B film.

*   *   *

When a group of airmen had come clumping down the companion ladder into the after cabin, Leo had already hidden under the bunks. The boat was under fire at the time, and, though they'd been mainly silent, occasionally they'd laughed together, a bit like boys before a beating. He'd been glad when the engines had burst into a deafening roar. Lying flat on his face, as Mike had told him to, he tried to imagine he was hiding behind the changing room lockers at school. But the chinstrap of his tin hat cut into him too painfully to give his imagination much chance.

At first when the aircraft attacked, Leo thought the tearing, wailing noise was coming from *Luciole*'s engines. Had her props been fouled, or was some vital piston seizing up? Only the brisk mutter of the ship's guns, and a series of violent lurches, persuaded him otherwise. A splintering crash near the bows was followed by a terrifying row overhead, as if the whole deck was being ploughed up. Every bone in his head was vibrating and ringing before the terrible aerial noise faded away.

Something had changed in the cabin. Leo was still in his old place, amongst the kitbags and spare life jackets, but now, because there was more light coming from somewhere, he could see into the cabin through the gaps. With one part of his mind, Leo knew what was happening – Mike had even warned him that they'd been seen by a spotter plane and could expect the worst – but he could not yet bring himself to imagine what an air attack might mean for so small a trawler. His heart began to pound so hard that his throat felt filled by its thumping. He remembered the burning cargo ship. Feeling the softness of his cheek and his slender fingers, he imagined them charred beyond recognition. Could it really happen? The freighter had been big, a sitting duck, but *Luciole* was small and weaving about at full speed.

And then the howling came back again, this time from a new direction. Seconds stretched like elastic. God, don't let me die, he begged again and again, thinking of his parents' grief. The gun on the deck above him was firing. He could hear it stuttering, until the sharper rattle of aerial cannon fire began. From the cabin came confused sounds; then screams. Somewhere outside the ship, a deep explosion shook her. He began to cry as he realised that *Luciole*'s engines were spluttering. The planes would return when she was motionless and that would be the end. What chance could they have? The ghostly silence that followed the dying tonk-tonk-tonk of the engines lasted until he heard more screams. Leo turned his face towards the cabin. Some of the gear in his line of sight had been shifted by the boat's gyrations.

He gazed in stupefaction. Bodies were strewn about the cabin. A jagged hole in the roof admitted a bright shaft of sunlight. Someone was trying to help the men, but they lay very still, like members of a collapsed rugger scrum before the referee blew his whistle. A pool of red liquid was leaking from under them and trickling a little closer to Leo with every roll of the ship. His stomach tightened to a fist, squeezing vomit into his mouth.

A sailor, bending over the tangle of limbs, managed to lift one of the men into a sitting position. This airman's nearest arm was attached to his shoulder by a few string-like sinews. A dazzling white bone stuck out from his sleeve. His lower arm was a bloody pulp. Something resembling a length of laboratory tubing had escaped from the clothing of one of the other men.

As Leo gazed uncomprehending at this man's intestines, he heard Mike call his name despairingly.

'I'm here,' gasped Leo, finding his mouth and tongue too stiff to function properly.

'Thank God you're okay.'

Mike knelt down beside the sailor who was trying to help the only surviving airman. Together they lifted him, and, after Mike had given him an injection, they knotted something round the top of his mangled limb. The wounded man went on crying out until Mike had used his syringe again. Then, having covered him with blankets, Mike beckoned to Leo.

'Follow me.'

As Leo obeyed he could not resist his desire to clutch Mike's hand for comfort. He was shivering with shock and longed to run away from what he'd seen. Though Mike appeared to be unhurt, his neck and hair were streaked with dry blood.

They emerged on deck in time to see a dory approaching very slowly, rowed by two bedraggled men. Several others were lying on her bottomboards. The top of the sun had risen above the horizon and Leo could see the people clearly.

'Who are they?' he whispered to Mike.

'Survivors from *Volonté*. They'd have sunk us, too, if we hadn't brought down one of the 109s.'

From the engine-room hatch, an oil-smeared head emerged, followed by a pair of broad shoulders.

'How goes it, Chief?'

'We've plugged the oil tank and are working on the manifold exhaust.'

'Is it still leaking over the distributor?'

'Not any more, sir. We should be able to supply fuel to the port engine with a hand pump.'

'Can we make fifteen knots?'

'Ten if we're lucky, sir.'

'How long till we can start up, Chief?'

'Twenty minutes.'

Mike raised his binoculars to the cloudless sky. The early morning light was a bluey-orange colour. To the west the sea was still dark.

'Will we be attacked again?' quavered Leo, wanting to cry. Memories of the attack and of the dead bodies increased his fear of seeing, at any moment, dark dots moving towards them. 'Please tell me,' he begged.

Mike placed a hand on his shoulder. 'I'm quite hopeful.'

When the dory was below the davits, Leo looked down and

saw a youngish woman in the stern. Her bandaged head was lolling against the shoulder of an airman. Her skin looked pale and lifeless. The airman stood up and lifted her very gently. Mike and two sailors got down onto the scramble nets to bring her aboard.

The airman maintained an unhappy silence as the woman was placed on the deck. Her underwear was visible through her soaking dress. All Leo noticed was her freckled face and the shallowness of her breathing. She looked slightly younger than his mother.

Mike faced the airman. 'What's wrong with her?'

'Shrapnel in her head.'

'Know who she is?'

'Mary Colwell. She's an agent, so it may be a cover name.'

After the woman had been carried below, Mike took Leo to the bridge, where he heard the engines burst into life. His relief lasted until he saw a black speck closing fast. Too shocked to utter, he raised a finger. Mike ignored him, as he rested both elbows on the rail to steady his binoculars. At last he lowered them and rumpled Leo's hair.

'Panic over. It's a Hurricane.' He thrust the binoculars at Leo. 'Our air escort. You'll see the other one shortly.'

'Friendly aircraft bearing Red three oh!' cried an officer with a heavily strapped arm, coming out of the wheelhouse.

'Thanks, Number One.'

Tears spilled down Leo's cheeks and he sobbed aloud. Why did he feel worse now they were safe? Staring at the deck to avoid looking at Mike, his eye fell on a bloodstained tarpaulin covering a body. An icy tingle went down his spine. In the wheelhouse, only yards away from this dead man, Mike and the fat Frenchman were chatting to the man with the strapped arm about their likely arrival time in Falmouth. A sailor in fisherman's clothing brought up cups of tea and handed them round.

'Condensed milk, I'm afraid,' Mike warned Leo. 'Want a drop of this?' He held up a rum bottle.

'Yes, please.' Mike splashed some into Leo's mug. 'A bit more, please.'

Mike gave him a second tot and then told the Frenchman something before going below. Deep folds of water were creaming away from the ship's bows as the engines throbbed reassuringly. The shadows of the circling aircraft moved across the waves, crossing and recrossing one another's paths. Leo rested his head on the rail and said a prayer for the wounded girl. But he had little confidence in his plea being answered. She was probably dead by now. He himself would certainly have died with the airmen, if Mike hadn't told him to get under the bunks.

Remembering what he had hoped to achieve by stealing on board a dozen hours ago, Leo felt the biggest fool alive. He had thought that if Mike found him on the trawler on the way to France, he would be shocked enough to end his affair. But now, he saw no reason why Mike should give a damn about anything except pleasing himself. If I had to go to France as many times as him, and I saw people die around me like he did, I'd come back to England and swear in the street at anyone who annoyed me, and I'd certainly go with any woman I wanted.

When the English coast appeared like a colourless smudge on the horizon, Leo felt as if every hope and feeling had drained out of him.

After the frenzy of the docks, with tugs hooting, engines shunting and men with bright welding torches working high on ships' sides, Leo found it unreal to be passing through peaceful countryside again. Cows grazed or lay under trees. People stopped to chat in village streets and walked into shops as if nothing had happened in the night. Seated beside Mike, on the back seat of the car, Leo gazed out with a fixed frown. They were being driven by a rating whose white-topped hat dazzled Leo as the sun caught it. He closed his eyes and thought of the chaotic scenes he had witnessed at the dockside on *Luciole*'s arrival. Ambulances, nurses and sailors galore: a mass of people, some of them cheering. Not that he'd had time to see much of this. Mike had rushed him away and locked him in a hut for almost two hours before returning for him.

What Mike would say to mum when they reached Trevean Barton, Leo didn't try to guess. He still felt fuddled after the rum. Mike would have telephoned her, so she must be out of her suspense by now. Leo tried to see Mike as a stranger might. He'd changed his clothes, and, in a clean white polo neck sweater, he might almost be a school gym instructor or tennis pro. But inside he must be crumbling and falling apart.

Mike's breath smelled of brandy, but his hair was brushed, and he'd even found time to shave. A few hours ago he'd been telling sailors what to do, and sticking needles into dying people. Now he was probably reckoning up the number of men who'd be alive today if he'd never showed up in France. Imagine feeling a failure after a night like that! The unfairness of it hit Leo hard. What Gold Star holiday could possibly be nice enough to reward someone like Mike? There couldn't be a treat that was half good enough. No strawberries and cream, no chocolate cake, no orchestra stalls for a favourite show, no cups or prizes – nothing would be any use at all. Leo thought of the happy, easy way Mike and mum had played tennis together, before he'd wrecked it for her by upsetting Justin. It came to him that mum had been Mike's Gold Star holiday.

CHAPTER 20

Andrea had been expecting their arrival ever since Mike had called, and had decided not to show the full extent of her joy and thankfulness until she could be alone with her son and with her lover in turn. But when she saw Leo coming up the path, with Mike walking just behind, Andrea was overwhelmed by emotion and ran to her son to hug him. As if experiencing all over again her grief on hearing that Leo was not in the house, tears filled her eyes and she could not speak. Almost immediately, Leo became tense in her arms, detaching himself as soon as he felt he could.

'I'm fine, mother,' he muttered, in a breathless undertone.

'It's so wonderful to see you, darling.' She dabbed at her eyes. 'When Rose told me you weren't in your bed, I was out of my mind with worry.'

'I'm sorry,' said Leo, standing stiff-faced and awkward.

'Why on earth did you do it, sweetheart? You *knew* how dangerous it would be.'

Leo did not answer. Conscious that Mike was standing just behind him, he moved away from his mother and went into the house.

'He knows about us, Andrea,' murmured Mike, as he followed her into the hall.

'Since when?' she gasped.

267

'Probably before I lied to him.' Andrea felt suddenly isolated, as if the two of them had long understood something she had only just grasped. She walked into the sitting room and saw Leo ahead of her, staring out of the window. Wanting to hug him and whisper reassuring words, she kept her distance, in case he rounded on her in front of her lover.

Mike said matter of factly to Leo, 'I'd like to talk to your mother for a few minutes. That all right with you?'

The boy nodded and left the room without speaking. As soon as Andrea heard her son's footsteps on the stairs, she flung herself into Mike's arms.

'Thank God you're alive,' she gasped, struggling with tears. 'Poor Mike, how awful to find him like that. I'm so happy you're both safe.'

'We damned nearly bought it.'

Mike's unhappy expression shocked Andrea as he sank down beside her on the sofa. In his pristine white sweater he called to mind some chaste and suffering knight from Malory's *Morte d'Arthur*. She put her face to his and murmured, 'I'm so terribly sorry he did this to you, darling.'

He took one of her hands in his and looked at her with disconcerting directness. 'Leo didn't stow away to get me in trouble, or hurt you, Andrea.' He closed his eyes for a moment as if overwhelmed by tiredness. Then he stared right into her eyes. 'He risked his life to stop us going on together. I really mean that.'

'You're wrong.' Her voice trembled despite her efforts to be calm. This *couldn't* mean the end of their affair. She wouldn't let it. 'He did it to wound me,' she cried. 'Remember how spiteful he was to Justin.'

Mike shook his head slowly. 'He risked his life to show how much he cared.'

'Cared for what?'

'For his father. For you two staying married.' Mike's resignation made Andrea's stomach lurch. Stay calm; stop him saying things he may find hard to retract.

268

'Do I have this right?' she asked with a brave smile. 'Leo will go on till he gets himself killed, unless I stop seeing you?'

'That's *not* my suggestion. Obviously he didn't mean to get killed, only to make sure we end it. He won't give up till we do.'

'He returns to school Friday. What can he do then?'

Mike looked at her with desperate sympathy. 'You expect him to stay there meekly for a whole term – a boy who's been under fire and seen men die?'

Andrea could feel control spinning away from her. Her face paled. 'Jesus Christ, Mike. He saw people die! I didn't know *that*!'

'I couldn't tell you on the 'phone.'

'Will he be scarred for life?'

'I doubt it. Look at the way kids have coped with the bombing.'

Filled with gratitude, she would have kissed his haggard face, if his manner hadn't made her hold back. 'I couldn't have borne it if you'd died,' she whispered.

He kissed her quickly and then got up. 'I'm afraid Leo posted a letter to his father the day before yesterday. He'll be on a train by now.'

'Don't look like that, Mike. You can't give in to him.' She left the sofa and rested her head against her lover's shoulder as he stood by the table. 'Darling,' she began confidently, 'we were going to tell Peter anyway. That's what *you* said you wanted. So what's changed?'

'I don't know,' he sighed, touching her hair. 'Maybe nothing. I'm too whacked to think straight.'

'But you *do* think *something's* changed.' She heard the fear in her voice and was appalled by it.

'I have to sleep a few hours. I've so much on my mind and can't seem able to . . .' He held his head in his hands.

'Darling, of course you must sleep. You *mustn't* think now.

269

Please don't. You'll wake up feeling quite different. I know you will.'

'Let's see what happens when Peter and Leo have talked,' he remarked almost to himself.

'We'll listen. Of course we will,' she replied, shaken by his tone. 'But, Mike, we don't have to do what they want.'

'That's true.'

'You don't sound sure.' At last her self-command was deserting her. 'It's not fair to hide what you're really thinking. It's wrong to lie to me.'

He turned away with a long sigh. 'I'm really thinking I've a report to write, and letters to bereaved relatives. And thanks to Leo, I'm wondering how to avoid an inquiry.' Exhausted and restrained, his voice seemed to scream 'don't press me'. But her anxiety was like a fever, banishing common sense; making her uncertainty seem unbearable. She *had* to know his thoughts, however exhausted he was.

'Is this the end for us?' she demanded, appalled that these dangerous words had left her lips.

'I can't go on with this now,' he snapped, losing patience at last.

'Darling,' she insisted, 'it'll be too late to discuss things after Peter joins forces with Leo. They'll tear us apart unless we have a plan.'

'For God's sake, Andrea. They'll be more confused than we are.'

He's right, she thought, amazed to be convinced. 'Peter's a realist,' she laughed. 'He may even accept that our marriage is over. What else can he do?' Her words seemed to fall between them, never reaching him.

Mike walked slowly to the door. 'I really have to sleep, Andrea. I'll 'phone you around eight.'

When he had driven away, Andrea stood on the path without moving. Through her tears, she saw the blood-red spears of peonies thrusting through the soil. How long had they been there, unnoticed by her? The apple blossom and the birdsong battered her senses as if she had been deaf and blind for days. She felt as though she were falling down a deep well.

Leo was sitting with Rose in the kitchen wondering how he could convince her he had been to France. But, so far, nothing he'd said had impressed her. And no report would appear in the papers to back him up. If he could have brought back wine, like Mike had that time, *that* would have made her sit up. Only there was no hope of getting a bottle from somewhere and pretending he'd brought it back with him. It was pretty hard to have nobody to boast to. A little admiration might have helped him forget some of the blood and guts.

At least, chatting to Rose, he was briefly able to stop worrying about how awful it would be when his father turned up – and dad certainly would turn up if he'd read the letter. He would be sure to beg mum to stop seeing Mike, and she would definitely refuse, making poor dad feel even worse. But the thought that made Leo cry in front of Rose wasn't to do with his father but was about the dying girl on the trawler. And then he found he couldn't stop.

'No call for that,' Rose told him, coming to sit beside him at the kitchen table. 'I don't hold with boys being that miserable.' And before he could get away, she was hugging him as if she was his mother; and though he knew that if anyone saw him like this, he would want the ground to open, he made no effort to push her off. And soon his sobs became shallower and less frequent, as if he was a child who'd been soothed after grazing a knee. Only with Rose he felt something else too: an extra nice sensation. He was savouring this feeling as a car drew up in the lane.

Leo left the kitchen, and from the scullery door, saw his father paying the taxi driver. He looked so crumpled and unhappy that Leo wanted to ask his forgiveness for telling him about mum. But when Peter limped into the sitting room and sank into an armchair, he said nothing.

271

His father muttered gruffly, 'Run along and get me a glass of water.'

Leo returned with a dripping tumbler which his father drained in a few gulps. As always in sunny weather, Peter looked hot and slightly bad tempered. Last week, in the papers, Leo had read a story about an army captain who had come home, and, finding his wife with another man, had shot them both. How scary it would be to have a dad who really might shoot someone dead. Peter produced a handkerchief from his pocket and mopped his forehead.

'It's good to see you in one piece. The best sight in the world. But what a damned silly thing to do.'

'I know, dad.'

'Pull up that chair.' Peter waited till Leo was sitting opposite. 'What's it all about? What did you see mum actually *doing*?'

'She'll admit if you ask her.'

'Answer my question.' His father's irritation shook Leo.

'Justin saw them kiss.'

'Is *that* your evidence?' Peter sounded stunned. 'For God's sake, boy, it could have been a peck on the cheek. Or Justin could have made it up.'

Leo blushed deeply. 'She's been using her pessary thing.'

Peter's lips tightened in distaste. 'You can't know that, Leo.'

'One day it was in the box, the next it wasn't.'

'There may be some perfectly innocent reason. And how come you were rooting about in her room in the first place?'

Upset at being doubted, Leo said fiercely, 'She took Justin's bike at night.'

'You saw her take it?'

'The saddle had been raised.'

'How do you know?'

'It was the bike Justin used.'

'So Justin noticed it, not you?'

'Yes,' cried Leo, squirming when he saw his father's sad and knowing smile.

272

Peter reached out a hand, which Leo did not take. 'I'm touched by your concern, really I am, but it wasn't your place to take things into your own hands without talking to me first. Even supposing you're right about mum and Harrington, how do you know you haven't made things worse by forcing a crisis? Mum'll be back in Oxford by the end of next week and Harrington won't be able to get away from here. It's often best to leave well alone.'

Leo felt tears pricking. 'I couldn't have let you go on not knowing.'

Peter said sharply, 'Just telling me would have been fine. You didn't have to gate-crash a secret mission, too, endangering your own life and maybe other people's. Whatever you think of Harrington personally, his work matters.'

'I only tried to help you,' gasped Leo, suddenly remembering what he should have told his father to start with. '*Mike told me*,' he cried eagerly. 'We were on the boat, and he said he loved mum.'

Peter let out a long low breath. 'What else did he say?'

'That you can't love mum like he does.'

His father covered his face with his hands and Leo looked away. He heard him sniffling and then blowing his nose loudly.

'Was Harrington unkind to you?'

'He was too busy. We were attacked by Messerschmitts, dad, and he had to give all the orders, and even had to stick injections into wounded men. And when our engines were hit, he decided what to do.'

Peter tried to smile. 'He didn't fix them, too, by any chance?'

Leo shook his head, not realising his father had been attempting a mild joke. 'The chief engineer did that.' His father's silence worried Leo. Perhaps he'd sounded too admiring.

At last, Peter remarked dryly, 'It's ironic really, but you've probably saved his life, in the long term.'

'Ha, ha, dad.'

'I'm serious. Because you made mincemeat of his security procedures, he'll be moved to other duties. A safe job on a destroyer. Something like that.'

'He'll get the sack?' Leo was appalled. He had wanted to give Mike a shock and make him stop seeing mum, but not lose his job.

'Secret operations can't be compromised, Leo. Anyway, he won't be too sorry to have a chance of surviving the war.'

Leo was taken aback by his father's bitterness. 'Isn't that good, dad?'

'I imagine your mother will think so.'

'I've made a total hash, is that it?' Leo's voice rose to a squeak. He was close to tears.

'I'm afraid *hash* is no word for it.' Leo had never seen his father look more downhearted. 'What you've done is put mum in a position where she'll have to choose between him and me. Do you fancy my chances?'

Leo was silent for a while. 'I could refuse to live with her if she chooses him.'

'Sweet of you. But no good, I'm afraid. Even if you make her feel guilty enough to stay with me for a time, it won't last.'

They both stared at the window as they heard the sound of an approaching car. The expression of anguish on his father's face was too much for Leo. 'Don't worry, dad. I really think she'll choose you in the end.'

'I wouldn't choose me,' muttered Peter, searching his pockets for a comb. When Leo knew what he was looking for, he ran upstairs to fetch his own. Peter was using it as Andrea entered the room.

'Peter! I thought you'd be on a later train.' She sounded shocked and painfully nervous. 'I haven't had time to think – to decide what to do.'

Peter sat up very straight on the sofa. 'Do you love him?'

'Yes, I do.'

Peter sagged. Leo wondered how his father could have

endured asking that question. Now that mum had given her answer, nothing could ever be how it had been. Perhaps dad was thinking this, too, because he looked terrible.

When Andrea said gently, 'You needn't stay, Leo sweetheart,' he realised that he must have been staring at his father in a grief-stricken sort of way.

'It's up to you, old chap,' said Peter.

'I'll stay,' he mumbled, and then started crying, though he hadn't known he would, even a moment earlier. He wanted to hug his mother and beg her to stay with them, but his father's calmness stopped him. Looking at his mother, with her hair loose on her shoulders, Leo knew she was beautiful. He hadn't always known it, but he could see it very clearly today. She was wearing her dress with the pattern of splotchy flowers that he had used to think was too low round the neck, but which was really just right.

'What do you want to do?' Peter asked Andrea, as if inquiring about her plans for the evening.

'I may not want what Mike wants.'

Peter said sharply, 'I asked what *you* want.'

'I'd prefer we talk later,' she replied, avoiding Peter's eyes.

'You should tell him right now,' Leo burst out, sensing her weakness.

'Why, darling?'

'Because we don't want to wait. Because it's cruel to make us.'

'I didn't want to say things till I knew they'd happen for sure. And I can't be certain till Mike and I talk some more. But I *can* tell you what *may* happen next. I guess I'd like to teach in Oxford weekdays and be with Mike weekends, if he can see me. I'd like you to be with me weekdays in your holidays, Leo, and with dad weekends.'

Leo looked at her in amazement. 'Where does dad go? Doesn't he come home now?'

'He's away a whole lot already, darling.'

'If dad can't come home, I won't either.'

'Mum's right about me being away lots,' said Peter in a level reasonable voice.

The sight of his father pretending everything was fine, when it wasn't, was too much for Leo. 'Don't give in, dad,' he gasped. 'You should fight for her.'

'Duels aren't legal these days, old chap.'

'They blooming should be,' shouted Leo, suddenly beside himself. Why couldn't his father refuse to do what mum wanted? Why wouldn't he tell her how miserable she was making him? Otherwise, how would she know?

'You're disgusting,' he shouted at his mother. 'I don't know why he cares.'

'Please, Leo,' pleaded Peter. 'It won't help me.'

'I don't want to see you, ever,' cried Leo, pointing a finger at his mother, like a witch doctor.

Before he reached the door, he could see he had upset her. Her mouth was open and her lips had gone floppy. She looked ugly, the way people did when they were about to cry but the sound hadn't come out yet.

Outside the door, Leo cannoned into Rose, whose ear had been applied to the keyhole. She caught him by the arm. 'You listen now, Master Leo. Do 'ee wan' to live with her? Because, after what 'ee said, she won' think so. She'll think 'ee won' mind if she lives with who she wants. You should caterwaul and cling if you wan' to keep her home with you and your dad.'

So, when his mother came to his room, Leo clutched at her legs and begged her to stay. He didn't look up, so wasn't sure if he'd impressed her. But when she'd gone out, he discovered some dark marks, a bit like tear drops, on his shirt.

CHAPTER 21

Mike had called Andrea at the time he had promised he would, and had explained that he would have to stay in Falmouth overnight. So she had driven the fifteen miles around the river, and had come to him. Leaving her car near the Green Bank Hotel, she walked down the hill to meet him on Prince of Wales Pier. The narrow streets were crowded with sailors, dockyard workers and local women going to market.

It was early evening and light rain was filtering down from a pewter sky. Mike was late, and so Andrea wandered onto the concrete pier. She could feel the rain on her cheeks and imagined it in her hair, as on the day when they had first kissed. Knowing how crucial this meeting would be for their future together, she felt breathless with nerves. Scarcely noticed by her, the grey-green water splashed against the pier's supports, spewing up cigarette packs, half-eaten sandwiches and bobbing bottles. Predatory gulls screeched overhead. An excursion steamer with a red funnel – evidently pressed into naval service – was taking on board a crowd of sailors, to return them to the great grey warship in the harbour.

When Andrea spotted Mike getting out of a black sedan, her legs shook. He put on his hat, and strode briskly towards her, an anonymous figure in his uniform. Arm in arm, they walked together to an hotel, exchanging self-conscious small talk en route. To have spoken about Leo and Peter in the street would have been unthinkable.

As Mike approached a building, set at an angle to the street, and pushed open a heavy glazed door, Andrea's heart started to race. The hotel already. Soon she would know what he wanted. From the corner of her eye, she saw little clipped trees in tubs, a red-carpeted entrance. He led the way across an almost empty lounge, from which guests were leaving for the dining room, and guided her into a deserted bar with panelled walls. Only when Mike had settled her into a brass-studded leather armchair and put a highball in her hand did Andrea gaze directly at his face. He had taken off his hat and looked drained and vulnerable. Sitting back in a chair identical to hers, he seemed further away than the physical distance between them.

'Darling,' she whispered, 'what's wrong?'

He put down his glass, and raised a hand to his brow. 'I've been given the boot. Leo isn't to blame. My crime was losing a ship and eight lives, including two agents. So it's curtains for my lot.'

'That's so unjust, Mike. The people who sent you are to blame, too.'

'That's not how they see it.'

'What will you do now, darling?'

'I've asked to go back to gunboats on the East Coast.'

To ease his depression, she smiled encouragingly. 'The East Coast's much nearer to Oxford than Cornwall, sweetheart.'

Unexpectedly, Mike grasped one of her hands. 'Did Peter come down this morning? I'm so sorry I didn't ask sooner.'

'He did. And he's being embarrassingly nice about everything.'

Mike nodded to himself, as if this was what he had feared. 'It's a ploy to give his lawyer more time.'

'Time for what?'

'To plan getting custody of Leo.'

'Darling, you don't understand.' Andrea freed her hand and said bravely, 'Leo wants to be with his father now.'

Mike's handsome features became stubborn. 'Andrea, you *cannot* give in to a boy his age. He can't properly know what he wants. Imagine how you'll feel if you hardly ever see him.'

'He loves his father more than me, and shares all his interests, so why shouldn't I be happy to let Leo live with him?'

Mike shook his head slowly. 'Because if he lives with Peter, you'll miss him terribly, whatever you may think now.'

'If you knew what Leo said to me, you wouldn't try to . . .' She paused, too upset to continue.

Mike leaned forward and kissed her cheek. 'He's angry, darling. But it won't last. Please do what's best. He goes back to school next week. So take him home with you first. Be sweet to him. It'll only be for a few days. And that way, you'll spare him a term spent brooding about his dad and you. In three months, he'll be far more forgiving about a split, and may even decide to live with you after all.'

For a moment, Andrea wanted to laugh. Mike sounded so wise and sensible, but he had completely missed the point. She said, as if speaking to a foreigner, '*Leo won't come home without his father*. He's said so, many times.'

'Then you must persuade Peter to come back for a few days.' Mike gripped her hand tightly. 'Listen to me, Andrea. I've done enough harm to my own son, and I don't want to hurt yours. Adults forget, but children never do. I adored being with Simon more than anything else in my life. But after his mother and I parted, she made him dread my visits. So he screamed and hit me when I came through the door. For his sake, I had to stop visiting.'

'That's so sad, darling, but it's not like my situation. Your son was too young to make a choice of his own, so you had to make it for him. But Leo's nearly thirteen, with a mind of

279

his own. So the choice must be his. If he decides to live with his father, I'll have to accept it.'

'You'll go through hell like I did, so don't kid yourself you won't. If he lives with Peter, you'll lose him completely. I can't let that happen to you, Andrea.'

His frown scared her. If she couldn't persuade Leo to return to Oxford with her, would their affair be over?

As if answering her question, his eyes met hers. 'Leo did an amazingly unselfish thing when he risked his life on that trawler. We owe it to him to get him through this mess with as little pain as possible. If that means being patient for a while, we'll damned well have to be.'

Andrea thought she understood. Mike admired courage more than every other quality, so Leo's brave act placed him on a pedestal, above the rest of them. Disagreeing deeply, she nonetheless couldn't argue. Not today, with his men disbanded and some dead or missing. She promised to do her best to take Leo home with her before his school term began. Before they parted, Andrea agreed to tell Mike, as soon as she knew whether she had succeeded.

After looking vainly for Peter all over the house, Andrea went into the bathroom and stifled a cry. He was lying stretched out in the tub, eyes closed, and for a moment she feared a Roman death. But the water was not red, merely dirty, and as he heard her he opened his eyes.

'I guess this isn't the best place to talk,' she murmured, disconcerted to see the tip of his penis bobbing like a small pink buoy.

'Don't go, I've been wanting to ask you something.' He soaped his chest and stomach thoughtfully. 'Is your affair with Harrington likely to last?'

'I don't know.'

'Would you like it to?' And now his voice shook ever so slightly.

280

'Yes, I would.'

He caught his breath as if winded, but rallied at once. 'Then what's the problem? Isn't *he* so keen?'

'I think he is.'

'You *think*!' His angry trembling made the water ripple. 'I want to know *now*. Is he fishing you out for good, or planning to throw you back? It's killing me, tell him that . . . please.'

She looked down at the cracked linoleum and said, 'Mike's worried I may lose Leo if he goes on with me. He cares what happens to him.'

'What a stinking hypocrite.' Andrea stared at the battered copper cylinder above her husband's head. Anything to take her eyes away from his penis, which, to her dismay, had started to jut clear of the water, like an artist's impression of the Loch Ness monster. Aware of it, he pulled himself into a sitting position. 'You know what gets me about your lover boy?' he said, bitterly. 'He's so falsely diffident about his looks.'

'You really liked him him, Peter; so why pretend you didn't?'

'Because I'm so bloody unhappy,' he shouted.

At home there were two handles on the wall above the bath. Here there was nothing, and Andrea had not thought of it till this moment. Knowing he would shout at her if she offered to help him get out, Andrea left the bathroom. As she closed the door, Leo appeared on the landing. Without looking at her, he turned and went downstairs. She guessed he had been listening. As they reached the hall, she said, 'I hope you won't mind me asking . . . but has dad said you can go live with him right now?'

'That's my business.' The grubby shorts and socks that had fallen to his ankles made his harsh grown-up manner all the harder to endure. Andrea imagined Leo walking about in clothes that didn't fit, and not eating enough.

'Do you think dad'll pack your trunk and sort your school clothes? Will he cook your food?'

'I suppose he can get a housekeeper,' her son remarked, in a worried voice that broke her heart.

She said eagerly, 'Sweetheart, come home with me till dad finds somewhere to live. Then go live with him in the summer vacation.'

'If dad doesn't come home, I won't come home either. I told you that, mum.' Leo walked towards the French doors and looked back at her for a moment, before going out. Andrea felt such pain that she longed to call out and remind him that they had loved one another too much in the past to drop every trace of affection now. If she had only spared him from going away to school, there might still be enough understanding left between them to prevent this rift becoming permanent.

Without meaning to follow him, she went out into the long grass under the apple trees. How could she ask Peter to come back to Oxford for a few days? There was no possible way she could, and Mike was plain wrong to think otherwise. Peter would consider it shabby to pretend to be reconciled with her, simply so that Leo could return to school in a state of happy delusion. After all, what would Leo think of his father later, when he realised he'd been deliberately deceived by him? Mike couldn't have thought of that.

When she saw Leo walking back towards the house from the lane, she came to a firm decision and went up to him. 'Darling, please don't try and persuade dad to come home with us.'

'I'll do what I want.'

'You're such a kind loving son, of course you want dad to come home. Maybe you haven't realised how hard that would be for me. One can't be in love with one man, and suddenly start to feel the same way about another without having time to oneself first. So you see, even if I stop seeing Mike tomorrow, I won't want to live with dad for a while.'

Leo's earlier bravado crumbled. 'Does dad know this?' he asked sadly.

'I'm sure he does, darling.'

As tears started to spill down his cheeks, Andrea could not bear it, and with a moan, clutched him to her breast. For a while, Leo remained limp in her arms and did not try to get away.

CHAPTER 22

Term had started again at the village school, so Andrea could not arrange to see Mike there. She would have liked to suggest meeting in a field or wood – somewhere entirely private – but, at the end of a hurried telephone call she had been too flustered to come up with precise directions. Instead, he had suggested the parish church, which he would be passing anyway en route to the station. He was due in London for what he had told her lugubriously would be 'my terminal bollocking by the old gents at NIDC' – whoever they were. As they walked up the nave together, she supposed that if this were a happier occasion she might start humming Mendelssohn's *Wedding March* in a mildly ironic way.

Mike glanced at the famous fourteenth-century wall-painting, with its gaggle of men and women being prodded into the fires of hell by assorted devils. 'At least medieval adulterers knew the score,' he muttered.

'I guess they did,' agreed Andrea, imagining he was thinking of sinners who'd loved and lost, and had always expected to. Héloïse and Abelard, Paolo and Francesca, falling unsurprised into the eternal flames. Whereas we *are* surprised to suffer, he seemed to be saying.

'My train's the three o'clock.' Mike looked at his watch. 'Doesn't leave us long, I'm afraid.'

285

They slid into a pew near the pulpit and an unhappy silence ensued. She wished he would do something loving, like kiss her, or at least hold her hand. Thoughts of legendary lovers and their losses had made his anxiety about train times seem less forgivable.

Wearing a tweed jacket and check shirt, Mike looked strange to her, though these ordinary clothes were probably more familiar to him than naval uniform. Suddenly she realised how nervous he was and felt a surge of sympathy. Mike was holding his hands together to keep them still. He looked at her imploringly, 'For God's sake, Andrea, what did Leo say? Is he coming home with you?'

'Dearest, I had to tell him his dad and I are going to be apart for a while.'

'Why did you say that?' His smile drooped and died. 'I'm staggered you imagine he'll come anywhere near you now.'

'Lying to him wouldn't have been right.' The forthright tone she had hoped for emerged as something less convincing.

His face was distraught. 'Who cares what's *right* if a white lie could have stopped him fretting all summer at that awful school?' Mike's fingers tightened on the back of the pew in front. 'You deliberately did the opposite of what I asked.'

Refusing to be cowed by his anger, she said, 'I can't believe you're blaming me because I didn't do something I thought wrong. He'll worry less if he feels he can trust what I say. Isn't it for *me* to worry about him?'

'Not when he's just risked his life because of *us*. That makes it *my* responsibility too.'

'Fair comment. But lying to Leo won't help him.'

'Come on, Andrea! I only asked you to hold back briefly so you wouldn't alienate him for good. It was the one thing I begged you to avoid.'

'Whatever happens, I'll never blame you, darling.' Andrea felt so shaky that her words came out blurred and breathless.

Mike held his head in his hands for a moment. 'That's

not the point at all,' he objected. 'I'd blame myself *anyway*, especially if I had to watch you go through what I did. I couldn't bear that.'

'What do you mean?' she cried, just then remembering what he had said about his own son.

A woman with a mop and pail came out of a door to the right of the altar and started to clatter about and splosh water over the chancel floor.

Mike whispered, 'I think we should see how we feel in a month.'

'And not meet till then?' Her head was spinning. He was slipping away from her, without even trying to reach out a delaying hand. 'You're so goddamn unfair,' she cried. 'You set me impossible conditions; told me I had to take Leo *and* Peter home with me till school started; and now, because I've failed to persuade them, which I was always sure to, you say I can't see you any more. That's pretty low.'

'Try to understand,' he murmured. 'I felt fine grabbing things for myself when I was in danger. But now I'm safe, everything's different. Peter and Leo deserve better than a rushed decision.'

Andrea felt hot and shivery as if she were running a fever. Giving up any attempt to speak softly, she burst out, 'Just when I don't want to live with them any more, you decide to leave me for *their* sake. Do I have that right?'

His dark eyes were full of tender appeal. 'All I'm saying is we should take stock after you've settled down again in Oxford, when I'll know about my new posting. The last few days have been hell for all of us.'

'You're being dishonest,' she cried, as the woman with the mop gawped at her. 'If we leave it a month, then that's the end. Be brave enough to admit it, instead of giving me false hope.'

'Please, Andrea, it's been the most beautiful time in my life, and I couldn't bear it if we . . .'

Scarcely knowing what she was doing, Andrea was on her

feet, stumbling over hassocks in her hurry to be gone before she began to rage or plead with him to reconsider. Above all she must *not* plead. From the graveyard, she saw, beyond the lych gate, a Wren driver and a weedy looking man in civilian clothes sitting in a familiar looking naval sedan. These people had been waiting for him. What reason had he given them for spending time in church? 'Got to tell the little lady the party's over'?

Her head throbbed with unshed tears. Either Mike had been incredibly unselfish to put a boy's interests before his own, or he had used Leo as an excuse to end it. But which was true? Ever since her appearance at naval headquarters, with Justin at her side, she had thought Mike honourable. Now she no longer knew. Deserted by his own wife, scared, lonely – wouldn't he have painted his self-portrait in any way he thought likely to lead to love? The hardest thing for her was knowing that, even if Mike *had* used Leo, she still wanted to find some magical excuse that would let her go on loving him, as she had done before Leo stuck his nose into her love affair and popped it like a child's balloon.

CHAPTER 23

In the first week of June, Peter and Andrea drove to Yorkshire for Leo's Sports Day. It was six weeks since Andrea had left Cornwall, and yet Peter had observed few improvements in her state of mind. On three occasions during May, he had stayed in Oxford overnight, and on none of them had he slept in the flat but always in his rooms in college. The reason had never varied: Andrea's grief over the loss of her lover had made it seem as distasteful to him, as it would have been to her, for him to share her bed. Initially, Peter had assured himself that Andrea would soon admit that he deserved, if not praise, at least appreciation for his restraint and understanding. But nothing she had said to date had given him any such encouragement. He would have become angry and resentful long ago, if he had not been so worried about her.

Because Andrea had always been an optimistic, buoyant person, with a gift for sniffing out self-delusion in others, it was horrible to see her with dark shadows under her eyes, looking so wretched. Not that Peter blamed her for thinking well of Harrington – he had, too. So well, in fact, that on reflection it seemed a little naïve of Andrea to have expected such a paragon to be with her for longer than a brief episode in his life. Had she ever asked herself why – when other women were plentiful, and many of them younger than herself, and

289

no less keen – Harrington should have been expected to bend over backwards for the sake of a thirty-five-year-old with a troublesome son and the kind of husband guaranteed to lie heavy on the conscience?

Hoping to comfort his wife, a few days ago Peter had suggested to her on the telephone that Harrington might be the kind of man who only desired unattainable women, and discarded them as soon as they had slept with him. Andrea had brushed this aside. Mike had been faithful to his wife till the day she left him, and was as far removed from Byronic poseurs and picaresque young fornicators from the *Tom Jones* stable as could be imagined.

Though she was pale and thin, and often tried his patience to its limits, Peter still loved Andrea too much to think of leaving her – if, strictly speaking, one could be said to leave someone already largely absent. Even now, unless careful, he could see in her lack of proportion something dogged and vital, as well as misguided.

Recently, without quite knowing why, Peter had used his contacts within the Admiralty to find out where Harrington was serving. Great Yarmouth, it turned out – commanding a squadron of motor torpedo boats, which were regularly in action off the Dutch and German coasts. Several evenings ago, Peter had caught an item on a BBC news report which he supposed was typical: 'Last night our Light Coastal Forces were in action off the Hook of Holland and sunk two armed trawlers and an E-boat, for the loss of two MTBS.' Mike seemed to be in greater danger than in Cornwall. At the time of his discovery, Peter had thought it best to keep the information to himself.

They had left York on the Helmsley road, and now were driving north, past fields where the hay was ready for cutting. Though Peter was happy to think that in less than an hour they would be seeing Leo, a sudden thought made him uneasy.

'Darling,' he asked gently, 'did you ever hear where Mike was sent after he left Cornwall?'

'I did,' she answered, turning her unhappy face towards him. Mike writes to Justin most weeks. And he told Leo.'

Peter was mortified. 'Why didn't you tell me the real reason why you've been so anxious?'

She seemed amazed by his question. 'I should've told you I was worrying about Mike?'

'Yes. Far better than leaving me thinking you'd no special reason to be sad, except missing him.'

'You're right. I'm sorry, Peter.' She touched his hand where it rested on the wheel. 'Mike's coming today.'

'To see you?'

She gave him the ghost of a smile, before shaking her head. 'Justin's spending half-term with him, so he's coming to get him.'

Peter frowned. 'Is Mike refusing to see you, Andrea?'

'He's not keen. Please don't ask me why.'

Even when gazing at the road ahead, through the yellowing mist of dead insects on the windscreen, Peter was aware of her lovely hair, flickering in the wind, as the elms sighed past, and the Howardian hills appeared, looking blue and misty in the summer haze. Andrea had caught the sun and there were faint freckles on the bridge of her nose. She's perfect, thought Peter. Yet to Harrington, she was only someone who'd given him pleasure, and was of no further use. Fear for her sanity made Peter shiver. Her need to know that the man was alive might go on as long as he lasted, or the war did. And, in the meantime, what about me?

Somewhere between Sheriff Hutton and Hovingham, it came to Peter that his marriage might be more satisfactory if Andrea were still seeing her lover.

Approaching the school, Peter was impressed by the number of parents arriving in cars. There had obviously been plenty of petrol coupons saved, or black market prices paid in order to acquire the necessary gallons for such a long journey. As a government scientist, he had faced no equivalent privations. Some boys were waiting at the end of the drive by the lodge gates, intending to jump onto the running boards of their parents' cars, so they could be swept, in glory, along the beech avenue to the school.

Since Peter's small Standard had no running board, Leo stood waiting to greet his mother and father under the shadow of the pseudo-Jacobean main building. As he saw the car, he ran forward and kissed them both through each open window, a clear demonstration of his delight at seeing them still together. And as they walked to the sports field, along with a growing crowd, he walked between them in his white shorts and singlet, his hands holding theirs, oblivious to the usual 'no touching' etiquette observed between parents and older boys on such occasions.

They were still linked in this way when Peter spotted Mike Harrington and another naval officer, both in uniform, walking on either side of Justin. At once Peter raised his stick in greeting, delighted to see Justin, and in no way resenting the boy for being the first to suspect Andrea. He had always admired Justin's sharp mind and still did. Leo's hand grasped his father's more tightly as he saw Mike.

Harrington's expression, when he saw Andrea, struck Peter as agonized. Andrea's face immediately grew pale, and, at first, Peter feared she might faint. Mike came up closer and calmly introduced his colleague as Tony Cassilis; and Justin started burbling to Leo about how Tony had escaped from France 'only a few days ago'. They were walking onto the mown field, where the running tracks were marked out in parallel white lines. By now, a master was hectoring the boys through a loudhailer, and Justin and Leo went off to take part in the first of the races.

Observing Cassilis talking to Andrea, Peter decided this was his moment to approach Mike. Why had the man refused to see Andrea, when a sympathetic explanation would have made it far easier for her to bear the pain of rejection? Peter reckoned that if he asked Harrington for a favour, he would not be disagreeable to him. But Mike began to walk away too fast for Peter to catch him before he reached the press of parents, clustering around the running track.

On seeing Mike, Andrea had been gripped, as firmly as ever, by her old delusion that he was *her* man, the only one meant for her. So she found it hard to focus on Tony Cassilis, who seemed to have stayed behind in order to talk to her. Suspecting that Mike had put him up to this, she waited for whatever message Tony had been asked to convey. But first, he treated her to unwanted highlights from his Great Escape. On ending his tale, Tony studied his shoes, and said, 'Mike's awfully cut up, you know.'

'He didn't look that way to me.'

'He misses you.'

'That's *my* fault?' Her voice rose angrily.

'He hates himself for the pain he's caused, and he's determined not to cause more.'

'A shame he didn't think of that before.'

Tony's pale grey eyes met hers. 'You're right. But I'd still do anything for him.' He rattled some coins in his pockets. 'It's dashed hard to do the right thing when one's feelings are pulling the other way.'

'I don't understand.'

'He still cares. That clear enough for you?'

She moved very close to Tony. 'Tell him that caring means nothing when a person isn't there. He couldn't even greet me when he was standing right here.'

The crack of a starting pistol was followed by shouts of encouragement and then by cheers. Andrea walked away from Tony without saying goodbye and headed for the track. On the way, she met Leo.

'Didn't you see the race, mum?'

'Sorry, darling.'

293

'I came second in the one-twenty yards.'

'That's great.'

'Where's dad? I don't believe he saw it either.'

'I expect he did. What's your next event?'

'Not the father's and son's race,' he told her dryly, before lowering his voice. 'Mike's running with Justin. He asked Captain Berty specially if he could.' Leo sounded so disapproving that Andrea guessed he was still jealous.

'Isn't that nice of Mike?'

'Oh, sure. But it's pathetic of Justin to let him. He'll feel a fraud if they win, and they probably will.'

In fact they came third. Andrea watched near the finish as the fathers thundered back on the final leg, the sons having run first. Mike had taken off his jacket, and looked like a Greek athlete with his head flung back as he finished. Though she thought less of him for not being prepared to talk to her himself, she admired him for keeping in touch with Justin. Part of her reason for loving him had been the knowledge that he was capable of such things.

The track and field events were over when Peter finally ran Mike to earth. He and Justin were emerging from the craft room. Peter guessed Mike was far from pleased to see him and didn't blame him. Cuckolds were rarely civil to their cuckolders but Peter felt at ease and, for the moment, cordial. If he could only have the guts to make a definite proposition to Harrington, a way to ease his present problems might be in sight.

As Peter approached him, Mike turned to Justin. 'Maybe you could say goodbye to a few people.' The boy took the hint and left them. The craft room was separated from the main school building by an open corridor, which was well frequented at present. Across a cinder yard lay the school's clay tennis court.

'Over there?' suggested Peter, indicating the deserted court.

The two men walked onto the gritty surface without speaking.

Peter stabbed the ferrule of his stick into the rust-coloured clay and muttered fiercely, 'She's still crazy about you, Harrington. Sleeps badly, hardly eats.'

'I don't sleep well myself.'

'Because you care for her?'

Mike clamped a hand to his brow. 'You just can't ask me that.'

'Why not?' Peter rested his back against the wire netting. 'You've made Andrea's life a misery. And mine, too.'

Mike took a deep breath. 'Your worries are over. I've decided to come to an understanding with my wife.'

'You're going back to her?' Peter was stunned to have his one hope shattered.

'It's not because I don't care for Andrea. I do. Making friends with Justin changed things for me; it told me how much my own son needs me.'

Peter cleared his throat. 'Does your wife need you, too?'

'Not really – though her latest bloke's just let her down.'

Peter moved closer to the naval officer and said very distinctly, 'Since it won't worry your wife, what about Andrea coming to see you every few weeks?'

Mike looked at him, dumbfounded. 'You wouldn't mind?'

'Of course I would. But it couldn't be worse than being with her the way she is now. She's so bloody low, she hardly speaks to me. I can't even spend a few hours at home. What have I got to lose?'

Mike thought for a moment. 'She might get fonder of me if we start meeting again.'

Peter laughed harshly. 'In Great Yarmouth? In November for one night a month?'

'She might decide to stay longer and come to London, too.'

Peter used his stick to scratch a line on the court's surface. 'If you let her do that, I'll muck up your plans to stay married.'

'How?'

'By suing for divorce and naming you.'

295

Mike raised his hands. 'Point taken. But will you really not mind if I fix up something with her before she leaves?'

'Go ahead.'

Mike reached out as if to shake Peter's hand, but withdrew it, in case he was rebuffed. 'You're a remarkable man,' he said instead.

Peter leaned heavily on his stick. 'I'm doing the best I can with the cards I've been dealt.'

Mike blushed. 'It's still damned generous of you to let her have what she wants.'

'I don't want her killing herself or going crazy.'

Before he could have second thoughts, Peter started limping towards the wire netting. But why should he think again? When he'd said he had nothing to lose, he'd been telling the truth. And, in any case, Andrea was more likely to get bored when routinely seeing the man, than when pining for an imaginary god.

CHAPTER 24

Early in July, the Headmaster's Indoor Games took place to celebrate Captain Berty's birthday. Because Leo was concentrating hard on playing 'Flip the Kipper' – a game in which cut-out paper fish were swooshed along with folded newspapers – he did not at first see Spud usher into the room a dark and beautiful woman in a wide-brimmed hat. It was her scent that made the boy look up, it smelled so foreign and out of place in this uncarpeted room with its bare light bulbs. The woman's skirt swept past, inches from his face, giving him a sense of extraordinary luxury. She was wearing white-rimmed dark glasses that made him think of film actresses. Later, Leo learned that this unforgettable apparition was Justin's mother. But, since Justin himself rarely spoke to Leo these days, he wasn't able to find out more about Mrs Matherson – not even how she'd reached Britain from Kenya. All he did hear, several days later, was that she would be settling in England, and that Justin would live with her in the holidays. When she gave two of Justin's newer friends a small native drum each, Leo was only a little envious.

A month ago, just after half-term, Mike Harrington had brought an MTB up to Scarborough and had whizzed Justin and four other boys along the coast to Whitby and back again. Leo had thought they would never stop chattering about their treat. Mercifully, he himself had had several things of his own to celebrate: he had done better than expected in mock Common Entrance; and the Sunday before Mrs Matherson's appearance, his parents had taken him out for the day.

They hadn't done the usual visit to Whitby or Robin Hood's Bay, but instead had walked for a mile across the moors, along the disused railway near Rosedale Abbey. Dad had managed this walk fairly well and had been unusually cheerful. His mother's mood had been totally different from her half-term gloom. She laughed a lot and told amusing stories about things that had happened at her school. She even held dad's hand several times and smiled at him. When she did, the purple heather and heath grass had become blurry for Leo when he'd looked away. His happiness had lasted right through the normally miserable hour that followed their departure.

Most of the milestones leading up to the end of term already lay in the past: the end of term exams, the General Knowledge Quiz, the Gold Star holiday. Only Matron's Treasure Hunt and the last home cricket match were to come – just one week to go. Out on the sunlit playing field, twenty boys were pushing the big roller up and down the pitch, supervised by the headmaster. Leo was strolling along under the shadow of the kitchen garden wall, hoping to nip in and grab some gooseberries. But, just then, the outside bell began ringing for supper. He walked towards the school across the front lawn, straight through a group of younger boys zooming about pretending to be fighter planes.

Outside the tuck box room, Leo saw a boy slumped against a radiator. He was in tears and caught at Leo's shirt as he passed. Leo pulled away, eager not to get involved with Hal Varney, who had replaced him as Justin's best friend, and had been taken out in the MTB.

'He's dead,' croaked Varney. 'Commander Harrington's dead.'

'How do you know?' gasped Leo.

'Spud told Justin.'

'Where is he?'

'In his dorm.'

Leo found Justin lying on his bed, staring at the ceiling. His eyes were red but he was not crying.

'Varney told me,' said Leo. 'What happened?'

'He attacked a German convoy in a fog and didn't come back. You needn't pretend to be upset. You didn't even like him.'

'You think you know everything,' snapped Leo. 'Well you're bloody wrong. I thought he was the . . .' But he couldn't say 'the tops', or anything like that, because of what Mike had done to his father, and because Justin knew what he'd done. And then Leo couldn't think of the right word to use, so he turned and left the room.

Later, when Justin didn't come down for supper or for prayers, Leo felt bad, and wished he'd been honest about how he felt over Mike. He guessed what had also stopped him had been his guilty conscience over telling Justin he couldn't come to Cornwall for the summer. Justin had wept then, because he'd been sure he wouldn't see Mike again. Leo thought back to the start of their friendship and how decent Justin had been. It made Leo sad to remember it. But though he wanted to explain to Justin that he'd only been mean to him because of what Mike and his mother had been doing, somehow he couldn't bring himself to go up to the dorm. After all, it wouldn't be long before Justin got over Mike's death. His mother had come back to England, so he'd soon be living with her. When the war ended, Justin would move among fashionable, good-looking people like his mum, spending the summer holidays in places where there were casinos and palm trees, and big yachts in the harbour.

When Leo returned home at the end of term, he found no litter of papers on the table by the sitting room window. Nor was his father's shaving brush and razor in the bathroom. He ran back to the sitting room where his mother was writing out cheques to tradesmen.

'Is dad in London again?' he asked, flopping down onto the deep sofa, among his mother's oriental cushions.

'He's in his rooms in college.'

'Why isn't he here?' demanded Leo shrilly. 'All the way in that beastly train, I looked forward to seeing him.'

'*I* didn't ask him to leave, sweetheart.'

'Then why did he?' Leo was alarmed and angry.

'Why don't you go ask him? He's staying in college till Sunday.'

Leo rang his father, who wouldn't tell him anything over the 'phone. They arranged to meet, not in college, but at 'the shack', his father's workshop in Mansfield Road. The ancient De Reszke cigarette adverts on the walls depicting girls in cloche hats (left by the previous owner) had always seemed homely to Leo, as had his father's yellowing inventors' patents, each with a red seal in the corner. The place had seen better days. There were dead flies on every window ledge, and a rose bush had grown up, blocking one of the windows. His father sank down in his battered 'thinking' chair, while Leo perched on the draughtsman's seat behind the sloping table. As a boy, Leo had enjoyed using his father's T-squares and protractors, and taking his silver drawing instruments out of their velvet lined case.

Outside, before his father had let him in, Leo had asked him why he was not living at home. Now Peter said gently, 'Mum's unhappy about Harrington's death. Frankly, it's easier for me to stay away for a bit.'

'Was she still seeing him, dad?' asked Leo, with a loud intake of breath.

'Every now and then,' said Peter, in the same tone he might have used to tell Leo how often his mother visited her hairdresser.

'You *knew* all the time.' Leo's face crumpled.

'I really didn't mind too much, old chap. She went on loving me in other ways. She'd only known him a few weeks, but I go back fifteen years. Time counts for something, you know.'

Leo was staring at him strangely. 'How could you stand it?'

'Because I love her.' Peter sat forward in his chair. 'Look at it this way, Leo: if you'd never brought Justin to Cornwall, she'd never have met Mike. It was pure chance. She never went looking for him. So how can she be such a bad person now?'

Leo gripped the table. 'She should have thought of us, and told him to shove off.'

'She was lonely, with me being in Falmouth, and you out with Justin most of the time.'

'That's a terrible excuse,' snapped the boy, his eye following a wasp that was bumping against one of the windows.

'I don't agree, Leo. She'd missed you all term, and it was very tough for her to see so little of you in Cornwall.'

'That's not fair, dad.'

'Maybe not. It's just a fact of life that children give their parents hope and interest when their own lives are running out of steam. So it's damned hard for mothers when their kids start growing away.'

Leo left his chair and swatted the wasp with an old notebook. 'She still didn't have to fall in love with him.'

Peter sighed. 'Some women need to believe they can be in love for the rest of their lives.'

'What about men, dad? What do we need?' Leo's freckled face was anxious.

'I wish I knew.' Peter hung his head for a while, and, when he raised it, smiled sheepishly at Leo. 'I do know one thing though. I was a bloody fool to send you away to that school.'

Andrea had first heard about Mike's fate from Tony Cassilis. He had come to Oxford one sunny evening and called up to ask her to meet him at the Randolph Hotel. She had known at once what news he must be bringing.

301

Mike had been commanding a flotilla of six MTBS ordered to make a night attack on a damaged destroyer, as she was being escorted along the Dutch coast by armed trawlers and a corvette. The action had taken place at night and at top speed. Mike himself went in last, and his boat's attack seemed to have succeeded, since a loud explosion was heard and the destroyer appeared to slow down afterwards.

Because Mike's attack was the last, it had lacked surprise. As he went in, he came under heavy fire. But the fact that there had been only a short burst of shooting after he fired his torpedoes had been considered a good sign, since it seemed to indicate that he had got away fast, leaving the German gunners with nothing to shoot at.

Mike had been called up by radio but had not answered. This had been no surprise to Tony. Aerials were often shot away in action and sets damaged. There'd been light fog over the sea when they'd reached the Dutch coast, and, since then, it had grown progressively worse. So, all they could do was stop their engines several miles away and listen. If Mike was in trouble, his engines should have remained audible, or at least his guns. But they could hear nothing, except the convoy chugging away to the north on its old course. Later, Tony and the others had gone back to the scene of the action but hadn't been able to make out anything in the thickening mist.

They had hoped Mike would be back at the quay when they returned there shortly before dawn, but his berth was empty. Engine failure seemed the likeliest explanation, or so they'd figured. But Mike wasn't back by noon, or even by six. Had he hit a mine on his way home and sunk? It was possible. Two MGB flotillas made a joint sweep with a similar number of MTBS, but nothing was spotted. Nor was it, ever. Tony suggested to Andrea that perhaps Mike's boat had been hit by one unlucky shell and blown apart. Indeed, the explosion they had heard might not have come from the destroyer at all.

Andrea had asked Tony where Mike's last attack had taken

302

place. A few miles out to sea from the Dutch port of Haarlem, had been his reply. So what was the name of the closest place on the English coast? He'd thought for a while. Aldeburgh, Leiston, Thorpeness. Somewhere in that part of Suffolk.

Two days later, since Peter had the car and Andrea had not wanted to ask if she could borrow it, she made the journey the hard way. She changed at Ipswich for Saxmundham. An obese and sweating soldier sat opposite her in the slow local train, reading *Blighty* and *Men Only* all the way, tin helmet and rifle beside him. She took a country bus to Leiston, and trudged the final mile on foot with her few wilting roses. All along the pebbly beach, concrete tank defences had been set up and barbed wire strung out, making her fear she would come upon a warning sign for mines. But she didn't, and, finally, found a way through the wire. The beach sloped down steeply to water that was brownish grey and streaked with froth.

A dull roar came from out to sea, merging with the closer rattle of stones and the thump of waves. It was a warm August afternoon but the breeze was cool. She sat down for a while and listened to the sea mumbling to itself – on and on, forever and ever, amen. She thought it the most desolate sound in the world. Poor handsome Mike. Her head bowed, she tossed her roses into the waves.

CHAPTER 25

Although the holidays were nearly over, Leo didn't seem as bothered as usual by the prospect of leaving home. Andrea knew that this was mainly because she and Peter had decided that, when this next term ended, his boarding days would be over. After the Christmas holidays, he would be staying on in Oxford and going to a new school, St Edward's, a short cycle ride from home.

Apart from complaining about a dull week spent with Peter's parents near Bath, Leo had been happy enough in Oxford, looking up old friends, and reading *No Orchids for Miss Blandish*, though Andrea had done her best to dissuade him, since it was reputed to contain descriptions of a rape and half a dozen murders.

'It's just cops and robbers,' he'd grumbled.

So Andrea had given in, thankful her relations with him were improving. This, she knew, was largely because she had hinted that his father would soon be coming home. But she had tried hard in other ways – for instance, coming to the Parks to witness the maiden flight of his model Beaufighter. Tennis had also become a bond between them, since they played two or three times a week; and, though Leo could not have forgotten her partnering Mike in Elspeth's tournament, he never spoke of it.

Returning to Park Town from the courts, after what would be the last game of the holidays, Andrea congratulated Leo on improving his service. Glancing at her son walking beside her, Andrea was more than ever aware of recent physical changes: the fuzz of hair above his upper lip, the more muscular legs, broader shoulders. During the holidays, Leo's voice had started to alter, fluctuating from alto to something indeterminately lower. Yet none of these alterations seemed threatening to her, as they would have done last year. Since that happy era, Leo had been lost to her, so completely it had seemed, that the partial return, taking place right now, was more than she could have hoped for even a month ago. Certainly the reconciliation was helping her get through the pain of losing Mike.

What helped most of all was her knowledge that Peter, her extraordinary husband, had told Mike he could go on seeing her, in effect giving his permission. In a bizarre fashion, Mike had become Peter's gift to her. Mike's death wasn't less tragic because of that, but she knew it would have been harder for her to bear if he had died six months earlier.

As mother and son walked into the dappled shadows cast by the trees in Park Town's central oval, Andrea sensed that the time had come to tell Leo that his father would soon be returning home. What forbearance they would have to show one another! Peter would have to admit that his working hours had been absurd, and his rearrangement of all their lives to suit his own needs, unspeakably selfish – just as she would have to confess that, by allowing herself to start an affair with a physically active younger man, she had been cruel, not only to Peter with his handicap, but to Leo, given his love for his father. She should *never* have been stupidly careless – revealing her guilt to Justin in a way that had caused Leo so much pain.

Peter, she had been glad to see, had lost weight in recent weeks – either because of the strains of his job or because of her affair – but, whatever the cause, he looked less jowly, and would not, she imagined, be so rotundly cumbersome in bed.

As she opened the hall door gripping the box of tennis balls and her racquet under one arm, Andrea was already imagining Leo's happiness when she told him the good news about his father. The afternoon post lay scattered at her feet. She bent down to pick up these letters, her bare knees brushing the bristles of the mat. One envelope was different, the jagged German script standing out: *Kriegsgefangenenpost*. The British Censor's crown with the word PASSED under it had been stamped near the bottom. Andrea's name and address were to the right of the envelope, the sender's to the left:

Absender:
Vor- und Zuname:
Lieut. Comm. Michael J. Harrington RNVR

The single flight of stairs up to the maisonette seemed to sway under her, as words leapt out from the envelope. *Gebuhrenfrei*! A German joke – delivered free! And what would Mike say? And what would she *want* him to say?

'Hurry up, mum,' complained Leo, treading on her heels. 'Any letters for me?'

'Sorry, sweetheart.'

In the bathroom, she sat on the old-fashioned wooden seat and opened the envelope along a gummed strip that the censor had used to reseal it. Her heart was hammering.

Kriegsgefangenenlager Datum: 24.08.41
Marlag VIIB

My darling,
If you haven't already heard that I'm a living, breathing POW, *and not a feast for the fishes, I hope you're sitting down! But it's the nicest kind of shock, I trust. Dearest, I've been so ridiculously lucky I really ought to start believing in something grander than common or garden chance to*

explain my resurrection. Only two of us were rescued after we blew up, though eight were still just about alive after the explosion. All I suffered was a cracked rib and a broken thumb.

Strange, isn't it, how I had premonitions the whole time in the West Country. Yet, recently, I'd begun to think I could go on forever. That's why I didn't get around to telling you lots of things, including how damned glad I am I never stuck to my earlier decision to stop seeing you. Those snatched meetings were wrong for us. But a complete break would have been even worse. Unthinkable, in fact. We're neither of us made for sharing, my love. It's all or nothing for the likes of you and me. In life one doesn't get what one wants most and *the second best thing.*

We had a bad time in the water before the E-boat found us. Such brave efforts to save the wounded men. But they all failed. Waiting for my turn to meet the man with the scythe, I felt everything you might expect: rage, fear, despair, but something unexpected, too – a longing for things to be better in the world, out of simple fairness. In a funny kind of way, I felt proud that this was how it would end, after what we'd been through already. I'd just about accepted that I wouldn't live to see the sun rise, when the E-boat showed up.

Six weeks on and I'm still euphoric in this drab place. We are taken to exercise in a clearing, deep in dark Teutonic woods straight out of the Brothers Grimm. A few leaves are already turning, and early this morning there was a mist among the trees that felt autumnal and made my heart ache for you. Because I risked everything (though I hardly chose to) my life has become incredibly valuable. I can't go back to the kind of marriage where the superficialities of social existence pass for life itself. Not even the attempt to be a decent father can justify going on paying the price I had to. I have to be with you *now, my darling.*

We have no curtains in our huts here; and in the evening, when our low voltage lights are on, I stare at the dark window panes. A pale image of myself peers back from the blue void outside. He sees me in captivity, and I see him in the future, in the dark. For what will I return to when I leave this place? What if in a few years you've grown happy without me?

Perhaps it would be better, kinder, to tell me now that I must not hope. Please write and tell me in the plainest words if that is the case. I must know, my love. You have lived my death; and now that I am alive again, am I still dead to you, or do I live and breathe?

Correspondence is restricted. I'm allowed to send three letters per month and a few more postcards. So will you please write to Justin with my news? Tell him I think of him, and will write next month. I love you, darling. And dream of you.

Mike

Several loud knocks on the bathroom door made Andrea jump.

'Hey, mum, it's dad. On the telephone.'

'Hang on a moment.'

Andrea rose and stood undecided. She imagined the letter in pieces, swirling in the lavatory pan, as she pulled the chain. Instead, she thrust it into her tennis blouse.

In the sitting room, Leo stood holding the receiver with his palm clamped over it.

'Tell dad when he can come back. Go on mum. *Please!*'

So Andrea told Peter that Friday would be good for her, and heard him catch his breath. In fact, he was silent for so long before agreeing to come home that she guessed he was crying with happiness. And he deserved to be happy, having been so generous to her. As for Mike – he might be shot escaping, or he might remain in the German forest for as many years as the war lasted. But by then Leo would be older, and would care less. So what would it matter if she made everyone happy now, even if later she had to disillusion one or more of them? The earliest months of his captivity would be the worst ones for Mike, and when he most needed her help.

Andrea thought of her first night with her lover, his flung-back hair, his deep-set eyes, his slenderness. How had she allowed her one great love to grow manageable? Maybe it would have happened anyway, even if Leo had never gone to sea. Romance always ended up as something else – becoming tragic, or mundane, or just stopping, and then being nothing at all. So she'd done better than that anyway.

'What did dad say?' cried Leo, the moment she had replaced the receiver on its cradle.

'Not a lot. You know dad.'

'He must have been happy.'

'He was, darling. Very happy.'

Later, playing a Chopin *Nocturne*, while Leo sprawled on the sofa, she imagined her reply to Mike. 'My lover – Nothing has ever made me happier than receiving your beautiful and moving letter . . .' And would it just be generous of her? Not really. By writing, she could still *be* that wonderful woman she had been in the spring, though leading another life entirely, day by day.

She stopped playing, and acknowledged Leo's brief but almost enthusiastic applause.